PRAISE FOR

The You I've Never Known

★"Hopkins creates a satisfying and moving story, and her carefully structured poems ensure that each word and phrase is savored."
—*Publishers Weekly*, starred review

★ "Delving into issues of teen pregnancy, scientology, bisexuality, same-sex marriage, family, and determination, this book is as substantial as it is beautifully written. Hopkins's fans will love the newest edition to her published works, a must for contemporary young adult collections."
—*VOYA*, starred review

"With trademark compassion, multidimensional characters, realistic teen behavior, and a slew of issues sympathetically explored, Hopkins has another winner here."
—*Booklist*

"A powerful, memorable, and honest look at how two girls navigate their troubled home lives. Ellen Hopkins once again reminds us why she's in a class all to herself—the gorgeous prose, the painfully authentic characters and their struggle to find where to fit in and how to be loved. No surprise . . . this book is beautiful and unforgettable!"
—*Justine* magazine

"Maya and Ariel's connection is among Hopkins's best. A page-turning exploration of independence, powerlessness, and secrets, with groundbreaking representation of bisexuality and queerness."
—*Kirkus Reviews*

"Writing in verse (Ariel's tale) and prose (Maya's), Hopkins uses skillful pacing and carefully chosen words to conceal the most important truth of the novel. The reveal arrives just as readers may be putting the pieces together themselves. VERDICT A sharp, gripping read sure to please Hopkins's legions of fans."
—*School Library Journal*

ALSO BY ELLEN HOPKINS

Crank

Burned

Impulse

Glass

Identical

Tricks

Fallout

Perfect

Tilt

Smoke

Traffick

Rumble

THE YOU I'VE NEVER KNOWN

ELLEN HOPKINS

Margaret K. McElderry Books

NEW YORK LONDON TORONTO SYDNEY NEW DELHI

MARGARET K. McELDERRY BOOKS | An imprint of Simon & Schuster Children's Publishing Division | 1230 Avenue of the Americas, New York, New York 10020 | This book is a work of fiction. Any references to historical events, real people, or real places are used fictitiously. Other names, characters, places, and events are products of the author's imagination, and any resemblance to actual events or places or persons, living or dead, is entirely coincidental. | Text copyright © 2017 by Ellen Hopkins | Cover art copyright © 2017 by Simon & Schuster, Inc. | Cover photograph copyright © 2013 by Marya May | All rights reserved, including the right of reproduction in whole or in part in any form. | MARGARET K. McELDERRY BOOKS is a trademark of Simon & Schuster, Inc. | For information about special discounts for bulk purchases, please contact Simon & Schuster Special Sales at 1-866-506-1949 or business@simonandschuster.com. | The Simon & Schuster Speakers Bureau can bring authors to your live event. For more information or to book an event, contact the Simon & Schuster Speakers Bureau at 1-866-248-3049 or visit our website at www.simonspeakers.com. | Also available in a Margaret K. McElderry Books hardcover edition | Interior design by Mike Rosamillia | Cover design by Greg Stadnyk | Book edited by Emma D. Dryden | The text for this book was set in Brandon Grotesque and Caecillia LT Std 45 Light. | Manufactured in the United States of America | First Margaret K. McElderry Books paperback edition January 2018 | 10 9 8 7 | The Library of Congress has cataloged the hardcover edition as follows: | Names: Hopkins, Ellen. | Title: The you I've never known / Ellen Hopkins. | Other titles: You I have never known | Description: First edition. | New York : Margaret K. McElderry Books, 2017. | Summary: With both joy and fear, seventeen-year-old Ariel begins to explore her sexuality, while living with her controlling, abusive father who has told Ariel that her mother deserted her years ago. | Identifiers: LCCN 2016027736 | ISBN 9781481442909 (hardback) | ISBN 9781481442916 (paperback) | ISBN 9781481442923 (eBook) | Subjects: CYAC: Parent and child—Fiction. | Identity—Fiction. | Sexual orientation—Fiction. | Lesbians—Fiction. | Psychopaths—Fiction. | Kidnapping—Fiction. | BISAC: JUVENILE FICTION / Social Issues / Physical & Emotional Abuse (see also Social Issues / Sexual Abuse). | JUVENILE FICTION / Family / Marriage & Divorce. | Classification: LCC PZ7.5.H67 Yo 2017 | DDC [Fic]—dc23 LC record available at https://lccn.loc.gov/2016027736

This book is dedicated to every child who has ever lost a parent, and every parent who has ever lost a child.

ACKNOWLEDGMENTS

With love and heartfelt appreciation to my husband, John, who steadfastly held my hand through the roller coaster ride so many years ago. Special thanks to my editing team—Emma, Ruta, and Annie—whose insights helped make this book the exceptional story it has become, and to my publisher, for offering understanding and patience when I desperately needed them. And a giant shout-out to my dear friend Susan Hart Lindquist, who listens to my rants and helps me sort through the reasons for them. Sometimes you just need an ear.

To Begin

Oh, to be given the gifts
of the chameleon!

Not only the ability
to match the vital facade
to circumstance at will,

but also the capacity
to see in two directions
simultaneously.

Left. Right.
Forward. Backward.

How much gentler
our time on this planet,
and how much more

certain of our place
in the world we would be,
drawing comfort

like water from the wells
of our homes.

Home

Four letters,
one silent.
A single syllable
pregnant with meaning.

Home   is more
than a leak-free roof
and insulated walls
that keep you warm
when the winter wind screams
and cool when summer
stomps all over you.

Home   is a clearing
in the forest,
a safe place to run
when the trees shutter
all light and the crunch
of leaves in deepening darkness
drills fear into your heart.

Home   is someone
or two who accepts you
for the person you believe
you are, and if that happens
to change, embraces the person
you ultimately find yourself to be.

I Can't Remember

Every place
Dad and I have
called home. When
I was real little, the two
of us sometimes lived in
our car. Those memories
are in motion. Always moving.

I don't think
I minded it so much
then, though mixed in
with happy recollections
are snippets of intense fear.
I didn't dare ask why one stretch
of sky wasn't good enough to settle

under. My dad
likes to say he came
into this world infected
with wanderlust. He claims
I'm lucky, that at one day till
I turn seventeen I've seen way
more places than most folks see

in an entire
lifetime. I'm sure
he's right on the most
basic level, and while I
can't dig up snapshots of
North Dakota, West Virginia, or
Nebraska, how could I ever forget

watching Old
Faithful spouting
way up into the bold
amethyst Yellowstone sky,
or the granddaddy alligator
ambling along beside our car
on a stretch of Everglade roadway?

I've inhaled
heavenly sweet
plumeria perfume,
dodging pedicab traffic
in the craziness of Waikiki.
I've picnicked in the shadows
of redwoods older than the rumored

son of God;
nudged up against
the edge of the Grand
Canyon as a pair of eagles
played tag in the warm air
currents; seen Atlantic whales
spy-hop; bodysurfed in the Pacific;

and picked spring-
inspired Death Valley
wildflowers. I've listened
to Niagara Falls percussion,
the haunting song of courting
loons. So I guess my dad is right.
I'm luckier than a whole lot of people.

Yeah, On Paper

All that sounds pretty damn
awesome. But here's the deal.
I'd trade every bit of it to touch
down somewhere Dad didn't insist

we leave as soon as we arrived.
I truly don't think I'm greedy.
All I want is a real home, with
a backyard and a bedroom

I can fix up any way I choose,
the chance to make a friend
or two, and invite them to spend
the night. Not so much to ask, is it?

Well, I guess you'd have to query Dad.
I know he only wants what's best
for me, but somehow he's never
cared about my soul-deep longing

for roots. *Home is where the two
of us are,* was a favorite saying, and,
*The sky is the best roof there is. Except
when it's leaking.* The rain reference

cracked me up when I was real young.
But after a time or twenty, stranded
in our car while it poured because
we had nowhere else dry to stay,

my sense of humor failed me.
Then he'd teach me a new card
game or let me win at the ones
I already knew. He could be nice

like that. But as I aged beyond
the adorable little girl stage,
the desire for "place" growing,
he grew tired of my whining.

That's what he called it. *Quit
your goddamn whining,* he'd say.
*You remind me of your mother. Why
don't you run off and leave me, too?*

*Who'd look out for you then, Miss
Nothing's Ever Good Enough?
No one, that's who! Not one person
on this planet cares about you.*

*No one but Daddy, who loves you
more than anything in the whole wide
world, and would lay down his life
for you. You remember that, hear me?*

I heard those words too often,
in any number of combinations.
Almost always they came floating
in a fog of alcohol and tobacco.

Once in a While

But not often, those words
came punctuated by a jab
to my arm or the shake
of my shoulders or a whack
against the back of my head.
I learned not to cry.

> *Soldier up*, he'd say. *Soldiers*
> *don't cry. They swallow pain.*
> *Keep blubbering, I'll give you*
> *something to bawl about.*

He would, too. Afterward
always came his idea
of an apology—a piece of gum
or a handful of peanuts or,
if he felt really bad, he might
spring for a Popsicle.
Never a spoken, "I'm sorry."

> Closest he ever came was,
> *I'm raising you the way*
> *I was raised. I didn't turn*
> *out so bad, and neither will you.*

Then he'd open the dog-eared
atlas and we'd choose our next
point of interest to explore.
Together. Just the two of us.
That's all either of us needed.

He always made that crystal
clear. Of course, he managed
to find plenty of female
companionship whenever
the desire struck.

It took me years
to understand the reasons
for those relationships
and how selfish
his motives were.

I've read about men
who use their cute dogs
to bait women
into hooking up.
Dad used me.

The result was temporary
housing, a shot at education,
though I changed schools
more often than most military
kids do. All that moving, though
Dad was out of the army.

At least we slept
in actual beds
and used bathrooms
that didn't have stalls.
But still, I always knew
those houses would never
be home.

I Might Say

We've actually found a real home
in a simple rented house only Dad

and I share, but I'd have to knock
damn hard on wood to eliminate

the jinx factor. We first came here
fifteen months ago on one sizzling

July day. I don't know why Dad
picked a California Gold Rush town,

but I like Sonora, and actually spent
my entire sophomore year, start

to finish, at Sonora High School.
Two whole summers, one complete

grade, well, that's a record, and
I'm praying I can finish my junior

year here, too. It's only just started,
and I'd say I'm probably doomed

to finish it elsewhere except for a couple
of things. One, Dad has a decent auto

mechanic job he likes. And, two, he has
an indecent woman he likes even better.

Indecency

Is subjective, I suppose,
and it's not like I'm listening
at Dad's bedroom door,
trying to figure out exactly
what the two of them might
be doing on the far side.

Truthfully, I don't care
that they have sex, or what
variety it might be. Vanilla
or kinky, doesn't matter
at all to me. I'm just glad
they're a couple, and that
they've stayed together

this long—six months
and counting. It gives me
hope that we won't pull up
stakes and hit the road anytime
soon. Plus, the regular
rutting seems to help Dad
blow off steam. His violent
outbursts are fewer and
further in between. The last
was a few weeks ago when
I made the mistake of asking
if I could bring a kitten home.

> *Kitten?* he actually bellowed. *No!*
> *Kittens turn into cats. Disgusting*
> *animals. Shitting in boxes, leaving*

shitty litter all over the floor.
And the smell! I don't work
my ass off to keep us from
living in a nasty, dirty car
to come home to cat stink.

I didn't mention his personal
body odor could rival any feline
stench. I wouldn't dare tell him
his cigarettes make me gag,
even though I finally convinced
him to smoke exclusively
outside, so it's only his nicotine
haze that I have to endure.

Instead, I shut my mouth,
resigned myself to the fact
I'd not share my bedroom
(complete with cat box)
with a furry companion.

Dad's never allowed me
to have pets. I assumed
it was due to our transient
lifestyle. Now I realize
it's at least in part because
of his impatience with dirt
and disorder. Or maybe

he's afraid to share
my affection. With anything.

It's Saturday Night

And Dad and Zelda are out
getting trashed. Some local
country band Zelda likes
is playing at Dad's favorite
"watering hole," as he calls it.

Sonora has brought out Dad's
inner Oklahoma hick, and that's okay
except when he's knocked back
a few too many and starts yelling
about "them goddamn Muslims"

or, worse, "fucking wetbacks."
I've made a few friends here,
and the one I'd call "best" happens
to be Latina. Dad probably thinks
I'm a traitor, but I don't care about

Monica's heritage, or if the Torres
family is one hundred percent legal.
Starting a new school, knowing
exactly no one, rates automatic Freak
Club membership. Monica had already

been inducted, for reasons I didn't
learn until later. Not that I cared
about why. She was the first person
at Sonora High to even say hello.
Freak-freak connection's a powerful thing.

Discovering the Reasons

For Monica's Freak
Club induction
made me discover
something about myself.

Something disquieting.
Disheartening, even,
at least at first,
because I found a facet

I never suspected
and, considering my history,
was not prepared for.

Sonora is small-town
conservative, especially
by California standards.
Accepting to a point,
but not exactly a mecca
for the LGBTQ crowd.

Monica Torres is not
only a lesbian, but also
a queer Mexican American,
and while she's mostly okay
carrying both banners,
they make her an outsider
in a school that takes great
pride in its Wild West spirit.

I would've run in the other
direction if I'd known she was
gay when I first met her.
The last thing I wanted
was a lezzie best friend.

For as long as I can remember,
I've hated my mother
for running off with her lesbian
lover. Dad has branded
that information into my brain,
and with it the concept
that queer equals vile.

But Monica is warm. Kind.
And funny. God, she makes
me laugh. I crave her company.
It was months before I figured
out the way she leaned,
and by then I already loved
her as a friend. Now, I'm afraid,

I'm starting to love her
as something much more,
not that we've explored
the places romance often
leads to. When we touch,
we don't touch there.

> When you're ready, *novia*,
> she tells me. *Only then.*

Monica understands
the reasons for my hesitation.
She's the only person I've ever
confided in about my parents—
both my mother's desertion
and my dad's instability.

Realizing I might in fact carry
some kind of queer gene,
not to mention a predisposition
toward imbalance, isn't easy
to accept. I still haven't exactly
embraced the idea, nor the theory
that one could very well lead
to the other.

Even if and when that finally
happens, I'll have to contend
with Dad, who will never admit
to himself or anyone else
that living inside his head
is a person prone to cruelty.

Despite that, I love him. Depend
on him. He's protected me.
Overprotected me, really.
I'm sure he only wants what's best
for me. I could never confess
to him the way I feel about Monica.
But I won't hide the fact
that we're Freak Club sisters.

Dad'll Have to Get Over It

He's the one who created
Freak Me to start with, so
however I choose to deal
with it had better be okay.

With him and Zelda (who
names their adorable newborn
Zelda, anyway?) busy elsewhere
for the evening, I invited
Monica over. She shows up
with a big foil-covered pan.

>   *Hope you're into tamales.*
>   *My mom doesn't know how*
>   *to make just a few, and I*
>   *figured these would be better*
>   *than frozen pizza.*

That would be our usual
go-to spend-the-night dinner.
"This is probably lame," I admit,
"but I've never tried tamales."

>   Monica walks past me on her
>   way to the kitchen. *Totally lame,*
>   she agrees. *Tamales are dope.*

I fall in line behind her, experience
a small sting of jealousy. What I
wouldn't give for her powerful,
compact build. I'm way too tall,

and thin to the point of looking
anorexic, not because I purposely
don't eat, but rather because
when I was growing up
there was never an excessive
amount of food around.
When we weren't bumming
meals off some sympathetic

woman, we survived on gas
station hot dogs, outlet store
bargains, and food pantry
handouts. On those lucky
days when I got fast food,
it was always kid's meals,
even after I outgrew kidhood.

I didn't dare complain,
of course, not even when
there was nothing at all.
I learned to make do with
whatever was offered.

And now my stomach still
can't quite accept larger-
than-child-size portions.
The Spartan rations are
enough to fuel my daily
activities, but don't allow
me a spare ounce of flesh.

I'm a Rectangle

Monica has curves,
and if tamales can round
out my straight lines
a little, I'm damn sure
going to give them a try.

Besides, when she peels
back the foil, the spicy-
sweet aroma arouses
a growl in the pit of my belly.

"Oh my God. If those taste
half as good as they smell,
my mouth's going to
have an orgasm."

> *Okay, that's kind of nasty.*
> *But I like it. And believe me,*
> *they taste better, so I'm gonna*
> *be watching your mouth.*

Straightforward interest,
barely disguised as humor.
That's fine. We've played
this game for a while now.
I can't win because Monica
knows exactly who she is.

I'm just starting
to figure out me.

I Just Graduated from Tacos

Because tamales *are* dope.
I polish off two without
thinking about it, am eyeing
a third when the doorbell rings.

> Monica looks up from her
> plate, where she's working
> on her fourth. *You expecting*
> *someone?* she mutters around

a big bite. I shake my head.
"I've got no clue who that can
be. But I guess I should find out.
Don't you dare finish those."

> She smiles. *Better hurry.*
> *Tamales disappear around me.*
> *Glad you like them, though.*
> *You could use a little meat—*

"On my skinny damn bones?
Yeah, I know. That's what Dad says."
I go to the front door, peek
out the adjacent window to make

sure I'm not opening it for a mass
murderer or something. But, no,
it's just Syrah, who's basically
my *other* friend. I unlock the dead bolt.

Speaking of Bolts

That's what Syrah does, right past
me. "Uh . . . come on in?" I offer.

> *Duh. I already did. Hey, what do*
> *I smell? Mexican food? Score!*

She zips straight toward the kitchen.
Syrah moves at two velocities:

freeway speed limit or stoned.
I trail her, feeling no jealous stab

at all as I watch her retreating form.
Monica has curves, but they're carved.

She's granite. Syrah's soft outside
and in. It's the inside that counts,

and that's why I like her, though
you wouldn't know how decent

she is if you only listened to her talk.
Sometimes she's got an obnoxious

mouth. Sometimes I do, too, courtesy
of my ex-military dad, who uses every

awful word in the book anytime
he gets a little wasted. *C'est la vie.*

By the Time

I reach the kitchen, Syrah
has already helped herself
to two tamales, leaving
the last three in the pan.
"Should we finish those
now, or save them for later?"

> *Better save 'em, says Syrah.*
> *We might get the munchies.*
> *I know your birthday's not*
> *till tomorrow, but I brought*
> *you a present. Two, in fact.*

She reaches into her purse
and, like magic, a full bottle
of vodka appears, along with
a couple of rolled cigarettes.
"I don't suppose that's tobacco."

> *Syrah laughs. It's a lot pricier.*
> *But I swiped these from my crack-*
> *brained brother. I'll catch hell*
> *for it later, but I don't give a shit.*

> *And that's why we love you.*
> *Monica takes her plate over*
> *to the sink, opens the vodka,*
> *and sniffs. Pee-yew. You stole*
> *this, too, I'm guessing. Yeah?*

Let's just call it borrowing,
not that I'll give it back, but
who cares? My mom stocks
up on this stuff five bottles at
a time. She was halfway to blitzed
when I left. She'll never miss it.

We finish eating and I take
the time to wash the dishes.
The last thing I want is to
invite one of Dad's ugly scenes.
He despises a dirty kitchen.
A dirty anything, really, except
maybe Zelda. Ooh. Ugly thought.

Got any OJ? Syrah pokes her
head into the fridge, withdraws
with a carton of orange juice.

Aw, come on. You don't like
vodka straight? But Monica
says it with a smile. Does
anyone like vodka straight?

I take three tumblers from
the cupboard, hand them to
Syrah. "We have to go outside.
I really don't need my dad
to smell booze, let alone weed."

We Pull Chairs

To the far side of the house,
away from the road. Luckily,
the manufactured homes in
this area sit on large lots.
We barely know our neighbors,
but then we never do.

Dad insists we keep our distance,
that we not invite
people living nearby
to borrow stuff or peek
in our windows. Okay by me.
Who needs a next-door spy,
especially when my girls
and I are sitting outside,
enjoying a toke or two?

Early October, the evening
is still really warm, made awesome
by little puffs of westerly breeze.
Said wind makes lighting the joint
something of a challenge, but one
Syrah is most definitely up to.

> *Got it.* She takes a big drag,
> holds it a very long time.
> She passes the blunt, finally
> exhales. *So where's your dad?*
> *He won't be home soon, will he?*

Dad almost caught us the last
time we indulged, and while
he isn't above maintaining
bad habits, he would not be
good with my having any.

"He went out dancing
with Zelda. They'll definitely
be out late, unless they have
an argument or something."
That's not out of the question,
which reminds me to remain
alert to the possibility.

*Zelda. Who in the actual fuck
names their kid Zelda?*

Considering my own thoughts
earlier, both the question and her
colorful phrasing make me smile.

*Monica snorts. Could be
the kind of mom who names
her kids Syrah and Chardonnay?*

*First of all, as you well know,
I pronounce my name SEER-uh,
not sir-AH. And second, so happens
Mom didn't name us. Dad did.*

First of all, just because you
mispronounce your name doesn't
mean it isn't actually sir-AH,
any more than your sister calling
herself char-DON-eye would
make her not Chardonnay.
And second, really? Your dad?
I thought your mom was the lush.

First off . . . Syrah raises her
hand for a high five. Touché,
bitch. And second, my dad used
to drink, same as Mom. After
they split up, he went all AA
because he fell for a churchy
straight-edge vegan chick
who never touched a damn
drop of booze in her life. Not
only that, but he married
her! Fucking unreal.

See, One Thing

About Freak Club membership,
no one's feelings are easily hurt.
We've all erected force fields
to keep the haters from our truths.

When it's just us we can lower
the barriers, allow our demons
a safe place to socialize, especially
when we're partying, too.

We pass the weed, chug down
our screwdrivers, listen to crickets,
a dog yapping in the distance. "How
come you don't you live with your dad?"

> Syrah gives me one of those *Are*
> *you effing out of your mind?* looks.
> *My mom would never let that happen.*
> *Dad actually pays child support.*
>
> *Anyway, we see him all the time,*
> *and it's not like he's nicer sober.*
> *In fact, he was a pretty cool drunk.*
> *Sobriety made him lose his sense*
>
> *of humor. Or maybe it made me*
> *lose mine. I always feel stressed*
> *when I'm around him. Of course,*
> *my stepmom's most of the problem.*

I've Never Met Her

Then again, I've never
met Syrah's dad, either,
just her mom, and I've
only bumped into her
a few times. We tend to
hang out when and where
our keepers aren't around.

"What's wrong with your
stepmom?" She's got me
curious now. "I mean, if
you don't mind telling us."

Syrah shrugs. *She and
Dad have two kids—twins,
and she's always fussing
about the boys' clothes and
hair, and don't forget those
teeth! She's a freaking tyrant,
and she thinks she can boss
me around, too. Just, nope.*

*Pretty sure that's what
moms, step or the regular
kind, are supposed to do,
observes Monica. My mom
is the bossiest person ever.
The only difference is she
does her bossing in Spanish.*

I've Met Monica's Mom

I've met her entire immediate
family, in fact. Dad. Two big
brothers, one little sister, good
Catholics all. Well, Monica
is probably the exception.
She says she's a Catholic in
constant need of confession.

> *What about your mom, Air?* asks
> Syrah. *Is she the overbearing type?*

The question hits square
in the diaphragm. Monica
shoots me a sympathetic look.
She knows about my mother,
but I've never talked to Syrah
about her. It's more than a sore
subject. It's a gaping wound,
barely scabbed over by time.

"For all I know, my mother's
dead. She hit the highway
when I was two, and we
haven't heard one word
from the bitch since."

> *Wow. That's shitty. Guess even
> a drunk mom is better than none.*

"Not necessarily." My voice
is razor-edged. "Speaking of
drunk, I vote we get that way."
I don't want to talk about
her anymore, so I head in
to fix more screwdrivers.

Syrah stays put, but Monica
stands. *I'll help.* She follows
me inside. *Hey. You okay?*

My hands shake as I pour
vodka. "Sure. Fine. Or I will be
soon." I lift my drink, toasting
my sudden rotten mood.

Monica comes closer, takes
the glass away, and places
it on the counter. *It's okay
to be angry, novia.*

The back of her hand
is a silk brushstroke
against my cheek,
so soft it invites tears.

The implication
makes me sway. But I can't go
there. Not now. Not yet.

Wait, Wrong

I don't dare
go there
ever.

Yes, I want
to fall hard
for someone,
experience love
and maybe
even lust.

However,
capital *H*,
it can't be
with a girl.

That's not
who I am.
Mustn't be
what I am.

Not only
because of Dad,
who'd happily
kick the crap
out of me after
calling me every
name in his antigay
slur book.

Beyond the universal
homo
fag
dyke
butch
muff diver
carpet muncher
etc.

would come words
he reserves for
my lesbian mother
and/or her girlfriend:

home wrecker
cheater
liar
whore

These things
are contrary
to everything
I know about me.
Though I have to admit
that knowledge
is elementary.

Who am I,
really?

Logic Suggests

I take a step back. Instinct
insists I hold my ground.
It feels good to be this close
to someone I care about.

And I do care
about Monica.

"It's stupid to be mad
at someone who means
nothing. Now let's go back
outside before SEER-uh
decides to come looking."

Monica takes two glasses.
I carry mine, plus the vodka
bottle, now registering
two-thirds empty. "Remind
me to stash this somewhere
once we finish it off, okay?"

       Like where? Under your bed?

"Ha-ha. Good question,
actually. Let me think
about it." Where indeed?
If Dad finds it, I'm toast,
not to be confused with
toasted, which is what
I'm rapidly becoming.

As We Start to Circle

To the far side of the house,
an engine in dire need
of a muffler comes coughing

and sputtering up the road,
working so hard there's zero
doubt it's going way too

fast at night where deer and
opossums and the occasional
bear often wander. The vehicle—

an old Chevy pickup that happens
to belong to Garrett Cole—slows
and the passenger window lowers.

> The head that pops out is attached
> to Keith Connelly. *Hey, girls!*
> *Is that vodka? Wanna party?*

Garrett and Keith are world-class
third-string pretend-to-be jocks.
"Not with you!" I yell in their direction.

> Now Garrett shouts his two cents.
> *Stupid lezbos. Bet what I got right*
> *here in my pants could cure you.*

"Maybe if you could actually
get it up!" I call cheerfully. "I mean,
for anyone besides each other."

Yeah! adds Monica. *Takes a queer
to know one.* She and I both find
the exchange immensely funny.

The guys, however, don't seem
to agree. Garrett punches the gas
pedal, kicking up a huge fog of dust

behind the farting exhaust pipe.
"Hope they forgot to roll up
the windows. What a couple

of dweebs." Giggling like complete
dweebs ourselves, we continue
around the house, where Syrah

has started to worry about the wait.
*What took so long? Thought you two
took off with what's left of the vodka.*

"Nah. We just got waylaid by Keith
and Garrett, who wanted to party
with us lesbians as long as we were

providing the booze and were willing
to try what was right there in their
pants. Garrett's sure he can 'cure' us."

*I have got to quit hanging out
with dykes. Just think. I could be
part of the popular crowd instead.*

"Don't call me a dyke. I mean, just
because one of my best friends
is queer doesn't make me that way."

I smile at Monica's obvious eye
roll. "Anyway, I bet if one of us
would give those boys head, we could

be popular, too." We look at one
another, all serious like, before we bust
up laughing again. "'Kay, never mind."

We finish off the vodka, and despite
the blooming buzz, a brilliant idea
jumps into my brain. "You guys up

for a little walk? I think I figured out
how to dispose of the evidence." I hold
up the empty bottle and outline my plan.

No one objects, so off we go down
the road to Garrett's house. By the time
we arrive, there's no sign of the guys,

though the bass boom of music tells
us they're inside. Easy peasy. "Think
I should wipe off our fingerprints?"

Without waiting for an answer, I use
my shirttail to do just that, then place
the bottle in the bed of Garrett's pickup.

Syrah Isn't Finished

Keep an eye out, she orders.

More quietly than I would've
thought possible, she opens
the truck's passenger door,
sticks her head inside.

She's making me nervous,
whispers Monica, and I agree.

Monica looks in one direction,
I keep tabs on the other,
while Syrah pokes around

in the glove box in search
of what, exactly, I have no clue.
Surely Garrett wouldn't leave
valuables in his truck.

Ha! It's not weed, but . . .

She exits the cab suddenly,
with a box in her hand, shuts
the door almost as noiselessly
as she opened it, nudges Monica.

Hurry up. Let's go.

We Quick-Time

Away from Garrett's,
where the music's still
blasting, obscuring all
the noise we've made.

I've got no idea what's
in Syrah's right hand,
but it must be amazing
because she's laughing
in a way that means
she's congratulating
herself. We trot

toward home at an easy
gait, but as we pass
the first neighbor's house,
his dog starts barking—
huge hoarse *hrrufs*
that make us pray
his fence is solid,

and send us sprinting
up the middle
of the road, howling
laughter in response.
"Don't look back!"
I urge, but of course
all of us keep glancing
over our shoulders.

See anything? hisses
Monica, trying not to trip
over obstacles obscured
by night's shadows.

"Nah. There's nothing
behind us." No dog.
No dweebs. No sputtering
truck. Looks like we
escaped in the clear.

Finally, damp-haired
with sweat and winded,
we turn into my driveway,
Syrah still in the lead.
Once we're on the porch,
I tap her shoulder.
"So, tell us, Sherlock.
What did you find?"

When she turns, the look
on her face is priceless.
Check it out. Why would
Garrett *need* these?

She lifts a small carton
up under the porch light.
Trojan condoms. Latex.
Ultrathin. Lubricated.
Thirty-six-count value pack.

"You stole Garrett's
condoms? What if he
actually does get lucky?"
We all look at one another
and totally bust up.

> Garrett would never get
> that *lucky*, says Monica
> when she finally stops
> hiccuping laughter.

> > *That's for sure. This right*
> > *here is a lifetime supply*
> > *of rubbers for Garrett,*
> > adds Syrah, and that makes

the three of us dissolve
into a fit of amusement
again. We go inside, still
laughing, retreat to my
room in case Dad comes
home. I put on some music

and for some crazy reason
that no doubt has everything
to do with vodka and weed,
Syrah decides to play with
the foil packets. She opens
one, extracts the condom,
stretches it full length.

Jeez, the guy thinks a lot
of himself. I kind of thought
he was dickless. Hey, think
fast! She tosses

a couple at Monica, who
catches them on the fly.
What am I supposed to do
with these? she complains.

Syrah shrugs. *Use 'em for*
water balloons? Give 'em to
your big brother? I just know
I don't need all of them.
I haven't gotten lucky
myself lately. Okay, ever.

Now she opens the drawer
in my nightstand, practices
sinking shots from across
the room before finally
growing bored with the game.

All right, everyone's stocked
up on latex. Everyone except
Garrett, that is. And . . .

We're laughing again. Hot
damn, is it great to have friends.

Maya

Funerals stink. Especially your daddy's funeral. Especially, especially when you have to sneak out to go because your crazy mother would totally flip if she had a clue that was your plan. And, hey, why not toss in the fact that your lunatic mom was most of the reason your dad drank himself to death to start with?

Mom chased Dad out of the house and all the way to San Antonio four years ago. Maybe it's just eighty miles from Austin, Texas, but it might as well have been eight hundred. I've only seen him a half dozen times since he left, and the only way I even know he died was because I happened to answer the phone when Uncle Wade called. Mom wouldn't have said a word. I didn't bother to tell her, either.

Instead, I bummed a ride with Tati, who only griped a little about spending her Saturday taking me to the funeral of a dude she's never even met. "What are best friends for?" I asked, when she hesitated to say she'd drive.

"Sex?" she answered, and all I could do was laugh.

I've been in love with Tatiana Holdridge since seventh grade, but that's not something I can say out loud, and it's got nothing to do with sex. Tati is the one person who knows me inside out, and sticks around anyway.

"Are you sad?" she whispered as we slipped into seats near the front of the mostly empty funeral parlor.

The simple question was hard to answer. Dad was in my life daily till I turned twelve, but even when he was home he was mostly absent. Kind of like how I am in chemistry class—there, but not. Still, he was gentle, funny, and offered himself up when Mom aimed her anger my way. The few times I've seen him since, he always did nice things—took me clothes shopping or to a movie, something Mom considers frivolous. That's her word for anything fun. "Frivolous." Things that qualify: movies, arcades, amusement parks. Even television.

Dad's funeral wasn't frivolous. It was spare. The only people there were his girlfriend Claire, his brother Wade, a few of the guys he worked with, and a couple of kids from the middle school where he was a janitor. That was sweet. They told me he didn't put up with the bullies who harassed them, and they wanted to pay their respects. I'm glad Dad was a hero to someone.

Throw pride into my jumble of feelings. Sadness was in there, of course. I also felt pity for Claire, who looked swallowed up by grief. She never said a word to me, or anyone else that I could see. But then, if I barely knew my dad, I didn't know her at all.

I felt grateful for Uncle Wade, who took care of all the details. His eyes watered as the minister recited his canned eulogy, and that made me remember the last funeral I went to. He was there, too, and Dad, when Grandma and Grandpa McCabe were killed in a car wreck. That must've been five years back.

Today, after the minister talked, everyone offered a

favorite memory. Claire talked about the day she met Dad, working at a car wash fund-raiser for the school. Uncle Wade told about going fishing when they were kids, and how Dad insisted on using stink bait so he wouldn't have to thread worms. One of the kids shared about the bullies.

And me? "Mostly what I remember about Dad is watching games on TV on weekends. He taught me baseball and football and basketball. Tried to get me to watch hockey, too, but it's not my thing. My best-ever memory was going to an Astros game and they creamed the Dodgers. My dad was so happy he sang all the way home. He could really sing."

That choked me up. When we were called forward and I bent to kiss Dad's white wax cheek, it was like the air got sucked from my lungs. It hurt to breathe. You always think you'll have more time, you'll get another chance to make things right with someone you should be closer to. Sometimes that doesn't happen. But why did it have to be Dad, and why so soon?

Tati escorted me to the open casket. I could tell she didn't want to, but in the moment I crumbled, she reached for me, propping me up with a subtle merge of fingers. "I'm here for you," she whispered. Well, of course she was, though as soon as we turned to leave, she let go of my hand. Considering where we were, that was necessary. But painful.

Outside, Uncle Wade stood sweating in the sweltering late August shade. "Would you like to follow the hearse to the cemetery and witness the lowering?"

Watch the earth swallow my dad, bait for my nightmares? I shook my head. "I have to get back to Austin or Mom will throw a fit."

He handed me a manila envelope. "Your father wanted you to have this. He loved you very much, you know. He was sorry he didn't have more to give you."

All I could do was nod and look inside. I'd thought every photo of my father was gone—trashed in one of Mom's rages. But Dad had kept a handful of the two of us, and now they'll be my hidden treasure. I have to hide them from Mom, along with Dad's handwritten apology for leaving me, and $1200 cash.

"He saved every penny he could," Uncle Wade said. "He hoped it might help you go to college, so try not to spend it all in one place." He winked, as if to say he knew college isn't in my plans. I'll be lucky to graduate high school. Not because I'm not smart enough to do the work, but as my counselor says, I lack motivation.

What I *am* motivated to do is find a way out from under my mother's heavy-handed rule. Case in point: when Tati dropped me off at home (she *never* comes inside, not that I blame her), I stashed my treasured envelope behind a bush outside my bedroom window, knowing it was sure to draw Mom's attention, and it would've. The second I walked in the door, she pounced. "Where have you been?" Spit pooled in the corners of her mouth.

I could've lied. But in that moment it seemed disrespectful. Not to her. To my father. "I went to Dad's funeral."

"That's the best you can do? You expect me to believe that?"

"I don't care if you do or you don't. He's dead. And by now he's buried. I didn't hang out to watch."

She didn't say she was sorry. Didn't ask how I found out he'd died. What she said was, "I'm surprised he lasted this long. He got more time than he deserved. Regardless, I'm extremely unhappy with you. How dare you leave this house without telling me where you're going, and who you'd be with?"

That's her Cardinal Rule, and I used to comply. Not so much anymore, though. Now I break it every chance I get, and if she happens to catch me, I come up with a good story. But I didn't think I needed an excuse to go to Dad's funeral. "I figured you'd say no."

She froze for a second, and in that moment her face morphed into something animal. Feral. When she spoke, it was a snarl. "Soon enough saying no won't be an option. We're moving to Sea Org in Los Angeles this spring. You'll live on campus, in youth housing. They won't put up with your shenanigans."

All I know about Sea Org is what I've overheard. It's where high-level Scientologists go to become even higher-level Scientologists. I guess I should've paid more attention, asked a few more questions. I should have pretended to care. But one thing's certain. "I'm not going anywhere. You might be sucked into that bullshit, but you can't make me."

"Bet me."

I didn't see the backhand coming. The prongs of her ring bit into my cheek, leaving four little red cuts to go with the ugly bruise meant to put me in my place. All it did was make me more determined than ever to leave this house behind as soon as I can figure out a way to go without her having me arrested.

I'm considering my next move now.

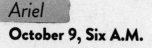
Ariel

October 9, Six A.M.

I rouse to a volley
of flimsy snores.
My friends are both
asleep on the floor,

Monica on the right
side of my bed; Syrah
on the left. She wanted
to drive herself home
last night. I said no way.
Friends don't let friends
drive loaded to the max.

Speaking of that, my head
feels like someone poured
cement inside it—thick
and churning. Hope it
doesn't set up. My skull's
already hammering.

Why do I drink again?
Why does anyone
drink to excess?

Not the best way
to start my seventeenth
year celebration. Hopefully
the day will improve quickly.

I Slide Out of Bed

Quietly, no more than a slight
creak of the aging wooden frame.

Tiptoe down the hall to the bathroom,
noticing the snoring on the far side

of my dad's bedroom door is much
louder than the tremulous snuffling

on the floor of my own room. He and
Zelda stumbled in really late last night.

Neither of them should have driven
home, but one of them must have.

Dad's LeSabre is parked just off the road,
not quite straight on the dirt shoulder,

as if trying to maneuver it into the driveway
was just too damn much to manage.

If they consumed that much alcohol,
they should've stayed over at Zelda's

in town. Dad probably figured I'd be
having a party, something he needed

to supervise. I'm glad the actual partying
part was well behind us when they arrived.

My girls and I were still awake when
we heard them come in bickering.

We quieted for a minute, trying to figure
out what, exactly, their problem was, but

Dad shushed Zelda long enough to move
their dispute to a more private location.

So we went back to yakking about our
upcoming varsity girls' basketball season.

All three of us are pretty great at the sport,
though Syrah has to work a lot harder.

Prior to starting Sonora High, I had no
clue I had any athletic ability to speak of.

But when we played in our regular PE
class last year, I found out I could shoot

with a high degree of accuracy, and I'm
quick on the court, too. Somehow word

got around and Coach Booker asked me
to try out for the team. When I argued

that I'd never participated in organized
sports before, she silenced me. "Talent

trumps experience, I've found. Show me
what you've got." So I did, and now, here

I am—starting center. I had to convince
Dad to let me join the team. He works

long days, and we live a fair distance
from town, so extracurricular activities

are difficult to accommodate. As for
basketball, transportation would

definitely be an issue except I stay after
school to practice and Syrah chauffeurs

me home, often with a stop for a burger
on the way, so there's less cooking to do.

I hope Dad will make time to come
to home games. He claims he's proud

of me, but I never see the truth of that
reflected in his eyes. Words are easy.

Maybe if he witnesses my ability
on the court, he'll recognize how hard

I've worked to rise above mediocrity,
and reward me with honest respect.

That Being the Case

I'd prefer he not realize the reason
I'm in the bathroom not long past
daybreak is because I need pain
relief for the residual effects of too
much vodka consumed rather quickly.

I swallow a couple of aspirin, chase
them with a whole lot of water, pee
out what I can, and return to my bed.
This time when I crawl over the foot
and across the mattress, the groan

>   of the frame wakes Monica. *Hey,*
>   she whispers softly. *Can I get in bed*
>   *with you? Sleeping on the floor sucks.*

I pull back the covers, invite her
beneath them. It's a double bed,
so there's plenty of room. Still,
our feet touch. Who knew toe
connection could create sparks?

>   It scares me, but I don't move, and
>   neither does Monica. *Happy birthday,*
>   *novia. Do you feel different this morning?*

We both keep our voices low, so we
don't disturb Syrah. "If you mean do
I feel older, not really. If you mean do I
feel hungover, damn straight. How
about you? Do you need some aspirin?"

I Expect Her

To admit she needs exactly
that. Instead, she shakes her head.

> *No. Te necesito. I need you.*
> She traces the line of my jaw

with one gentle finger. Now
I'm terrified. But I stay very still
and she presses no further.

> In fact, she turns over. *Maybe
> now I can finally get some sleep.*

"You were sleeping before.
I know because you snore."

> *Lo sé,* she sighs. *Get used to it.*
> She sighs again, dips into slumber.

I lie back against my pillow,
inhaling the cologne of sun-toasted
skin and coconut oil lifting off

her shiny black satin hair. The scent
rustles leaves of memory in a forest
too dark to enter. Longing, not sexual,

but more a need for connection
stirs, upwelling suddenly at Monica's
dream-driven sigh. *Novia. Te necesito.*

I Wake Again

This time to a window bright
with sunlight and some foreign
movement disturbing my sheets.
Monica. Yes. Everything comes
tumbling back in one moment
of clear consciousness. "Morning."

> Still prone on the floor, Syrah
> peeks up through heavy lashes.
> *Oh, man. My mouth tastes like*
> *rotten potatoes. And I need coffee.*

> Monica sits up beside me. *Coffee?*
> *Si, lo quiero también. And I'm starving.*
> *Wish we had leftover tamales instead*
> *of pigging out on them last night.*

"You guys actually drink coffee?
Like, to wake up in the morning?
The only way I can choke it down is
cut with cream and enough sugar
to trigger a diabetic coma."

I vow to attempt the Mr. Coffee anyway,
and we pad to the kitchen in our pj's.
My pj's, actually, as neither Monica nor
Syrah brought theirs to the impromptu

> slumber party. Both fight the extra
> leg length, especially Syrah, who says,
> *Jeez, Ariel. How tall are you, anyway?*

"Five ten plus. Hopefully I'm done
growing now. As my dad always says,
it's hard for tall girls to find dates."

Maybe dates with boys, corrects
Monica. Personally, I kind of like
my women built like Amazons.

Shut up! exclaims Syrah. Listen,
I am a total ally. But here's the deal.
I really don't want to hear details.

That's 'cause you're dumb, says
Monica. The details are the best
part. She's claimed the Mr. Coffee,
located the Folgers, and poured water
into the reservoir. You got filters?

It takes a couple of cupboard
explorations to find them, and
while I'm looking it occurs to me
that I wouldn't trade my Freak
Club friends for membership

in the Popular Pack, even without
a required BJ initiation. Monica's
queer, Syrah swears she's not, but
she doesn't judge or question or get
all fake about liking Monica anyway.

And neither has insisted I declare
myself gay, straight, or just confused.

I'm Confused

About a lot of things,
including the coffee-
making process, but
I am totally clear on
how to make a killer
omelet for three, and

that's what I'm working
on when Dad and Zelda
materialize, scarlet-eyed
and crazy-haired. They
must have gotten past
bickering long enough

to engage in (yeesh!)
creepy old-people sex.
I don't care what that
involves, don't want to
consider the visuals.
The vague smell of
rutting is more than
enough to stimulate
a gigantic yuck factor.

Morning, girls, says Dad.
Smelled the coffee and
thought we'd come help
ourselves. That okay?

When we agree that it
is, he comes over and

nudges me. *When did you
start drinking coffee, anyway?*

I could say I didn't really,
that this pot was mostly
meant for my friends.
Instead, I tell him, "This
seemed like as good a day
as any. Seventeen and
still a coffee virgin? I'd
never live that down."

*Seventeen? When did that
happen?* He grins like a total
goober. *Oh. That's right. Today's
your birthday, isn't it? Well,
happy, happy, Ari Fairy.*

"Dad!" Inevitable laughter
spills from the mouths
of my so-called friends.
Nothing to do but laugh
along with them. "God, Dad,
I'm not, like, four anymore."

*Too bad, too. You were such
an adorable little girl.* He
watches Zelda pour coffee
and put two spoons of sugar
in each mug. *What the hell
do you think you're doing?!*

All Laughter

And pleasant conversation
brake to a complete standstill.

> Zelda freezes. *What do you
> mean? What did I do now?*

*You put all that goddamn sugar
in my coffee. What the fuck for?*

> Zelda's jaw drops. *But Mark,
> you always put sugar in your coffee.*

*Only in the sludge they serve
in town. I told you before . . .*

> Her head is twisting side to side.
> *Are you saying no milk, either?*

*That's exactly what I'm saying.
I don't know why you're acting*

*like this is some big surprise.
It's not like we haven't had coffee*

*at home before. Brew Folgers right,
no need to make it fucking sweet.*

"Here, I'll take the one with sugar,"
I offer, mostly to make them shut up.

What a Strange Exchange

It's unsettling, and I really wish
they'd stop. Monica and Syrah
are trying not to participate as
spectators, but that's pretty hard.

"Eggs are done. You guys want
to eat outside?" I don't wait for
them to answer because I know
they must be as uncomfortable

as I am. I divide the omelet into
three portions, put them on paper
plates, and hand them out. "Don't
forget your coffee." I grab my own

syrupy cup, and we head off for
our alfresco dining experience.
We've barely cleared the door
when Monica says, *What was that*

all about? How long have they been
together? Like, six months?
You'd think she'd know how your
dad likes his coffee by now, right?

I settle into a chair, take a bite
before I answer. "No one said
she's the brightest bulb, but yeah,
seems like she ought to by now."

Well, I'm not positive, but it looked
like your dad wanted to pick a fight,
says Syrah. Is he always so argumentative?
And what about that Ari Fairy thing?

My face ignites. "He hasn't called
me that since I was really little.
He just wanted to embarrass me.
And yes, he enjoys a good argument."

Saying it out loud makes me realize
just how true the statement is.
Sometimes he insists things are
honest-to-God facts, when I know

they're not. It's like a big game
for him. Regular entertainment.
The point is to make his opponent
question her beliefs. Maybe even

her sanity. I use the feminine
pronoun because it's almost
always a female he coerces
into playing. That includes me.

I take a sip of coffee, now cooled
to lukewarm. "Hey. This isn't bad. I
don't get what Dad was griping
about." Actually, now I consider it,

I think Zelda was right. I remember
sneaking a sip of his coffee a couple
of times. It was always sweet.
And milky. It reminded me of hot

cocoa, only made with coffee ice
cream. Has he really changed
the way he drinks his Folgers?
Never mind. I already know

the answer. But why mess with
Zelda, and why exactly then?
I wish I could figure out the rules
to Dad's confounding games.

What I do know is if you call him
on his bullshit, first thing he does
is deny he ever said it in the first
place. If that doesn't work, he'll swear

you misunderstood. And if you still
hold your ground, he'll go all-out
verbal attack, doing his best to
convince you that *you're* victimizing

him. If you don't back off then, things
can progress quickly to physical
violence. I learned the hard way
to zip it sooner rather than later.

But Then Comes

The inevitable apology,
and it's always so sincere
there's no possible way
not to forgive him.

He swears everything
he does, he does for me,
and how can I not
believe him, when
he loves me more
than life itself—
another regular vow.

Up to a point,
I understand where
his cruel streak began.
As a soldier, he saw things
that, God willing, I'll never see—
flesh-chewed corpses
and people left living,
but missing limbs
or lacking intact brains.

So, yeah, I cut him
a lot of slack, and anyway,
he's been around the block
a time or two, as the saying
goes. He knows things
I've yet to learn,
so I listen to his advice,
even when it confuses me.

Omelet Finished

We're still sitting outside
in my pj's, warmed by tepid
October sunshine,
when Garrett and Keith
go chug-chugging by,
headed toward town.

> Garrett honks, Keith opens
> his window long enough to
> give us the finger, and Syrah
> says, *Hell yeah! Now I can say*
> *those assholes saw me in lingerie.*
> *I still have a chance at popularity.*

That cracks me up, and Monica
actually spits out a mouthful
of coffee. *Lingerie! Oh, baby,*
these are some sexy jammies.
She pronounces the *j* like
an *h*, Spanish language–style.

> *Probably the sexiest hammies*
> *those boys have ever seen, at*
> *least on real flesh-and-blood girls.*
> *Porn star bitches don't count.*

"Girl, I happen to be attached
to these pahamas, and at least
they know we wear them. They
probably fantasized all night

about the naked lesbian party
happening just down the road.
Hey. You think they spotted
the Popov bottle in back?"

We decide that's highly unlikely,
considering their general state
of awareness. "And that stinking
exhaust is so loud, I doubt
they'd hear it rolling around."

>*Oh*, says Syrah. *What time is it,*
>*anyway? I'm supposed to be at*
>*work by eleven. They've got me*
>*doing the lunch shift today.*
>She waits tables at the Diamondback
>Grill. Best cheeseburgers in town.

"It's probably around ten.
We were up a little after nine."
Much later than I usually get up.
I'm an early riser for the most part.

>*Can I catch a ride?* asks Monica.
>*My brother said he'd pick me up,*
>*but I could be waiting forever.*

"So sorry my company sucks."
I pout, pretending to be hurt.
But I get it. Dad and Zelda
are way too present inside.

I Expect Zelda

To hang out all day, in fact.
She usually stays the weekend.
So I'm surprised when she asks
for a ride back into town with
Syrah. Not sure if it's because
of the earlier stress or what.

> She claims something else.
> *My nephew's coming to visit*
> *for a while. His father passed*
> *away recently, and my sister's*
> *having a real tough time dealing*
> *with everything. I want you to*
> *meet Gabe. You two will get along.*

We're waiting for Monica
and Syrah to exit my bedroom
dressed in something other
than hammies. "I'm sorry,"
I tell her, because that's what
you say to someone dealing
with a loss, even peripherally.
"Is Gabe going to go to SHS?"

> *No. He's nineteen. Your dad*
> *said he'd try and get him on*
> *at the shop. Gabe's a pretty good*
> *mechanic himself. And this might*
> *sound weird, coming from his old*
> *aunt, but he's easy on the eyes.*

Awesome

She wants to set me up with
her nephew, who's too old,
too greasy, and too connected

to Zelda to possibly be the man
of my dreams, as if I'm dreaming
about men to start with. But since

she's being nice, and since I feel
sorry for the way Dad talked to her
earlier, I find myself agreeing to stop

by her house tomorrow after practice
to meet him. "As long as I can
convince Syrah to give me a ride."

> She offers a knowing smile.
> *I hear you'll be able to drive*
> *yourself around pretty soon.*

I stop my eyes mid-roll. "Really?
How's that supposed to happen?"
I don't have a license, not to mention

> a vehicle. Zelda lowers her voice.
> *I'm not supposed to say anything,*
> *but Mark's been looking at used cars.*

Before she can say more, Dad
comes blustering down the hall.
He looks at Zelda. *Ready to go?*

She Holds Up One Hand

As if to say stop. *No worries.*
You don't have to take me.
Ari's friend offered to give
me a ride home. Oh . . .
She glances at me nervously.
Is it okay to call you Ari?

I'm not big on nicknames,
but at least she asked,
and it kind of feels warm.
I'd say like family, but that's
something I don't have much
experience with. I start to tell
her it's fine, but before I can open

my mouth, Dad interjects,
No, it's not okay, it's way
too goddamn familiar.
She's my daughter and
I don't even call her Ari.

Unless he attaches
"Fairy" to it, apparently,
but I'm not jumping into
this round of his game
except to say, "I don't mind,"
disregarding the eye arrows
he shoots in my direction.

Zelda Ducks Them, Too

Choosing to use my un-nicked
name. Anyway, I'll go ahead
and ride back into town with

Ariel's friends so I don't
interrupt your day. I know
you've made other plans.

Dad scowls. *What the hell are*
you talking about, woman? My plan
was to buy some beer, take you

home, and watch the Astros game
at your house. She's got a big-screen
TV. We don't. Houston's on a roll.

Zelda shoots me a sympathetic
glance. *It's your daughter's*
birthday, Mark. Spend it with her.

Now you're telling me what to
do? But when he notices the hurt
in my eyes, he says, *Fine, goddamn it.*

Stung to the core, tears threaten.
I push them away. "It's okay, Dad.
You watch the game. I'm good."

No, no, he backtracks. *Zelda's right.*
A girl only turns seventeen once.
What would you like to do today?

Hard Question

I'm considering my answer
when Syrah and Monica finally
appear, dressed in yesterday's
clothing, which is wrinkled
and carries vague essences
of tamales, vodka, and weed.

Emphasis on the Mexican food,
thank goodness, and maybe
the rest is all in my head. Dad
and Zelda don't seem to notice.

> *Okay, says Syrah. Better hustle.*
> *I have to stop at home and change.*
> *Come by the restaurant later and*
> *we'll do something cool for your day.*

> *Something cool like a sundae?*
> *asks Monica. 'Cause you can count*
> *me in! Let me know what time*
> *if you're going, okay? I'll even*
> *bring the candles.* She comes over.

Gives me a hug.
A long hug.
Long enough
to make me squirm,
hoping Dad doesn't
notice and take it
the wrong way.

Which would be
the correct way.
But he's too busy
sloppy kissing Zelda
to notice anyway.

Let's blow this joint! orders
Syrah, and Monica reluctantly
lets go. Zelda, on the other hand,
seems happy enough to disconnect.

Trouble in paradise?
I hope not. Even though
she's only been tethered
to Dad for a few short
months, she's an anchor,
holding us in place here.
Just to be safe, I offer again,
"Dad, if you want to take
Zelda home and watch
the game, I'm good with
it. We can do a movie
and dinner in town later."

He thinks it over, but finally
says, Nah. I'd have to come
back out and pick you up.
I've got a better idea. You girls
go ahead. We'll talk about
dinner and give you a time.

Once the Others Leave

Dad tells me to get dressed,
we're going for a drive, and as
I don a pair of loose-fitting jeans
and my favorite camouflage tee,
I can't help but think about Zelda's
comment. Could Dad be taking
us shopping for a used car?

Because that would make this
birthday just about perfect.
A car that belongs to me.
How awesome would that be?

Not because of some grand
desire to hit the road and explore
the country. I've already done
that, and so if I inherited Dad's
wanderlust, it's already been
satisfied. But just the ability
to drive myself to school, or
home after practice, without
asking for help or permission.
That, to me, defines freedom.

Not just the independence part,
but also the ability to decide
it's time to go and find my own way

home.

I've Been Old Enough

To get my license
for a year now.
Everybody I know
already has one.

That includes Monica,
though she rarely
gets to use it because
she doesn't own a car.

That's been Dad's
excuse, too.
No vehicle to drive,
why bother with
all that paperwork?

But I'm pretty sure
Dad wants to control
how I come and go
so he can inform
my every decision.

To be honest,
I used to think
that was okay.
I believed I needed
a decent keeper,
that independence
was too much
responsibility.

It was easy,
being told what to do.

But now that I've had
a taste of free will,
my appetite
for self-discovery
is growing.

I'll never figure out
who I am and what
I want from life
if I keep relying
on Dad's input.

Time to leap
from the nest,
experience flight,
even if it means
a crash landing or two.

I don't say anything
like that to Dad, of course.
He enjoys his role
as overseer.

But maybe,
if I've played my cards
perfectly, he'll loosen
the reins and let me try
to find my flight path.

But as It Turns Out

That's not exactly what Dad's got
in mind. In fact, it's not even close.

He grabs a six-pack of Budweiser
from the fridge, tells me to get

> behind the wheel of his LeSabre.
> *You drive. You can use the practice.*

That has me going for a few, but
now he tells me to turn up country

rather than toward town. "Where're we
going?" I ask, still hoping he'll tell me

> to look at a car. Instead, he says,
> *We haven't taken a nice long ride*

> *in a while, and I've been wanting*
> *to check out this place called Indigeny*

> *Reserve. It's apple season, you know.*
> *Plus I've got a hankering for cider.*

Well, at least he's letting me drive.
Once in a while when I was little,

he used to sit me on his lap and have
me steer while he worked the pedals.

Then later, when my legs grew long
enough to reach the gas and brake,

on way-out-of-the-way roads, usually
dirt, he'd let me handle it all. So I mostly

know what I'm doing. "When can I get
my license?" I nudge. "I can pass the test."

> Yes, I know. You just need my signature
> on the application. You've been saying
>
> the same thing for months. But since
> you don't happen to own a car—

"But Zelda said . . ." I realize suddenly
maybe I should've kept quiet about it.

> Zelda said what? Open-container
> laws be damned, he pops a beer.

Too late to turn back. "Oh, kind of in
passing she mentioned you've been

looking at used cars. Guess I assumed—
or hoped, really—it was for me."

> He splashes into a big pond of anger,
> comes up stuttering. Bigmouthed bitch.

Damn, Damn, Damn

I've done it now. Last thing
I wanted to do was get him
angry at Zelda. "Don't be mad,
Dad. She's just excited for me.
If she was wrong about your
intentions, it's no big deal."

> He slurps his beer, reels
> himself in. *Look, Air, I'd like to*
> *get you a car, but I haven't been*
> *able to find an affordable vehicle*
> *worthy of the investment. I can*
> *do the labor if something goes*
> *wrong, but parts are expensive,*
> *plus there's insurance and gas.*

Way to explode my zeppelin,
Dad. But, hey, here's an idea.
"What if I get a job?" I expect

> him to embrace the concept,
> but his immediate reaction is,
> *No frigging way. Not on my watch.*
> *If I can't pay for it, you don't need it.*

Pride? I don't think so. But if
not that, what then? "Lots of kids
get jobs, Dad. In fact, lots of parents
require their offspring to prove
how responsible they actually are."

Except for a Slurp

Of his beer, he's quiet for a good
half mile. Okay, it's more like three
or four slurps, before he finally says,

> *I've failed you in so many ways,*
> *little girl. I simply can't let you work*
> *when I'm responsible for your needs.*

"But, Dad, you said it's important
for women to make their own way
in the world and not rely on a man."

> He thinks that over for a second.
> *I don't believe I've ever said that, and*
> *definitely not when it comes to you.*

An uneasy silence bloats the space
between us. I heard him say those precise
words before, and now I search my memory

vault to dig up exactly when. I've got it.
We were staying with Cecilia, one
of several women Dad hooked up with

along the way during our nomadic days.
That was a pattern. Touch down
somewhere he felt like hanging

around, he'd pick up a woman hungry
for a man and willing to put up with
his kid. Dad was all charm, and the world

offered up plenty of lonely ladies.
Talking them into putting us up for a while
was something he accomplished easily.

When I was really young, I totally
thought he was seeking a replacement
mom for me, but as I got older, I came

to realize the relationships were never
meant to become permanent. Rather,
they allowed us periods of home-cooked

meals, regular showers, and a temporary
address that accommodated school.
Oh, not to mention fairly frequent sex

for Dad, who happily accepted all benefits
as long as they didn't require monetary
compensation. Once in a while he took

part-time work, but that was rare, and as
far as I know, he contributed very little
of his paychecks to our upkeep.

Things were no different at Cecilia's, where
we'd stayed for a couple of months. I guess
I was twelve because I got to ride the bus

to school for a whole sixth-grade semester.
Maybe if Cecilia had just accepted Dad
being a lazy ass, we would've stayed longer.

She'd recently lost her job, and while
unemployment might have been enough
to provide for a single woman, it stretched

awfully thin for two hard-drinking adults
and one kid—even one who ate like a bird.
I'm not sure about Dad's criteria when it

came to working or not, but at Cecilia's
he heaped one excuse on top of another
for not finding a job. Finally, she decided

enough was enough, and as was often
the case, everything came to a head
after a night out at a local tavern.

They'd left me alone and I was asleep
when they bungled in, already immersed
in a heated argument loud enough to yank

> me out of an indigo ocean of dreams.
> . . . do you think you are, you goddamn
> leech? I'm sick of buying your beer.

> Come on, pretty baby, Dad soothed.
> You know you never had it so good.
> Besides, you want to be independent.

> It's not good for a woman to rely
> on a man. Independence! That's what
> you want. Celebrate your freedom.

She Celebrated

By kicking us out
a few weeks later.
When it became clear
that's where things
were headed, I begged
her for enough time
to finish the school year.

Kindly, she agreed,
but tension hung like
a static curtain in that
little house. Summer
was heating up, and
along with it tempers,
and I was very glad
the day Dad and I piled
into his car and took off.

We spent June and July
mostly camping out,
and by the time school
started in the fall,
we'd shifted states again,
from Idaho to Oregon.
I celebrated my thirteenth
birthday in a Corvallis trailer
park, with a whole new woman
attached to Dad's hip.

School blows, man. The first quarter is almost over and I shudder to think what my report card will look like, though Mom probably won't even ask to see it. She's so blinded by her "church" work she barely remembers I'm here. Bad for her. Good for me, except when she tries to draw me into that insanity. All I've got to say about that is hell no, at least behind her back.

Mom got lured into Scientology by one of the women she works with at the credit union. Bethany convinced Mom that L. Ron Hubbard's brand of pseudoscience could fix her "ruin," which at the time was marriage to an uncommunicative husband. Of course, Mom never mentioned that the reason Dad didn't talk much was because she never shut up long enough to give him the chance. Just bitch, bitch, bitch. I learned to tune her out around kindergarten.

Dad chose gin as his way to cope, and as he relied more and more on that habit, Mom retreated further and further into the belly of her cult, and that is exactly what Scientology is. She paid for their books. Paid for their courses and seminars. Moved from member to counselor to auditor and hopes to climb even higher in the organization. Whatever turns her on.

Personally, the whole thing turns me off. I was ten when she first fell prey to the hype, but Dad managed to buffer me for two years, and I listened to his warnings about the bizarre nature of the "not-religion," as he called it. "They say they want to clear you of negative thoughts and events," he told me. "But all they do is baffle you with their bullshit and keep banking your money."

After Dad left, Mom coerced me into a couple of auditing sessions, where strangers tried to erase a few of my personal negatives by asking questions designed to induce guilt in children. The first was, "Do you have a secret?"

What kid doesn't? I already knew that saying no wouldn't cut it, but I also realized whatever I said would probably get back to my mom. So I answered, "I said a bad word." When pressed, I admitted that word was "damn." At twelve, I'd been practicing cussing for a while, and "damn" was not the worst of it, but that was all I was copping to.

The guy made me tell him where I said it (school), when I said it (at lunch), to whom I said it (a girl who bullied me). He was older, and tufts of gray hair poked out of his ears, so when he insisted I repeat the story, I wondered if he had trouble hearing. But when he asked me to tell it yet again, he wanted me to add stuff—what did I have for lunch that day, who was with the girl, what were the two of them wearing? Each detail was supposed to lighten the burden of carrying the memory around. Maybe it did. Who knows?

But, as I suspected, Mom scrubbed my mouth with soap on a nail brush. I guess it could've been worse, which is why I chose *that* secret to share. The one about letting our next-door teenage neighbor touch my boobs for a dollar? Yeah, not so much. I quit going anywhere near Mom's "church" after I was stupid enough to admit shoplifting a pack of gum. Details. Juicy Fruit. The guy in line ahead of me was a large man, easily big enough to hide me from the cashier while I stuffed the gum in the front of my pants. Jeans.

When Mom found out, I couldn't wear jeans for days. They irritated the welts. So now, when she's busy training or auditing or whatever she's doing, I use the unsupervised time to enjoy things I'll never confess to her or her minions. Especially not in Los Angeles. Uh-uh. I'm not going anywhere. I've done a little research. Lots of horror stories out there about freaking Sea Org. It swallows people whole, and those who somehow find their way out are stalked. Harassed. Billed beaucoup dollars for supposed training. No sir, not me. I'm still working on a solid getaway scheme.

Today Tati and I headed downtown to see if we could scare up a good time. One of the bars had put together an unofficial Oktoberfest. Beer and barbecued sausages. Now that's my idea of fun, especially when someone else is buying.

Technically we weren't allowed to drink, of course. We have fake IDs, thanks to Tati's big brother, who's got connections, but we're kind of scared to use them. But luck was with us, because we hooked up with a couple of soldiers from Fort Hood. They were sitting at a table outside, sucking suds and half listening to the National League Championship baseball game onscreen inside.

"Who's winning?" I asked as we approached.

"Atlanta. Fuckers."

"Hey, now," said the other guy. "That's no way to talk to a lady. Sorry, girls. Robin's a little pissed at the Braves."

Robin. Weird name for an overbuilt hulk with a dark buzz cut and an iron jaw.

"Houston was in over their heads," I said, showing off just a little. "Atlanta was bound to beat 'em."

Mr. Polite checked me out. "You like baseball?"

"Yeah. Football, too. Hockey, not so much."

Sergeant Jason Baxter laughed and introduced himself. "Sit down, if you want." He turned his full attention to me, while Robin homed in on Tati.

"Buy us a beer?" I asked boldly.

"How old are you, anyway?"

I flashed my bogus ID. "Old enough."

He rolled his eyes, but laughed again and went inside, returning with two frosty mugs of foamy brew. "So tell me how come you like sports. Most sports," he corrected.

We drank and talked for a couple of hours, exchanging information cautiously. I talked about Dad, and recently losing him, avoiding much mention of Mom. He talked about himself, mostly.

Jason's twenty-seven, and a Texas boy through and through. Tati thought I was crazy for picking a guy so much older than me, but I liked his manners and the way he made me feel like the prettiest girl in the whole place.

"But he's shorter than you," Tati said.

"Who isn't?" I replied.

"Plus, he's got crazy eyes."

I have to admit that's true. They're the color of gunmetal, and ghosts live inside them. Haunted, that's what they are, and I guess he might be, too. Not like I knew him well enough to ask. Anyway, he was fun to spend time with. Good-looking, and charming, too. And, while Robin got aggressive after several beers, Jason remained polite.

In fact, at one point Tati was pushing Robin's hands away and Jason stepped in. "Ain't no fun if the lady's not into it, you know?"

Robin thought about making trouble, reconsidered, and stomped off. Tati was upset and wanted to leave. I thanked Jason for a nice day, and for reeling in his friend. "Only what's right," he said. "A man's gotta do what's right. Any chance you'd want to see me again? I have most weekends off and the base is only an hour away."

Uh, yeah! But I had to think of a way to be in touch without him calling the house. I asked Tati if he could call her and leave me a message. She looked at me as if I'd totally lost it, but agreed anyway.

Jason took my hand, pulled me off to one side. "Okay if I kiss you?"

I've kissed a boy or five, but none has ever asked if it was okay. That surprised me, and so did the kiss. I expected a soldier's lips—rough, harsh. But his were gentle, at least at first, and it might have stopped right there, except I wanted more. It was me who moved toward urgency, not that he complained.

Truthfully, instinct drove me. His lack of demand pushed me forward, as if I had something to prove. And when he responded as men do, or at least as much as they can in a public place, I felt vindicated. More than that, I felt desirable.

And since I got home, I've been carefully considering how Sergeant Jason Baxter might fit into my escape plan.

I Don't Get a Car

For my birthday.
I do get a couple of cards.

Monica gives me one
at dinner. On the front
it shows two girls holding
hands, getting ready to go
down a giant waterslide,
and it says: FRIENDS DON'T LET
FRIENDS DO STUPID SHIT ALONE.

Inside, she wrote: *Let's do*
something stupid together.
          Te amo, Monica.

Dad follows that up with
one of his own—a generic
birthday card decorated with
pink roses, and too few candles
to accurately represent the day.

Inside is a twenty-dollar bill
and: *Roses are pink, money*
is green. I can't believe my
little girl is seventeen.
Happy birthday. Love, Dad.
PS: Don't spend it all in one place.

Dad's Lame Attempt

At humor is not amusing.
Twenty bucks wouldn't buy
a movie with popcorn and Skittles.

I suppose I have to give him credit
for treating Monica and me to
a post-dinner flick, no popcorn

or Skittles included, unless I want
to spend the twenty. That's cool.
Syrah comped our dinner, with

sundaes for dessert. Mine had
a candle, and there was singing.
So I'm full as we walk into the theater,

which is pretty busy. Not surprising
considering it's Saturday night. What
is surprising is Dad doesn't go in.

> *You girls have fun,* he says. *I'm going
> out for a couple of beers with Zelda.
> I'll pick you up after the show.*

Excellent! He's not mad at Zelda
after all. "You have your phone,
right? In case I need to remind you."

> *Aw, come on. I only forgot you one
> or two times. More like a dozen
> over the years, but why argue?*

I Pick a Horror Flick

About a girl who gets called to babysit
for strangers, clueless that the adorable

little boy's in serious need of an exorcism.
Of course the house is at the end of a road

in an unpopulated area, surrounded by
dark, scary woods, and when she finally

finds enough sense to run, she discovers
the giant creepster trees could use the help

of a good priest, too. It's one of those movies
where you're expecting stuff to happen, but

when it does it makes you jump anyway.
We sit way in the back, with no one behind

to bother us, and during a particularly tense
scene, Monica snakes her fingers into mine,

pulls my hand against the taut muscles
of her belly. Beneath her shirt, her body

is warm, and the connection is comforting,
and this feels so right it makes me sigh

contentment. At the sound, she unknots
our fingers, allowing hers to softly explore

the skin on the back of my hand. Back
and forth they travel, inviting mine to

reciprocate. And just as I do, the kid on
screen grabs hold of his babysitter's foot

and starts to drag her backward toward
the leering house and our hands fly up

in response, and after we scream
we both bust up at our over-the-top

reaction. I believe that's what people call
a mood breaker, and I'm fine with it

because I've got no idea what to do with
what just happened between us. Every

small movement was saturated with
importance. But what does that mean?

Another question looms even larger.
Where, oh where, do we go from here?

To Start With

We go home.
Dad's even out front
close to on time, no
reminder necessary.

It surprises me,
but what doesn't is
the smell inside the car,
which just about knocks me

over. Amazing
how much beer he
must've consumed
in the last couple of hours.

He looks a little
unsteady, and Monica
seems unsure, so I offer,
"Hey, Dad. Want me to drive?"

> *Hells to the no.*
> *If you messed up*
> *and your friend got*
> *hurt, I'd be held liable.*

Flawed logic.
Just who'd be held
liable if he messed up
while driving a little tipsy?

Tipsy or not,
he's not changing
his mind, so I sit in back,
wishing Monica and I could

hold hands
or maybe attempt
something more. Now I
wonder if she's ever tried

something more,
and if so, with whom.
We've never discussed it,
for whatever reasons, but since

I've lived here,
she hasn't been with
anyone else, at least not
that I'm aware of. I do know

> she's not out to
> her family. *No,* she said
> when I asked. *Mis padres*
> *wouldn't understand, or accept.*

Yet she accepts
herself just as she is,
doesn't try to hide from
the truth of who she is inside.

I Want to Be

That sure of the truth of me.
I feel like I'm teetering
on the edge
of semi-certainty,
which is pretty
much meaningless.

But I've got lots of time
to figure it out, so for now
I'll resign myself
to enjoying the research.

When Dad pulls up in front
of Monica's house,
I jump out to claim shotgun.
Totally aware of spying
eyes nearby, Monica and I
exchange an awkward good-bye.

"Thanks for the card."
I wink. "Let's do something
stupid together soon."

Monica smiles. *How stupid
can we get? You better think
about that. Happy birthday,
novia.* She turns and motors
on up the walk, calling over
her shoulder, *See you mañana.*

In the Car

Dad's singing along
with Garth Brooks.
His voice carries a hint
of the twang that has almost
disappeared with time
and distance from his home state.
When he starts a slow cruise,
I ask, "Do you ever miss Oklahoma?"

> He keeps humming
> for a second or two, but
> finally answers, *Not much.*
> *I left a lot of bad behind*
> *there. Nothing in Oklahoma*
> *but pain and worry, and that*
> *includes your grandparents.*

Boom. He never talks
about Pops and Ma-maw—
that's what they insisted
I call them. "Do you ever hear
from them?" I'm not aware
of any communication.

> His hands tense
> on the steering wheel,
> and his jaw juts forward.
> *Every once in a while.*
> *Look, Air, there's no love*
> *lost between them and me.*

Not sure that's true.
Ma-maw griped about Dad,
but affectionately, at least
from what I can remember.
It's been a long while
since I've seen her.

"What about . . ."
I don't know if I'm allowed
to ask. Ah, why not?
"What about your brother?
I mean, don't you want
to stay in touch
with any of your family?"

You're my family, Air.
Besides . . . He trails off,
then continues. *Okay,*
I never told you this because
it didn't seem important
for you to know, but Drew
was killed in the line of duty
a few years ago. He was a damn
good cop, but he messed up
bad that day. Never assume
someone with their hands in the air
isn't concealing a weapon.

Uncle Drew

I can scarcely picture him, and what
surrounds the memory is the smell
of tobacco on his fingers when he held me.

"Of course it was important for me
to know, Dad! You and I have always
been so isolated. So insulated.

And you're the one who kept us
that way. I'd like to think I have family
outside of just the two of us."

> *Family is a recipe for heartbreak,*
> *Ariel. A recipe for heartbreak,*
> he repeats, louder, for emphasis.

We're almost home before I finally
find the courage to ask the question
that prickles on every birthday.

"Do you suppose my mother's missing
me today? Not that I really care, but
do you think she wonders about me?"

I expect his usual barrage of expletives.
Instead, he sits quietly for several
long seconds. Finally, he sighs heavily.

> *You know, sometimes I ponder*
> *that. When you first came along,*
> *Jenny seemed like such a good mama.*

My Jaw Drops

I
am
blown
away.

I can't remember
him saying one
nice thing about her.
He hardly ever even
mentions her name.

"Really?"
I hope I didn't sound
too eager. But I know
nothing about my babyhood.
It's not something he discusses,
and he doesn't have
a single picture of me
before the age of three.

> Yeah. Jesus, did she
> have me fooled! You know,
> I've been with a lot of women
> in my time. Enjoyed the company
> of ladies near and far.
>
> But Jenny was the only one
> I ever let myself love.
> I'll never make that mistake again.

The Confession

Materializes from inner
space, so unrecognizable
it's totally alien.

And yet it makes Dad human.

"You were in love with my mother."
The simple declarative sentence
pushes Dad over the edge.

> *Goddamn straight. Why*
> *does that surprise you?*

"I don't know. I just never
heard you say so before."

> *I had to pretend she meant*
> *nothing, or lose my mind.*
> *She used me. Played me.*
>
> *But even if I could've gotten*
> *past that, I'll never forgive*
> *her for screwing you over.*
>
> *Not one goddamn word in all*
> *these years! Too damn busy playing*
> *bushwhacker with her girlfriend.*

Bushwhacker?

No comment. But now I have
to hear the story again.
I pretend to listen, catching
snatches (ooh, bad word in
context here) of his recitation:

> . . . from deployment, no one
> there to greet me.

> . . . got home and Jenny
> says she's moving out.

> . . . in with her girlfriend. Girl.
> Friend. She left me—and you—
> for a goddamn dyke!

> . . . out the door, not so much as
> a good-bye kiss for her baby girl.
> Wish I'd have seen it coming.
> How could a mama do such
> a vile thing to her child?

I've asked myself that very
question many, many times,
invariably after Dad repeats
the tale. Usually, he's two sheets
into the wind, and today he's
at least a sheet-and-a-half-way
there. How can he drive like this?

It's Nothing New

Of course, and for the most part
we've been lucky. I mean, considering

the miles we've traveled, oftentimes
with him drinking either before we got

into the car or even after we were on
our way, most of his beer-fueled faux

pas were relatively minor. There was
one time I can barely remember. I couldn't

have been older than three. It wasn't
long after we first started road tripping.

Dad let me sit up front, where I was, for
sure, not safe, despite the fact that his car

was too old to have air bags. Luckily,
it was equipped with seat belts. Thankfully,

I was wearing mine when he swerved
to miss something in the road, overcorrected,

and skidded off the highway, rolling us
down a muddy bank. We landed on the tires,

and Dad was drunk enough to start laughing,
even though he'd broken bones in one arm

and one leg. Except for peeing my panties,
I was totally fine. But we weren't going

anywhere, not in that wreck. Which is
how we came to live with Leona, who

witnessed the entire incident and stopped
to ascertain the extent of our injuries.

Funny, but I can see her face peering
into my window as clear as water, and

                    I can make out her razor-voiced words.
                    Everyone okay in there? I'm a nurse.

The details blur after that, but Leona
helped us out of the car, noting Dad's

                    extremities. *You stay right here. Don't try
                    to get up. I'll go call for an ambulance.*

          Ah, no, we don't need that, insisted
          Dad. *Give me an ACE Bandage, I'm good.*

                    *Mister, you've got a couple of hellacious
                    fractures. ACE Bandages won't fix those.*

                    *But don't you worry. We're a long way
                    from town. It will take them at least*

an hour to get here. You should be
sobered up by then. You ought to know

better than to take a chance hurting
your beautiful daughter. I'll be right back.

Dad wanted to protest, but he couldn't
stand on his leg, let alone climb back up

the embankment. I remember hating
the way I felt, wearing pee-stinking

clothes. But when Leona returned,
she confirmed the ambulance was on

its way before locating clean undies and
pants in the car, and helping me into them.

By the time the EMTs came scrambling
down to the rescue, Dad had realized

he'd be staying in the hospital for
a few days. *What about my little girl?*

I don't know why, but Leona volunteered,
If you can trust me, I'll take her home.

Everyone at the hospital knows who I am.
These guys right here can vouch for me.

They Could and They Did

Besides, Dad didn't really have much
of a choice, so he said why not. Leona
was nice—she even took a couple
of days off work so she could care
for me—but I cried and cried,
terrified I'd never see my daddy again.

I clung to him and begged to stay
right there in the hospital. Promised
I'd be very good. I'd already lost
my mommy. What would happen
if Daddy didn't come back? Leona pulled
me into her lap, stroked my hair, soothed

my fears with the motherly touch
I must've been missing. After enough
time absorbing Leona's kind attention,
I said okay, she could take me with her.
Mid-hysteria, something meaningful
must've passed between Dad and her,

something a little girl wouldn't realize,
because after surgery to repair
his damaged limbs and a couple days
recovering in the hospital, Dad joined
me at Leona's place, which is a bare-bones
sketch in my memory. It was small, but

I got my own bed, and I remember
the sheets smelled sweet citrusy,
like Ma-maw's lemon meringue pie.
There were trees outside the window
that looked like giants with big groping
hands reaching for me when the light

was low and the wind blew strong.
I can't pull images of the furniture,
except for a recliner that had seen
better days. I wasn't allowed to sit
in it. Leona said it belonged to her
resident ghosts, not that I understood

right away. Eventually, the reference
became clear, in recollections of framed
photos that hung on every wall—
a series featuring a mustached man
and a curly-haired blond toddler, even
younger than I. Turned out Leona's husband

and child had died in a train derailment
a couple of years before. She didn't like
to talk about them, and enough time had
passed that loneliness made her ripe fruit
for Dad to pluck. I don't know what drove
us to finally leave, but his injuries had healed,

and we went in her dead husband's car.

Over the Years

We've probably switched
cars three dozen times.
One way Dad made a few
extra bucks was by selling
a car for more than he'd
invested in it, then finding
another "deal" he could fix,
drive, and dispose of again.
He's an ace mechanic. Once,
I asked him how he knew
so much about engine repair.

> *Pops taught me the basics,*
> he explained. *And I took auto*
> *shop in high school. I might've*
> *dropped out and made my living*
> *the way I'm making it now, but*
> *the army wanted to see a diploma.*

That's about as much as he
ever told me about his teen
years. He doesn't talk much
about his time in the service,
either, but oh, the alcohol-induced
stories I've heard about the ins
and outs of helicopter rotor repair!

All that thinking about cars
brings me back to why I can't
have one. That has to change.

But It Won't Today

This birthday is just about
over, no car for me, and what
the hell was I thinking? I'll have
to find my own way to autonomy.

But then, I always understood
that, didn't I? We bump into
the driveway, safe and sound
despite Dad's compromised state.

"The sleigh knows the way,"
I say out loud, "so Santa, please
don't sweat it." The sentiment
floats up from out of the depths,

> disturbing Dad, who throws
> the gearshift into park, turns
> off the ignition. He turns to look
> at me. *What did you just say?*

I repeat the sentence while
trying to discern what's got
him so riled up. "I have no idea
where it came from. Do you?"

> He sits in silent contemplation,
> as if searching for the right thing
> to say, but ultimately comes back
> with, *Nope, never heard it before.*

My Gut Reaction

To his answer
        is one word:

                bullshit.

I'm dying to
        respond with

that single
        word exactly:

                Bullshit.

Except that word
        requires all caps:

                BULLSHIT.

No, more effectively,
        rapid all-cap fire:

                BULLSHIT
                BULLSHIT
                BULLSHIT

But that's my gut,
        not my brain, and

my brain is
        where my own

                bullshit
comes from,
        at least, according

                to Dad.

I Don't Dare

Vocalize that, of course,
and not because of bad
language. Dad doesn't
appreciate my pushing
back on anything. If he
utters it, I'm supposed
to believe every word.

        Sometimes I think he
        wants to own my brain,
        manage it, housekeep it,
        scrub it until it's polished
        to a contemplation-free
        sheen, then reprogram
        every single opinion.

At times I feel he'd like
to keep me in a box, tied
up with a pretty bow,
and truthfully, existing
stuffed in a cube would
be easier than mustering
the will to shake down

        the invisible walls, break
        free from my history, go
        in search of the woman
        I want to become, with or
        without Dad's blessing.
        Oh, who am I kidding?
        Forget the damn "with."

Dad Will Never

Willingly let me go. Never encourage
me to grow up and detach myself

from his greedy grasp. No, I'll have
to wrest myself away forcibly.

But then what? It's not like I've got
a whole lot of options. Graduating

high school is goal number one,
and I've still got a way to go. I can

barely consider what's beyond that
horizon. Placid ocean? Tsunami? Icebergs?

I can't imagine life without my dad
in control. He's definitely an overbearing

admiral, but what if I'm the kind of captain
who can't avoid sideswiping the glacier

and sinking the ship? Oh, look. Here I go
again. Whenever I converse with myself

I talk a great game, but when I take a firm
mental stand, eventually I chicken out.

I really need to quit that. Dependency
isn't only self-defeating. It's self-perpetuating.

As Dad and I Go Inside

That silly Santa sentence keeps knocking
on the door to a corridor in my brain
I can never quite access. I swear I'll unlock

the portal one day. Dad asks about TV,
but I'm tired and it's approaching late,
and algebra comes with a test tomorrow.

I take a quick shower, brush my teeth,
don my pj's, and climb into bed with
my math notes, not that they'll do me

much good. Math and I have agreed
to disagree. The only reason I care at all
is I have to keep up my grades so I can

play basketball. The main problem
is, with all the school I missed growing
up, I never got the basics down very well.

Dad, who sometimes played the role
of homeschooler, tried his best to teach
me what he could, but his own education

was lacking. Some people might write
that off as Oklahoma ranchers not caring
about reading, writing, and arithmetic,

but Ma-maw and Pops valued school
learning. Uncle Drew was a good
student, according to Ma-maw, but Dad

always preferred messing around
with engines to building his brain.
That boy always did as little schoolwork

as possible. Just barely enough to get by,
she told me once. *Then he'd sweet-talk*
his teachers into passing him anyway.

That isn't so hard to believe, especially
if his teachers were female. Knowing
this now doesn't bother me much,

but when I was young it used to make
me mad because I loved when I got
to go to school. It made me feel like

a normal kid. Whenever I had actual
classroom time, I gathered every bit
of knowledge I could, and held it close.

But English and social studies came easier
than math and science, so I guess
I'll always lag in anything numbers related.

One Thing Math Is Good For

Is making me drowsy.
Can't sleep? You don't need
melatonin or Lunestra.
Twenty minutes staring
vacantly at notes about
algebraic equations

does the trick every time.
I click off my bedside lamp,
drop my head on the pillow,
close my eyes, and burrow
into the darkness. The faint
sound of Dad's TV show

is soothing, and somewhere
outside an owl cries *whoo-
whoo* over wind tapping
against window glass.
A pleasant lull wraps itself
around me and as I wait

      for sleep to find me, that
      silly refrain surfaces again.
      The sleigh knows the way, so
      Santa, please don't sweat it.
      Only this time, the faintest
      hint of a voice is attached.

It's a clear, warm soprano,
familiar but not, and now
she sings, *You better watch
out. You better not cry. You
better not pout, I'm telling
you why. Santa Claus is coming . . .*

It's at once unsettling and
comforting. The latter because
I know the words are meant
for my ears; the former
because I can't match a face
with the voice, and I must.

One of Dad's women? Maybe,
but I don't remember any of them
singing, at least not like this,
and definitely not to me. I know,
somehow, this person's song
is meant specifically for my ears.

My mother. That's who it is,
and I don't want to listen to this
remnant of my earlier musing.
I put the pillow over my head
so the only thing left to hear
is the rasp of my breathing.

By Morning

My heart
                    has mostly glued
                    itself back together,
                    and my brain

has excised
                    last night's unbidden
                    memory, scrubbed
                    away most of

the remains,
                    leaving me slightly
                    off-kilter. I've never
                    embraced the idea of

chasing
                    after the past when
                    the present is difficult
                    enough. Besides, I want no

specters
                    inhabiting my future,
                    so I've determined to
                    exorcise them, banish them

into the realm of nightmares.

I Wake Late

Stumble out of bed
and into clothes.
No time for breakfast,
I grab my backpack,
yell, "Hurry, Dad!"
and go wait for him
in the car.

It's either ride
with him
or take a seat
on the school bus
that passes by
around the same time
he leaves for work
every day.

Buses are for kids.
Okay, technically
I still qualify,
but considering I
was robbed
of a normal childhood,
I've never really felt
like much of a kid.

Once upon a time,
I wanted to. I dreamed
of playing with other kids.
Dolls. Trucks. Princesses.
Army. Go Fish.

Anything but solitaire.

I wished I could share
the playground with someone
about my size who'd swing
beside me, higher and
higher, a race to the sky.

I yearned to ride
a bike or roller-skate
around a block
busy with children
eager for my company.

But anytime
I actually managed
to make a buddy,
it wouldn't be long
before we'd leave
her in a cloud of exhaust
as we hit the highway again.

I learned not to bother
with connections.
Even once we moved here
and it seemed like we might
hang around a while,
it was months
before I allowed myself
the joy of friendship.

Without Monica's Persistence

That never would've happened.
I have zero clue why she decided

to make me her pet project.
She reached out before she knew

my background, so it couldn't have
been because she felt sorry for me.

I must've looked starved for company.
By then it was much too late to go

back and try to reclaim some kind
of childhood. Nope, I've never been

a kid. More like a dad-sitter, and God
knows he needed one. Still does.

Someone to cook and clean, a substitute
wife to make up for the one who split.

Someone to set his workday alarm
when he forgets, to quiet the house

on weekends when he wants to sleep
in. He always says he couldn't make it

without me, that he needs a small voice
of reason, not to mention a keeper.

Case in Point

Here he comes hustling
out the door. With luck,
neither of us will be tardy.

But I don't count on luck.

Which is why I'm relatively
sure the stinking algebra test
is going to get the best of me.

Then again, you never know.

Dad jumps in the car, starts
it, and as the engine idles
to "warm," I remind him,

"Zelda's making me dinner."

> Obviously, he's forgotten,
> if he ever really knew. *What?*
> *She didn't invite me, did she?*

"Um, I wouldn't know, Dad."

Definitely in need of a keeper.
"But I'm going over after practice.
She wants me to meet her nephew."

> *Oh yeah. I remember now.*

He turns, gives me a long, hard
assessment. *That's not what
you're planning to wear, is it?*

I glance down at myself,

unsure of what his concern
might be. "What's wrong with
what I'm wearing? It's clean."

Is that supposed to be a joke?

Why is he so pissed? "No, Dad.
I just don't understand why
my outfit bothers you."

It's a little too provocative.

Jeans and a peasant blouse?
Everything's covered, though
the blouse is a gauzy material.

I could argue, but maybe he's right.

"One sec." I run into the house,
change into a long-sleeved
T-shirt, hoping we won't be late.

That's better, Dad says when I get
back. *Never forget . . .* He winks
at me. *All guys only want one thing.*

Not Exactly a Problem

But it could be if I protest too much.
So I nod and wink back. "I'll remember,
Dad. But don't worry. Zelda will supervise."

> Engine suitably tepid, he puts the car
> in gear, backs out onto the main road.
> Guns it. *You'll need a ride home, though.*

"Not sure. Maybe Zelda will bring me,
or maybe Gabe has a car. First day,
he probably won't go for that one thing."

> *Yeah, well, if he does—if any dude ever
> does—you tell me, hear? I'll take care of it
> so it never happens again, that's for sure.*

If I ever experience something like that,
I think I'll deal with it and keep it to myself.
I have to admit I'm pretty naive about sex.

Other than a few leering comments, guys
haven't exactly lined up to take interest
in me. I've never even been to first base,

let alone circled the field. Not with a boy.
Not with a girl. I've come closer with Monica
than I should have, because I know as soon

as I fall in love, Dad'll find a reason to move.
Moving away from "home" would be bad.
Moving away from love would be devastating.

School Isn't So Bad Today

Even algebra goes smoothly.
I know the test answers, or
at least think I do. Pretty sure
I'll pass anyway. History
is interesting for a change,
and psychology is fascinating.

I took psych as an elective.
Syrah says I'm dumb, that art
would be easier, and I guess
she's right. But dissecting
the human mind is something
I might choose as a career path.

God knows, just checking out
the people in the halls, mental
health issues are everywhere.
Substance abuse. Eating disorders.
Depression. Thoughts of suicide.
It's a bottomless bowl of nuts.

Okay, I know a health-care
professional wouldn't use
the term "nuts," but right now,
picturing Hillary as a pecan
makes me smile. Usually when
I see her I want to run for cover.

Hillary Grantham

Is one of those girls
everyone pretends to like,
though actually liking her
would be extremely hard.

Hillary's parents own a huge
ranch. Thoroughbred horses
and black Angus cattle dot
the rolling hillsides, requiring

the oversight of a decent-size
crew of laborers. Local kids
sometimes get jobs out there,
mucking stalls and tossing hay.

Hillary would never stoop so low,
despite her love of all things
equine. The girl defines arrogance,
which isn't totally her fault.

Not only is she privileged, but
she also happens to be smart,
talented, and a decent athlete.
The all-around rich American girl.

I'm not nearly as intelligent,
have no real talents to speak of.
The only place I've got her beat
is on the basketball court.

Today, However

She holds her own in practice,
which makes me work that much

harder, not that I have one damn
thing to prove, except to myself.

Coach loves me just as I am,
and so do my teammates (especially

one of them, who I'm dangerously
close to loving back). And honestly,

even Hillary treats me with respect
on the court, though she ignores me

anywhere else, other than to maybe
nod slightly, the way she might reward

the hired help. Regardless, we play
together on a team, and our shared

goals matter there. Guess you don't
have to like someone to appreciate

their ability. I do admire Hillary's.
But I have to admit I'm glad mine

is at least marginally better. If that
makes me immature, sticks and stones.

After Practice

I take the time to shower off the sweat
and wash my hair. Sometimes I'll wait
until I get home to clean up, knowing
Syrah smells just as bad as I do, but
I don't think Zelda would appreciate

me showing up scented like effort.
Or Gabe, either, not that I care
what he thinks. I'm not dressing to
impress some random guy, though
it's only polite to show up clean.

> On the way over to Zelda's, Syrah
> comments, *So, you've never met this
> Gabe guy, right?* When I agree that
> I haven't, she actually asks, *What if
> he's a knockout? You swing both ways?*

"I don't 'swing' at all. If you mean
have I ever been attracted to a guy,
well, yeah. But I've never acted
on it, or on any attraction, for that
matter." The statement rings

true, and when she asks why
not, I'm straightforward. "Before
Sonora, we never lived one place long
enough for me to hook up with anyone.
And now, I guess, I'm a little scared."

Afraid

Of lust, its recent bloom
inside of me. Powerful.
How do I control it?
Do I even want to try?

Anxious

about the mechanics,
seventeen and never
been kissed, at least not
in the context of romance.

Nervous

I'll make an improper move.
Choose the wrong person
and not be able to correct
a dire mistake of the heart.

Uncertain

of outcomes. The future,
and my place in it, with
little to zero ability
to take charge of its direction.

Petrified

of falling all the way in love.
Lacking anything like a role
model, commitment isn't
something I understand.

124

Beyond This Fear

Exists bone-deep trepidation
about my dad's reaction
if he finds out I've fallen
for anyone at all.

Sharing isn't his best thing,
and I'm pretty sure the idea
of divvying my affection
with someone else would
drive him totally crazy.

A guy would present a certain
kind of threat, of course.
But a girl? How can I ever
confess *that*? It would push
him all the way over the edge,
and that's a shadowy, perilous
place I'd rather not revisit.
There's teeth-rattling pain
there, wrapped in the skin
of my father's hands.

I'm sure the vast majority
of parents expect their kids
to partner up eventually,
but Dad isn't like most people.
The topic is off-limits.
Inaccessible. And I'm a whole
lot safer keeping it that way.

I Don't Share

These intimate details
about my hesitant psyche
with Syrah. I'm not sure
I could confess them
to Monica, and probably
shouldn't. The last thing
I want to do is hurt her.

Besides, as I recently read
in a book, *Taking no chances
means wasting your dreams.*
It's past time to take chances.
I'm considering my dreams
when Syrah drops me off.

Stuck mid-musing about
my first kiss, I rap my knuckles
on Zelda's front door, fully
anticipating she'll answer it.
But when it opens, the face
on the far side is unexpected,
and so is my reaction to it.

> *Oh, hi. You must be Ariel.
> I'm Gabe. Come in.* His smile
> softens his angular face, and
> when I look into the deep ponds
> of his eyes, interest surfaces.
> In him. In me. It's instant connection.
> But what, exactly, can that mean?

Tomorrow will be three months since I met Jason. We've seen each other almost every weekend, and our relationship moved quickly to love. I mean, I guess it's love, though I'm not sure it's exactly the "deep, forever" kind, at least not yet. I'm willing to give it time, especially now. Meanwhile, he's buying the beer, and the sex is amazing.

Jason wasn't my first. I've been with other guys, all around my age or a little older, but hurried backseat sex, fumbling with belt buckles and condoms, didn't really do much for me. Jason springs for a room, or sometimes borrows one from a friend who lives here in Austin. With plenty of space and no prying eyes, we can be relaxed about making love. It feels closer to that than rutting. Plus, we always do something frivolous before and after.

A sergeant expects to be in charge, so I've been subtle about how I've directed things, not that it's exactly difficult to maneuver a guy into sex. But high school boys don't care that they're being played, mostly because they don't believe a girl is capable of such a thing. A man like Jason has been around the block a time or two, experienced decent partnering, and awful.

He's never been married, but has been engaged twice. The first time he was still in boot camp, but when his back was turned, she hooked up with a guy who owned a car lot. "More money in selling beaters than my lousy paychecks could compete with," he told me. The second time, his fiancée couldn't cope with his deployment to the Gulf War. "She was sure I'd come home in a body bag," he explained. "Too bad. I loved that damn woman."

He claims he's been waiting for someone to love ever since, and that was six years ago. Pretty sure he hasn't been waiting for someone to sleep with, but that's okay. He's with me now, and with luck he'll decide to stay once I share my news. If not, there's always abortion.

I confided in Tati, of course. At the moment she isn't speaking to me. The last thing she said was, "Are you fucking insane? This is *not* the way to stay in Austin. You could've just run away and stayed with me until you turn eighteen."

Like Mom couldn't figure out that's where I went? Like she wouldn't happily have me arrested? I've got a whole fourteen months before I can split legally. But maybe if Jason does the right thing, like a decent country boy might, I'll become Mrs. Baxter. Mom will have to sign off on it, but why wouldn't she? It's not like she wants to be my mother. All she cares about is going "Clear" and climbing higher up the Scientology ladder. Plus, she wants to take me along.

She keeps insisting I go to auditing to deal with Dad's death, but I'm not swallowing the Kool-Aid. I went one time, just to shut her up, but I'll never, ever go again. She'd have to tie me up and drag me. The auditor managed to tap into a memory of the Christmas right before

Dad left. Mom quit celebrating any holidays other than the sanctioned Scientology ones like L. Ron Hubbard's birthday, but Dad and I held on to Christmas, with or without her participation.

Lots of details about that day floated out of my brain. I wore lilac-colored pajamas to open the two presents under the little tinsel-trimmed tree. Both were for me, and both from Dad. One was a skateboard—black with a red hawk logo. The other was a journal bound in dark green leather, and on the first page was a message from Dad: *Write down everything important that happens so you can share it with me.*

He didn't say he was leaving. Not that day. But even at twelve I could read between the lines, and I couldn't blame him. I kept that journal, and several since, always meaning to share them with him one day. Too bad, so sad, miss you, Dad.

I didn't confide that information to the auditor. Last thing I need is Mom digging around in my stuff, looking for written confessions. Instead, I told him about learning to ride a skateboard—a lot of painful memories there, all involving scrapes and bruises.

Now it's my time to get away. I did a little research. A US Army sergeant, Grade E-5 with almost ten years in, earns around $1700 a month. With perks like base housing, commissary shopping, and military health care, we should live comfortably.

I'll have to drop out of school, but I can get a GED or something. Not like I'm Harvard-bound. Not like I have a chance at any job other than waitressing or bagging groceries.

It isn't the greatest plan, and I totally get that. I'm turning seventeen in a couple of weeks, and that's young to be a wife, not to mention a mom. I don't know what military life is like, but I'm sure it's kind of confining. Still, lots of people manage it, and no matter what it will offer more freedom than staying in my mother's house, struggling with school and sneaking out to have any fun at all.

I'm sorry to use you, baby-inside-me, but this seems like the best move for my future.

Our future.

That thought slams into me suddenly.

Our future.

Mine.

Jason's.

Our baby's.

Almost Three Weeks

Since I first met Gabe
and he has proven to be
a complication I really
didn't need. Every time
I start to think I know who
I am, something clouds
my already hazy POV.

My feelings for Monica
haven't changed. She is
a comet in the night sky,
and the moment I see her
my mood becomes brighter.
I can't deny that I love her.

I don't think I'm in love
with Gabe, but I adore
spending time with him.
He's the first guy I've ever
met who actually listens
when I talk, and at least
pretends interest. Plus

Zelda was totally right.
He's easy on the eyes.

Speaking of Eyes

His are unique.
They remind me
of opals—a mottled
mixture of green
and blue, and when

the light hits them
just so, you can see
glints of orange
circling the pupils
in a narrow band.

The condition is called
heterochromia, he tells
me. There are different
kinds. Some people or
other animals have eyes

that are totally dissimilar
colors. That's complete
heterochromia. Sectoral
is when the eyes have
spikes of pigment that

look like spots. Gabe's
type, where the centers
are a different hue than
the rest of the irises,
is central heterochromia.

Sometimes science rocks.
Gabe inherited his condition,
and as he explains it, he
grows pensive because it
makes him talk about his father.

> *My dad gave me his eyes,*
> he says. *It was the best*
> *gift of all, because I can*
> *keep it forever, and if I ever*
> *have children they might*
>
> *get it passed on to them,*
> *too. I like that because*
> *it helps me feel like a part*
> *of him is still alive in me,*
> *and carried in my genes.*

We're sitting on Zelda's
porch swing. She and
Dad are inside, doing
whatever while waiting
for the coals in the barbecue

to ash over. We can hear
them bellowing inebriated
laughter. I'm embarrassed,
but it would be worse if
Zelda was Gabe's mom

instead of his aunt.
This way there's a single
layer of separation, at
least. But thinking about
Gabe's family makes me

ask, "Is your mom okay?
I heard she's having
a tough time dealing with . . .
Oh, man. I'm sorry."
Okay, that was awkward,

> but even so, he says, *Hey.*
> *Don't be sorry. Look, we just*
> *never expected to lose him,*
> *you know? Dad was such*
> *a solid fixture in our lives.*
>
> *Not rich or highly educated,*
> *but he was a hard worker*
> *and a really nice guy. It might*
> *sound like a cliché, but*
> *everyone truly loved him.*

Suddenly, it strikes me
that if something awful
happened to Dad I wouldn't
have the slightest clue
what to do. Find a way

to bury him, I suppose,
and then . . . What?
I don't even know how
to get hold of Ma-maw
and Pops. That makes me

feel very alone and a little
scared. One time when I was
maybe eight I got off the school
bus and no one was there to
meet me, so I walked back

to the house where we were
living. Dad's woman du jour
was gone. So was he, and it
was hours before he got back.
I was petrified I'd be alone forever.

I inch closer to Gabe,
till our legs almost touch.
The autumn air is cool, and
the heat of his body through
his jeans and Levi's shirt

is noticeable. Couple that
with the clean, leathery
scent lifting off his skin,
it's borderline sensory
overload. It's a good thing.

So, Naturally

I backpedal immediately.
        Put distance between us.
                Quick, change the subject.

I ask how he likes his job,
        the one my dad helped him
                get—part-time work at the shop.

He says other than the grease
        and porn on the wall it's decent.
                There's a joke there somewhere

because he grins and then
        hot damn, man, is he gorgeous.
                I push that thought aside and

search for the humor, and
        when I finally understand,
                reward him with rich laughter.

Now a single word surfaces
        inside my head: comfortable.
                That's the way I feel with Gabe.

No. Not right. More like half
        the way I feel. The other half
                is uncomfortably turned on.

I Command

That half to remain very, very quiet,
and am more than a little relieved
when Dad bombs through the door,
carrying a platter of sausages.

> Gabe jumps to his feet. *Here, let me
> help. Barbecue is one thing I'm pretty
> darn good at. Dad was a great teacher.*

>> *Oh, he must have been,* agrees Zelda.
>> *I remember this one time . . .* She takes
>> Gabe's arm and steers him toward
>> the grill. Dad follows, weaving slightly.

I cross my fingers that our dinner
doesn't crash-land on the ground,
but my luck or Dad's, the hot dogs

end up dirt free on the barbie. Watching
the scene unfold initiates my huge sigh
at the domesticity of it all—something
I struggle to reconcile in connection

to Dad and me. The idea of extended
family is totally foreign. I command
my inner voice to shut the hell up

and let me enjoy what's left of this
day without overthinking or dissecting
or second-guessing or otherwise closing
myself off to perhaps very real possibilities.

After We Eat

Dad switches from beer
to tequila. This will turn
into a long Saturday night,
and I don't really want
to spend the rest of the day
watching Dad and Zelda
get blotto, so I ask Gabe
for a ride home. When

        he agrees, Dad insists,
        I'll have an eye on the clock.
        I know exactly how long it
        takes to get there and back,
        so don't get cocky, hear?

    No worries. Straight there
    and back, and I promise
    to be the perfect gentleman.
    Your daughter is safe with me.

        Dad slaps Zelda on the butt.
        Wish I could promise your
        aunt is safe with me, but I am
        a man of my word. The two
        of them cackle like crows.

I'm glad to be out of there,
and grateful to Gabe for
taking me home. His junker

is what some people call
a classic, but I mostly see
it as just plain old. It could
use some body work, not
to mention upholstery.
"What kind of car is this?"

> *It's a '67 GTO, and it's fast.*
> He starts it up, and any doubt
> of its speed dissolves with
> the rev of its well-tuned engine.

"Well, in that case, maybe
I should remind you that
you said I'd be safe in your care."

> *You don't like speed?* He pulls
> out onto the road carefully, putts
> through town. *Is this slow enough?*

"You don't have to drive like
an old woman. I won't jump
out or do anything stupid.
I guess I'm a bit overcautious."
Always worried about losing
whatever advantage I might've
recently gained. Sad really.

What Fun Is That?

That's what he asks, and it's a valid
question. Wasn't I only recently thinking

about the folly of taking no chances?
So when we get far enough out of town,

I tell him, "So, go for it. Show me what
she can do. I'll even keep my eyes open."

> He grins. *Okay, if you're sure. Hold
> on to your hat!* Pedal to the metal,

we're over a hundred in mere seconds
flat. The acceleration forces me back

into the seat and the landscape outside
the windows blurs. The rush is incredible.

If I ever do get my own car, I'd better
settle for a clunker with an engine half

this size or expect regular ticketing.
When Gabe dials back, regret descends.

"Wow. That was awesome. I'd never
have guessed this car could do *that*."

> *Never judge a book by its cover. But
> I'm glad Fiona and I could impress you.*

"Wait, wait, wait. Fiona? Are you,
like, a *Shrek* fan or something?"

*Is anyone not a Shrek fan? But hey,
I've got an idea. Wanna drive? Fast?*

He'd let me drive his car? Of course,
he has no idea. "I don't have my license."

*Why not? No one ever taught you how,
or you flunked the test, or what?*

"Actually, I've got my permit, and logged in
my hours, but Dad won't sign the application."

*You live pretty far out here. You'd think
he'd want you to have transportation.*

"I guess it's his way of keeping me close
to home. Doesn't really matter. I don't

have a car or any way to buy one. No car,
no job. No job, no car. Catch-22."

*If you're comfortable behind the wheel,
you can still take Fiona for a short spin.*

*I won't ask to see your license. It's a tempting
invitation, and I'm thinking it over when . . .*

I Spy Something

"Hey. Take it easy. What's that?"
It's hard to see in the failing light,
but it's in the road, moving toward us.

I think it's a horse. But no rider.

The saddle on the tall trotting
chestnut is, indeed, empty. "Can you
angle the car across the road and stop?"

He manages to block most of
both lanes diagonally, and when
the winded horse notices, it slows

to a walk. I get out of the car, approach
the sweating mare carefully. "Whoa,
now," I tell her. "Hold on, big girl."

She tilts her head, perhaps considering
escape. But when I hold out my hand,
something makes her decide to come

toward me and allow me to take hold
of her reins. I stroke the length
of her wide pale blaze. "Atta girl."

I steer her to the shoulder, allowing
Gabe to park the GTO off the asphalt.
When he gets out and joins me, he says,

That was awesome. You know horses?

"Some. My Oklahoma grandparents own
them, or did. Pops taught me to ride when
I was little. And one of Dad's girlfriends

lived on a ranch. Nadia, who worshipped
her warmbloods, showed me a lot more.
So yes, I'm acquainted with horses."

Well, this one must've left someone behind.

"I'd say that's a given. Tell you what.
You take the car and see if you can find
them. I'll ride the horse in that direction.

She's awfully tall, though. Can you please
give me a boost?" I'd try it without help
but my jeans are kind of tight, and I don't

want to rip the butt seam. I had no idea
I'd go riding today. I expect an awkward
attempt, but he immediately interlocks

his fingers, creating a pocket for my foot,
and launches me into the saddle. "Okay,
wait. I take it you know horses, too?"

I do. I'll tell you about it later, though.

The Mare Argues

When I try to turn her around.
That means home, or at least
whatever she's focused on
reaching, is in the opposite
direction. I do my best to talk
her into acquiescing. "Come on,
girl. Your person needs a ride."

Reluctantly, she lets me head
the other way. Rather than hurry,
we walk to cool her off, and I
think about Nadia, who was
the last person I saw tossed
off a horse into the dirt, not
that she didn't deserve it.

The woman was a piece of work.
Dad hooked up with her in
Arizona, where ranch life is only
pleasant seasonally. Maybe
that was part of her problem.

While Pops insisted I ride
his beautifully trained
quarter horses using nothing
more than halters for reining,
Nadia got off on spade bits
in her bridles, and I'm pretty
sure that's how she dealt
with men—pain as control.

I've no clue if Dad gets off
on pain, but relinquishing
the reins, so to speak, is for
sure not his thing, and YAY!
Since he didn't fit Nadia's profile,
the relationship quickly went
south. Still, I loved being there.

Her horses were stunning—
big Spanish mounts. I learned
not to fear their size. And, unlike
Nadia, I didn't rely on ugly bits
to gain their cooperation.

What I discovered was how
easily horses worked using
nothing but subtle shifts
of weight, and once in a while,
for punctuation, a gentle
touch of knees or hands.
This was their instinct
and, somehow, mine.

But then, no surprise, Dad
decided it was time to leave,
or Nadia did. That was more
than two years ago, and I haven't
been anywhere near a horse
since. Until now. Guess
it's like riding a bike.
Once you've accomplished
the skill, you never forget how.

We Crest a Small Rise

And up ahead in the distance,
I can see Gabe's GTO, pulled over
on the shoulder. I squint and discover
him in an open expanse, well off

the road, kneeling over something
on the ground. I urge the mare into
a gallop and when we get closer,
I notice a person, lying motionless

in the dirt. Doubtless they were
ejected from the saddle I'm currently
occupying. "Everything okay?" I shout,
though it's a ridiculous question.

>   Even from here, Gabe's concern
>   is obvious. *She's in shock,* he yells.
>   *Get my jacket off the backseat.*
>   *I've already called 9-1-1.*

I hop down off the horse and loop
her reins through the door handle.
If she really wants to get loose,
she will, I guess. I grab Gabe's coat

and hustle on foot to join him. When
I reach his side, he pulls back, and
I recognize the person he's tending
to. Hillary. Damn. "Is she conscious?"

No. Not sure if she's got head or neck
injuries, so I don't want to raise
her feet. For now, we'll just keep her
warm and let the EMTs figure it out.

I'm torn between joining his vigil
and taking better care of the horse,
who might spook if a car goes by or at
an approaching siren and flashing lights.

Not much I can do for Hillary, and
I know she'd be worried about the mare.
"I'm going to move her horse away
from the road. I'll be right back."

        He tucks the coat carefully around
        Hillary. *Call your dad and let him know*
        why I won't be back right away, okay?
        Don't want him to get the wrong idea.

I wouldn't have even thought
about calling Dad, but it's a good
idea. When he answers his phone,
he's skeptical at first, like we'd go

to such lengths to try and deceive
him. "Listen. Hillary's on the basketball
team, and it's a pretty great coincidence
that we found her when we did."

He Asks

About a dozen questions,
most of which I can only
answer with, "I don't know."

> How bad is she hurt?
> What was she doing out there?
> How long till the ambulance arrives?
> What are you going to do after that?
> Have you called her parents?

Okay, that last one deserves
some thought. I don't know
her parents at all, but their
number must be listed.
Their ranch is what's known
in the trade as a "going concern."

"Listen, Dad, I'll get back to you
when I've got more answers.
I'll try calling her parents now."
I can't believe I didn't think
about doing that myself.

I ask information for "Grantham,"
but the operator can't find a listing.
I can't remember the name
of the ranch. Something with a G.
The Lazy G? Crooked G? No,
not right. Then it strikes me
that Hillary's probably carrying

a cell phone, with relevant
numbers programmed in.
I take hold of the horse, whose
breathing has slowed to warm
puffs of steam exhaled into
the rapidly cooling air. Just

as we turn away from the road,
an old pickup belches by, and
I know without looking who
it belongs to. Garrett doesn't
even slow down to see what's
going on. In fact, he picks up
speed, hoping, I'm sure, to kick
up some dust. The mare reacts

with a nervous skitter, and
I'm glad Garrett's timing isn't
worse. "Easy, lady," I tell her.
"He's a jerk, but you're okay."
I lead her out into the field,
close to the girl she left lying
there. "Hey, Gabe. See if Hillary
has a phone on her, would you?"

When he asks why and I explain,
he says, *Would you please do it?*
I'm uncomfortable reaching into
her pockets. I'll hold on to the horse.

He's Comfortable

With that, at least, so we trade places
and as I kneel beside my not-quite-friend
he walks the mare to keep her calm.

Hillary's wearing a Windbreaker,
and I try those pockets first, come
up empty. I'm scared to move her

too much, but the front pockets
on her jeans yield nothing, so I reach
under her and find what I'm looking

for. She moans a little as I extract
it, and I have no clue if that's bad
or good. Maybe she's coming to?

"Hillary? It's Ariel. Don't move,
okay?" There's no sign she hears
me, but perhaps the sound of a familiar

voice will comfort her somehow.
When I go into her contacts, the first
one to pop up is "Daddy."

"Answer. Answer," I pray, but it goes
to voice mail. "Um, Mr. Grantham?
This is Ariel Pearson. I'm one of

Hillary's teammates. There's been
an accident. Looks like Hillary
was tossed from her horse and . . ."

I offer the spotty details, and as
I disconnect I can hear the not-so-
subtle approach of the ambulance.

Noting the horse's reaction, I offer
to take charge of her while Gabe
goes to wave down the EMTs.

As I move her farther away from
the scene, I look for another contact
and find a Peg Grantham under favorites.

*She answers on the fourth ring, but
freaks at the unfamiliar voice. What
are you doing with Hillary's phone?*

Her accusatory shriek pisses me off.
"Okay, listen. Hillary's horse threw her.
My friend and I found her, and called

9-1-1. The ambulance just got here,
so she'll be on her way to the hospital
soon. I've got the mare and can bring her

to you, or you can come get her. Just
tell me what I should do. By the way,
I'm not into stealing horses or phones."

*Well, that's certainly good to hear.
Do you know where the ranch is located?
The foreman can meet you at the gate.*

Okay, That Was Weird

I guess maybe expecting
an apology was too much,
but, "I know where you are,
and I'm happy to deliver
the horse, but don't you
want to know how Hillary is?"

>   *Well, of course. You just upset*
>   *me and I forgot to ask. Is she*
>   *okay? Any bones broken?*

"I'm really not sure, but I
can tell you she's unconscious."
And now I really have to ask,
"Are you Hillary's mother?"
I realize I know nothing about
her family except the rumors
passed around about her dad:

He's a real estate developer
who owns a sizable chunk
of the state, and has powerful
friends in California politics.
Who knows how much is true?

>   *No, I happen to be Hillary's aunt.*
>   *Her father's out of town and left*
>   *me in charge, but I'll let him know*
>   *what happened. Oh, and I guess*
>   *I ought to thank you for your help.*

I'm Glad

Dear, sweet Peg Grantham
isn't Hillary's actual mom.
Such a caring individual!
Now I feel sorry for Hillary.

Busy dad. Ice-blooded aunt,
who's apparently her caretaker.
No wonder Hillary is so cool.
Gabe, on the other hand,

impresses me with
not only his warmth, but
also his bank of knowledge:
treatment for shock;

equine handling; giving
a girl a decent boost.
I watch as they strap
Hillary to a backboard,

under Gabe's watchful eye.
She's moving a little, and
they warn her to stop.
Does that mean she's come

>around? Yes. She's asking
>about her horse. *Niagara?*
>*Where's Niagara? Is she okay?*
>At the sound of Hillary's voice,

the mare's ears start twitching.
I lead her a little closer, hoping
Hillary can see her. "It's me,
Ariel. Don't worry about Niagara.

I've got her, and I've already
talked to your aunt and
arranged to take her home.
You concentrate on getting well."

As the EMTs lift the backboard
onto a gurney, then roll it toward
the ambulance's maw, Hillary
says, *Ariel? But . . . how?*

"Just a strange coincidence.
Everything's going to be fine,
okay? Oh, wait. Here's your phone."
Before I hand it off, I take the time

to send myself a text with the phone
number I found for her father,
just in case ol' Peg is a no-show.
Somehow, I wouldn't put it past her,

though I guess I shouldn't judge
a book without actually *seeing*
its cover, either. Meanwhile,
I focus on delivering Niagara.

The Ranch

Is over a mile back toward town.
By the time we start in that direction

the sun has dropped below the horizon
and it's turned damned cold. The EMTs

returned Gabe's jacket, so I bum it
to mitigate the teeth-chattering ride

ahead. "Follow me, but not too close,"
I tell him. The mare's game for a fast

pace home and, in Thoroughbred style,
gallops long-legged strides most

of the way there. Despite the chill,
it's exhilarating in a way few things

are. Going fast in a car is exciting,
but this is elemental. Approaching

the gate, I slow her to let her catch
her breath and cool off gradually,

though she'd rather hurry to the barn.
It's dinnertime, after all. I brake her

under the big over-the-driveway arch
bearing the ranch's name: the Triple G.

Triple! That's it. I've been past here
so many times I can't believe I forgot.

As promised, a man who I assume
is the foreman comes trotting up on

a stocky bay gelding. I dismount and hand
him Niagara's reins. "Great horse."

> *Thank you, young lady. She is, and we*
> *appreciate your intervention. I'd sure*

> *hate it if anything bad had happened*
> *to her, not to mention to Miss Hillary.*

> *A lot of people would've kept on going.*
> *Be sure and thank your friend for us, too.*

He nods toward Gabe, who's sitting
in his idling car, where I hope it's warm.

"I will. I think Hillary's okay. She was awake
and talking when they took her away."

> *That's real good to hear. The Lord*
> *willing, I'm sure Miss Hillary will be fine.*

> *By the way, Niagara here is a handful.*
> *You're not looking for a job, are you?*

Mucking Stalls

Wouldn't be the worst job
in the world. But he offers
to let me exercise horses,
and that would definitely
interest me. However,

"I'd love the work, but
I'm afraid transportation
would be a problem. I don't
have a car or a way to get one.
My dad can't help out, so I'm
stuck riding with friends."

> *Shame. Well, if something*
> *changes, please let me know.*
> *My name's Max, by the way.*
> *I'm in charge of the barn.*

"Thanks, Max. I'll for sure
get in touch with you if
anything happens to change."

Wow. Getting paid to ride
horses, and top-flight
Thoroughbreds at that?
Great proposition. Too bad
I can't take advantage of it.
Catch-22 sucks.

I broke the baby news to Jason a week ago. At first I thought he was going to freak out. His expression mutated a few times, like he was trying on masks. But he held it together. "Are you sure it's mine?"

"Positive." Once I might've had to guess, but I haven't been with anyone else since I met Jason, and that's what I told him. He seemed to believe me. So then we played the Q & A game.

Question: "How far along are you?"

Answer: "Ten weeks, I think."

Question: "How did it happen?"

That one made me laugh. I don't think he appreciated it. I coughed back the giggles and tried again.

Answer: "I must've forgotten to take a pill." Total lie. I've never been on birth control, and I have no idea if skipping one time can result in pregnancy. But Jason didn't call me on it.

Biggest question: "What do you want to do about it?"

Answer: "Keep it. It's the only thing I can do." Okay, the second sentence wasn't accurate, but I wanted him to believe there could only be one choice for me, so I added, "I love you, Jason, and this is your baby. No way could I kill it or give it away. I'll raise it on my own if I have to. Not sure how I'd manage it by myself, but I'd figure it out."

At first he didn't say a word, just stared off into space for probably five minutes. I gave him that time. Not like a life-changing event gets dropped in your lap every day. Finally, he reached for my hand. "I guess it's time I had a son."

I dropped my head against his chest. "I'm scared, Jason. When my mom finds out . . ."

He kissed me gently and said, "Everything will be okay. I promise."

We had another hour together, and spent it in bed. No discussion of babies or just *how* everything will be okay. It only crossed my mind once to wonder if having sex could hurt the baby inside me. Don't think Jason worried about it at all. I have no idea who to ask about it, at least not until I see a doctor. Now I guess I should.

So yesterday I turned seventeen. It started off as expected, with little recognition from my human incubator. She barely looked up from her newspaper when I sat down at the breakfast table. I worked real hard to come up with the right thing to say. "Hey, Mom. What was it like having me? I mean, the birth experience. Did it hurt like everyone says it does?"

I studied her face as she considered the question. Despite all the ugliness inside her, she's actually kind of pretty for forty-two. Her hair is like brass—shiny, with just a few hints of gray—and the few wrinkles she has are thin filaments. Maybe all that clarifying is good for the skin, if not the psyche.

"It was god-awful, if you want to know the truth. Felt

like you were going to pull my insides out. I don't recommend childbirth."

Not exactly comforting. And I realized we'd never discussed it before. Of course, we've never discussed lots of things before. What did I have to lose? "Did you breast-feed me?"

She snorted. "Are you kidding? A nurse talked me into trying it at the hospital. 'Your baby needs colostrum,' she insisted. I tried, but all it did was give me sore nipples and frustrate you. You sputtered and cried. Wailed. Finally she gave up and offered you formula. You were happy with that."

"How long did you stay in the hospital?"

"Overnight. Why are you asking me all these questions?"

"Just curious. I mean, I guess because it's my birthday, and . . ." I couldn't figure out where to go from there, so I shoveled cereal into my mouth.

"It is, isn't it? And look how gloomy it is outside. Just like the day you were born. Do you have plans?"

I almost got excited, thinking for once she might offer to spend quality time with me. Yeah, right. "Not really. Tati and I will probably chill." I figured a guilt trip wouldn't hurt, though. "Unless you've got something in mind."

Guilt is not in Mom's vocabulary. "I'll be tied up at services most of the day. You should come. Birthdays are good days for audits. Lots of people tap into past lives." The crazy rose up in her eyes.

"One life at a time, thanks."

She got up and went to the hook by the door, reached into the purse hanging there. "Here's ten dollars. Have a pizza with your friend. And happy birthday."

I took the money and didn't mention I was actually planning to hang out with my boyfriend. Tati's still upset with me, though she has forwarded Jason's messages as promised, and doesn't sound quite as pissy. She has a hard time staying mad at me. Still, when she called to wish me a happy birthday, it was a nice surprise.

"I know you're going to see Jason today, but I was hoping we could get together for a little while. I've got a present for you."

"Of course!" Knowing she'd forgiven me, at least mostly, would've been enough of a gift, but it wasn't all she gave me. She picked me up midmorning and we drove to a little park, which was mostly deserted. Late January, too cool for kids to swing or slide, there were only a few people walking their dogs, and I was happy for fewer distractions so we could finally talk.

We sat quietly for a few minutes before she asked, "You're really pregnant?"

I nodded. "Yep."

"And you're going to stay that way?"

"For six more months, give or take."

"Aren't you scared?"

"Totally."

"Have you told your mom?"

"Not yet. I wanted to make sure . . ." I paused because

I realized I still wasn't sure. "Jason says everything will be okay, but I don't know what that means yet."

"I'm jealous."

That one stopped me. "You're jealous I'm pregnant? You want a baby?"

"Don't be dense. I'm jealous of Jason. I hate that you love him. And if you've got a baby to love, too . . ." Her voice cracked, but she pulled it back together. "What will happen to me?"

I reached for her hand. "Tati, you're my best friend. I will always love you, and I need you now more than ever!" My eyes stung. I let the tears fall. I've held them back too long.

Tati leaned across the seat, opened her arms, and I pleated myself into them, gathering warmth and strength. Dove soap perfumed her skin and her breath was cinnamon. *Home,* that's what I thought. *Tati smells like home.*

Finally, she pushed me away. "Okay, I know you've got plans, so let's get the birthday stuff over with." She handed me a silly card with kittens eating birthday cake, and inside it were two tickets to an Astros-Rockies game. "It's Houston's first home stand this season. I was going to try for opening day, but this one is on Saturday. You can take Jason instead of me if you want."

My jaw actually dropped. "No way. I want to go with you. But since when do you like baseball?"

"I don't really, but maybe if you teach me about it . . . I know they have cute players." She sighed. "I just . . . when you told your favorite memory of your dad, I wanted to make a memory like that with you."

Happiness poured into my heart, like water from a pitcher.

It was a strange sensation, one I've never experienced before. I didn't exactly know what to do with it. "This is the best present, ever. And I'm damn sure going to go with you, as long as you're driving." I reminded myself to put the tickets in my secret stash spot under my dresser, along with Dad's manila envelope. "Mom gave me ten bucks. Let's have lunch before I meet Jason."

We opted for subs rather than pizza, which makes me queasy at this point in time. Then she dropped me off at Jason's friend's apartment. Jason was there, beer in hand. He'd had a few before I arrived. "What took you so long?" he demanded.

I was only a half hour late, so I'm not sure why I felt compelled to apologize. "Sorry. I had lunch with Tati. She wanted to give me a present."

"Just so you know, I've got something for you, too. Come here."

"Can I get a beer first?"

"No. Not good for the kid."

It was the first time he'd ever denied me, and even though he might have had a valid point, it pissed me off. "I don't think one beer will hurt her."

"Him. And it's not up to you. I'm saying no. Now come here." He softened slightly. "Please."

Everything about Jason seemed different, and I

hesitated to go closer at first. But then he smiled and held out his hand, which held a little box, gift wrapped in blue-and-silver foil. Inside it was a sapphire-and-diamond ring. Small stones, but real, and set in fourteen-carat gold.

"Let's do it," he said. "Maya McCabe, will you marry me?"

Headed Home Again

It's almost like nothing unusual
happened. Well, except it's later,
and now Gabe and I know a lot
more about each other than we did
before. Still, we're both on the hunt

for information. Before diving
into that dialogue, however, I
put in a call to the hospital and
ask about Hillary. Whoever's on
the answering end of the phone

can't—or won't—tell me much
except she's still in Emergency.
"Maybe I should've told her
I was Peg Grantham," I joke.
"Although the real Peg would

probably have me arrested
for impersonating her if she
ever found out." I give Gabe
a quick overview of my earlier
conversation with the shrew.

> *Maybe she was having a bad*
> *day. And, face it, your call wouldn't*
> *have made it any better, you know?*

He's Got a Point

"You're right," I admit. "Maybe—
maybe—I'm too quick to judge. I think
it's a defense mechanism I designed

somewhere back in my childhood.
Better to push people away than get
too close and then have to leave them."

Gabe has skeletal knowledge
of Dad's and my prior nomadic
existence, but we haven't discussed

it in depth. Now, however, he asks,
Why did you move around so much
anyway? That must've been hard.

Remembering some of the people
I allowed myself to call friends,
a fog of wistfulness blossoms.

"I didn't always mind, but once in
a while we stuck around long enough
for me to connect with someone and

it hurt to know I'd probably never
see them again. I can't really tell you
why Dad refused to put down roots.

He said it was itchy feet, but there
were times it felt more like he was trying
to run from ghosts of his past."

The Danger

In opening up is allowing too much
to spill out. Because now Gabe feels

> comfortable asking, *What kind
> of ghosts? You mean, like, your mom?*

I take a deep breath, hoping to slow
the stumble. "She's one, I guess."

> *You never talk about her. Do you
> ever see her? Where is she now?*

All vestiges of my earlier regret
disappear, blown away by a giant

hot wind of rage. "No, I don't see her,
and I have no idea where she is.

For all I know, she's rotting in jail
or hell, and I couldn't care less

because the bitch never gave one
good goddamn about me." Out of

> air and steam, I pause and he says,
> *Hey, take it easy. How do you know?*

My temples pulse noticeably.
"How do I know what, exactly?"

How do you know she never cared?
When was the last time you talked to her?

"I don't know. Let me see. Guess
I must have been two. That's when

she walked out of my life. Fifteen
years, no calls, no letters, no visits.

Hmm. Wonder why I might assume
I'm not a bullet point on her priority

list. I mean, how would you feel if one
of your parents up and deserted you?"

  I realize my mistake just as he says,
  Desertion might be preferable to death.

  At least it's reversible. But I didn't mean
  to upset you. Let's change the subject.

Anger cools, dissipates into a reddish
haze, and I'm not sure if what's left

is directed toward Gabe or my mother.
Most likely the latter, because now that

we're talking about fast cars again,
a small blush of desire paints my cheeks.

I Have a Hard Time

Believing he can
make me feel this
way at any time,
let alone after stoking
such an overwhelming
inferno of negative
emotions. He must
be a warlock, hungry
for a bite of my soul.

"I don't suppose you
have a cauldron and
broom somewhere?"

> *That was off the wall.*
> *Are you accusing me*
> *of witchcraft or what?*

"Not exactly. It's just
you have this strange
effect on me, and I was
wondering if you cast
spells in your spare time."

> *If I do, it's my secret.*
> *But I'm curious about*
> *this strange effect.*
> *Care to elaborate?*

"Better not. Anyway,
there's the house."

Gabe Steers the GTO

Into the driveway, pulls close
to the walk, stops the car.
When he turns in his seat
to look at me, the orange
rings in his eyes almost glow,
and I think maybe he actually
is a creature born of magic.

"Thanks for the ride. And for
the adventure." I should exit
the automobile, go on inside,
but suddenly I don't want him
to leave. Can't stand the idea
of spending the evening alone.

As a way to delay the inevitable,
I ask, "Would you like to come in
for a little while? To talk, that is."
Don't want him to get the wrong
idea, not that he's ever offered
anything more than conversation.

> I'd like to, but what about your
> dad? He's probably expecting
> me back any minute now.

"He can't know how long it
took for the ambulance, or
getting Niagara home. Besides,
he and Zelda are probably. . . tied up."

Both of them? He grins at
my puzzled look. *That was
a little bondage humor and,
yes, I realize it's not a pretty
picture, so try to unsee it.
But if you think we can get
away with it, I'd like to keep
you company for a while.*

He follows me to the door, so close
behind I feel his breath, warm
through my hair to the skin of my neck,
sparking delicious little shivers.
What's going on? Is this me?

Dad turned down the heat
before we left, and the air inside
is almost as cold as outside.
I dial up the thermostat, kick off
my shoes, ask Gabe to do the same.

"My dad insists. Says it's the only
way to keep the floor clean enough
not to vacuum. Just so you know,
I vacuum anyway." I gesture toward
the living room. "Go sit and try to stay
warm. Want something to drink?"

He shrugs. *Sure. Whatever
you're having is fine, except
I don't drink soda. It's poison.*

Rules Out

Jack Daniel's and Coke, I guess, not
that I should be drinking with Gabe.
So why is that exactly what I want

to do? I go check out Dad's alcohol
stash. He's got a big bottle of some
generic rum, maybe two-thirds full.

I think I can get away with swiping
a little. Hot drinks, that's what we'll
have. I microwave two mugs of water,

add single shots (okay, big single
shots) of cheap liquor, taste. Yech!
Add sugar. Taste. Much better, if still

not great. Dash of cinnamon, dab
of butter. Hot buttered rums, and
I'm sticking to that. I carry them into

the other room, where Gabe has
planted himself on the sofa. Luckily
he chose the not-sagging end.

I offer a mug. "You can only have one,
since you have to drive eventually.
You're not into prohibition, are you?"

> *I don't imbibe very often, but we've*
> *got something to celebrate today,*
> *don't we? Plus, it's still cold in here.*

I'm Thinking

His reference to a celebration
was about Hillary, though we still
have no clue what's up with her.
"I wish I knew how she's doing.
You probably have a better idea
about that than I do, though."

> *Not really.* He sips his drink.
> *Mmm. Not bad. You do this often?*

"Do what? Make drinks?"

> *Not just make them, but invite*
> *guys in to share them with you*
> *when you're sure your dad's away.*

I almost snort out the liquid
in my mouth. "Dude, you are, in
fact, the very first guy I've invited
into this house, or any place
we've lived. Are you kidding me?"
I must sound as hurt as I feel,

> because he apologizes ASAP.
> *Oh God. I'm sorry. I didn't mean*
> *to offend you. Holy crap. Twice*
> *in one day! It was supposed to be*
> *a joke. Obviously I'm not as funny*
> *as I think I am. Forgive me?*

He's so sincere, what can I do but
say, "Of course I do, and I'm sorry,
too. Apparently I never developed
a viable sense of humor. My dad
thinks he's funny, but only
when he's drunk. So maybe
I should just drink more."

I do, and the hot crawl down
my throat feels pretty damn
great. In fact, it opens my mouth.

"Listen, Gabe, and if this is TMI,
just tell me to shut up, okay?
Between moving so much and
Dad overprotecting me, until
we came to Sonora I've never
had friends, so I was also denied
any kind of deeper connection.

Inviting a guy—or a girl, for
that matter—to share drinks,
or weed, or a kiss, or more, has
never even been a consideration
until now, and it's all so new I
have no clue how to deal with it.
I have zero experience. Truth is,
I'm operating totally on instinct."

And Now I Need More to Drink

I think I just bombed it. You don't say
stuff like that to a guy, especially one
you're sort of semi trying to impress.

> But as I start to offer another apology,
> he smiles. *For someone claiming to be*
> *a relationship virgin, you're amazingly*
>
> *self-possessed. Don't get me wrong, that's*
> *a good thing, and relying on your instinct*
> *is the best possible thing you can do.*

I probably don't want to know this,
but I've got nothing, really, to lose: "What
about you? Are you a player or a stayer?"

> *Player or stayer. I see what you did there.*
> *I got around a little in high school. Then,*
> *in my senior year, I became pretty serious*
>
> *with this girl named Meredith. She was*
> *a horsewoman, by the way, which is how*
> *I know anything about them. My dad worked*
>
> *construction, and my mom's a receptionist.*
> *Pony rides were the closest I ever came*
> *to horses before I met Merry, who was*
>
> *an equestrian through and through.*
> *She might've loved me, but not nearly*
> *as much as . . . wait. Does this bother you?*

"What? Hearing about your girlfriend?
Not even. I don't read romance,
but I don't mind a good romantic story."

Even one that ends without a happily
ever after? At my nod, he continues,
It wasn't her fault we broke up. Not really.

When Dad died, it was such a shock.
I mean he left for work like every other
day. Except that day he didn't come home.

He fell from the roof of a three-story house,
and hit his head completely wrong. It was
quick, they said, not enough time to feel pain.

I'm glad Dad didn't feel pain, but Mom and
I did. I couldn't process what happened at
first, and when I finally did, I melted down.

Merry tried to help, but all that did was make
me push her away. I got so sick of hearing shit
like "things happen for a reason" and "it was

God's will," and she repeated them too many
times until finally I told her to get the fuck
out of my life. I probably didn't mean it,

but that's exactly what she did, and to tell
you the truth I was so engaged in my Pityville
vacation I didn't even notice she'd gone.

By the Time

He did notice, and tried to make
amends, she'd decided trying to
work things out would be too
labor-intensive. Besides, she was
tired of seeing him miserable.

> I don't blame her. She's intrinsically
> happy, and right then all that good
> cheer totally pissed me off.
> When someone you love dies,
> it's easy fold up into yourself.

"I've never lost anyone, not like
that, anyway, but I understand
climbing into your own head
and hanging out there for a while.
It's a great defense mechanism.

I'm really sorry about your dad.
I was thinking earlier that if
something happened to mine
I'd have no idea what to do or
where I could go. I'd be an orphan."

> Gabe inches a little closer. I'd let
> you move in with me, although
> at the moment that would mean
> moving in with Aunt Zelda, not
> that it's such a bad place to live.

Rapid-Fire Q & A Begins

Q: How long will you be at Zelda's?

> A: I'm not exactly sure, but at least
> until my mom gets out of the hospital.

Q: Hospital?

> A: Yeah. Mom had kind of a breakdown.
> I wanted to stay and take care of her,
> or at least watch the house, but she said
> she'd be uncomfortable with me all alone.

Q: When will she be released?

> A: I don't know. She's been there almost
> a month. I guess until she feels strong
> again, or until the insurance runs out.

Q: Then what? Are you going home?

> A: That's my plan. I'd always thought
> I'd get to college, but I'm afraid Mom will
> need me. Dad left her okay financially,
> but she'll require emotional support.

Q: How far from Sonora is Stockton?

> A: Not so far. A little over an hour if you
> don't speed. Why? Will you miss me?

I Admit I Would

Though the funny thing
is, knowing he'll probably
not stay around actually
relieves some pressure.
Whatever our connection,
I can play this game my way,
and not have to pretend
I'm anyone except who I am.

Which turns out to be
a good thing, because now
it's Gabe's turn to ask questions,
including one I've never
had to answer out loud.

> *Something you said interested*
> *me. When you were talking*
> *about inviting people to share*
> *a drink or a kiss, you included*
> *girls in the comment. Are you*
> *into women or did my dirty*
> *little mind make that up?*

I try to form the proper
sentences, but swallow
the first words that surface.
Forming cohesive thoughts
around my frequent musings
isn't something I'm practiced
at. Honesty. Let's start there.

"I wish I was one hundred
percent sure about who
or what I'm 'into,' as you put
it. As I mentioned, I've never
actually tried either boys or
girls, but truthfully, I seem
to be attracted to both.

I've got an excellent friend
who happens to be a lesbian,
and our relationship is very
close to love at this point,
but whether or not that will
become sexual, I don't know."

*I see. So then, what about
guys? Or, I suppose more
accurately, what about me?*

"Jeez, are you always
so blunt? Okay, well,
to return the favor,
you're the first guy
of my approximate age
who I've ever had fun
just being around. I don't
think I'm allowed to confess
anything more because
the game isn't played
that way, is it?"

Those Exceptional Eyes

Lock mine. I couldn't look
away if I wanted to, but
right this moment I don't.

I don't like games.

He puts his drink on the table,
removes mine from my grasp,
and places it just touching his.

And I don't require confessions.

He reaches for my hand.
His skin is warm and rough
in the way of someone who

labors for a living. It's not
unpleasant. Now he lifts
my fingers to his lips, kisses

the tips individually. One. By.
One. The intimate gesture
makes my heart tremble and lifts

goose bumps. I never thought
my first real kiss would be
with a boy, but this boy says,

*And I don't care if you love someone
else. I really want to kiss you. Okay?*

My Head

Doesn't ask
for permission
to nod. It bobs
all on its own.

Gabe turns his hands
heel-to-heel, palms
facing upward, cups
my jaws and lifts,
tilting my mouth
toward his. Unlike

his hands, his lips
are soft when they
cover mine, and if
I had any doubt
about my ability
to kiss, he erases
it immediately.

It's instinctive.
It's gentle at first.
Its intensity grows.

The flutter in my chest
swells into a quake,
one I don't want to quell.

But now he pulls away.

Wow. Not bad for an amateur.

I Kissed a Boy

And I liked it. A lot. Wonder
if I'll like kissing a girl as much.

"I thought it would be trickier.
Maybe you're just a good teacher."

      Maybe you've got a high kissing IQ?
      Anyway, I wouldn't mind doing it

      again. But I think I'd better go before
      your father comes looking for me

      with a shotgun or something. Hey.
      Wait. Does your dad own a gun?

I laugh, happy he has no plans
to pressure me for anything beyond

kissing. I know I'm not ready for more.
"Not that I'm aware of, and I think

I'd know about it if he did." Thank
God. Dad isn't a very good drunk.

I'd hate to see him go off half-cocked
with a deadly weapon in hand.

      Well, I'm leaving anyway, so I guess
      we're probably safe. A kiss good-bye?

My Second Kiss

Is a subtle echo of the first—quiet,
caring, and a promise of something
more to come, if I extend the invitation.

But I won't do that right now.

After Gabe leaves, I sit for a while
in contemplation, seeking the meaning
of what just happened between us,

its relevance to my quest for identity.

Is it really possible to lean both ways?
If it is, and I do, that must make me bi,
but is multi-gendered attraction

an actual, viable thing?

I've heard people say that's bull,
that those who claim to be bisexual
are nothing more than nymphos

indulging unencumbered greed.

Maybe I'm greedy, borderline
gluttonous. Or maybe I'm just
curious to know if I have a preference.

One thing's certain: I'm confused.

The Worst Thing

Is I can't talk to Monica about this.
Any other subject, she'd be my go-

to confessor. But she wouldn't
understand and the last thing I
want is to make her crumble.

Funny, but I've always thought
she was the tough one, and she is

on the surface. But just beneath
the crust is a layer of liquid goo,
one that's hard to tap into.

It's where she buries her pride
when she must, which is usually

around her family. At school
she's fine claiming her unique
personal vision, and I covet

the bold self-acceptance
she presents to our classmates.

I just wish she were strong enough
to shed her hetero mask at home.
Sometimes when I consider stuff

like that, I wonder if I'm thinking
about my best friend. Or myself.

Either Way

I know I've got to call Monica,
who I haven't talked to since
yesterday. I need to hear the rasp
of her voice—rich and warm
and fringed with accent.

But when she picks up, she's
anything but her usual soft-

>   spoken self. *Oh, hey, where*
>   *have you been? Did you hear*
>   *about Hillary? She fell off*
>   *her horse and cracked her*
>   *head on a rock or something.*

"Wait. What? Slow down,
hermana. How do you know
what happened to Hillary?"

>   *Seriously? It's on the news.*
>   *They said if some local kids*
>   *hadn't found her, she probably*
>   *would have "succumbed to*
>   *the elements." That means died.*

"Holy shit. I didn't realize
she was hurt that bad. Good
thing Gabe knew some basic
first aid from his lifeguard days."

She pauses long enough
for my words to sink in. *Gabe?*
Zelda's nephew? What does he
have to do with this? Hey . . .
You mean you and Gabe were
the ones who found Hillary?

"Yeah. He was bringing me
home from Zelda's 'cause Dad
wanted to stay for an after-dinner
boink. This horse came trotting
up the street so we stopped her
and went looking for her rider.
I didn't know it was Hillary
until Gabe spotted her in the dirt."

I tell what's left of the story,
right up through meeting Max
and him offering me a job,
which I can't accept because
I'm a loser without wheels.

"I can't believe it made the news,
though. Must've been a slow day."

> *Girl, Hillary's dad is running for*
> *senator or governor or one of*
> *those politics things. I'm not sure.*
> *But anything that happens to*
> *a Grantham's gonna make the news.*

Who Knew?

Guess I should pay more attention
to politics, or at least current events,

especially if I'm going to end up
smack in the middle of one.

> They said on the news they were trying
> to figure out who the Good Samaritans
>
> are. Didn't you tell them your names?
> What's wrong? Don't want to be famous?

"Famous? What are you talking about?
All we wanted to do was help Hillary

and get Niagara home safely. I didn't
purposely *not* tell them. I just never

thought it mattered. And, in fact, I
did tell Hillary it was me, but maybe—"

> They said she was just out of surgery,
> and the details were still sketchy.

"Our identities can't be a secret. I'm sure
the ambulance guys took Gabe's name

when they asked him what happened,
not that it wasn't pretty obvious."

Well, I think you ought to tell them
it was you. You could be famous

for real, and I could be the hero's
girlfriend. Yeah, I like that idea.

Guilt bulldozes into me. Monica's
excitement made me totally forget

the postscript of my day's activities,
and her certainty about the "we" of us

unsettles me. Still, there's familiarity
wrapped up in there, and that I like.

"My dad always says if it comes down
to a choice between wealth and fame

to choose money. Fame, he says, relies
on the whims of others, and people

love you one minute, despise you
the next. That always made sense to me."

Te amo hoy y te amaré mañana.
She loves me today and she'll love

me tomorrow. She just leveled me.
"Y te amo también." And I love her, too.

I'm getting married.

That should have an exclamation mark, shouldn't it?

I guess a small part of me is excited to leave my current existence behind in favor of something brand-new. But the closer I get to the appointed time, the more I think I might've made an awful mistake.

Okay, I'm not big on school, but it's familiar, and despite the daily boredom there's a certain comfort in routine and recognizable faces. The only person I'll know at Fort Hood is Jason, and while I'm not a member of the popular crowd here, I'm not exactly a hermit, either. I miss Tati already, and I haven't left Austin yet.

Oh, and the baby stuff is overwhelming. I went to Planned Parenthood and found out that, one, I'm definitely pregnant (duh) and, two, I despise gynecological exams. Does anyone like them? You'd have to be kind of depraved.

As instructed, I took off my clothes, and slipped into this paper robe thing, trying to figure out how to tie it. But it didn't matter anyway, because within ten seconds every inch of me was exposed so a strange man in a lab coat could feel up my boobs, looking for lumps or whatever.

Then the nurse said, "Put your feet in the stirrups,

honey. Now scooch your rear end forward." I scooched. "Farther, please." Right up into the cute young doctor's face. Oh my God. So embarrassing! There were fingers and instruments and who knows what else?

Probably nothing too weird, with the nurse standing there watching it all.

I stared up at the ceiling the whole time, face burning. Luckily it didn't take very long. After he let me lower my legs and sit up, he said, "Everything looks just fine. Your weight is good, and it's important for you to maintain that if you plan to continue the pregnancy. You're fourteen weeks now, so you'll have to decide very soon."

"My fiancé and I want to keep the baby."

He looked unconvinced, but continued, "Then you'll want to stay healthy. Remember everything you put into your body also affects your baby, so eat well and avoid alcohol, tobacco products, and unnecessary medications. I'll write you a prescription for prenatal vitamins." He smiled. "And don't worry. You won't need another pelvic for a while."

That was a relief. And so is the fact that the morning sickness I've been fighting should ease at this point. I hate waking up, knowing as soon as I move my head off the pillow I'll have to dash for the bathroom and spend way too much time making out with the toilet before heading off to school. It does seem to be getting better, so hopefully I won't puke before exchanging I do's.

It won't be a fancy wedding. Just Jason and me down at the courthouse. Well, Tati will be there as my witness, and Jason's brother will stand up for him. But I'll wear a pretty, new dress that I bought with seventy-eight dollars of the money Dad left me. It's pale green, with lots of flowing fabric to semi-conceal my blossoming belly. Oh, Mom won't be attending.

Jason wanted to go with me to break the news, but I figured I'd better handle it on my own, and I'm glad I did. Mom did not take it well. I gave her the worst of it first. Too bad I was standing so close. She grabbed me by the hair, yanked my face toward hers. "Pregnant? You disgusting little whore! I knew you were sneaking around. How will I ever live this down?"

"You don't have to tell anyone, Mom. All you have to do is sign the marriage license application. Jason asked me to be his wife." I flashed my ring, which she somehow hadn't even noticed.

She pushed me away. "You call that an engagement ring? Diamond chips and blue glass? I bet he got it at a pawnshop. And who is this Jason, anyway?"

"He's a soldier, Mom, like you care. Do you want to meet him?"

"I do not. In fact, I'd better not find him in my house. I'm going to call and make an appointment for you to get an abortion. And then I'll see about moving to L.A. right away. You obviously need supervision."

"No way, Mom. I'll be going to Fort Hood as soon as the ink on the license is dry."

"I don't believe I agreed to this ridiculous idea. I'm still your mother, you know."

I backed up a step. "You haven't been my mother since you went searching for your inner alien."

Her fists clenched and unclenched, and I moved closer to the door.

"No need to start now, though. All you have to do is sign the application."

"What if I won't?"

"You know that audit partner of yours? What's his name again? Oh, yeah. Royce." I knew I had her when she went stiff and her face turned the color of ripe watermelon. "I wonder how Sea Org would feel about your relationship. Not to mention his wife. They're moving to L.A., too, aren't they?"

I happened to pick up the phone one day when she and her fuck buddy were in deep conversation. Let's just say extramarital relationships are frowned on within the Scientology organization, especially among higher-ranking members. I saved the information for a rainy day, and the storm had arrived.

"Anyway," I continued without explaining further, "I'm happy to keep my mouth shut. Just let me go and everyone will be satisfied. Including Royce and you, obviously."

Rarely have I seen her so mad, and it made me so happy. "You would resort to blackmail, wouldn't you?"

I smiled. "Oh, yeah."

"Okay, then. You deserve every bad thing that will come from this, and don't you dare come crawling back when you realize the enormity of this mistake. I wash my hands of you. Understand?"

"Totally."

All I am is dirt under her fingernails, anyway.

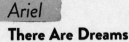

Ariel

There Are Dreams

You never want to wake
up from. Doesn't matter
if you find yourself in

                        some

cloud forest or at a country
fair, it's all about who
you're with in those

                        dreams.

Regardless of what you're
doing—slow dancing or
riding a carousel—it's how

                        you

feel just being with them,
like finally you're whole.
But then dawn insists you

                        have to

let go of the fantasy,
cleave in two again, leave
that half behind while you

                        claw up

into the real-world realm,
sweat clinging to you like
the regret you can't run away

                        from.

The Dream

I fight my way out of is tinted
green. Not dark like evergreen
but more the hue of summer
leaves. It's familiar, but discomfiting.

And I don't have a clue why.

I do know it belongs to a place
I've been before. A place I'm very
sure I called home once upon
a long time ago. I lie in bed now,

hair damp with sweat.

Try to identify the reason
for my apprehension.
On the far side of one of those
green walls, people were arguing.

Of course my dad was one of them.

The other must've been one
of his female companions.
I can't quite conjure her face.
But the voice that matches

the color was soft. Throaty.

I Cycle Back Through

The places
I remember
us living, recalling
my temporary bedrooms.

At Nadia's,
where the smell
of horses permeated
everything, every wall
in every room was white.

At Cecilia's,
which was plain
and squat and stuck
in some bygone era, dark
wood paneling covered the walls.

At Leona's,
I slept in her dead
daughter's bedroom,
where beneath the photo
tributes, the walls were blue.

Azure.
The very color
of Leona's husband's
eyes. That floats up from
nowhere. Maybe eventually

the source of the green will, too.

What Pops

Into my head now is Monica.
We talked on the phone late
into last night, right up until
Dad tripped on something
coming through the front door.

       Most likely it was his feet.
       But when he yelled, *Goddamn*
       it, Ariel! I quickly promised
       Monica I'd see her today, and hung
       up to go see what was wrong.

I found Dad trying to sit
up from his recent sprawl
across the threshold. "God, Dad,
what did you do? And did you
really drive yourself home?"

       Even from ten feet away,
       the stink of alcohol almost
       knocked me onto my butt.
       Still, he denied being wasted.
       I'm fucking fine. Don't you dare

       talk down to me. Why the hell
       did you leave your shoes in front
       of the door? Trying to kill me?
       You lazy bitch. I'm gonna kick
       the shit out of you. Come here.

Instead, I quickstepped backward
a couple of paces. My father was drunk
the few times he actually hit me,
and probably no more so than
he was last night. "Dad, I took off

my shoes, just like you want me
to, and put them where I always
do, which is not right in front
of the door. I leave them under
the coatrack." I wouldn't dare do

anything else, and I've had years
of practice. "In fact, I specifically
remember . . ." My mouth snaps
shut. I don't want to mention
Gabe coming in and leaving

his Vans beside my Nikes. Anyway,
it's not totally out of the question
that he might have accidentally
moved my shoes when he left.
"Never mind. I'm sorry you fell."

> *Goddamn straight. Better be*
> *more careful. I can't afford to*
> *crack my skull open, you know.*
> He pushed himself up onto his
> feet. *You get to bed now, hear?*

That Was That

And I'm grateful. Those post-alcohol-
soaked night encounters can end
worse. Thankfully that's mostly

the anomaly. Dad's only a vicious
drunk once in a while and last night
was not one of those occasions.

Of course everything feels more logical
when you can gain a little perspective
on it. Last night I experienced a few

apprehensive seconds. But all is well
in the bright spotlight of day. And
in a short while I'll spend time

with my best friend. I need to see
if kissing Gabe changed anything
between Monica and me, not that

I mentioned it to her. That does
bother me. I feel like I two-timed.
Does kissing person-on-the-left

count as cheating when person-on-
the-right has never even offered,
though you're sure she's wanted to?

Relationships are weird. You can
believe you understand them
when in fact you haven't got a clue.

So Far

I've spent seventeen years
clueless. It's past time to start
figuring stuff out. I told Monica
I'd meet her at the hospital.
I want to check on Hillary,
which is also strange. Not like
I cared one bit about her until
now. Why should possibly
saving her from freezing to
death change anything at all?

I just have to convince Dad
to drive me into town, which
accomplishes a couple of things.
One, he'll know for sure I was
telling the truth about why Gabe
got back to Zelda's so late. And, two,
I'll have the transportation I require.
It shouldn't be too hard. He and
Zelda usually hang out on Sunday.

Now that I know how, I put a filter,
coffee, and water into the pot, turn
it on, hoping the smell will convince
Dad to get out of bed. He can doctor
it any way he wants. Don't want to
repeat the Zelda episode, which
reminds me again of last night's
shoe tirade. They never tripped him
at all. At least, I'm pretty sure not.

As I Work

To seduce my father's consciousness,
I think about a couple of times when

he convinced me something happened
when I knew—or thought I did—he'd

fabricated the story. One time his then
girlfriend, Rhonda, was at the grocery

store. I was little enough not to think
about right versus wrong, so I wandered

into her bedroom. As women often do,
she kept her jewelry box on an end table

beside her bed, and I decided to play
dress-up with some of it. I put a string

of pearls around my neck and a ring
or two on fingers much too small

to hold them. Then I went into the closet
and found a ridiculous black straw hat

with shiny blue feathers and put that on
before spinning circles. I didn't see Dad

      come into the room until he snatched
      the hat off my head. *Stop that!* he yelled.

I remember crying from the shock
of his reaction, which even at such

a young age seemed over the top.
"But . . . but . . ." I tried to articulate

something I knew was right, but his
demeanor silenced my mouth, my brain.

> *Don't you ever come in here again!*
> he yelled, flipping the pearls over

my neck and yanking the rings off
my fingers. I ran from the room, crying.

Why was Daddy so mad? He was the one
who told me it would be all right

to play dress-up with Rhonda's things.
When I finally emerged, still confused,

Dad and Rhonda were in the kitchen
talking about nothing in particular.

I let myself forget the awful experience,
at least until Rhonda later came screaming

about her emerald ring gone missing.
I denied. Dad denied. I swore I never saw

the darn thing, knowing Dad had taken
it from me. But neither of us mentioned

that, and somehow Dad convinced her
some burglar must have stolen it.

We only stayed at Rhonda's a few more
days, and after we left I saw that green

stone ring exactly one more time—
right before Dad pawned it. That night,

as we enjoyed a steak dinner, I asked,
"Daddy? Why did you tell me Rhonda

said it was okay to play dress-up with
her stuff? I think it made her mad."

Across the table, he lowered his eyes,
and what I saw inside them made

> me want to duck. *You listen to me.*
> *I never told you it was okay to go*
>
> *in that woman's room. You're making*
> *that up, and I won't have my daughter*
>
> *turn into a lying whore like her mother.*
> *Do you understand me? You'd better.*

I Didn't Know

Exactly what a whore
was, but I understood
him just fine, and never
brought it up again.

Some things don't need
a detailed explanation.

But it wasn't the last
time he made me believe
one thing, then yanked
my certainty right out

from under me. He's sort
of an expert, and even
though I realize it, I
always seem to give him

the benefit of the doubt
and heap blame on myself.

Does that make me crazy,
or only sympathetic to
his own eccentricities?
I think maybe he's only testing

my sense of loyalty.
I hope I rate an A-plus.

Especially Because

I need his cooperation now.
The coffee idea seems to have
worked because he comes
padding into the kitchen,
wearing flannel pajamas
that have seen better days.

"God, Dad. Buy yourself
some new pj's, would you
please? That material is so
thin, I can see your hairy
legs right through it."

> *Didn't anyone ever tell you*
> *it's creepy to check out your*
> *old man's leg hair? I didn't*
> *raise a pervert, did I? Now,*
> *how about a cup of that coffee?*

"I'll pour it for you, but you
have to decide if you want
sugar and cream in it. I'm not
exactly experienced at
barista-ing. It could be gross."

> *Maybe I should make you*
> *take a sip first, prove it's not*
> *poison . . . or piss. Pretty sure*
> *that's how they make it*
> *at the so-called coffee shop*
> *Zelda is so damn fond of.*

I hand him a cup without
tasting it first, and he takes
a tentative slurp. His eyes fly
open wide and his upper lip
snarls and I'm thinking I did
something terribly wrong

> until he smiles. *Just kidding.*
> *It's not bad at all. If your little*
> *girlfriend was the one who taught*
> *you how to make coffee, please*
> *give her a big thank-you kiss*
> *for me.* Did he really just say that?

Does that mean he suspects?
But, no. It must be another
of his not-so-funny jokes,
or else I would've heard
judgment in his voice.

> He carries his cup over to
> the table, sits. *What've you got*
> *going on today? You planning*
> *on seeing that boy or what?*

Uh-oh. This could go a number
of ways, so I'll head him off
at the pass. "No. But now that
you've asked, I'm hoping you'll
drive me into town. I want to go
to the hospital and visit Hillary."

He Looks at Me

Long and hard, but apparently
doesn't discern anything
suspicious in my body language.

       Still, he comments, *I didn't realize*
       that girl was a friend of yours.

I avoid saying she isn't exactly.
"She's starting guard on our team.
I want to find out how she's doing."

       He shrugs. *Okay by me. I was*
       going over to Zelda's anyway.

Ka-ching. "I'm going to meet
Monica there and we'll hang out
somewhere until you're ready
to come get me, if that's all right?"

       As long as the two of you
       aren't picking up strange men.

No problem there, Dad, and
now I can quit worrying
that you've intuited our secret.
"When can we leave? I want
to give Monica a time frame."

       Time frame? How about when
       I'm damn good and ready?

To Be Fair

He answered my question.
I go shower,
brush my teeth,
dress in my usual
jeans and tee, this
time a long-sleeved
shirt in pastel teal.

The shade of a sunrise sea.

Monica likes this
color on me, says
it contrasts nicely
with the quiet titian
of my hair. Well, not
in those exact words.

She said it en español.

I'm starting to like
the Spanish language,
not that I know much
of it yet, but it's soft
and rolling and mostly
logical, near as I can tell.

If I were more fluent,

I'd make this call
in Monica's family's
native tongue. One day.

This Day

I manage a simple, "Hola,
novia. ¿Cómo estás?" Most
tourists would know how
to ask how someone's doing

so I don't feel especially
smug about remembering
that much. And now I switch
to the language I'm fluent in.

"Dad says he'll bring me
to town when he's 'damn
good and ready.' At least
he's willing to get dressed

and drive. I'll text you when
we're about to go, okay?"
I expect her usual cheerful
banter, and a positive sign-

      off, but her reply takes me
      by surprise. *Let me know*
      a little ahead of time. And
      can you bring that boy?

"Boy? You mean Gabe?"
The last thing I want to do
is introduce those two.
What's up her sleeve? "Why?"

I can almost hear her shrug.
I want to meet him is all.
You've been spending lots
of time with him. Sometimes

I'm kind of jealous, and I want
to make sure I've got nothing
to worry about. Maybe we could
hang out together once in a while.

Usually I find her honesty
refreshing. Today it's unsettling,
but I don't see how I can say no
unless I go ahead and lie to her.

Which I refuse to do. Anyway,
upon further consideration,
maybe it would be good to put
the pair of them in the same

place, if only for comparison's
sake. And maybe a wider buffer
zone between Gabe's kiss yesterday
and the one I wanted to coax

from Monica today would be
an okay thing. "I'll give him a call
and see if he's free, then I'll go
give Dad a nudge. See you soon."

She Makes Me Promise

I'll follow through,
which is weird for
Monica, but whatever.
When I call Gabe
it's almost like he's
been waiting for
the phone to ring.

> And apparently he was.
> *I was hoping you'd call.*
> *You've been on my mind*
> *since I left yesterday.*

There's something
new in his voice—
a hint of affection
that puts me slightly
on edge. Pretty sure
this is where I'm
supposed to get
all flirty. "Yeah? And
what exactly have
you been thinking?"

> *That I wish I would've*
> *chanced the shotgun*
> *and stayed longer.*
> *I'm craving more of you.*

Straightforward

Five simple words.
        Five direct words.
                I'm craving more of you.

I've been honest with
        him, I've shared secrets.
                I've confessed misgivings.

He might not understand
        that's what they were.
                He might pretend to consent.

And now he's waiting
        for me to respond, hoping
                I'll say what he wants to hear.

The crazy thing is, at
        the sound of his voice,
                my heart stutters, my pulse

quickens, and minute
        electric jolts prickle
                my skin, make me shiver.

The reaction is almost
        as intense as interlacing
                my fingers with Monica's.

It Comes Close

But as Dad always says, close
only counts in horseshoes and
hand grenades. I rein it in. Rein
him in, too. "You want to meet
me at the hospital in a little while?

I'm going to try to get in and see
Hillary, or at least find out how
she's doing." I take a deep breath.
"Oh, and Monica wants to meet you."

> Who's Monica?

"My friend."

> Your best friend?

"That's the one."

> Who's a lesbian?

"That is correct."

> She wants to meet me?

"That's what she said."

> I don't get it. Why?

"She said so she can stop
being jealous of you."

Did you tell her I kissed you?

"I did not tell her that, no."

So why is she jealous of me?

"Because she knows I like you."

She doesn't own a shotgun, does she?

I have to laugh at that. "No way,
and don't worry. You'll be safe
with me." I glance at the clock.

"Okay, it's quarter to ten now.
I'll light a fire under my dad
and try to be there by eleven
thirty. Does that work for you?"

I didn't say I was coming.

"No. But you and I both know
you want to meet Monica, too,
if only to satisfy your curiosity."
He's quiet for a moment.

Are you going to satisfy your curiosity?

I'm quiet for a longer moment.
"Probably. But not today. And not
in front of you. We're good to go?"

He Agrees We Are

And that is an unspoken vow
between us to leave intact
this odd web of friendships.

His and mine.
Mine and hers.
Hers and his,
soon to come.

The logical side of me says
I'm playing with dynamite,
that sooner or later:

He'll get hurt.
She'll get hurt.
I'll get hurt, and
the fault will be mine.

The emotional half tries
to insist there's no such
thing as too much connection.

One plus one.
Plus one plus one.
Totals four, and
that's better than three.

But when Gabe leaves,
is that four minus one, or two?
Math was never my best subject.

I Make an Executive Decision

Call Monica and tell her we'll meet
(the "we" including Gabe) in front
of the hospital in an hour and a half, so
now I have to nag Dad into the shower.

"The game starts at one," I remind him.
"You have to drop me off first," I underline.
"Zelda never has enough beer," I push,
"so you have to stop at the store."

> *Stop bitching at me,* he insists.
> *Okay, maybe you're right,* he concedes.
> But now it sinks in. *What've you got
> up your sleeve? You planning mischief?*

Mischief? Is that word in actual
circulation? "Nothing up my sleeve
but . . . pesto!" It's an old joke,
something to do with an ancient

cartoon Dad watched in reruns
as a kid. Can't remember the name,
but "moose and squirrel" comes
to mind, and even then I don't have

> it right. *Not pesto. Presto. You know,
> like magic? Presto-change-o? I've got
> to find Bullwinkle online somewhere.
> They don't make 'em like that anymore.*

Pretty Sure

There's a reason for that,
but I stuff the thought and

shut my mouth. Listening to
Dad go on about Russian spies

and genius dogs who were
cast members in *The Rocky*

and Bullwinkle Show buys
me a ticket into town within

the relative time frame I had
in mind. We arrive at the hospital

at 11:40, and it's swirling
with activity. "What the . . . ?"

Almost as soon as Dad puts the car
in park, Gabe raps on my window,

> opens the door. *So, I met Monica*
> *and that . . .* He points toward
>
> the front doors, where a small knot
> of people, including what looks to be
>
> a cameraman, have gathered.
> *That right there is all her doing.*

Monica spots us, waves us over.
Dad gets out of the car, audibly

sputtering, but before he can say
anything, Gabe nudges me forward.

>   Over my shoulder, I hear Dad say,
>   *What the holy hell is going on?*

>   Now Monica sprints toward us.
>   *Come on, baby. They're waiting.*

"Who's waiting?" The words barely
clear my lips before she grabs hold

of my right arm, tugs me toward
the scene at the front of the building.

Gabe hustles along at my left,
leaving Dad to bring up the rear,

still demanding an explanation
he won't receive from Monica.

As we approach the group, a man
peels off and comes toward us.

>   He extends a hand. *You must be*
>   *Ariel. I'm Charles Grantham.*

Hillary's Father

Is tall, fit, and extremely handsome
for a man in his fifties. I always
considered Dad, who is forty-eight,
"older," at least compared to my peers'
parents. But Mr. Grantham has at least
six or seven years on my father.

"Good to meet you, sir. How is Hillary?
They wouldn't tell me anything
when I called for information yesterday."

> First of all, please call me Charles.
> Hillary has a concussion and some
> swelling around the brain, which
> they'll monitor for a few days. But
> they expect a full recovery, thanks
> to you two. I'm extremely grateful.

My dad wanders up and I take
the time to introduce him to Charles.
Charles. Huh. First time a man his age
has invited a first-name basis.

> Before Dad has a chance to say anything,
> a well-dressed woman in her early twenties
> comes over and says, *I'm Kelly Waits*
> *from KCRA, and I'd like to do an on-camera*
> *interview with you and your friend*
> *for our six o'clock newscast. Just a couple*
> *of questions. Would that be okay?*

I'm going to be on TV? Good thing I
put on makeup. "Well, sure. I guess."
As she goes to round up her crew,
I can't help but notice Monica's gleeful
smile, and I've got no doubt about who
called the press. She's downright giddy.

Dad, however, is anything but.
He's breathing hard, in the way
that I know means he's pissed,
and big ropy veins have popped
out on his face, which is the color
of ripe persimmons. He looks
about ready to have a stroke.

> You don't want to be on TV,
> he hisses, eyes darting around
> to see who might've heard him.

> Sure she does! argues Monica.
> Ariel and Gabe are heroes.

> Don't talk to me about heroism.
> Dad fights to control the anger
> in his voice. I was in the army.
> I knew real heroes, and none
> of them went looking for publicity.

"I didn't go looking for publicity,
Dad. It found me." With help from
Monica. "You don't really care, do you?"

He does, I can tell, but before he can
make a scene the news crew gathers.
Next thing I know, Gabe and I are
standing in front of a camera, telling
our story. Then the young reporter
moves over to interview Charles,
who informs her of his undying gratitude
to the young people who went out of
their way to go looking for his daughter.

> While that happens, a guy from
> the *Union Democrat* comes over
> and gets comments. He's nice
> enough to interview Monica,
> too. *Ariel, she's my friend, and*
> *a real hero. I love this girl.*
> *She's good at basketball, too.*

Okay, that was random, but
he writes it down anyway.
Then he turns to talk to Dad,
who struggles to maintain
his cool, especially when
the newspaper photographer
snaps a shot of Gabe and me.

> *Listen. Of course I'm proud*
> *of Ariel. I've tried to raise*
> *her right. Looks like I succeeded.*
> *That's really all I have to say.*

Utter Garbage

But I suppose
he's just spouting
what's expected,
and the first thing
to come to mind
when thrust into
a situation like this.

I sure wouldn't
know. It's the first
time it's happened
to me, and very
likely the last.

Both reporters
make sure our names
are spelled correctly
before returning
to their studio/
office, respectively.

> At this point, Monica's
> bouncing up and down.
> *Now you're famous.*
> *Maybe it'll rub off*
> *on me. Oh, by the way,*
> *I like your boyfriend.*

The label's unsettling.
Hope she doesn't notice
my furious blush.

The News Crews Leave

Dad yanks me off to one side
with a sharp jerk of my left
arm. *Why didn't you tell me
this was going to be a circus?*

Each word is punctuated
with rage. "I had no idea,
Dad. Monica thought Gabe
and I should be recognized.
It was a complete surprise."

*Yeah, well, I hate surprises. And
I have a damn hard time believing
you were clueless about all this.
Look at your clothes and makeup.*

I don't want to confide
my wardrobe choices were
meant to impress not one,
but two people who are close
to me. Instead I try, "I thought
I should look nice to visit
Hillary. It's only respectful."

*I don't like being lied to either, not
by my flesh and blood. Your need
for the spotlight isn't a good thing,
and if people weren't watching
us right now, I'd take this further.*
He turns away. *Get your own ride home.*

Suddenly I'm Very Glad

People were watching.

    Why'd he get so pissed off?

    What made him think this was *my* idea?

    How can he believe I'd flat-out lie?

I'm beginning to question Dad's sanity.

    Is he drinking more heavily than I realized?

    Does he have a secret prescription pill stash?

    Can dementia be creeping in early?

Or maybe I should question my own sanity.

    Might I have encouraged Monica to invite TV time?

    Did I leave my shoes where Dad could trip on them?

    What about Santa's sleigh knowing the way?

Was the last a total invention of my subconscious?

    What wasn't was Dad's overreaction.

    What wasn't was Dad's hideous anger.

    I hope it's safe to go home tonight.

Honeymoons are supposed to be memorable. Mine totally was, but not in the way most people think of. After our frill-free wedding, Jason and I went to an early dinner with Tati and Jason's brother at Matt's El Rancho. Killer Mexican food, which was good because my new husband started drinking margaritas right away. I was glad he put a huge burrito in his gut to absorb some of the alcohol.

I let Jason decide on the honeymoon, which he said was all he could afford. I thought about breaking into my cash stash to spring for a nice hotel room instead, but listened to Tati's advice. "Keep that money for emergencies," she said. "Don't even mention it to Jason. As my grandma says, every woman needs a secret rainy-day fund, just in case."

I don't want to think about "just in case," but it makes sense, especially considering Jason and I are relative strangers. For instance, his brother informed me at dinner that the reason their parents didn't attend the ceremony was because they had committed to judging a stock show.

"None of us realized Jason had gotten serious about someone," he said. "Shocked the hell out of me, to be honest."

Seems Jason's family communicates about as well as mine.

Once we finished our delicious pralines and tres leches

desserts, Jason escorted me to a borrowed pickup, pulling a rented pop-up tent trailer, and off we went to McKinney Falls State Park for a long weekend of camping. The park isn't very far from town, and it's pretty enough, with a creek and two waterfalls and plenty of places to hike, if that's your thing. Apparently it isn't Jason's.

"I get plenty of 'hiking' at work," he said, setting up a couple of folding chairs. "Three days off, I want to relax. But first, how about a roll in the honeymoon hay?"

He pulled me inside the trailer, where his hands went straight to the zipper of his slacks. They were off before we hit the bed, which was roomy enough but the foam was thin and carried solid hints of the people who'd slept—not to mention rolled in the hay—in it before. That, plus the tequila-and-beans clinging to his breath, put me on the verge of nausea.

"Can we open a window?" I asked quietly. "I don't feel so good."

"What? Now I make you sick?" He rolled away and jammed open the window over the bed.

"Not you," I tried. "Between the baby and the wedding excitement and the spicy food. And it smells kind of . . . stale in here."

He rolled over again, coaxed me backward into the heat of his body, and that did feel good, especially with the cool breeze now blowing over our skin, raising goose bumps and soothing my upset stomach. He trailed his hand down over the small hill of my belly. Gently. Lovingly. "What will we name him?"

"Don't be mad, but I think it's a girl."

"Nope. Can't be."

"Well, we'd better pick a name that will work for either one, just in case. And if it is a girl, will you love her as much as if she was a boy?"

He hesitated, but then said, "Well, sure."

We kicked a lot of names around. Alex. Jamie. Avery. Riley. Emory. Ryan. But finally we settled on Casey. If it's a boy, Casey David. If it's a girl, which it is, Casey Nicole. Strong, and feminine. It makes me happy.

What pleased me that evening was feeling like Jason and I had discussed something important, and come to a mutual decision. It struck me how few conversations of real importance I'd shared with him—or anyone, straight from struggling high school student to wife and soon-to-be mother. Does that make me an actual adult, despite being just seventeen?

The rest of the weekend was pretty cool. I even talked Jason into hiking, and decided I liked camping okay. Except for the stinky mattress. He dropped me off Sunday evening at home and drove back to Fort Hood, where we're waiting for an affordable house big enough to suit a family of three.

Meanwhile, I'm doing my best to stay out of my mother's way. If she was cold before, she's a corpse now—frigid, hard, unmoving. She did agree to let me live here until I move or she does, and her plans are to go end of this month. April. Spring. New lives beginning.

Yesterday, Tati and I drove to Houston for the Astros-

Rockies game she bought tickets to for my birthday. I was pretty excited because the day before the Astros had routed the Rockies, 15–2. But that must've used up their home run allotment for the week, because they lost 5–3.

Still, I got to spend the whole day with Tati, gorging on junk food and soda, things I never enjoy at home and am supposed to limit now. I figured one day wouldn't make me or the baby fat. And Tati, of course, couldn't care less.

"These are the best hot dogs I've ever had!" she said, and she must've meant it, because she ate three over the course of the afternoon. I limited myself to two. Plus a soft pretzel, peanuts, and an ice cream bar.

Apparently, something I ate made Casey happy, because bottom of the ninth, while Tati and I yelled at our team to get it together, there was a stuttering movement inside me. At first I thought it must be hot-dog gas, but then it happened again, and I knew my baby was saying hello to me, and to Tati, and to the Astros, despite their dismal performance.

"Oh my God!" I exclaimed.

"Hey, it's just a game," Tati said.

"No. Put your hand right there and wait." I guided her to a spot just beneath my belly button.

It didn't take long. "Holy shit," she said. "It's alive."

We laughed and laughed.

Pretty sure Casey was giggling, too.

Ariel
Life Just Got Weird

Good weird, but still . . .
I've no idea how to react.

So, the other day, post-TV
and newspaper interviews,

I asked Charles, aka
Mr. Grantham, aka Hillary's

dad, if we could visit her,
and despite a tepid protest

from the nurse on duty,
Charles's insistence paid off.

Gabe and I were allowed
a couple of bedside minutes.

Guess pulling strings isn't hard
when you're an important

politician, someone with a name
people recognize. Or maybe

it's more about the clout of money.
Either way, we got to say hi.

Hillary Looked Awful

Her skin was the color of chalk
on a blackboard. Mostly gray.
Tubes threaded into her arm
delivered some sort of fluid
sustenance—mostly sugar
water would be my guess,
but what do I know, except
for what I've seen on TV shows?

> Regardless, when she opened
> her eyes, which were shut
> against the glare or maybe
> to invite unconsciousness,
> she smiled. *Ariel. Thank you.*

Her eyes didn't seem focused,
so I wasn't sure why she was
thanking me. "For what, Hillary?"

> But she didn't hesitate. *For
> taking care of Niagara. That
> horse means everything to me.
> She's, like, my best friend.
> That sounds stupid, I know,
> but if something bad would've
> happened to her . . .*

It didn't sound stupid at all.
I understand not having friends,
and relying on the next best thing.

Then Her Attention Turned

Toward Gabe, and that was when
I realized that whatever liquid
her IV pumped was supplying her
with more than sugar. Major painkillers

        were involved. Oh. I remember
        you. Except, I don't know you.
        Except I think I should. You were
        there, weren't you? Who . . .

    I'm Gabe, and I'm Ariel's friend.
    Yes, I was there, too. Ariel sent me
    to find you while she reasoned with
    Niagara. I know nothing about horses.

"Well, that's not exactly true,"
I argue. "But we can talk about it
when you're better. We just came
to say we care about you." So. Weird.

        Strange enough she barely knew
        how to respond, especially with
        that feel-good drip. *I . . . uh . . . really?*
        She about choked on the last word.

For whatever reason, "Of course"
fell out of my mouth, and I still
don't really understand why.
Is it because she looked so fragile?

Fragile

```
Insubstantial
      a
      r
      even there
      l           p
      y           h
                  e
                  m
                  e
                  r
                  a  s a whisper of
                  l            u
                               m m
                                   e
              a   in November
              d
              I
              h
              also felt this way
              v
              e
```

I'm Feeling That Way

Now, in fact, and it has everything
to do with my growing confusion.

I'm being yanked in two directions,
and either way I go offers conflict.

To my left, Gabe.
Soft-spoken.
Smart.
Funny.

> To my right, Monica.
> Opinionated.
> Smart-ass.
> Hilarious.

Left.
Ambition.
Loyalty.
Patience.

> Right.
> Talent.
> Honesty.
> Comfort.

Left.
Boy.
> Right.
> Girl.

The Last Comparison

Means the least, honestly,
and I'm more and more sure
about that, though I still haven't
given in to the growing desire
to go all the way either way.

I want to.
I'm scared to.
Because it would
feel like commitment.

Maybe I don't want to choose,
and I'm not talking about left
or right. I'm talking about Gabe
or Monica. I don't think I'm allowed

to have both.
I hear people talk.
I know how they feel
about "someone like me."

> There's no such thing as "bi."
> That means they'll fuck anything.
> They're . . . (depending on who's
> talking) *straight* or *gay, and going*
>
> *through a phase*
> or *in total denial.*
> *They're full of shit.*
> *They're mentally ill.*

These Sentiments

Bother me
not because I think
they're wrong,
but because I worry
they might be
right, in whatever ways.

What if

- my brain is in serious
  need of rewiring?

- I'm totally topped off
  with manure?

- I'm straight—or gay—
  and keep denying that
  obvious fact?

- all I really want to do
  is screw indiscriminately?

- there's no such thing as bi?

All I Know

For sure is I'm totally distracted
from the things I should be thinking
about—schoolwork, teamwork—

while trying to figure this stuff out,
not to mention keeping Dad in total
darkness about this major change in me.

Paying attention in my classes today
was a losing battle. Mr. Santos called
me on it, too, in third-period Spanish.

> *Señorita Pearson. ¿Dónde estás?*
> *Por favor, únete a nosotros aquí*
> *en el planeta tierra.* Or, roughly

> translated, *Miss Pearson. Where*
> *are you? Please join us here*
> *on planet earth.* Which, of course,

tore everyone else out of their
personal stupors, busting them

up like they weren't just as guilty,
though I doubt their thoughts had

strayed anywhere close to mine.
Then again, I can't be certain. Maybe

every single person in that class
is an oversexed full-of-shit lunatic.

One of the Hardest Things

About my left/right dilemma
is balancing spending time with
Monica and Gabe. I love being
with both, but not in the same
space. The right/left day I tried

was one of the strangest ever.
I mean, they attempted to be nice
to each other, but the narrow
stream of jealousy that flowed
between them burgeoned into a

regular river before the afternoon
was through, and I'm afraid
the fault was mostly mine.
I tried not to flirt, which probably
made it even more obvious that

I really wanted to. After we left
the hospital, first we went for
burgers, and it wasn't so bad
while all of us were stuffing
our faces. Then we decided

to play tourist and walk around
downtown Sonora. It's mostly
just shops and places to eat,
but the fun was supposed to be
the company, and it was for a while.

Then stupid me, walking between
them, I slipped one of my hands
into Monica's, the other into
Gabe's, and all I could do as
we strolled along the sidewalk

was compare the two. Size.
Softness. Texture. The weight
of the pressure each applied.
Monica's fingers felt like eels—
smooth and cool and slender.

Gabe's were more like sausages—
plump and warm and dimpled,
and they gripped mine tightly.
Securely. That's it. He made
me feel safe. Monica kept

slipping hers up and down,
in and out of mine, the way
a little child might. Playful.
That's right. She's my one
true source of fun. I love her.

I do. And the screwed-up thing
is I think I'm falling hard
for Gabe, too. Is there such
a thing as promiscuous love,
or does it only apply to sex?

My Brain's Relentless

It really needs to stop processing
anything other than basketball drills
at the moment, and all it does is argue

> with me. *Earth to Pearson!* yells
> Coach Booker, echoing Mr. Santos,
> only in English. *You've made that shot*
>
> *a hundred times. Yank your head out*
> *of your butt, would you, please?*
> It takes force of will, but I do as

she so bluntly requests, managing
to land a three-pointer, not that those
count in practice. "How's that

for an apology?" I shout back.
But I'm so busy being a smart-ass
that I don't notice Syrah right in

> front of me. I crash into her at
> decent speed and we both hit
> the floor. *Jesus freaking Buddha!*
>
> Syrah screeches, using the Spanish
> *Hey-suess* pronunciation. That
> makes everyone laugh, including

Syrah and me, despite what
I'm sure will become awesome
bruises on both our rear ends.

Monica Sprints Over

Holds out her hands,
offering to help me
up from the floor.
When they connect
with mine, the subsequent
electric arcs almost make
me pull away. Instead,
I let her tug me to my feet.

> *That had to hurt,*
> she says. *You should*
> *pay better attention.*
> *I've got plans for you later.*

> Her words are sinking in,
> seeking meaning, when
> Syrah, who's still splayed
> on the court, complains,
> *Hey, what about me?*

> *Sorry, I got no plans for you,*
> jokes Monica, letting go
> of my hands so she can pull
> Syrah off the hardwood, too.

Coach Booker tells us to hit
the locker room, and as I
limp from the gym, I try
not to think too much about
what Monica's got in mind.

I Also Do My Damn Best

Not to gawk at her
in the shower, hot
water coursing through
her waist-length dark
hair and down
over her suede skin.

She wouldn't care,
of course. But, while
most of the girls must
suspect the gravitational
pull between Monica
and me, I'd rather keep
them guessing, at least
until I've eliminated
all personal doubt.

The temptation to stare
has become harder and
harder, however, and now
she turns to face me,
a soft soap lather barely
disguising the sinews
of her breasts and
black curls beneath
her belly button, and

I have to close my eyes,
pretending shampoo
is what I'm worried about
getting inside them.

Something Shifts

Inside me,
something elemental,

as if
the earth
has tilted,

barely perceptibly,
on its axis,

bringing it right again.

Don't know what this
means, but the motion

tips me
slightly
off-kilter.

I inhale boldly,
exhale slowly, then,

just as I regain balance

she brushes by and
the cartwheeling inside

is like
dropping
from a high dive.

Thrilling. Electrifying.
Borderline terrifying.

Not sure
I'll ever be
vertical again.

The Whole Time

We get dressed, I keep my eyes
turned away from her. I don't want
to tumble off that cliff again, despite
enjoying the strange, precipitous fall.

Clean panties and bra on, I take
a few seconds to brush through
my tangled hair before buttoning
into an oversize plaid flannel shirt.

I manage to catch a glimpse of Syrah,
sliding into her jeans. "Whoa. Tell me
my butt doesn't look like that! Yours
looks like grape jelly. The color, that is."

> She snorts. *Thanks for clarifying.*
> *Anyway, whose fault is that?* She shuts
> her locker. *I'll meet you guys outside.*
> Most of the other girls have gone,

> and the couple remaining are not close
> by, something Monica notes before coming
> over. *Turn around. Let me see.* When I do,
> her hand slithers down my thigh. *Feo.*

"Hey. Who're you calling ugly?" I force
my voice light, hoping she doesn't notice
the way I'm trembling at her touch.
But when I turn to face her, her smile

tells me she's seen it. Now I'm staring
at her lips, and it's all I can do not
to kiss them. No. Not here. This is
not the time. This is not the place.

I clear my throat. "Syrah's waiting.
We'd better go or we'll lose our ride."
She nods, but is reluctant to move,
and I dare to whisper, "Later."

       Her eyes widen, and her smile
       deepens. *Sí, novia. Más tarde.*
       At the far end of the row, Darla
       slams her locker door shut,

a reminder that we've almost
completely blown our cover.
Monica goes to put on her shoes
and I finish dressing, too.

I believe I just gave her a promise,
wrapped in a single five-letter
word. I hope it's not more
than I'm truly willing to deliver.

On Our Way

To the parking lot, we walk
so close to each other
her jeans whisper
against mine, promising
much more to come
más tarde.

The obvious energy
exchange makes me dizzy
with anticipation.

I'm so focused
on imagining what that
might mean I barely notice
the knot of people
standing on the sidewalk.

As we start past them
Garrett steps in front
of us, blocking our path.

> *Why don't you girls*
> *give us a little show?*
> *I've always wanted*
> *to watch lezzie action*
> *up close and personal.*

> *Cállate, idiota,* responds
> Monica. *Shut up, idiot.*
> *And move the hell out*
> *of our way.*

Or what, bitch? He draws
himself tall and wide
and puffs out his chest.

Most of the group shrinks
back against the wall,
but Keith moves into place
at Garrett's right elbow.

"What's the problem, Garrett?
We weren't bothering you."
I pretend courage
I'm really not feeling.

*The problem is I don't like
gays. It ain't natural.
Besides . . .* He dares to run
his hand down over my left
breast. *It's a waste of pussy.*

Monica steps in between
Garrett and me. *Don't you
touch her. And what would
you know about pussy?
I've never seen you with
a girl. Only with your friend
there.* She points to Keith.

The Other Kids Laugh

At the implication.
Keith hurls an expletive.
Garrett's face ignites
and he starts to lift
his right hand, but
thinks better of striking
a girl—lesbian or not—
in front of so many people.

Monica stays in place,
as if willing to jump
one-on-one with this
arrogant prick, but
I won't let it go that far.

"Come on. Syrah's waiting.
Sorry, Garrett, no show
for you. You'll have to do
what you always do and
find it on pay-per-view."

I steer Monica around
Garrett and Keith, off
the sidewalk, and into
the parking lot. "What
were you thinking?
He could have hurt you."

> *No estaba pensando.*
> *I wasn't thinking. I just*
> *wanted to protect you.*

I Don't Care Who's Looking

I reach for her hand, weave
my fingers into hers as we head
toward Syrah's car. "That was
dumb. But thank you."

What's his problem, anyway?

I shrug. "Maybe you got it
right. They say the biggest
homophobes are often
closet queers."

Who says that?

"I don't know. I just read it
somewhere. You take shotgun."
I let go of her hand, slide into
the backseat where I can think.

While Monica explains to Syrah
what happened with Garrett,
I consider the homophobe theory,
which can't apply to all of them,

or my dad would be totally gay.
Pretty sure he's not, but wouldn't
that be crazy? What if my queer
gene came from his side of the family?

When We Get to My House

There's a strange car in the driveway.
What's even weirder, Dad isn't home,

and I don't see anyone around. "Do
you guys think there's someone inside?"

> *I don't know,* says Monica. *You and
> your dad lock your doors, don't you?*

"Yeah. Dad's all paranoid about it,
in fact. Kind of obsessive compulsive."

> Syrah jumps out. *One way to know.
> Come on. There's safety in numbers.*

We circle the house, looking for any
sign of a break-in, but the windows

are intact, both doors still locked, and
we find no hint of possible covert entry,

so I use my key and one by one, we cross
the threshold to take a look inside. The house

> is empty. *Let's check out the car,* Monica
> suggests. *Hope there's no dead bodies inside.*

> *That's dumb,* says Syrah. *Who leaves
> corpses in some stranger's driveway?*

We Don't Find Corpses

But on the front seat
of the candy-red Ford
Focus is an envelope,
and it's addressed to me.

Inside is a thank-you
card, and a note which
reads:

> DEAR ARIEL,
>
> I REALLY CAN'T THANK YOU
> ENOUGH FOR WHAT YOU DID
> FOR HILLARY. PLEASE ACCEPT
> THIS GENTLY USED TOKEN
> OF MY THANKS. I'VE TAKEN
> THE LIBERTY OF REGISTERING
> THE CAR IN YOUR NAME AND
> PAID UP THE INSURANCE FOR
> SIX MONTHS. ENJOY!
>
> CHARLES GRANTHAM
>
> P.S. I TOLD THEM YOU WERE
> MY NIECE, SO PLEASE LET'S KEEP
> THAT OUR SECRET. ALSO, TO BE
> HONEST, THIS WAS HILLARY'S
> CAR. SHE'S GETTING A NEW ONE.
> IT WAS HER IDEA TO GIVE THIS
> TO YOU.

No Freaking Way!

Hillary Grantham's given me
her car? This has got to be
some kind of joke. The girls
and I exchange incredulous
looks. "This can't be real, can it?"

> *Sure looks real to me,*
> comments Syrah. *And*
> *"gently used" is right.*
> *The odometer only has*
> *38,000 miles. She opens*
> *the glove box and pulls*
> *out the owner's manual.*
> *It's a 2012. Hillary must've*
> *only driven it to school.*

"I don't think I can keep
it. It's way too extravagant.
Besides, I didn't do anything
to earn it. Not really." Even
if I did, what'll Dad say?

> *What? You saved Hillary's*
> *life. Do you want to hurt*
> *her feelings? Anyway, you*
> *gotta keep it. He put it in*
> *your name and everything,*
> *so it's already yours.*

Every Argument

I can think of gets shot down:

"I still don't have my license."

*So get one. All you have
to do is pass the driving
test. You know how.*

"Dad'll have to sign for it.
(Which means he'll have to
approve this whole thing.)"

*Talk him into it. How can
he say no? He won't have
to take you places.*

"Even with the insurance
paid, I'll have to come up
with money for gas."

*Do what everyone does.
Go out and find a job.*

"Dad doesn't want me
to work. He insists he's
responsible for my needs."

*Point out if you're earning
your spending cash, he'll
have more of his own money
to spend on booze. Or maybe
say Zelda instead. No need
to underline the obvious.*

Excellent Point

Not that I'm sure it—any of it—
will work. But, hey, what have
I got to lose, and I already know
where I can apply for a job I'd like.

> Syrah hatches a more imminent
> plan. *Let's take her for a spin.*
> *The keys are in the ignition.*
> *You might as well get used to her.*

"You think we should? What if
we get caught?" We most definitely
shouldn't, of course. But I really,
really want to. I still can't believe it.

> *No cops out here,* insists Monica.
> *Anyway, don't drive like an ass.*
> *They can't tell if you got a license*
> *just by looking at you, can they?*

Another excellent point.
"Okay. Let's go." The girls argue
over shotgun, and eventually
reach a compromise. Syrah

will claim it first, then switch,
with Monica on the inbound.
It takes a few minutes to orient
to the strange vehicle, figure out

254

important stuff like how to turn
on the heater, not to mention
the radio. I let Syrah take charge
of choosing the station. It's late

afternoon, and the November
light has faded into an auburn
sky, so we'll be doing this with
headlights on. Luckily, they work

fine. In fact, everything seems
to be working fine. The engine
turns over easily, hums like
a beehive, and while the Focus

isn't exactly a performance car,
it's got plenty of pep when I hit
the gas pedal. Speaking of gas,
"Check it out. The tank is full."

> Which leads to bickering. Syrah takes
> the lead. *We could go all the way to Sac.*

Don't be stupid. Two hours each way?
That's too far. Her dad will be home.

> *He never gets home before midnight*
> *on Friday. In fact, that's early for him.*

How do you know? You're not there every
Friday. Him and Zelda could get in a fight.

The Suggestion

Makes me pull over onto
the shoulder. "Okay. Change
seats. Let's go back. I feel like
a criminal. Besides, I'm getting
hungry, aren't you?"

> *You crack me up, says Syrah,*
> *exiting the front. You underage*
> *drink, you smoke weed and inhale,*
> *but driving without a license*
> *makes you a criminal? Whatever.*

> Monica settles in and as we
> turn toward home, she says,
> *Hey. How come you got the car?*
> *What about your boyfriend?*
> *Did he get one, too?*

"Will you please stop
calling Gabe my boyfriend?
I have no idea why I got the car,
or if he got one, too. Are you
in a different time zone?
We found out about this
together, remember?"

> Her fingers tiptoe across the seat,
> to my knee and up my leg, then
> come to rest on the inner thigh
> curve. *I'm glad he's not your*
> *boyfriend. He's so not your type.*

I Won't Argue That

Not with our current connection.
I don't want to quarrel, don't want
to feel confused, and at this moment

I'm totally sure that Monica *is* my type,
so I'm relieved to see the only vehicle
parked in our driveway belongs to Syrah.

Monica was right. When Dad and Zelda
do fight, his early return can upset
our plans. I'm glad tonight doesn't

seem to be one of those times. Of course,
it's early. "You coming in, Syrah? Afraid
we're stuck with frozen pizza rolls."

> *Yech. No thanks. Anyway, I promised*
> *Dad I'd babysit the twins so he and*
> *Marla can go out for their anniversary.*

That both relieves me and makes
me a little queasy with anticipation
about alone time with Monica.

> We grab our stuff out of Syrah's car,
> start toward the house. *Did you bring*
> *your keys?* asks Monica. *It would suck*
>
> *if your car got stolen the first day.*
> True, and to be safe, I lock the doors
> of my 2012 candy-red Ford Focus.

Thinking About Dad

Coming home early
reminds me I'd better
give him a heads-up.
First I click up the furnace.
As always, it's freezing
inside when I get home.

"Get comfy," I tell Monica,
"while I call my dad and
tell him about the car.
Otherwise, he'd probably
freak out if he saw
it in the driveway."

> *Okay. But do we really*
> *have to eat pizza rolls?*
> *Is there anything fresh*
> *in the 'frigerator?*
> *I can cook, you know.*

"Not sure. But my fridge
is your fridge. If you find
something to whip up, I'll
eat it. I trust you know how."

> *Bueno, pero primero . . .*
> Yes, but first she positions
> herself so close to me there
> are barely molecules between
> us. She lifts up on her toes
> to match my height, and . . .

I've Dreamed About This Kiss

For days.
For weeks.
For months.

And, just maybe,
for the entire part
of my life
that had any
clear notion
of what a kiss
could—or
should—be.

Oh.
My.
Serious.
God.

Our mouths fuse.
Tongues converge.
But there's more.
So much more.

And, yes, there's longing,
upwelling from places
we've yet to explore,
but that's not the genesis.

Because the bond between
us begins heart to heart.

This, My Third Kiss

Takes my literal breath
away. I so want to tell her
I love her, but I know if I do
I'll jinx us, and this duality
we've merged into.

> But Monica doesn't hesitate
> to declare, *Te amo más que
> la vida misma. Tú eres
> mi amiga y mi corazón.*

She loves me more than
life itself. I am her friend
and her heart. That draws
my smile. "A chef and poet,
too. How lucky am I?"

> *Luck isn't random.
> It's something you create.
> You call your dad and I'll
> go see what I can create
> in the kitchen. I'm starving.*

I watch her go, try not
to think too much about
where the rest of this night
might lead us. Temptation
is a powerful force. Succumbing
to it scares the hell out of me.

It Also Excites Me

Because, as scared
as I am that Dad will find
out, and try to beat
that sex demon out of me,
or disown me for it,
or both,

the need to embrace
this part of myself
is escalating.

Lately, my dreams
are inhabited
by lust-infused images.

Feminine.
Masculine.
Both.
Right. Left.
Up. Down.
Over.
Beneath.

Sometimes I wake
to find myself touching
the most intimate
parts of my body,
satiating a hunger
so deep, so vital,
feeding it is integral
to my well-being.

The sensation is incredible,
but I could never find
the courage
to do it consciously.
My programming insists
it's wrong.
Wrong.
Wrong.

So why
does it feel
so right?
Right?
Right?

Now I need
to know what it's like
with someone else.
Someone I trust.
Someone I care about,
and believe they care about me.

I think it could be tonight.
I'm terrified.
Thrilled.
Determined.

But First Things First

I locate my phone, dial Zelda's number
and, still caught up in the tempest

of carnal confusion, when Gabe answers,
a serious outbreak of guilt erupts.

It feels almost as if he's been peeking
in the windows. "Oh, hey. Is Dad there?"

> *No. He and Aunt Zelda ran into town*
> *to pick up some groceries. They should*

> *be back soon, though. Should I take*
> *a message or do you want to try his cell?*

"I should probably talk to him.
You won't believe this, but—"

> *Wait. Don't tell me. Let me guess.*
> *Hillary Grantham gave you her car.*

I just found out myself less than
an hour ago. "How do you know?"

> *Her father told me. I didn't get a car,*
> *by the way, but he did offer to pay*

> *for bodywork, paint, and an all-new*
> *interior for the GTO. Pretty cool, huh?*

I agree that it's totally cool, then
ask, "So, Dad knows about the car?"

> Actually, yeah, he does. He answered
> the door when Mr. Grantham came by.

> Oh, I got to meet Hillary's aunt, too.
> Believe it or not, she's kind of attractive.

Why does the remark sting a little?
"Is that so? Well, maybe on the outside.

Anyway, what did Dad say about
the car? Was he pissed?" Bet he was.

> Not that I could tell. He was nice
> enough to the Granthams, and after

> they left, all I heard him say was,
> "Huh. Can you imagine that?"

That doesn't sound too bad, but
I'll have to wait until he gets home

to know for sure. Dad's squirrelly.
"So, are you going to fix up the GTO?"

> Does a duck quack? Hell yeah!
> It's like an early Christmas present.

I Tell Him

A gently used car
is like making up
for every Christmas
present, plus
every birthday
present, I never got.

There
were
lots
of
them.

Too often there
wasn't enough
money for Dad
to buy them.
Of course,
there was always
enough cash
to cover his booze
and cigarettes.

Once I was old
enough to figure
that out,
disappointment
swelled into anger.
Not that it mattered.
My silent seething
rarely bothered Dad.

The few times
I mentioned how awful
it made me feel to be
ignored on the days
other kids celebrated
with parties and gifts,
Dad would shrug.

Sorry. I'm not much,
and I admit that.
But I'm all you've
got, aren't I?
It's me or foster care.
Take your pick.
Besides, you know
you love your old man.

Despite all the bad,
I did love him. Still do,
though sometimes
I can't figure out why.
Maybe I've always
been desperate
to love anyone at all.

I Don't Offer Gabe

That extended
addendum.

We decide to hang
out on Sunday,
designated football
day at Zelda's.

He wants me to help
him pick out
a classic GTO
paint color,
plus complementary
interior options.

I ask if he'll give
the Focus a once-over,
not that I think
the Granthams
would keep it in less
than perfect mechanical shape.
I just want to spend time
with Gabe.

Because, whatever does
or doesn't happen
with Monica after this,

I
care about
him, too.

The First Thing

That happens with Monica
is dinner. I can't believe
what she's put together
with the meager ingredients
we have available.

On the menu:
Homemade mac
(unburied from the cupboard)
and cheddar cheese
(one of the few things in the fridge)
with baby peas and pearl onions
(found in a freezer drawer).
She even digs up bacon
to add, crumbled,
to the main dish.

> *It needs to bake thirty or forty*
> *minutes.* She slides the casserole
> into the preheated oven, then
> turns back to me. *What did*
> *your dad say about the car?*

I relate what Gabe told me.
"So, things could either be
A-OK, or totally not. You never
know where Dad's concerned.
At least the car won't be a surprise."

> She sets the oven timer. *We've got*
> *a little time. What you want to do?*

I Hesitate

But not for long, because if I lose
my nerve now, who knows when
I might find it again? I take her hand,

lead her into the living room,
notice we both still have our shoes
on, something we'd better remedy.

"Shoes by the door in case Dad
decides to surprise us. Besides,
socks are sexier." Did I just say that?

> Monica laughs. *I never heard*
> *that one before, and you haven't*
> *seen my socks. They could be gross.*

They're not. They're fluffy pink and
totally clean, at least until she has
to walk around the house in them.

Vacuuming is my Saturday job,
so there's almost a week's worth
of dust on the floor. Oh well.

"Okay, this is the very first time
I've ever asked anyone this, but
you wanna make out or what?"

> *Pensé que nunca lo preguntarías.*
> She thought I'd never ask, and
> before I can change my mind

she pulls me over to the couch,
gently sits me down. *Oh, wait.*
She goes over to the window, closes

the blinds. *This is a private show.*
Wouldn't want your neighbors
to see. Recostarte, novia. Lie back.

I like that she's taking charge,
mostly because I have no idea
what to do next. I close my eyes,

accept her lead. It begins with
the expected kiss, except this one
moves quickly beyond invitation,

all the way into the danger zone.
Just as I think my heart will pound
out of my chest, the tip of her tongue

traces the outline of my mouth
before her lips kiss the excited pulse
beneath my right ear, then move

to the matching throb under the left.
When she kisses down my neck,
to the small cleft between my breasts,

my instinct is to protest. *No!*
she commands. *¡Déjame hacer*
esto! She says to let her do this.

And "This"

Might be something
I've thought about,
dreamed about, but
had no clear idea about

     how it would look,
          how it would feel,
               how it would happen to me.

How it looks is beautiful.
When she rises up over me,
I can see she is a creature
not of this world, an angel—
half-dark, half-light—fallen
to earth from the autumn sky.

     Flawless but for the barely
          perceptible blemishes
               I am privileged to see.

How it feels is unlike
anything my imagination
could have invented.
She fumbles the mechanics
of clothing and positions,
but I don't mind because

     if she isn't practiced
          we can learn together;
               there is discovery to share.

Driven by Instinct

Fueled by solid lust
    we are skin to skin
    tongue to tongue
    and tongue to skin

She kisses in circles
    the arc of my neck
    the curves of my breasts
    the smaller circumferences
    of my nipples.

She licks in lines
    tracking contours
    down my right side
    back up my left and, finally,
    straight from chin to belly button.

She touches tentatively
    in lines and circles
    show me what you like
    gaining momentum
    building intensity

She nudges me
    closer and closer
    right up against the brink
    and, no way to hold back,
    pushes me over the cliff.

It's one hell of a trip.

Crash Landing

The buzzer goes off in the kitchen.
I smile. "Does that mean I made
my eight-second ride?"

> Monica looks confused.
> *No, that means our dinner*
> *is done. You must be hungry?*

"Starving. But what about you?"
I reach out and stroke the cleft
that would be cleavage if there

was more flesh there, not that
I'd prefer it. "I think I owe you
one." I wink and she laughs,

> but shakes her head. *Later.*
> *We've got lots of time, not like*
> *the mac and cheese, which will burn.*

I watch her straighten up
and go into the kitchen, but
take my time following her.

Everything between us has
changed. This thing we have
is more serious now, and while

that's not necessarily bad,
I wonder if Monica and I have
been irrevocably altered, too.

Maya

I've been at Fort Hood almost four months now. It's been a long, hot, boring summer, nothing much to do but make plans for the baby. She's due in about a week, and I want everything perfect before she gets here.

The house is a small two-bedroom, with a cute little kitchen and one decent-size bathroom, plenty for two adults and one infant. It's not very modern, and looks almost identical to the one next door, but what do I care, as long as the appliances work and the toilet flushes? That's critical, since I have to pee way more often than anyone should. I even get up a couple of times at night. It's so annoying.

Jason thinks it's funny. "Maybe we should be buying adult diapers, instead of stocking up on the baby kind. Do they make maternity diapers?"

Ha-ha.

I definitely need maternity clothes. I've kept my weight pretty well in check, but over these last few weeks Casey has grown exponentially. My stomach is stretched to the max.

Jason makes fun of that, too. "Girl, you get any bigger I'll have to put you out to pasture till you drop that foal."

Country-boy humor.

Speaking of country, Casey seems to love Garth Brooks and Clint Black. Play those boys, and she gets to kicking so hard I'm sure she must be line dancing. Thinking like that makes me homesick for Tati, who taught me most of the moves I know.

Tati calls to talk a couple times a week. I'd call her, but Jason gets mad. "What do you think I am, made of money? We can barely afford the phone bill without long distance charges." He's right, money is tight. My calculations neglected to factor in things like baby furniture and clothes. Most we managed to pick up "gently used," but even so it was an investment.

Our finances make things like movies impossible, too, except the ones we watch on TV. If it wasn't for the library, my brain would be mush by now. I've tried to make friends with the neighbor ladies, but theirs is a tight-knit sorority. Seems they're not looking for new members.

I wish I could visit Tati, but I don't have access to a car and even if I did, I don't have a driver's license. I'm going to get one, though. I've been practicing. Jason won't let me drive, but when Tati visits—she's been out here five times—she puts me behind the wheel of her Malibu, with her standing joke. "Let's go cruising for soldiers."

They're not hard to find. But we're not really looking. Even if I wanted to cheat on Jason, what man in his right mind would want to have sex with me? It would kind of be like having sex with the baby, too. The idea is cringe-worthy.

Truthfully, I have zero desire to even look at a penis, let alone touch one. But Jason insists. "I'm your husband, aren't I? What good is a wife who won't please her man? The least you can do is jack me off."

Actually, it's the most I can do.

Especially considering how hard it's been to get Jason to cooperate with me. It's not like I ask for much, but one thing I insisted on was him taking natural child-birth classes with me. I practically had to beg him to be my coach.

"Coach? What does that mean? Feed you plays?"

"Sort of, I guess. You stay by my side. Encourage me. Remind me to breathe, that sort of thing."

He laughed. "How could you forget to breathe?"

"Not regular breathing," I huffed. "There are tech-niques to help me relax through the contractions."

"I've got a better idea. It's called medication."

"If I'm on drugs, the baby is, too. I don't want Casey to arrive all doped up. She won't nurse right."

I've done tons of research, obviously. Jason couldn't care less, though. "Nurse? You want to breast-feed and wreck those pretty titties?"

"Jason, it's not like this is the first time I've discussed this with you."

"Guess I wasn't listening."

I had to work hard to quell the anger rising up inside of me. I already had the arguments in place, however. "First of all, it might be the only time I ever have big breasts.

You'll enjoy them. And second, formula is expensive. Breast milk is free, not to mention healthier for the baby. It will also help me lose weight more quickly."

"Well, aren't we just the expert?" He popped a beer, slurping it loudly for effect.

I chose to lower my voice, and my blood pressure. "I'm no expert, Jason. That's why I'm asking for your help. You're all I have here at Fort Hood, and you know that. Please promise you'll be there for me."

He got drunk and passed out without promising, but he did go to a couple of Lamaze classes. Together we learned the stages of labor. Practiced relaxed breathing techniques: in through the nose, out through the mouth, pretending to sink into beach sand beneath a blanket of September sunshine. Deeper. Deeper. Relax. Relax. The more you tense, fighting the cramping of contractions, the harder they'll fight back.

After three sessions, Jason claimed he'd learned all he needed to know. But he never even heard about transition, let alone how to help me push when the doctor tells me it's time. That's okay. I've managed to make it this far mostly on my own.

Why change anything up now?

Except . . .

What I'm determined to change is family dynamics, at least where my child is concerned. Though I lived in my mother's house until recently, she's been missing from my life for years.

I'm not sure what kind of mother I can be, but I swear I'll never desert my baby, or keep secrets from her.

I bought a new journal today, and I'll write this one for Casey, so she'll always know her mommy has nothing to hide.

Ariel

Altered

Changed.
Different.
Transformed.

Irrevocably.

Irreversibly.
Permanently.
Forever.

Trinity.

Troika.
Triad.
Trio.

Triangle.

Monica.
Gabe.
Me.

I'm Desperately Trying

To maneuver this territory—
the landscape of three.
But it doesn't show up
on a GPS, and there are no
maps, no guidebooks.

Not only that, but the terrain
is uneven, the trail unbroken.
The travel might be smooth
for a while, but eventually
I'll trip on a half-buried rock

or step in a pothole, and once
in a while a veritable sinkhole
opens up and it's all I can do
not to get swallowed. The weird
thing is, the longer I journey,

the less important right or left
seems. And that's what confuses
me. Shouldn't one path make
more sense than the other?
If I keep walking in separate

directions, won't I split in two?
It's not that I can't accept the fact
that I'm bi. I can. The problem
I keep returning to is commitment.
Shouldn't that be part of my identity?

Until Recently

Identity wasn't something
I thought much about, at least
not anything beyond the concept
of a name. I mean, I always felt

like a girl, and not just because
Dad was very clear that's what I was.
(And not a dyke, like my mother.)
When I was little, he wanted me

to wear dresses, and keep
my hair long, though I hated
brushing through it every
morning and again before bed.

But even after I was old enough
to choose my own wardrobe
and cut my hair if that's what
I wanted, I felt right in my body.

As for attraction, I thought some
girls were prettier than others,
and ditto for good-looking boys,
but didn't everyone think that way?

With sexual awareness came new
understanding, but that arrived
relatively late, and not only
because moving so much prevented

any real connection, but there
also seemed to be physiological
reasons for that. I never even had
a period until I was almost fifteen.

When I talked to my health teacher
about it, she suggested I see a doctor.
That took some convincing for Dad
to finally let me go to Planned

Parenthood, which was the only
place we could afford. PP did a whole
workup, and the ob-gyn told me
the delay was probably because of

a lack of early nutrition. Thanks
so much, Father-of-the-Decade.
At least it wasn't a true hormonal
problem, something my height

and decent breast development
denied. I was ecstatic to know
things were mostly right with
my body. Not like I ever had anyone

I could really talk to about things
like periods. Dad, of course, would
swear otherwise, insist I could discuss
anything with him. Yeah, right.

A Few Years Ago

Just about the time
I first really noticed
there was a difference
between boys and girls,
we were living with
Jewel, the only one
of Dad's women who
had kids of her own
in the same house.

Debra was younger
than I was, but Shayla
was three years older,
and had a boyfriend
who came over once
in a while, mostly when
Dad and Jewel were out.

One time I made
the mistake of telling
Dad I thought Carlos
was kind of cute.

> Cute! he roared. Boys
> are not cute, they're wild
> animals, and I'd better
> not ever catch you with
> a Mexican, understand
> me, missy? He shook me
> hard for emphasis.

I heard, but even with
the jaw-snapping reminder,
didn't understand.
What I took away
from the experience
was the message that
I should never bring up
anything about boys
to my dad. Especially
not Mexican boys, or
Mexican anything.

So the time Debra and
I were playing hide-and-
seek, and I burst into
Shayla's room while
she and Carlos were
doing some naked thing
together, I kept my mouth
sealed. And when she
wound up pregnant at
the tender age of fourteen,
I barely knew enough
to put the two things
together. And only later

did I realize had I said
something sooner, Shayla
might've escaped that fate.

So, No

Dad is totally unavailable
        to in-need-of-a-confessor,
                completely confused me.

Can't talk to Monica
        about Gabe, and
                though Gabe claims

an open mind about
        my thing with Monica,
                in-depth conversation

about it would feel
        all wrong. The only other
                person I can maybe discuss

it with is Syrah, except
        she's not the most
                discreet girl in the world.

For now, I guess,
        I'll keep dissecting
                it internally and hope

the process doesn't
        devour me alive,
                from the inside out.

Even Beyond the Triad

Something primitive,
feral, really,
has taken possession
of me.

Sometimes
it feels like a superpower.
Sometimes
it feels like an Achilles' heel.

At school, when I cruise
the hallways,
I view people through
a new lens.

It's not just are they cute,
or do they smile
at me. It's how they make
me feel.

Turned off?
Turned on? More and more
it's the latter.
Guys. Girls. Doesn't matter.

That both intrigues and scares
the hell out of me.
What's truly terrifying
is they notice it.

That Transparency

Is beyond my ability to control.
It's like living inside one of those dreams
where you're naked in a public place,
except skinned in plastic wrap.

People can see your heartbeat
quicken or the way your breath falls
shallow inside the draw of your lungs,
or the acceleration of your brain's

electric impulses which signals
an unexpected blush of desire.
Sometimes they look away.
Sometimes they stop and gaze.

Once in a while the person
you catch staring puts you straight
on edge. Yesterday on my way
to the gym, I felt eyes laser in,

and when I glanced around
in search of them, it was Garrett
I found studying me, intently,
as if finding something new.

I expected an ugly remark
or a flipped middle finger, maybe
two. Instead, he smiled, creeping
me out with his undisguised interest.

Today Is Gobbler Day

As Dad likes to call Thanksgiving.
I'll be spending it with Gabe, doing

most of the cooking at Zelda's. She has
a big oven and all the pots, pans, and

various utensils we need. Dad and I
have never cooked an actual turkey

ourselves, on our own. In the past
we either went out or relied on whoever

we were living with to provide dinner.
I'm thankful for the chance to try not

to ruin a turkey myself this year. Gabe
swears he's helped his mom roast one

in the past, and it's not as hard as people
make it out to be. Last night I went over

to Zelda's and watched him brine the bird.
He claims it "infuses the white meat with

flavor and juiciness." I have no clue if it
works or not, but I can't stand dry turkey,

so I'm hopeful I'll be thankful about that,
too. Truthfully, I have much to be grateful

for. Friends. Relationships. A decent home.
Good grades. A brilliant basketball team

to be part of. Coach Booker says we'll kill
the league this year, and she could be right.

We're hard-core, even without Hillary,
who'll have to sit the season out.

And, hey, I've got a car. Dad decided to let
me keep it, though he still hasn't agreed

to take me in for the driving test that'll
net the coveted license. With me behind

the wheel of the Focus this morning,
I figure I'll give him a nudge. "So, Dad.

I was thinking. Basketball season
starts soon. With practices and games,

transportation could be a problem.
I thought maybe one day

next week we could meet at the DMV
after school and work. Coach'll let

me take off a little early if I give her
a heads-up. I'll make the appointment."

He Grunts

Which is his way of saying
he's considering it, and
that's better than a straight

no, so I nudge, "California
is strict about teen drivers,
and I can't drive with any

of my friends in the car for
a year, you won't have to
worry about me doing bad

things, especially since if
I do I'll lose my license
until I turn eighteen, and—"

> *Okay, I get it. It's just, kids*
> *die in accidents all the time.*
> *If I lost you it would kill me, too.*

Is that what he's worried
about? "Oh, Dad. I'll be very
careful. I promise. Please?"

> *Best I can give you right*
> *now is a definite maybe.*
> *Still better than a straight no.*

At Zelda's

Gabe and I go directly to work
in the kitchen while the so-called
adults disappear, ostensibly to

watch at least most of the Macy's
Parade. If that's really what they're
up to, it's a definite first for Dad.

Has Zelda domesticated the man?

Gabe attempts to domesticate
me, giving instructions on how
much celery and onion to chop

and sauté for the stuffing while
he rinses the turkey and pats
it dry so the skin will crisp.

His expertise soon becomes evident.

"You'll make some woman
a very good wife," I kid. "In fact,
will you marry me? I could use one

of those." That was totally off
the wall, and he wastes little time
pouncing on the obvious.

        Thought you wanted a female wife.

I absorb the remark, consider
its implications. Rather than respond
right away, I watch Gabe lift the stuffed,

trussed bird into the oven, admiring
both his culinary talent and the muscle
required to heft eighteen pounds of poultry.

"I'm not interested in matrimony."

I realize there's truth in the statement.
With the rare exception of Monica's
parents, I've never seen marriage work.

I've witnessed divorce. Widowhood.
Spinsterhood. Remarriage, and failure
repeated. Oh, and of course, desertion.

"Anyway, what if you flip me straight?"

That almost sounds like a challenge,
doesn't it? Not surprisingly, he takes
it that way, and I appreciate that.

He crosses the kitchen in two long
strides, pulls me into his arms, kisses
me in a decisively masculine way.

    I'm willing to give it a try if you are.

We've Been Borderline

A time or two, but still
haven't gone all the way,
mostly because I'm scared.

Scared it will hurt.
Scared it will define me.
Scared I might like it too much.

Pressed tightly together,
heart rates rising in sync,
I can feel him grow rigid

against me and it would be
a lie if I said it didn't excite
me, and in a completely

different way than Monica
did. If we were somewhere
private, I'd give him the chance,

despite my trepidation, to try
and flip me right this minute.
But that isn't the case, so we

cool things off, mutually satisfied
that a wordless promise was just
exchanged between the two of us.

For Now

We pour eggnogs, discuss
spiking them, decide to wait
until later for alcohol, if we
choose to imbibe at all.

We carry drinks into the living
room, which is empty except
for the giant balloons floating
along a New York City avenue

twenty-five hundred miles away,
yet visible right here in California,
thanks to technology. We sit
to watch the end of the parade

and eventually Dad and Zelda
escape her bedroom, and head
outside for a smoke. I'm not sure
if it's Gabe's regular presence here

or mine once in a while, but
Zelda's house never seems to wear
the intolerable scent of tobacco.
She's a polite smoker by choice.

> *Eggnog, huh?* Dad stops on
> the way by, lifts my glass, and
> sniffs. *It's no good without booze.*
> Pretty sure I'm glad it's virgin.

Apparently Brining Works

Because the turkey is juicy
and flavorful, and the stuffing
absorbs much deliciousness.
I skip the mashed potatoes,
reach instead for yams, not
candied but simply baked
and dripping melted butter.

"This is the most I've ever
eaten in one sitting by far!"
Still, I mop up the last drips
of gravy with a dinner roll.

> Dad watches, then comments,
> *If you ate like that every day*
> *you'd need bigger clothes.*
> *Better skip the pumpkin pie.*

> Gabe shoots me a sympathetic
> eye roll. *Ariel eats like a canary.*
> *I think she can manage one piece*
> *of pie without requiring*
> *a whole new wardrobe.*

As much as I appreciate Gabe
sticking up for me, Dad's been
drinking for hours. This could
could go badly or he could
laugh it off. I cringe, waiting.

But it's Zelda who takes on Dad.
*Hey, Mark. Isn't it you who always
says you like your women with
a little extra padding? Or was
that something you made up
to make little ol' me feel better?
Either way, this girl's having
pie, though it might have
to wait for an hour or so.*

Dad chooses to plaster a grin
on his face. *Y'all are right. My
girl is a little bird. One meal
won't make her a blimp, will it?*

He stares across the table at me,
and with one sudden vicious
verbal blow knocks the air
from my gut, and from my lungs:
*Too damn bad she looks so much
like her fucking whore mother.*

I push back from the table
hard, a reservoir of invective
threatening to burst the dam.
But just as I'm about to free
it, a thought dashes across my
mind: What if this is his way
of proving me too irrational
to merit a driver's license?

I Stay in My Chair

Zelda jumps to her feet,
inviting Dad's anger
simply by warning,
Mark . . .

And Gabe stands slowly,
puts out one hand to
steady me, and asks,
*Do you really think
that was called for?*

And Dad sits very still,
ignoring the others
while measuring my
reaction to his absolute
invitation to tell his sorry
ass totally off.

Now I stand, scoot
my chair back under
the table. "Know what,
Dad? That was the first
time you've ever mentioned
what Mom looks like.
Interesting to know
I resemble her.
Thank you for that."

I amble over to the counter.
"I think I'll have some pie."

And That's the First Time

I can remember
calling my mother
Mom. Not "my mom."
Not "my mother."

Mom.

I hope that hurts
my bastard father.
I'm reeling, though
I don't dare show it.

My father

is a carrion eater.
Maybe I've seen it before.
But I'm not sure
I truly realized
until now that

bone picking

might, in fact, be
his favorite hobby
and that his victims
are as varied as his

W   o   m   e   N

                              and me.

Wordlessly

My pie and I retreat to the living
room. I turn on the TV, mostly
for noise, which works perfectly,
because what comes on is football.

I flop down onto the too-soft sofa,
stare at big dudes in tight pants
and helmets running into one another,
pick at pumpkin filling in need

of more cinnamon or nutmeg
or whatever. I'm glad I decided
not to drink earlier. That little scene
was an excellent reminder

of the importance of self-control.
I'm thankful I could manage it.
I think I'll save inebriation for when
I'm positive there won't be a need

to parry with Dad, or with anyone,
for that matter. I'm wounded,
but not fatally, and with any luck
at all, I'm still on track to get

my driver's license this coming
week. Once mobility is assured,
I won't require anyone in my life.
I'll be picky about who I keep.

Gabe Will Probably Be a Keeper

He joins me on the sofa now,
tilting the sagging cushion, and
so also me, toward the center.

> *Wow. That was ugly. I'm sorry*
> *he said those things to you.*

I shrug. Try to think of a proper
response, but no words seem
appropriate. What finally comes
out of my mouth is, "Want some
pie? I'd hate for it to go to waste."

> *You don't like it? I made it from*
> *scratch. Well, except for the crust.*
> *That came from a mix, but a good one.*

I don't mention the need for
more spices. "It's yummy, but
I don't have room for dessert
after all. You're an awesome
cook, by the way. I hope I can
be as good as you one day."

> *Stick with me, baby, and I'll impart*
> *my entire repertoire of culinary*
> *secrets. You'll be a master chef.*

I can't help it. "But then I'd need
a plus-size wardrobe, wouldn't I?"

I don't know if that is, in fact,
a subconscious plea for
reassurance, but Gabe takes it
that way, and I'm happy when
he reaches for my hand.

> *You listen to me.* His whisper
> is fierce. *I don't know what
> your dad's problem is or was,
> but that attack was bullshit.
> You're an incredible girl, and
> if you put on a pound or two
> no one would notice because
> you'd still be the exact same
> funny, bright, loving person.*

Funny? I guess.
Bright? Enough.
Loving? Am I?

"Okay. If you say so. I'll save
the pie and eat it later. With
whipped cream. And I'll wash it
down with full-strength eggnog.
None of that light shit for me."

> *Atta girl. Now, who's winning
> the game?* He chances a quick
> kiss. Last thing we need is
> Dad's commentary on *that.*

After a While

Dad stumbles into the room,
holding a glass of what might
have a thimbleful of eggnog
combined with some amber
liquid. Whiskey, is what Dad's

> breath announces, when he says,
> *Move over there, would ya?*

Gabe excuses himself to go
call his mom and wish her
a happy Thanksgiving. When
he gets up off the sofa, I do, too.
"I'll help Zelda with the dishes."

> Dad snorts. *Was it something
> I said? Hey! Touchdown!*

I ignore him, and the touchdown,
wander back into the kitchen,
where Zelda has already managed
to clean up the Gobbler Day mess.
"I didn't know you were a magician."

> *It wasn't so bad. Mark cleared
> while I washed and put stuff away.*

Dad Played Busboy?

That's hard to believe.
Maybe Zelda gave him
hell. Funny, but I think
the magician comment
is the most words I've
ever offered her at once.

"Dad never helps clear
at home. You really must
be able to work magic."
There. Real conversation.

> *Believe it or not, I think*
> *he felt guilty about blowing*
> *up at the dinner table, not*
> *that he bothered to apologize.*
> *He didn't tell you he was sorry,*
> *did he? I told him he should.*

"No, but it doesn't matter,
and empty apologies
don't count anyway.
I'll do what I always do,
and chalk it up to alcohol."
Zelda, who isn't nearly as
buzzed, nods understanding.

> *You and I don't talk much,*
> *but I want you to know if you*
> *ever need an ear, I'm here, okay?*

Actual Kindness

That's how that feels.
Not just lip service.
And lacking ulterior motive.

What can she want
from me, anyway?

"Thanks, Zelda. Appreciate it."

Not that I'd ever take
her up on it. Not like I
ever want to grow close

to one of Dad's women.
That would spell doom.

"And thanks for a great Turkey Day."

I don't mention it's the first time
I've ever felt like part of a family
bigger than just Dad and me.

Why did he have to ruin it?
Why was I the person he chose

to shove so forcefully away?

Between the L-Tryptophan

In the turkey and the alcohol
in his eggnog, Dad passes out,
snoring, before the game ends.

I don't need to stay and listen
to his rumbling, so I ask Gabe
for a ride home, and to make
sure Dad stays put, I bring
the keys to the Focus with me.

"I'll send them back with Gabe,"
I assure Zelda. "But you might
want to hang on to them until
tomorrow. Dad shouldn't drive
tonight, and I'm fine home alone."

The first third of the drive
is silent, Gabe and I both lost
in introspection. He's rarely

so pensive, and when I finally
pull myself out of myself,
I ask, "Is everything okay?"

> Yeah. I just miss my mom, and
> talking to her only makes me
> miss her more. She's doing better,
> though. Says she'll probably go
> home after the first of the year.

"That's great. Sounds like progress.
Oh, hey . . . Look. There's Niagara."
Gabe slows as we pass the Triple G,

where a woman's riding the mare
in a paddock. An attractive woman.
Gabe confirms it's Peg Grantham.

"Pull over a second. Please."
When the GTO brakes to a halt,
I jump out and go over to the fence,
wave, and Niagara, plus rider,
come trotting over. I introduce
myself, then ask, "How's Hillary?"

> Her injuries are healing well.
> But she's antsy. And lonely.
> You should come visit her.

"Would tomorrow be okay?"
I say it before realizing I might
not have a way to get here.

> Oh, absolutely. Also, I hear
> you're a horsewoman. I'll take you
> on a tour of the barn if you'd like.

"Sounds like a plan. I'd love it."
Deal struck, I figure I'll just have
to talk Gabe into giving me a ride.

Home Again

Straight into the routine.
Shoes off by the door.
Click heater up.
Go into the kitchen
for something to drink
while Gabe settles in
on the couch to wait.

Except this time what
I return with are two
steaming mugs of tea,
sugar on the side.
While I wouldn't mind
something stronger,
I want to see if kissing
him is as good minus
any trace of alcohol.

> He looks at me quizzically.
> *Earl Grey? That's new.*

"You know your tea,
which doesn't surprise
me. But, yeah, I guess
this is the mostly new me.
I'll put on some music.
Any special requests?"

> *Don't suppose you have any*
> *Cold War Kids? Or Muse?*

This makes me smile.
"I do, actually, and I rarely
get to play them without
headphones on. Dad only
listens to country."

I plug my phone into
the speaker dock Dad gave
me for Christmas last year,
an interesting gift choice,
considering he hates my music.
Then I sit close to Gabe,
who pulls my legs across
his. We sip tea, listening
to music we both appreciate,
and the importance of this
particular connection
soon becomes obvious.

I need to feel cared
about. Gabe needs to
feel not alone. We don't
have to give voice to those
feelings. It's enough we
acknowledge them. We do,
and I know we do, because
simultaneously we set
our cups down so they
can't interfere in what's
coming next. "Wait."

Not on the Couch

Not fast.
Not half-clothed.
Not a throwaway.

I lead Gabe down
the short hallway
to my room, happy
for once to have made
the bed when I got up.

I turn on the night-
light I rarely rely on.
That will be enough.
I don't want to bathe
in harsh artificial glare,
but I do want to see.

      He stops me just inside
      the door. *Are you sure?*

"Is it too late to change
my mind?" I grin. "No.
I'm sure. At least I think so."

      Now he smiles. *Way to be*
      definitive. Well, if you're
      almost, sort of, kinda sure,
      let's give it a try. But first . . .

I've Lost Track

Of what number kiss
this could be, but it
doesn't matter. This kiss
will lead somewhere new,
and that's a place I must explore.

This kiss isn't sweet.
Isn't gentle, and yet,
the kind of need infusing
it is anything but selfish.
He's giving to me.
I'm giving to him.
And when one accepts
what the other offers,
it is with gratitude.

His arms encircle
my waist, lift, and carry
me to the bed, where
he lays me down
carefully, treasure.

I watch him peel off
clothing—his shirt,
his Wranglers—until there's
nothing left but the gray
boxers that hide nothing.

He has a blue-collar body,
toned by physical labor,
not gym equipment.

He also has goose bumps.
The heater hasn't quite
managed to shake the chill.
I laugh. "Better get under
the covers before you freeze."

Good idea. But first . . .

He reaches down, unzips
my jeans, tugs them off
by the cuffs. I wish I'd worn
Victoria's Secret panties
instead of the garden
variety cotton, but that's
all I've got in my drawer.

Gabe doesn't seem to care.
His hands travel my legs,
knees to hips, then push
up over the slight rise
of my belly to the small
hills jutting just above.

Take off your sweater.

He helps lift it over my head,
then unhooks my bra before
covering our exposed skin
with sheet and quilt and
lying beside me, facing me,
and he pauses there.

You can still change your mind.

In response, I kiss him,
plead for his lips and tongue
and fingers to touch places
only one other person
has ever been given explicit
permission to explore.

He isn't Monica, no, not at all.
She is silk. He is leather.
She is lithe. He is brawn.
She is low tide. He is high.
She quivers. He quakes.

The giving is different.
He directs, and I follow
the script, learn the action,
rehearse until I get it right.

The final act is approaching.
I thought I would be scared
but I'm anxious for the gift
of knowledge denied by God
in the book of Genesis.
Instead, Gabe is the denier.

Stop. I don't have a condom.

Condom, Right

I definitely don't want
to take a chance on
getting pregnant.
Oh, but . . .
"Hold on a sec."

I roll over toward
the nightstand, open
the drawer, which is
still well-stocked with
Trojans I haven't had
a use for, up until now.

When I hand one to
Gabe, he gives me
an *oh really?* look.
"You can thank Syrah.
Long story. Tell you
later. Meanwhile . . ."

The pause has resulted
in a need to start over,
and that's okay by me.
I'm enjoying circling
the bases. Home plate,
now safe, can wait.

We Take Our Time

And we both score twice.
And the seismic waves
are incredible. Massive.
Nothing like the gentle
temblors with Monica.

My bed, my room, the entire
house, are plenty warm now.
I kick off the covers, skin
cooling slowly within
the circlet of Gabe's arms.

> *So, what do you think?*
> The words fall against
> my cheek, carried in warm
> Earl Grey–scented puffs.

"I think that was pretty
great. And I'm glad you
were my first." I don't add
the masculine reference.
Let him assume what he will.

Eventually

And much too soon,
Gabe's arms release
their hold on me.

I should probably go.

"You probably should.
Do you have any plans
for tomorrow?"

No. Why? Miss me already?

"You're still here, in case
you missed that, dude.
I know I'm a pain, but
I need a ride out to see
Hillary. And her horses."

Happy to chauffeur you anytime.

Deal struck, I struggle
with what to say now.
Is it always so awkward
after you have sex?

I watch Gabe get dressed,
admiring again the cut
of his muscles. And again
I'm bulldozed by guilt.
Everything's changed
between him and me now.
But what about Monica?

Maya

For Casey

You arrived today. Every minute is seared into my memory.

I woke from dreams of drowning in quicksand—a slow suck under, no one I could trust to take my hand and pull—to nightmare cramps fifteen minutes apart. I wasn't sure what labor felt like, if that was it or the fake-you-out kind. But, at a week beyond my due date, you seemed anxious to find your way into the world.

When I reached out for your daddy, his side of the bed was empty. He went out with his buddies last night and never made it home. I called and called, scared the worst had happened, but finally he answered and explained, "I was too drunk to drive, so I slept in the car."

Something to be grateful for, I guess.

"You have to come home right now," I told him. "It's time to go to the hospital."

"Are you sure?"

Seriously? "Positive."

"I'll be right there," he promised.

But he wasn't. I hate to break this to you, but Daddy isn't very reliable. It took me a while to figure that out. It's what happens when you marry someone you barely know. It wasn't the best idea I've ever had. Hopefully it won't be the worst. At least I'm not in L.A.

I suppose I kind of used you, but I promise to make that up the only way I know how—by loving you more than anything in the whole universe. Half of me can't wait to cuddle you, play dress-up with cute little outfits. Watch you grow. Mold your life.

The other half is scared shitless. What if I can't do this? What if being an awful mother is genetic?

Yesterday I painted your room. Your daddy and I argued about color. He wanted "cornflower" because he was sure you'd be a boy. I knew better, not that it matters, but either way, I didn't want to resort to stereotypes. Blue doesn't have to represent maleness any more than pink is the only suitable hue for a girl.

So I chose a pretty golden yellow, almost the exact shade of the roses that bloomed outside my windows back home in Austin. Despite the ugliness inside our house, those flowers gifted me with snapshots of beauty I could carry anywhere. I brought their memory here, and call it up when the need arises. That happens often.

Like this morning.

I waited and waited for your daddy to get home, breathing in through the nose, out through the mouth, just like I learned in Lamaze. That part was easy, but trying to relax through the clench-build-release of contractions designed by some unearthly power to move a baby closer to viable life outside its mother's body proved impossible.

They got stronger. Closer together. When they were maybe seven minutes apart, you shifted inside me and I knew your tumbling act was wrong. Suddenly, it felt like someone stuck me with a knife right below my belly button, only from the inside out. Luckily the phone was in my hand. I dialed 9-1-1.

The ambulance was there in less than ten minutes, but it seemed like hours, and the whole time I prayed you'd be okay. A very nice EMT (that's "emergency medical technician") sat in back and talked to me on the drive to the hospital. "Don't worry," she said. "Every baby comes into the world in his or her own way."

Your way was the hard way.

We got to the hospital and your vitals weren't the best. The ER doc said you were in fetal distress and he needed to perform a C-section. Fast. I wanted so much to deliver you the way I'd practiced. But the pain was incredible, and once the epidural kicked in, I couldn't feel a thing from my waist down. I did like that. In fact, since I could barely sleep last night, I dozed off. Next thing I knew, I heard you cry and the nurse said, "It's a girl."

Then you were in my arms, all seven pounds, eleven ounces of you, and I smiled at the titian waves of downy hair that promised you belonged to me. Jason arrived not long after that, still smelling of last night's beer and pool-hall sweat. He didn't want to hold you, said he was afraid of breaking you, but he did pet your pretty amber curls. "She looks like you," he said, and that was the best compliment he could've ever given me.

But then, after they took you away to be cleaned and dressed and swaddled, he blew up. "They said you agreed to a Cesarean. Why would you do that?"

"I didn't have a choice."

"Liar!" His voice was sharp and way too loud.

It was like being smacked upside the head. Again. Only, no lunatic mother involved. But I don't guess you need to know any of that, at least not right now. One day, when you're old enough to understand, I'll tell you, because girls have to grow up smart.

I try not to argue with your daddy. If facts get in the way of his opinion, he won't believe they're true, so disagreeing with him is pointless. But I said, "I did it for our baby. She was in trouble."

You know what he said?

"Don't be ridiculous. She was fine. And now you'll have a scar."

I will have a scar, a flaw in his eyes, but to me it's a forever reminder of my connection to you. Casey, my beautiful, perfect baby girl. Jason's contempt for your birth journey is painful. And right now, everything hurts, but that doesn't matter because you're here. You're safe. You're perfect. And you're mine.

Ariel
I've Got a Problem

Okay, I've got several problems,
and this one might actually
not be an issue at all,
though I think it has to be.

I like sex.

I mean, maybe it can become
a horrible habit, if that's all
I ever think about in the future.
Right now, there's other stuff, too.

But I like sex.

I like it with Monica. I like it
with Gabe, though the two
experiences were not the same.
At the moment
I'm not interested in liking
it with anyone else.

But if I like sex

as much as I do, what if
I can't turn off this person
I've lately turned on—
pun most definitely intended?

After Gabe Left

Last night, I lay in bed
worrying. Not about the fact
that we'd made love,
or even that I'd enjoyed it
so much, but about how
it might change the way
we relate to each other.

Part of the attraction
was not acting on it, and
now that isn't an option.

So what happens next
time we're together?
Does having sex once
make it a requirement
going forward? I don't
even know if that would
be such a bad thing.

But I don't want to feel
trapped. Sex should be
spontaneous, I think, not
something expected.

And on the far end of all
that, what if I'm the one
who comes to expect it?

Look at Me

I'm a regular sex expert.
Not.

The thought is hilarious.
Totally.

I've barely done two positions.
Lame.

But then, I've done a girl and a guy.
True.

I should really stop thinking about this.
Duh.

It could become an obsession.
Maybe.

I'm going to see Gabe today.
Awesome.

I should hang out with Monica tomorrow.
Definitely.

Can we chill with no sex involved?
Only one way to find out.

What's that?
Just say no.

But what fun is that?

Dad Still Isn't Home

By midmorning, when Gabe picks me up.
I'm ready to go as soon as the GTO pulls

in the driveway, and I meet him outside,
denying any chance at a roll in the hay,

as Dad likes to call it, at least when talking
to me. Once I asked if he'd ever actually

done it in the hay, because it sounded itchy.
He didn't think the question was funny,

coming from his daughter. I didn't think
the discussion was merited, coming from

my dad, who was warning me against
rolling anywhere, anytime, with anybody.

I listened pretty well for quite a while,
though once I understood the way of things,

I thought him quite the hypocrite. I still do,
but maybe now I can forgive him some.

Meanwhile, I hop into Gabe's car, allow
him to lean across the seat for a kiss hello.

It is sweet. Not demanding, or even requesting.
I'm a little relieved I don't want to jump his bones.

At Least Not Right This Minute

As he backs out onto the road
I ask, "So, have you seen Dad
this morning? He survived
the eggnog, I take it?"

> *Yeah, but barely. He looked*
> *beat-up hungover.*

"That doesn't surprise me.
When he gets three sheets
to the squall, a nasty hangover
is guaranteed. He deserves it."

> *Yeah, he was pretty shitty*
> *yesterday. Sorry he did that.*

"Not your fault. Don't be sorry.
Besides, I'm used to it. Sort of."
I'm tired of talking about Dad,
and this conversation could go
somewhere I'd rather it didn't.

"Thanks for picking me up."
We bump along out toward
the highway, and it strikes me,
"I should probably give you
some money for gas."

> He smiles. *Do you have any*
> *money? No, I didn't think so.*

*No worries. It's okay. I planned
to see you again, and besides,
who wants to spend the day
with your dad and Zelda?*

That makes me laugh. "I get
your point. But you know,
I think you need a hobby."

*He grins. How about I make
you my hobby? You, girl,
are quite entertaining.*

"Entertaining? I don't think
anyone's ever called me that
before. It's a good thing, right?"

*A very good thing. You're funny.
And smart. Not only smart, but you
know lots of stuff, and the two don't
always go together. In fact, I've wondered
how you know as much as you do.
Didn't you change schools a lot?*

"Yeah, I did, and that was hard,
especially as I got older. But
there's something to be said for
seeing a lot of the country and
learning that way. Plus, someone
invented these great things called
books. I read all the time."

I Don't Add the Part

About swiping books.
Dad called it "borrowing,"
but what we did was steal
them, sometimes from
the people we were mooching
off of, and other times

from libraries. Either Dad
would scrounge a library card,
or, if we stayed in one place
long enough, he'd get one
of his own. Once in a while
those books would get returned,

but more often they'd move on
across the country when we
did. Then Dad would make
a game of removing any pages
with a name stamped on them
and dropping the well-read books

into a return slot at a library
in another town. *Rotating
books into their catalog
can only be a good thing, right?*

On some level, that was true,
and it never struck me that
what we were doing was wrong
until I hit maybe fifth grade.

Books are definite necessities,
says Gabe. I spend a fair amount
of time reading myself, especially
at Zelda's. Either that or indulge
in her steady diet of reality TV.

"Dad jokes about that. Says
if he wanted to watch people
hooking up he'd rather do it
at a bar, and as for surviving,
he's already done that in the army."

Your dad was in the army?
He sounds incredulous.

"Well, yeah. He was a mechanic.
Worked on helicopters, mostly
here in the States, but I guess
he went to Iraq for the Gulf War.
He doesn't talk about it much.
Only when he gets really drunk."

Wow. I never would've guessed.
He doesn't seem like the type
who can take orders very well.

"Probably why he's not still
in the army. He hated it, actually.
Said it's for losers and fools."

We Reach the Triple G

Turn into the driveway, where
we're stopped by the mammoth
wrought-iron gates. Gabe pushes

the buzzer on the intercom,
and when he informs whoever's
on the other end that we're here,

> a remote opens the barricade
> to let us in, then shuts it behind
> us. *Is that to keep people out or in?*

"Probably both. And to keep
their animals more secure.
Horses are great escape artists."

The driveway is recently paved
and lined with tall deciduous trees,
wearing not a single leaf. On either

side, white fences enclose large
paddocks where elegant horses and
grass-fattened cattle graze. Maybe

a quarter mile in, the road splits.
To the right is the training barn,
which is huge. To the left looms

the main house, plus two smaller
cottages for guests or hired help,
at least that's what I'm guessing.

"This place is ridiculous. Can't wait
to see what the house is like inside.
It looks big enough for thirty people.

Pretty sure there are only three,
plus maybe a maid or twenty."
Despite all the miles Dad and

I logged, I've never seen anything
like this up close. I wrap up
my musing out loud. "Bet it's lonely."

> *Nah. They probably have huge*
> *parties and stuff. Mr. Grantham*
> *is connected.* Gabe parks in the circle,

as instructed, and before we
reach the front door, it opens.
"Don't tell me. Security cameras."

> Peg Grantham greets us on
> the front step. *Come in, come in.*
> *Hillary's excited to see you.*

She leads the way into a formal
living room, where the centerpiece
is a huge fireplace, burning some

> fragrant wood. *Make yourselves*
> *at home. I'll go help Hillary down*
> *the stairs. She's still a little shaky.*

How Do You Feel at Home

In a single room the approximate
size of an entire apartment,
minus the walls, of course.
Not surprisingly, the decor
looks straight out of the pages
of a chic glossy magazine.

The navy-blue sofas (three!)
don't sag, and their upholstery
is perfect. Ditto the contrasting
cream-colored overstuffed chairs.
The tables gleam under thick
coats of polish. The caramel
carpet is spotless, the cathedral
windows show no streaks
or water marks. I'm afraid
to touch anything for fear
of leaving fingerprints behind.

I'm contemplating how to sit
without leaving butt indentations
on the cushions when Hillary
limps into the room, aided by
her aunt. She looks like hell—
gaunt, pallid, and uncertain
of her balance. But I keep that
to myself and smile. "Hey, Hillary.
How are you feeling?" Lame.

Marginally better than I look.

Peg guides her into a chair, says
she'll return in a few. I sit on
the adjacent sofa, call Gabe over.
"I don't think you two have met
officially yet. Hillary, this is Gabe.
I'm not sure how much you remember,
but he's the one who found you."

She stares at him for several
long seconds. *I remember your eyes.*
Finally, she twists her attention
in my direction. *And I remember
you telling me Niagara was okay.
Things are blurry before and after.*

*Well, I'm glad we found you when
we did.* Gabe has been studying
her intently, eliciting a small barb

of jealousy, an emotion relatively
novel to me. I do my best to ignore
it. "The team sure misses you. Syrah
tries hard, but she can't match
your speed. We've got a tourney
in two weeks. Wish you could play."

*Me too. And ride. I'm turning
into a regular slug. But I can't take
a chance on an accident, and my
equilibrium will be off for a while.*

We Talk for Twenty Minutes

All the time Peg
Grantham will allow.
Gabe and I learn:

Only three people do,
in fact, live there, in
the eight-thousand-square-
foot house—her dad,
Aunt Peg, and Hillary.

Her dad, who's a high-
powered lawyer, spends
long stretches of time
in Sacramento, where
he practices. He's also
running for the California
State Attorney General's
office. Which is why Peg
is living with them.

As long as she can keep
up with her schoolwork
despite her injury, Hillary
will graduate in June
and go on to Stanford,
her parents' alma mater,
and where the two met.

Her mother and older
brother are dead.

They Were Killed

On September 11, 2001,
when the twin towers of
the World Trade Center
were leveled by terrorists.

> *I barely remember Mama,*
> *says Hillary, and if not*
> *for photos, I wouldn't be*
> *able to picture Brent at all.*
> *I was only three when it*
> *happened. We were visiting*
> *Aunt Peg in upstate New*
> *York, and I came down*
> *with some virus, or I might*
> *have been there, too.*
>
> *Mama had taken Brent*
> *into the city to sightsee.*
> *They were staying at*
> *the Marriott at the foot*
> *of the WTC. When the towers*
> *fell, the hotel was sliced*
> *in two. Everyone on one*
> *side lived; but on the other . . .*

She shakes her head sadly,
but her eyes don't tear up,
and it's obvious many years
have passed—enough for
a young child's grief to
be swallowed up by time.

Wow, says Gabe. It's weird
to know someone personally
affected by 9/11. I was little,
like not quite five, but I totally
remember my mom glued to
the TV, praying and crying.

Not for anyone she knew,
but just because of how many
people died, including first
responders. It hit her hard.

I overheard my dad and her
talking, saying how terror
was not supposed to affect
us at home, and no American
would ever feel safe again.
I didn't get it then. It took
years to understand.

The only thing I can think
to say is, "I'm really sorry,
Hillary. That sucks so bad."
Gabe's right. It's strange
to find out someone you know
was personally affected by such
an infamous piece of history.

All I Know About 9/11

Is what I've learned in school,
usually on the anniversary.
I asked Dad about it one time.

> *It didn't surprise me, he said.*
> *The only thing that did was*
> *that it took them so long,*
> *and that Saudi Arabia*
> *masterminded the whole*
> *dirty thing. I figured it would*
> *be Iran or Iraq, and shit, who*
> *knows? Maybe their stinking*
> *fingers were in it, too.*

In the years that followed,
as American casualty counts
grew in Iraq and Afghanistan,

> *Dad commented once, Hell,*
> *it could've been me over there.*
> *And for what? Upsetting*
> *the power structure is only*
> *going to fuck things up even*
> *worse, you mark my words.*
> *Shit's gonna get ugly, and,*
> *intelligence or not, the US*
> *of A is not immune. There*
> *will be more attacks at home.*

Guess he knew a thing or two.

We Change the Subject

And now we learn
that Hillary's new car
is on order. It's an
all-wheel-drive
Long Beach Blue
BMW X6 M,
not that I've got a clue
what that is, except

> Gabe says, *Holy crap!*
> *Those are beautiful*
> *cars. Definitely a step*
> *up from a Ford.*

"Hey, now, without
that Ford, I'd probably
be on foot forever.
This is the first chance
I've had to thank you
in person for the Focus.
No one's ever given me
a gift like this. Not sure
how I can repay you."

> *The debt was mine to pay,*
> *Ariel. You and Gabe didn't*
> *have to stop. A lot of people*
> *would've driven right past.*
> *So, thank you. Both of you.*

It's a Natural Break

In the conversation, and Peg
must've been listening for one
because she comes bustling in.

> *Okay, we'd better let Hillary*
> *rest now. This is the most*
> *stimulation she's had in a while.*

We say our good-byes and I
comment, "Next time I see you,
I'll be driving a pretty red car."

> *Wait by the door, says Peg. I'll take*
> *Hillary up to her room and then*
> *give you that tour of the barn.*

> When they go upstairs, Gabe
> asks, *So did your dad commit*
> *to signing off on your driver's license?*

"Not yet. But I'm not taking no
for an answer. You don't happen
to have any ideas about blackmail?"

> He grins. *Maybe I could wait till*
> *he and Zelda are busy in the bedroom*
> *and sneak a pic with my phone?*

"I don't think that would work.
Where are you going to post it, for one
thing? Like, who would care?"

Just Stating the Obvious

And Gabe can only agree.
Peg returns, wearing riding
boots in place of her earlier
slippers. She gestures for us
to come along with her.

>   *It's kind of a hike to the barn,*
>   *she says. If you'd rather drive,*
>   *go ahead. I can use the exercise.*

It is a decent walk, but the sun
has warmed the autumn air,
which is scented with the sweet
wood smoke that has escaped
the chimney. For no other reason
than to make conversation, I ask
Peg, "Do you like California?"

>   *Well enough. I've been out here*
>   *for fifteen years, so it pretty much*
>   *feels like home. Why do you ask?*

"Just wondering. Hillary told us
about her mom and brother.
I figured that's why you're here."

>   *You figured right. I'd probably still*
>   *be in New York if Charles didn't need*
>   *me to take care of Hillary. When she*
>   *goes off to college, I could leave, but*
>   *I won't. All that I am is right here.*

All That I Am

Interesting turn of phrase.
I'll have to dissect it later
because we've reached
the barn, which is massive.

In the center is a huge indoor
arena with a decent block
of seats. "Do you put on shows
here, or just use it for training?"

> We used to host regular events, but
> then life got busy. Maybe we'll do
> it again in the future. Who knows?
> Meanwhile, it's good to be able
>
> to work the horses year round,
> not that Sonora rain can rival
> upstate New York snow. I would've
> killed for this facility in Albany.

We follow her to the long row
of stalls edging the barn. As we
stroll, I ask, "So you trained
horses in New York, too?"

> Oh, yes. I moved there to be with
> my fiancé. We were both Olympic
> equestrians and met at a competition.
> Love blossomed over dressage.

She's Human After All

I'd love to know more of the story,
but I don't know her well enough
to ask her to tell it. Shame.
My curiosity is screaming, *ASK!*
But my logical side wins out.

We walk down the line of stalls,
studying the horses inside them.
Most are Thoroughbreds—tall
and fine-boned, with chiseled
heads and the quick tempers
associated with hot-blood horses.

But a couple of warmbloods
stand out. Though a bit shorter
than their stable mates, they're
obviously athletes, and strength
is what makes them beautiful.
"What breed are they?"

> *Hanoverian. I brought the mare's
> dam with me from the East Coast
> and bred her here. The stallion
> I found in Oregon. He's amazing,
> not only handsome, but he has
> an unparalleled temperament.
> We plan on breeding the pair next
> time the mare comes into heat. These
> horses practically beg to do dressage,
> and they're talented hunters, too.*

It is Gabe who asks, *Do you*
show anymore? You, I mean.

> No. It's a time-consuming hobby,
> and I don't have a lot of spare time.
> The Thoroughbred breeding program
> is our bread and butter. Hillary
> showed Niagara, but most of the colts
> are racetrack-bound. Now Peg does
> a double take. *You like horses, too?*

> *More like I put up with them —*
> *and the people I know who like*
> *them.* He winks at me. *Actually,*
> *horse lovers tend to be pretty great.*

We pass Niagara's stall and
the mare comes over, as if
she recognizes me and wants
to say hello. Maybe she does, because
she sticks her nose over the door
and nickers softly. "Hello to you,
too. Sorry. Fresh out of carrots."

> *Funny,* says Peg. *She's picky about*
> *who she relates to. Max said he offered*
> *you a job here. Hope you'll consider*
> *taking it. Niagara would appreciate*
> *it, and so would I. Hillary won't be*
> *able to ride for quite a while, I'm afraid.*

Job Offer Assured

I ask what my duties
would be if I came
to work at the Triple G.
It would come down to:

> exercising horses
> brushing horses
> feeding horses
> moving horses

from stall to paddock
and back again, no
manure shoveling involved.

Plus, if I'm interested,
Peg is willing to

> teach me dressage
> teach me to jump
> teach me to hunt
> teach me cross-country

which add up to eventing,
something she did as a member
of the US Equestrian Team.

I'm not sure I'm equal
to all of that, but I kind
of want to give it a try.
And that's what I tell her.

Once Again

It comes down to
convincing Dad to let
me work, and allow
me to transport myself.
And, if I can manage that,
to finding the time
commitment. Basketball

finishes in February,
and that will free up
my after-school hours.
Meanwhile, it would
just be weekends. Oh,
one final question,
"How much could I
expect to get paid?"

A pragmatist. I like that.
I'd have to check in
with Max, but I think
we could start you at
twelve dollars an hour,
as long as you're an able
rider. Some of the colts
are pretty green.

"Sounds fair. I'll talk
it over with my dad
and let you know
as soon as I can."

We Wrap It Up

Head back toward the house.
But the rest of her story
is gnawing at me, and I know
it won't let go unless I shake
it off, so what the hell. "May
I ask a personal question?"

> *You can always ask. I can't*
> *guarantee I'll answer it, though.*

"What happened with your
fiancé? I mean, when you
decided to move out west,
why didn't he come, too?"

> She considers her reply,
> and her sigh is heavyweight.
> *He and I had planned our*
> *future, start to finish, and*
> *for him that meant eventing,*
> *and New York, not babysitting*
> *in California. In his eyes, I chose*
>
> *family over him, and I guess*
> *that was accurate enough,*
> *though I didn't feel I had*
> *a choice, and begged him*
> *to come along. I learned*
> *love can't always weather*
> *the circumstances of our lives.*

Such Loyalty

To family is humbling,
and also completely alien.

The only family I own
is Dad, and though of course

he loves me, I'm sure of
that, sometimes he makes

me feel like a burden
he'd rather not shoulder.

Yes, he stepped up when
my mother deserted us,

but should he ever actually
fall in love again, would he put

me first? Could he love Zelda?
I don't know, and thinking

back over the years, it's odd
he hooked up with so many

women, but never connected
on a deep emotional level

with even one. Is my father
really capable of falling in love?

Maya

For Casey

I haven't updated your journal in a while, but it's been a hard few months. Your daddy was transferred to a new army base, so we're just getting used to life at Fort Bragg. North Carolina is a long way from Texas, and part of me doesn't mind that so much. I left a lot of bad memories in Texas.

In North Carolina, the weather is different. The people are different. The twang of their voices is different from our gentle drawl. And there's new stuff to see when Daddy puts us in the old Chevy he bought and takes us for drives. There's even an ocean—the Atlantic.

We've been to the beach a couple of times. You're so cute when you sit on the sand and it shifts under you. Your eyes go wide, you coo surprise, and try to grab a handful. Of course Daddy cusses about that. "Keep her on the blanket, would you? That crap'll get everywhere!"

He uses worse words, but I'm cleaning up his language here in your journal. Too bad you have to hear it sometimes. I've asked him to please not swear in front of you. He tells me I'm "f***ing" crazy, that you're too little to understand. To be totally honest, I had to scrub my own vocab, too. You listen to everything. I want your very first word to be "mama," not the f-word.

Our new house is a little bigger, a little newer. But it's still just like the one right next door. Soldiers might be creative in how they fight, but not so much in how they live.

I did change things up for you. Instead of the yellow I painted your first bedroom with, I chose bright green for this one because it reminded me of new grass. We moved here in March, right before the official first day of spring.

345

Spring in Texas meant bluebonnets stretching as far as you could see. One day I'll show you bluebonnets, but they don't have them in North Carolina. Here there are columbines and bleeding hearts and wild geraniums. I hoped the blooming flowers would ease my growing depression, but they haven't helped much.

I'm so lonely, only you and your daddy to talk to.

I never made a lot of friends at Fort Hood, but here I don't even have Auntie Tati nearby. She isn't your real aunt, just my very best friend in the world. Austin was only an hour away, and sometimes she'd drive out to the base. Boy, did she ever love you!

As soon as she walked through the door, she'd beg, "Let me hold her! Please?" You'd snuggle right into her arms, look up at her with your huge brown eyes, and smile. Pretty sure she got your first real smile. That only made me a little jealous.

Tati's favorite thing was buying you pretty dresses, something I can't really afford. You're wearing one of them now, in fact, as you push across the tile in your walker. I've read it's not good to keep you inside it too long, but you love moving so much! You're seven months old, and not quite ready to walk yet, but I can tell how much you want to.

Oh, Casey, you are such a beautiful little girl, and always happy. Tati says it's from all the good breast milk you scarf, and I think that's probably true. I don't think your daddy likes sharing, though. He keeps saying, "That baby's getting too big for boob sucking. Time to take her off the teat."

But I can't stand the thought of weaning you. Not yet. You're eating cereal and mashed bananas and applesauce, and we're working on carrots, too. You should see what that does to your poo! Is that gross to say to a baby?

I don't know what's right or wrong. I'm running totally on instinct. Well, instinct and love. The connection we have is amazing, and you are the one thing keeping me sane. I hate military life. Some people like the order, the routine, the sameness.

Your daddy loves all of that. I think he wants to be the handsome soldier in magazine pictures. He likes polishing his boots and cleaning his rifle. He makes me keep his uniform spotless, and ironed. I never used an iron in my life before I married Sergeant Jason Baxter. But I don't dare argue with him. He isn't nice when he's angry. Sometimes he scares me a little.

I'm supposed to feel safe here. You know, because soldiers with guns behind fences provide lots of security. But soldiers flip out sometimes. Just a few years ago, right here on this base, one of them went off and shot nineteen people. Only one unlucky officer died, but you never know where a stray bullet lost in a barrage of gunfire might go. Maybe even through our living room windows.

"You're nuts," Daddy says. "There isn't a more secure place on the planet."

I try to believe him. Try not to worry. I take you out for walks in your stroller and put you in a baby seat on the back of my bike. You even have a baby helmet, just in case. If anything ever happened to you, I would take the easy way out.

But you're here, and safe, so I'll keep going for you. You're really all I have. I don't count your daddy, but I wish I could. Once upon a time I thought I loved him and that he loved me. But even after I knew that wasn't true, I married him anyway. It was my only chance at escape. I figured one way or another we'd make it work.

Maybe we will. Who knows?

December Delivers Short Days

And counting down toward
the end of another year, things
are very different from even
a month ago. Let's see.

I've got a car.
A car I can drive
because I got
my license,
passed the test
with only one
little mistake.

It was Zelda who talked Dad
into showing up at the DMV
right when I needed him.
I made the appointment,

told him when
to be there. At first
he said he couldn't
get off work, but
Zelda dropped by
the shop, asked
his boss to comply,
and then he had
no real excuse.

Later, he was mad, of course.
You and that bitch double-
teamed me. Admit it, you planned
it together, didn't you?

I reminded him
that Zelda and I
rarely even speak,
and when we do,
he's pretty much
always around,
so, no, we made
no secret pact.

"Maybe she believes I deserve
the privilege, or maybe she just
wants you to be a little freer
to feed your, uh, appetites."

Then it got really
strange because
he went totally
silent, and stayed
that way until I
saw him again
the next evening
and then he said,

Wash up for dinner.
One of my appetites
needs to be fed.

Dad Holds Grudges

I've known that, like, forever,
and have tried to make sense
of them. He harbors hate

for my mother, which is well
enough deserved; bitterness
for Nadia, Cecilia, Jewel, and

more than a few whose names
I don't remember, despite
dredging up their faces

in random daydreams. I'm only
marginally aware of the details,
but it seems the splits were mutually

acceptable, so I can't explain
his reasons. Rhonda he escaped
from, contraband in pocket; and

Leona is little more than a sketch
in my memory notebook. These two
he rarely mentions. Still, as far

as I can tell, none of them deserved
his abuse, verbal or otherwise.
And beyond every single one

of them, I can't help but ask myself
what it is I've done to make
my dad hold grudges against me.

What Hurts Most

Is I think his main grudge
against me is . . .

me.

For someone so determined
to maintain a desperate hold,

he

would rather I not be here
at all, at least that's how

I

feel much of the time.
It hurts. And the longer

we

are entrenched here, where
attachment is available to

me,

the lonelier this house
seems with just the two of

us

sharing these rooms.

Sometimes, in Fact

I vastly prefer being alone
to subjugation, and for Dad,
winning is everything. I tried
playing chess with him exactly
three times. The first, I'd never
played before and didn't know
the rules. What he taught me

was how the pieces moved,
and that was enough that time.
The second, I'd learned some
basics from a teacher I can
barely recall. Strategy wasn't
something I could define, let
alone make sense of. What

Dad showed me that time
was the cruelty of make-believe
war, and oh, how he made fun
of my childish upset. After that
I refused to sit across the board
from him until I had the chance
to read up on possible moves

and probable outcomes. I truly
believed I had that game won
until Dad's bishop managed an end
run and put me in checkmate.
He laughed and laughed, and
what he made very clear that
time was I'd better not lose and cry.

Crybabies

Top Dad's most-
disgusted-by list. Right
below come:

queers
(zero exceptions)

foreigners
(white Europeans mostly exempt)

pussies
(except the feminine kind)

cheaters
(his cheating excepted)

whiners
(drunk whining forgiven, depending)

know-it-alls
(generally in reference to me).

Over the years, I've made
that list more times than
I care to remember.

He's my dad, and he loves me.
Most of the time we get along fine.

But once in a while I feel like
he would've preferred to stay child free.

But Everything's Better with Wheels

School, because I can come
and go on my own schedule,
not have to worry about
waiting for Dad in the morning
or Syrah after practice.

Work. I started at the Triple G
last Saturday, and so far, so good,
even though I have to get up early
on my weekends. They want me
there no later than eight,

which makes sense considering
the number of horses I'm expected
to exercise within two six-hour days.
Over the course of twelve hours,
I rode nine, twice each. Boy,

was my butt sore come Sunday
night, but I figure that'll get
better once I develop some
gluteal calluses. Peg was right.
Most of the Thoroughbreds

are green, which means challenging
because their training is elementary,
so it's mostly about staying astride
while they gallop out their excess
energy. In comparison, Niagara

is a lope around the carousel.
I'm looking forward to working
with her more. This week I'll only
get Sunday in because of the game,
but Peg and Max are understanding

about prior commitments. I had
to talk Dad into the work thing myself,
but once the car was accomplished,
it wasn't hard. "Twelve bucks an hour,
and even only working weekends,

I can pay for my own gas. Besides,
it'll keep me busy. You prefer me
busy, don't you?" He agreed that
he does, and I know it's true,
especially considering how much

time I've been spending with Gabe.
Monica, too, but Dad doesn't notice
her the same way, which is kind
of odd, all things considered.
But I'm not going to question it.

Tomorrow is Monica's birthday,
and tonight Syrah's mom is out
of town, so I'm going over there
for a party, though I phrased it
"cake and ice cream" to Dad.

I Even Baked the Cake

Not from scratch. I'm not that
great of a cook, but the mix
stuff isn't so bad. I'm frosting
it (canned icing, of course)
when Dad comes into the kitchen.

> *That there looks pretty good.*
> *Save me a piece. A big one.*

"Sure thing, Dad. Like there'll
be any left. Hey, don't forget
about my game tomorrow."
It starts at noon, and since I
figure we'll party fairly late,
I'm spending the night at Syrah's.

> *Since when do high schools play*
> *girls' basketball on Saturday?*

"We only have a couple of weekend
games. The rest are Monday or Friday
nights. But this is a tournament."

> *Well, I'll try, but no promises.*
> *Saturday's my day off, you know.*

In other words, he'd rather drink
beer and play with Zelda. Thanks
so much for all your support, Dad.

I Leave the Cake

On the counter, with a stern warning
to Dad, "Do. Not. Touch. The. Cake."

I mitigate that and increase the odds
of its survival by adding, "Please."

> *I'll be good*, he says, taking a package
> of hot dogs out of the fridge. He puts two

on a plate, takes them to the table. "Raw?
You could microwave those, you know."

> He shrugs. *It don't matter to me. I'll*
> *eat something hot with Zelda later.*

"Nice picture, Dad. I'm going to get
my jacket and take off. Be right back."

On the way to my room, the telephone
rings. That is a strange occurrence.

We only have a landline because it
came with the cable bundle, and our

cell service can be iffy out here. I must
sound surprised when I answer, "Hello?"

The woman on the other end mutters
something incoherent. Drinking, obviously.

She apologizes, tries again, asks to
talk to someone I've never heard of.

"Sorry. You have the wrong number.
No one here with that name."

I hang up as Dad yells, *Stupid jerk
telemarketers. Tell 'em to buzz off.*

"Wrong number," I call, correcting
him before finishing my mission.

I grab my jacket, and by the time I get
back to the kitchen Dad has finished

his disgusting snack and popped
a beer. I'm glad I can drive myself

into town. Thinking about how many
times I've ridden in a car with him

driving under the influence is the stuff
of nightmares. We're both damn lucky

to be alive and all in one piece. "Okay.
I'm off. You be careful, okay, Dad?"

He takes a long slurp. *What makes you
say that? Careful's my middle name.*

"Okay, then. See you tomorrow
at my game. Noon. Go to bed early."

Careful

Go to bed early.
Don't eat raw hot dogs.
Sheesh, I sound like his mom.

Still, I'm careful
with the cake, carrying
it to my car and cautiously

stashing it on
the front passenger seat.
I drive into town judiciously,

vigilant about
speed limits and hairy
curves. I park sensibly, well off

the road in Syrah's
driveway. I don't plan on
leaving tonight, so if I get blocked

in by some partyer
it won't much matter
until tomorrow morning.

I'm wary about
announcing my arrival
until I'm sure Syrah's mom

has already left.
So maybe careful is,
in fact, my middle name.

The Mom Unit Is Gone

And seems like half the school
knows Syrah's place is an open
invitation to fun, because within
two hours her house is overrun.
So much for anything resembling
a private party. The one thing

      I insist on is Monica having a piece
      of her birthday cake. I don't mind
      skipping, but she does, cutting
      a giant slice. *Compartiremos.*
      We'll share. If I get fat, you do, too.

We share cake. We share drinks.
We share weed, but only a little
because we both want to be on
our game tomorrow. Syrah
doesn't much seem to care
about that, though she's starting
in Hillary's position, and should.

The problem with this kind
of party is nobody worries
about trashing the place or
making too much noise. Not
surprisingly, Garrett and Keith
show up, and they are two
of the worst offenders,
especially since they're mostly
soused when they get here.

At first, Syrah not only goes
along with their obnoxious
crap, but actually flirts a little
with Keith. When he goes to
take a piss, I pull her aside.
"What are you doing? Keith?
He's disgusting. Whatever you
do, don't let him kiss you. Who
knows what goes in that mouth?"

> *He could probably say the same*
> *thing about you.* She's borderline
> wasted. *But that's okay. I like you*
> *anyway. And don't worry, I'd rather*
> *kiss* him. She points to Gabe,
> who's just come through the door.

Shit. Gabe and Monica together
again, and at Syrah's party,
no less. I'd ask him how he found
out about it, but it's obvious
something's happening here.
Oh, and my Focus is in the driveway.
"I'll be right back," I tell Monica,
before making my way over to Gabe.

> When he sees me headed in his
> direction, he smiles and meets me
> halfway. *Hey there. Noticed your car*
> *among the fleet outside. Thought*
> *I'd stop in and say hello and also . . .*

Don't Kiss Me, Don't Kiss Me

Not in front of this crowd.
Not in front of Syrah.
Not in front of Monica.
But he knows better,
and besides that, he
has important news.

> I was just at the AM/PM.
> Overheard some cops
> talking about this party.
> Someone called about
> the noise. They'll either
> show up knocking or
> wait around the corner
> for people to leave.

"Thanks for letting us know.
I'll spread the word.
Maybe it'll help clear
the place out. This isn't
the kind of party we had
in mind, at least not in
my mind. It's Monica's
birthday. I was just thinking
cake, ice cream, and a drink
or two. Big game tomorrow."

> He smiles. I know. I'll be
> there, at least if you want
> me to be. And I'll help
> clear the place out.

It's a Grudging Exodus

But most everyone leaves
peacefully. Monica and Syrah
disappear into the kitchen

and now Gabe comes over.
He kisses me, but not on the lips.
Instead, the warmth of his mouth

> caresses my forehead. *I've got
> something to tell you, but not here.
> Not tonight. Not at your friend's*

> *birthday party. Can we talk after
> your game tomorrow?* Even in
> the low light, an air of sadness

is evident in his beautiful eyes.
"Sure. But is everything okay?"
His nod is not at all convincing.

> *Nothing to worry about.
> In fact, I hope you'll be happy
> for me, but that's all I'm saying*

> *now.* He steps back. *Better go.
> Good luck tomorrow. I'll be cheering
> for you.* He turns and walks out the door.

That Sounded Vaguely Ominous

What can he possibly want
to tell me that he thinks
it needs to wait for a more
private moment? Concern
manifests itself in a sudden
need to pee. I wander down

the hall to the bathroom,
relieve my body, if not my mind,
and when I exit, find myself
face to face with Garrett.

> *Feeling better?* His grin
> is an actual leer, and he
> bumps into me. Hard.

"What are you doing here?
Didn't you hear the cops
are on their way?"
I try to step around him.

He pushes me backward
against the wall, pins me
with his substantial bulk.

> *Ain't no cops gonna bother us*
> *now everyone else is gone.*
> *How 'bout we have a little fun?*
> The alcohol on his breath
> almost buckles my knees.

I look him straight in the eye.
"The last thing I want is
a little fun with you, Garrett.
Now please get out of my way."

His eyes flash a strange
combination of anger and
amusement. *Aw, come on.
You been flirting something
awful. You a cock tease?*

"Flirting? With you?"
My brain scrambles to think
what I might've done to give
him that impression. "Garrett,
you know that's not true.
I've got a girlfriend."

*Maybe, but I saw you with
that dude, too. And I watch
the way you check out guys
at school. You a switch-hitter?*

He actually licks his lips.
"What I am or am not
is none of your business.
Now leave me the hell alone."
I hold my ground, fight hard
not to look scared, but the way
I'm trembling is obvious.

Ooh. Tough girl, huh? Tough
goddamn dyke. Let's see
if you're into guys or girls.
Bet I could eat you better.

He pushes me sideways
and back, into a nearby
bedroom, and is on me
so suddenly I can't react.
Next thing I know, I'm on
the bed beneath him, held
fast by the weight of his body.
"No, Garrett, no! Stop!"

But the words are trapped
by the booze-flavored drool
inside his mouth. His teeth
rake my lips and one hand
snares my hair, snaps my head
against the mattress.

Don't fight, baby. I'll make
you feel so good you'll never
want a girl again. Here,
check this thing out.

His free hand unzips
his jeans, and just as I start
to panic, a familiar voice
interrupts the scene.

I don't think that's a good idea.

Suddenly, Forcefully

Garrett is lifted into the air,
freeing me. I jump up and
away from the bed. "Gabe!"

> He ignores me completely,
> too busy with Garrett. *What
> the hell do you think you're doing?*

Garrett doesn't back down.
*What the fuck's it to you?
I'm just breaking her in a little.*

*And, hey, if you want, you can
take a turn, too. A good screw
or two might flip her totally.*

> Gabe assesses the front
> of Garrett's pants. *Breaking
> her in? With what you've got there?*

> *Nah, I don't think so. What
> I witnessed looked like assault.
> You like forcing yourself on girls?*

Garrett shakes his head. *Nope.
Can't assault the willing.
Goddamn cock teaser wanted it.*

"That's a lie! You're the last
person on this planet I'd want
to have sex with. The last!"

Behind them, backup arrives.
Monica and Syrah in my corner,
Keith, of course, in Garrett's.

And that makes Garrett a little
too eager to force an ugly
confrontation. He forms fists.

> *You really don't want to do
> that,* says Gabe, pushing him
> out of the bedroom, into the hall.

Monica and Syrah hustle out
of the way. Keith, who's drunk
enough to get brave, steps closer.

> *Who the hell are you, anyway?*
> says Garrett, obviously fortified.
> *I don't answer to pansy-ass jerk-offs.*

> Gabe draws himself up, maximizing
> both height and menace. *I'm Ariel's
> friend. Friends don't let friends get raped.*

Garrett glances at Keith, who
nods. *What're you gonna do?*
asks Garrett. *Take both of us on?*

> *Yeah, dickwad,* agrees Keith,
> moving into position on the opposite
> side of Gabe. *You don't want to do that.*

Gabe Sizes Up the Situation

There are two of them,
yes. But they're wasted,
and I think he senses
that neither is a true threat,
at least not on his own.
Still, there *are* two of them.

> *Look, I really don't want to*
> *hurt you, no matter how much*
> *you deserve it. Why don't you*
> *tuck your teensy pecker back*
> *into your pants and get the hell*
> *out of here?* He takes a step toward

Garrett, who's too dense to
understand what that means,
though he does make sure his pants
are zipped. *Ooh. I'm so scared.*
Come and get me, asshole.

Gabe doesn't hesitate. He swings
a fist straight into Keith's gut,
doubling him over. That enrages
Garrett, who wades into Gabe.

That proves to be a huge mistake.

Up Close

Isn't how you want to observe
a fistfight. Garrett manages to land
a punch or two, but this is no contest.

I'm not two feet away from Gabe.
and I can see his eyes glaze over, as
if he's vacating this dimension.

He steps into Garrett and as I watch,
I swear he morphs into something
just this side of human, a boxing

machine, like those kids' robots, only
full size. *Bam, bam, bam!* Three straight
to the face, and the sound of knuckles

connecting to flesh and the bone
beneath makes me wobble. I've heard
it before, only last time it was Dad's

fist, and the person he was pounding
was a woman. Like she did then,
Garrett now lowers his hands, defeated.

And like Dad then, Gabe isn't finished,
throwing a flurry of impressive blows
that drop Garrett all the way to the floor,

blood and snot pouring from his nose.
The coppery smell gags me, but I manage
to choke back the impending vomit.

Meanwhile, Keith has found breath
and regained some strength. Stupidly,
he ducks his head and charges Gabe,

who dances to one side. Keith loses
his balance, slips, and bashes his skull
against the wall, and Gabe advances.

"Stop!" I yell. "Enough! God, do you
want to kill them? Please, just leave
them alone. They're finished, can't you

see that?" I'm shriveling. Shrinking.
Folding up into myself, stumbling
backward. I'm a sniveling ten-year-old

again, pleading with someone I thought
I knew to dig down for his humanity,
find mercy, and end the carnage.

It doesn't matter that he's doing
this to defend me. It's savage.
I actually feel sorry for Garrett.

Gabe stops, straightens, but when
he turns and looks at me, I find
something terrible in his eyes—

satisfaction.

He Bends Over

Careful
to avoid the bodily
fluids on the floor,
lifts Garrett to his feet
by the back of his shirt.

> *Never assume a stranger*
> *is a pansy-ass jerk-off.*
> *How about I call you a taxi?*
> *You're in no condition to drive.*

> *Fuck you, shithead.*
> Garrett does his best
> to shake it off. He points
> at me. *You good*
> *with this, bitch?*

> Gabe leans closer.
> *That's no way to talk*
> *to a lady. I suggest you*
> *apologize. You too,*
> he says to Keith,

who's struggling
to get up on his feet.
The guys must've read
the pleasure factor
in Gabe's eyes,
because both mutter
halfhearted apologies
before limping away.

Still, they refuse
to accept complete
defeat, extending middle
fingers before vanishing
into the dark of night.

Monica rushes to my side.
¿Estás bien? ¿Que pasó?

I reach for her, and
discover how badly
I'm shaking. "I'm okay,"
I lie, falling into her arms.
"Garrett thought I should prove
whether I'm into guys or girls."

What? For real? Did he . . .?

"No, thanks to Gabe.
But he would have.
At least, I think so."

Do you want to call the cops?
asks Gabe. *You probably should.*

"And tell them what?
Nothing happened?
And even if it had,
they'd write it off as drunk
kids getting carried away."

What I Hold Very Close

Unable to share, even
with these, my best and only
friends, is that I don't dare
call the cops.

Ever.

My dad's programmed
that into me for as long
as I can remember.

Why?

I have no clue.
All I know is it's near
the top of his rules
list, just below
"Don't question me."

Ever.

Once, when he left me
with Ma-maw and Pops,
he drilled into me
that should flashing red
and blue lights ever appear
on the horizon,
I was to dash out into
the alfalfa fields.

Hide.

I never had to do that.
Never had to deal
with law enforcement
one way or another.
Somehow, Dad's managed
to avoid any kind
of run-in, too.

How?

Sheer luck,
I suppose. I know
he's done things in the past
that should've
resulted in some kind
of punitive measures.
Rhonda's emerald ring,
for instance.

Pawned.

If tonight
had resulted in actual
penetration—rape—
would I feel differently
and report it?
Excellent

question.

Monica Holds Me Close

Until I finally stop quivering.
Then, heedless of spectators,

she reaches up and kisses me
so sweetly I momentarily forget

the ugliness I'm mere minutes
beyond. She wraps me in love,

and it's almost enough to smother
the residual fear and outrage.

Gabe looks vaguely uncomfortable
at our emotional exchange.

Syrah is her usual underwhelmed
self. She ignores us, rushes over to Gabe.

> *Wow! You were amazing! The words*
> *escape in a rush of breath. I've never*
>
> *seen anything like that. Hey, wanna*
> *be my bodyguard? Then, totally as*
>
> *an afterthought, Oh, and are you*
> *okay? Giddy, that's how she sounds.*

Gabe blushes crimson. *Other than*
sore knuckles, I'm fine. At least one

of them has granite-strength bones.
He looks down. *Sorry about your floor.*

Hey, no problem, gushes Syrah.
That's why they invented paper

towels and cleanser. It's gross, though.
She goes to find the necessary items.

I push away from Monica, swallow
my disgust at the bodily fluids

pooled on the tile. What I really
want to do is crawl into a corner

and sleep so I won't think about
the images solidifying in my mind,

resurrected by visions of Garrett's
and Keith's faces. Blood gushing.

Snot dripping. Bruises resembling
thunderheads rearing up. A woman,

dropped down on her knees, sobbing
apologies for "inviting" my dad's abuse.

I can see her broken face clearly.
But I don't remember her name.

Funny How the Brain

Manages damage control,
conveniently curtaining
windows that overlook
certain footpaths into the past.
I try to keep the shades drawn.

> Monica notices, however.
> She moves closer again,
> a drift of solace, claims
> her place at my side.
> *Estás bien, novia? No te ves*
> *tan bien. You look a little sick.*

"I'm queasy," I admit.
"I'm not real good with blood,
and watching someone get
pummeled is more than
I can take. I mean, I've seen
random guys involved
in altercations, but never
that close. I didn't realize
how brutal it is."

> *I'm s-sorry, sputters Gabe.*
> *I couldn't see another way out.*

"No. It's okay. Not your fault,
and not like they didn't deserve it,
especially Garrett. But where did
you learn to fight like that?
That wasn't, like, amateur night."

Where I grew up you either
decided to be a tough guy
or you let the tough guys
take you down. I chose to be
strong, and Dad encouraged
me to learn to box. He put in
extra hours to pay for gym
time and a trainer, even.

Golden Gloves could've been
my ticket out. I worked all
the way up to state, and would've
been a finalist except
Dad's accident made that
impossible. My dream died
along with him, but hey,
at least I'm still here.

"You could go back to it,
couldn't you?" I ask, even
though the idea of regularly
beating people up makes me
even more nauseous than
the mess on Syrah's floor.

Don't think so. I have to get
real about life some time,
and with Mom coming home
at some point soon, now
is probably the right time.

Sounds Way Too Adult

As does cleaning up the mess
on the floor, and when Syrah
returns with the supplies,
Gabe volunteers for the job.

I don't offer to help, don't dare
get too close or I'll only add
to the ugly puddle on the tile.
At least they managed to miss

the carpet. There's that, I guess.
Instead, I start tidying tables
and countertops, tossing cups
and cans, some with cigarette

butts floating inside. Monica
joins in the effort. "Why are people
so gross?" I ask, only to make
conversation. No answer really

      required, Monica shrugs in reply.
      Parties bring out the bad in some
      and the worst in others. You sure
      you don't want to report Garrett?

"No. Let it drop. We should open
some windows. It stinks in here."
It does. It smells like sweat and weed
and old booze with a float of tobacco.

We finish the cleanup, windows
open, Syrah flirting obnoxiously
with Gabe all the while, and
the strange thing about that is

I don't seem to care. To his credit,
Gabe doesn't bite, but if it's only
to impress me, I almost want
him to know it's okay if he does.

Almost. Shouldn't I feel more
possessive? Is it just because
I discovered something about
him tonight I never expected?

I'd say something completely
foreign, but it's not. It's something
I'm intimately aware of, having lived
with it all my life. Dad hides it well

most of the time, and obviously
Gabe does, too. In fact, he disguises
it better, or maybe it only seems
that way because I've known him

for such a short while. But beneath
his gentle exterior, way down
in the depths of those lizard eyes,
roils a red-hot mantle of rage.

Maya

For Casey

Oh my God! What's happening? We're a long way from New York City, but if it could happen there, maybe it could happen right here. It seems like the whole world's gone crazy. NYC. North Carolina. There. Here. Everywhere. Crazy. Who would do such a despicable thing? Who? And why?

It's September 11. Your birthday. I got up early to see your daddy off to work and bake a cake for your party. It's Tuesday, so I didn't plan anything big, just a few of your playgroup buddies and their moms, who I can more rightly call acquaintances than friends.

Daddy said we should've waited until Saturday, but I think a girl should celebrate the actual day she was born, rather than hold off to accommodate other people's schedules. But now your party is on indefinite hold.

Not too long after your daddy left, he called me. "Turn on the TV."

"Why? What channel?"

"All of them. Just do it."

Every channel showed the same thing. The twin towers of the World Trade Center, the biggest buildings in this whole country, were in flames. Smoking. Falling apart. Someone flew planes into them. On purpose. Big planes. Jetliners.

They showed it in slow motion.

I couldn't stop watching. Still can't turn it off, even though I know people are dead. They keep repeating footage of them screaming. Falling. Jumping. Jumping from so high up in the air they could never survive, but they preferred that to burning to death.

One of the towers crumbled. Crashed to the ground, nothing left but rubble, dust, and smoke. And bodies. In pieces. So much carnage. How do you escape when you're seventy stories up in the air, only stairs to get you down, not knowing what's below, or if what's above you will crush you?

Then the second tower broke apart, too. There were—are—people trapped inside. Some are first responders—cops, firefighters. Trying to save the others. You don't know, baby girl, you don't know.

It's like a scene from a movie. Some awful disaster flick. Only it's real life. Real death. So many must have perished. Men. Women. Little kids. Babies. What if you and I were there in that building or on the ground, when it all came tumbling down?

Now they're saying another plane crashed into the Pentagon, and yet another in a field somewhere. Hijacked, all of them. Passengers and crew, minding their own business, traveling to or away from home.

"Collateral damage." That's what the military spokesman called them. Not wives or parents or brothers. Cold as a mortuary slab. "Collateral damage."

A pretty newswoman, coaxed not to smile as she usually would, says, "These are concerted acts of terrorism."

Well, yeah. What else could they be? We don't know who these terrorists were, or what motivated them to commit this kind of atrocity, and we won't for a while. But our country is under attack. That means we—you and I—are under attack. This isn't supposed to happen on American soil.

I've never considered myself patriotic. Definitely not a fan of the military. I married a soldier so I could divorce my mother, not because of his uniform or because I believed in some noble cause. But since this morning, love for my country has skyrocketed.

I don't know a single soul in New York City, but as I sit

glued to the television, watching them run for their lives or stand there, staring in shock, I'm crying for all of them, and for every American. We're afraid. So very afraid.

The base is scrambling, all personnel on high alert, and I'm sure every active installation in the country is the same way. The threat feels foreign, and what might happen next, not to mention when, is anyone's guess.

Four different people managed to fly four domestic jet aircraft into four separate targets. Well, the one that went down in Pennsylvania probably missed whatever it was aiming for. Even so, how is this possible?

"Don't worry," your daddy tells me. "Everything will be fine. You're safe. I'll see to it, no matter what."

I wish I could believe him, but anxiety surrounds me like a prickly aura, vaguely electric. I work very hard to keep you from sensing it. You've played and napped through the whole thing, happily unaware.

While you were sleeping, Tati called, and we talked for a long, long time. One of her cousins is a New York City policeman. She doesn't know if he's all right. "Air travel will probably be tough for a while," she said. "But when it eases up, I want to come visit. Think that would be okay?"

It was the best thing I heard all day, other than you trying out new words that you happened to overhear. "Pre-zi-den?"

"Close. President."

I wouldn't want to be President Bush right now. Or anyone in charge of anything. I just want to shut the blinds and hide.

Daddy won't be home, so I fix your favorite dinner—mini corn dogs and Fritos. After you finish, I go ahead and light the three candles on your cake, and as I watch you licking chocolate frosting off your fingers, I wonder about your future in a world gone totally insane.

What will you face tomorrow? In a year, or five, or a

decade? How can I possibly keep you safe when I don't know what might fall from the sky? Will I spend the rest of my life looking up, or scanning the horizon for incoming planes?

Before today, I was only really afraid of two people. My mother. And your daddy. Sometimes he stares at me and I think he wants to take me apart, and I don't know why except there's a piece of him that only appears when roused by anger. So I try very hard not to make him mad. Now, with everything going on, he'll be ridiculously on edge. As long as he doesn't take it out on you, I'll make it all right.

Happy birthday, my angel. I'm sorry this day will always be linked to this awful event, but with time the fear will fade and I'll do everything I can to make our celebrations happy ones. For now, I'll share a piece of cake with you. Then we'll watch Dora the Explorer until you're ready for bed, and after I tuck you in tonight, I'll worry about tomorrow.

Ariel
Last Night

Post Gabe-and-Garrett nightmare
I immersed myself in the dream

that is Monica. Once Syrah's house
emptied we smoked a little weed,

> and then it was past time for bed.
> *You two take my mom's bed,* urged Syrah.

"You're sure she and her boyfriend are
out of town? I'd hate to surprise them."

> *I'm sure. She and the nimrod don't have
> sex here. I think she's afraid I'll learn*
>
> *something a girl shouldn't by listening
> in on her mom. So when they're in the mood*
>
> *they get a room. And, lucky you, that
> also means the sheets are mostly clean.*

> *Where's your sister tonight?* asks
> Monica. *One of us could take her bed.*
>
> *She spent the night with a friend, and if
> you'd rather sleep separately, okay by me.*

No Judgment

Either way. I love that about
Syrah. She went off to her own
bed to dream about Gabe
or whatever. I was so happy
when he finished the cleanup,
then begged off for the night.

Not sure if he intuited my
negative reaction or if the act
of beating people to a bloody
pulp tired him out, but he left
right away, reminding me
we'd talk after my game.

Once Syrah shut her door,
I asked, "You want to be alone
tonight? It's okay if you do."
It would've hurt my feelings
terribly, but I wasn't about
to say so. "Feliz cumpleaños,

mi bella amiga." Happy birthday,
my beautiful friend, and that's
exactly how she looked there
in the low lamplight. Beautiful—
wild and dark and unpredictable,
like some creature of the forest.

> She held out her hand.
> *Quiero pasar la noche contigo.*
> We spent the night together.

Monica's Beauty

Was blanketed by darkness,
but every unique inch of her
is pressed into my memory.

All the recent ugliness melted
beneath the luscious mocha
of her skin, a whisper against

mine, promising tomorrows
saturated with love. Love. I hardly
know how to accept the possibility

that it's real, and available to me.
We had no need to hurry, and
in the tarrying, I found something

unexpected—an exchange of energy
so intense I think we could have
come without even touching.

But touch we did, with mouths
and tongues and, oh, you can hardly
imagine the incredible sensuousness

of the lowly fingertip when bringing
pleasure to a partner is your entire
realm of being for an hour or more.

More. Much more, until, completely
spent, we fell asleep, safe in each other's
arms. Oh, that was sex as it should be.

What I Can Say

In retrospect
is I still like sex.
But I think it's better
with trust involved.

I didn't have to worry
about doing anything
right

or

wrong.

I just had to trust
we'd take care of each
other, there in bed,
but also after,

when maybe cake
becomes the determining factor,
or tamales or a horror flick.
Anything except

orgasm

which is not

necessarily dependent

on someone wanting
to spend the night with you.

What I Can't Say

With certainty is how
I feel about Gabe
this morning.
Maybe I overreacted
on a purely emotional level.

I mean, he was protecting me,
and had he not stepped up,
who knows what might
have happened?

Still, pulling back
from the situation and
dissecting his response,
I come away
not only disappointed
but also a little scared.

Not so much scared
that Gabe would hurt me.
I've never felt threatened
by him before. But then
again, how would I know
exactly what might
set him off?

And that's what
really scares me—
that I never noticed
even hints of warning
signs before.

Or Maybe

It was just a fluke
and I'm way overthinking it,
when right now
what I should be thinking
about is the game.

I take my car.
Syrah follows with Monica
in hers. I'm sure sooner
or later I'll try to cheat
the system and allow
someone under twenty-five
to ride with me
before my provisional license
becomes unrestricted
in a year. But for now
I'll play by the rules.

The high school isn't far,
and when we pull into
the parking lot, I'm gratified
to see it's already filling
with spectator vehicles.
A quick scan
doesn't reveal Dad's car,
but it's still an hour
to game time,
so maybe he'll show.
The GTO, now sporting
a fresh coat of racing green
paint, is noticeable, however.

I park close to the locker
room, go in to suit up
in my shiny blue uniform,
nerves tingling.
This will be my first
actual game
and as starting center
the pressure to perform
well is building.

Coach Booker gives
a short pep talk
that does little to alleviate
the tension bloating the space
between the locker rows.
At least it's not just me
who's nervous.
We're all pacing
or bouncing up and down
on our toes.

It's a relief
when Coach calls us
to go warm up.
At least until we file
into the gym,
where the bleachers
seem to sag beneath
the weight of so many people.
But hey, it's cool.
No reason to think we'll blow it.

From Tip-Off to Halftime

It's a fairly even match,
the scoring shifting back
and forth between teams.
Syrah misses a couple
of rebounds; I miss a shot
or two, and so does Monica.

But on the upside, I sink
four two-pointers and one
from outside the key that
nets us three. Monica scores
a half-dozen times,
including the free throw
that puts us ahead
going into the locker
room at the half.

As we start in that direction,
I scan the bleachers.
No sign of Dad. Big surprise.
I do catch sight of Hillary,
who's sitting between Peg
and Gabe. They're laughing.

One other person stands out,
mostly because she holds
herself painfully straight, which
puts her a good six inches
taller than the man beside her,
and if I'm not mistaken,
she's staring at me.

When she sees me notice
her, she smiles warmly,
as if we know each other,
which we definitely don't.
If she wasn't so pretty,
I might think she was
some creepy stalker.
Maybe she just likes
watching stellar girls'
basketball play.

In the locker room,
Syrah comes puffing up,
water bottle in hand.
*Did you see Gabe, all over
Hillary? What's up with that?*

Why do you care? asks
Monica. *Not like he's yours.*

*But maybe he could be.
I mean, as long as you're finished
with him.* Addressed to me.

"Listen, if you can snag him,
go for it." Seems doubtful.
"Anyway, I don't think
he and Hillary are *together*
together. Just sitting together."

Coach Rallies Us

For the third quarter,
figuratively slapping us
on the back and promising:

> *You girls got this.*
> *Now get on out there*
> *and take 'em down!*

We don't exactly drop
them to their knees,
but two quarters of hard
play put us ahead by four
at the end of the game,

and I can personally take
credit for nineteen points,
second only to Monica.
Syrah even scored six,
so we're all happy

when that final buzzer
rings. As we slap hands
with the other team, the crowd
begins to desert the stands
and I notice Zelda's with
Gabe now, no Hillary, Peg,
or Dad in view.

Thanks, Dad. Glad I mean
so much to you.

But as I Shower

It occurs to me that Dad
might have come with Zelda.

He could have been in
the bathroom taking a piss.

He could have been outside
polluting his lungs.

He could have been at
the snack bar buying popcorn.

Nah. The snack shack
would have been closed.

But the other two options
are still valid, so I'll go in search

of my father, hoping, if not
believing, he'll be here somewhere.

A phrase that materializes
from the ether: *glutton for*

punishment. And right behind
that: *none so blind as those*

who will not see. Wonder if
the idioms will prove wrong.

If He's Here

He's here, so I'm not in a hurry,
and I wait for Monica to slide into
her deliciously tight jeans.

I wish I could straight-up go over
and kiss her, but this is small-town
girls' basketball in a small-town

high school in small-town Sonora,
California, so the most I'll do
is lick my lips seductively (like I

know anything about seduction
beyond what Monica herself
has managed to teach me) and

invite, "Come with me? I know
it's stupid but I'm not-quite-
hoping my dad is out there,

pretending to have watched
the game. If he is, you can help
me celebrate. If he isn't, we can

go find something to do to make
me feel better. Unless you've got
plans for an after-game party?"

> She laughs. *Last night taught me
> I'm not the party type. Except
> maybe private parties with you.*

We Cut Back

Through the gym,
where several people
are still milling around,
including Monica's family.

All of them.
Mom. Dad.
Two big brothers.
One little sister.

> Carolina comes jogging
> up now. *Hey! You guys
> were awesome.*

She holds up two hands
for high fives—one from
her sister and one from me.
Now the rest of the Torres
family surrounds us,
chattering half in English,
half in Spanish, happily
congratulating us. Glad
somebody's kin cares.

> Now Monica's mom says,
> *Esta noche vamos a celebrar
> el cumpleaños de Mónica.
> Por favor, venga a cenar.*

I've Just Been Invited

To a birthday dinner celebration
for Monica. How can I turn that down?

Maybe there will even be tamales.
"Muchas gracias. Me encantaría ir."

> *Tu español es bueno*, says Mrs. Torres.
> *Muy bueno. We will see you tonight.*

We follow the family out to the parking
lot, where Syrah is leaning against her car,

flirting with Gabe, which reminds me
he and I are supposed to talk.

> *I think maybe you lost your boyfriend,*
> comments Monica, grinning broadly.

"I think that's okay by me." And I'm not
sure it's all about what I saw last night.

"Who needs a boyfriend when I've got
you?" Did I just offer a confession? Two?

> *I thought you'd never figure that out.*
> *Pero mejor tarde que nunca, ¿no?*

But better late than never, yes.
Now do I have to confess to Gabe, too?

I'm Thinking That Over

When someone taps me on
the shoulder. I turn to face
the tall redhead who smiled
at me from the bleachers,
and when I do, she sways
as if momentarily dizzy.

> The spiky-haired woman
> beside her extends a hand
> to steady her. *Take it easy.*
> *Everything's going to be fine.*

"Are you okay?"

> She pulls herself together.
> *Oh, yes. Sorry. Are you . . .*
> She holds out a newspaper
> clipping. It's the story about
> Gabe and me finding Hillary.
> *Are you Ariel Pearson?*

"That would be me."

> *And this . . .* She points to
> Dad, who's standing behind
> us in the picture. *This is your*
> *father? It says Mark Pearson.*

"That's my dad, yes."

> *Mark Pearson,* she repeats,
> sounding totally confused.

What does this woman
want? She's studying me
like a scientist getting
ready to dissect a frog.

       I'm Maya McCabe. Does
       the name sound familiar?
       Her voice is a bit too eager.

"Not really, no. Should it?"

But before she can answer,
Dad and Zelda come strolling
up behind her. Guess he made
it to the game after all.

"Hey, Dad. Didn't think you were here."

       At my greeting, Maya McCabe
       spins to face Dad. *Jason.*

           Dad's face drains every hint
           of color and his eyes narrow
           into serpent-like slits. *Fuck no.*

"What is it, Dad? Who's Jason?"

       But it's Maya who answers,
       Jason is your father. Jason Baxter.
       And I'm your mother, Casey.

Casey. The wrong-number name.

Denial

No.

"I'm Ariel Pearson."

No.

"He's Mark Pearson."

No.

"You can't be my mother."

Except.

There was Dad's reaction.

Except.

This woman has no reason to lie.

Except.

There's something about her voice.

Except.

She looks like me.

And now it's my turn to sway.

Why Now?

That's what I want to know.
Why here? Why today?
But all I manage to say is,
"I don't understand. Dad . . . ?"

> Immediately, Dad pushes
> between Maya and me.
> *Ariel, you get in your car*
> *and leave here right now.*
> *Don't say another word.*

Everyone moves at once.
Zelda, toward Dad.
Spiky hair, between him and Maya.
Monica, to my right.
Gabe and Syrah, who can't help
but notice the commotion,
start across the parking lot.

"Why are you here?" I demand.

> *Casey . . .*

"My name is Ariel."

> *No. It's not. It's Casey Baxter,*
> *and I'm your mom. I've been*
> *looking for you for fifteen years,*
> *ever since he kidnapped you.*
> *It was only a fluke that I found you.*

It's a lie! thunders Dad.
Don't you listen to her.
She'll just hurt you again.
Go, Ari . . . I'll take care of this.

He tries to circle Spiky, but
she and Zelda form a wall
between him and Maya,
who reaches out for me.

I jerk my arm away.
"Leave me alone! What
do you want from me?"

       All I want is the chance
       to be your mom. Please.

              Shut the fuck up, you
              cheating whore, and leave
              my daughter alone. Get out
              of here, Ariel. I mean it.

       Or what, Jason? You going
       to hurt her? Does he hurt you,
       Casey? Because if he does—

"Stop calling me Casey!
Who the hell do you think
you are? You can't just show
up out of the blue, fifteen damn
years without a single word,

pretending to be my mom.
You are not my mom. A real
mom does not desert her kid
and run off with her girlfriend. . . ."

At that, Maya looks down
and Spiky slides an arm around
her shoulders, confirmation.

> *See?* demands Dad. *See?*
> *She never gave a damn*
> *about you. Only about her.*

> *Oh, Casey. That's not true.*
> *I've never, ever stopped*
> *loving you or searching—*

"Screw you! I don't want you
in my life. I've never had a mom,
and I don't need one now!"
Goddamn it. I'm crying.

Tears stream from my puffing
eyes, down my superheated
cheeks. I must look like shit,
not that I care, because
I definitely feel like a huge
steaming mound of crap.

Leering Faces

Masks
of real people
surround me in
a wide semicircle.

I glance face to face to face.

Maya looks pummeled.
Spiky looks sad.
Zelda looks stunned.
My friends look confused.

Dad looks ready to detonate.

And when Maya lifts her eyes
from the ground,
meeting mine to beg compassion,
he does.

> *I will kill you, bitch!*

He lunges toward her,
hands outstretched
as if seeking her neck,
and I scream, "No, Dad, stop!"

This time it's Gabe who steps in.

> *Hold it right there, Mark.*
> *You wouldn't really hurt*
> *her, would you? Let's work*
> *this out like civilized people.*

Dad Looks More

Like a caged wolf.
Wary. Confused.
Bone-deep pissed.
Hatred shimmers
in his eyes.

Also fear.
And like a trapped animal,
fear makes him dangerous.
Still, he pretends courage.

> *Get out of my way, kid.*
> *I ain't afraid of you.*

He steps into Gabe,
swinging wildly.
But Dad has grown
slow and is out of practice.
Gabe steps to one side
and Dad's momentum
carries him too far forward.
He goes down on one knee
as everyone else scatters.

> *I don't want to hurt you,*
> *Mark. Don't get up.*

Dad doesn't understand
the danger, springs to his feet.
I picture Garrett and Keith,
just last night.
"No, no, no, no, no!"

I Can't Watch

I turn.
Run for my car.
Don't look back.
Don't look back.
People shout my name.

Ariel!
Casey!

Who am I?
Who am I?

"Leave me alone!"
Don't follow me.
Don't follow me.

What just happened?
What the fuck
just happened?

I don't get it.
I don't get it.

I jam the keys in
the ignition.
Start, car, start.
It does, no problem,
despite my quaking hands.

The space in front
is empty. I gun the car,
barely glancing

at the group splintering
in different directions.
Monica comes running,
waving to stop.
Dad is right on her heels.

Don't hurt her.
Don't hurt her.

He won't.
Gabe won't let him.
I drive right past.
Can't stop.
Won't stop.

How do I process this?
Maya McCabe.
Who is this woman
who claims to be my mom?
My mom?
Impossible.

Shows up.
At my game.
Just like that.
Materializes
out of thin air.
How the hell does that happen
after all this time?

And Casey? Who is she?

My Name

Is Ariel.
Ariel Pearson.
And my dad
is Mark Pearson.
Not Jason Baxter.

Why does Maya McCabe,
who so can't be my mother,
let alone my mom,
insist my name is Casey?
I've never even met
a Casey. I can't be one.

She's crazy.
That's it.
Maya McCabe is crazy.

My name is Ariel.
Air. Ari.
I'll even take Ari Fairy.

Which circles me
right back to Dad.
Mark Pearson.
Not Jason Baxter.
Right?
He couldn't have—
wouldn't have?—
woven my entire history
into a tapestry of lies.

I Drive

And drive, looking
in the rearview mirror,
but there's no sign
of anyone following me.

Head spinning, I cycle
through snapshots
of my past.
All those women.
My teachers.
Ma-maw and Pops.
None of them ever called
me Casey. None
I can remember.
No, I must be Ariel.

I drive until I notice
my gas gauge registers
under a half tank.
Work tomorrow.
School all week.
I have no money
and won't get paid
until the eighteenth.

That's Ariel thinking.

Casey's asking:
Work?
School?
You're kidding, right?

Pertinent Question

Who am I kidding?
How can I go to work?
How can I go to school?
How can I play basketball,
or hang out with my friends
or fall in love or dare
to dream about my future?

How can anything
be normal again?

In fact, what's normal?
How would I know
when I can't even be sure
who the fuck I am?

Casey. Casey Baxter.
Are you a part of me?
Are you who I am?

"This is who I am!"
That's what I want to yell,
but I need certainty.

I need the truth of me.
But who can I believe?

I Stop the Car

In a wide turnout,
try to decide where
to go from here.
My cell has buzzed
messages for over an hour.

I scroll through them while
I consider my next move.
Everyone wants to talk.

>   Dad: *WE HAVE TO TALK. COME HOME RIGHT NOW.*

At some point. But not yet.

>   From Syrah: *WOW. THAT WAS WEIRD. I'M HERE IF YOU*
>   *WANT TO TALK.*

Maybe later.

>   From Monica: *LO SIENTO, NOVIA. YOU'RE STILL*
>   *COMING OVER, YEAH? YOU CAN TALK TO ME, OKAY?*

I know. But not now.

And I can't even consider
a boisterous Torres crowd
when all I want to do is fall
into bed and sleep this away.

>   From Gabe: *AUNT ZELDA WOULD LIKE TO TALK TO*
>   *YOU. I KNOW YOU'RE UPSET. SO IS SHE.*

Upset

Yeah. I bet she is.
I get it completely.
Upset.
Confused.
In need of a giant dose
of truth.

I've always known
Dad was unreliable.
Self-centered.
Deceitful, yes, even that.

But there are lies,
and there are lies.
Identity isn't something
that should be trifled with.
I can't believe he's been
lying about who he is
all this time.

Oh yeah, and who I am, too.
Because as much
as I'd like to blame
this on Maya's insanity,
the name thing
somehow resonates.

Holy shit.
What if I really am
Casey Baxter?

There's One More Message

From an unknown number,
which can only belong
to Maya McCabe, and it does:

> YOUR FRIEND GAVE ME YOUR NUMBER. HOPE THAT'S
> OKAY. I'M SORRY I WASN'T MORE CIRCUMSPECT. TATI
> SAID I SHOULD WAIT, BUT I WAS SO EXCITED TO
> HAVE FINALLY FOUND YOU I JUST COULDN'T. YOU
> DON'T KNOW, CASEY, YOU CAN'T POSSIBLY KNOW
> HOW HARD I'VE LOOKED FOR YOU. NOTHING I TOLD
> YOU WAS A LIE. I'M SURE THIS COMES AS A SHOCK
> AND AM WILLING TO GIVE YOU AS MUCH TIME AS
> YOU NEED.

Friend, huh? Wonder
which so-called friend
that might have been.
Syrah, probably.
Who else would feel
the need to stick her nose
where it doesn't belong?

And what the hell does Maya
mean, as much time as I need?
To what? Decide she is, in
fact, my mother? A blood
test can prove that.

What does it take to prove
you're an actual mom?

Where Do I Go Now?

Not home. Not ready
to listen to Dad's bullshit
excuses and lies.

How could he do
this to me?

How can I ever believe
a single word
he utters again?

Not going to Syrah's
or Monica's.

What would I say?
Hey, don't sweat it.
(Santa please . . .)

Everything's cool.
Nothing's changed.
Oh, except
don't forget
to call me Casey.

Can I just keep being
Ariel instead?

I'll go to Zelda's.
We have something
in common: betrayal.

The GTO

Is nowhere in sight.
Gabe must be off somewhere,
and that's fine by me.
I'm here to commiserate
with Zelda and don't need
a distraction.

She must have been
waiting for me,
because she answers
my knock right away.
I realize this is the first
time I've been here
without Dad and/or Gabe.

> *I hoped you'd come,* she says.
> *How about a drink?*
> *God knows I've had a couple.*

I think it over, but decide,
"Better not. At some point
I'll have to drive. You go
right ahead, though."

I follow her inside,
where it looks like Christmas.
Red and green garlands sway
over doorways and windows,
and in the living room
is one of those pop-up trees,
all trimmed and lit.

"When did this happen?
How did this happen?"
It didn't look like this
last time I was here.
"Don't tell me it was elves."

> She snorts. *Wish it were*
> *that easy. Gabe and I have*
> *been working on it. He's done*
> *most of it, in fact. So maybe*
> *I do have an elf, though*
> *he's a pretty tall specimen.*

Christmas is still two weeks
away, but it's not like Dad
and I ever put up a tree
or hang stockings. I've never
even considered doing such
things. "Well, it's pretty."

> *It seemed prettier a few hours*
> *ago. Have a seat. There's stuff*
> *you should know.* She gulps
> whatever it is she's drinking.

I perch on the edge of the sofa,
rather than settle in. Not sure
I'll let myself feel comfortable
again. At least with discomfort
you're clear on the truth. Suddenly
I don't know why I came here.
What can I say, really?

The Feeling Must Be Mutual

Because even as Zelda sits
in the adjacent recliner,
a huge sheet of Arctic ice
coalesces in the silence
between us. To break it,
I ask, "Where's Gabe?"

> This is not what I'm here
> to talk about, but Zelda's all in.
> *Gabe went out to the ranch*
> *to visit Hillary. I'm being direct*
> *here, because it's one of the things*
> *you should know. Lately they've*
> *been spending time together.*

Glacier broken, a big chunk
sinks. *Glub-glub*. Gabe and
Hillary. Wow. Didn't see that
one coming. It's crushing,
but why? Not like he and I
are an actual couple, just
friends with privileges.

And only a few hours ago,
I thought I didn't care about
Syrah flirting with him.
Is it because that was out
in the open, and this definitely
wasn't? Are all guys sneaks?
"Why didn't he tell me?"

He should have, and I'm sure
he would have eventually.
I think he was waiting to see
how things panned out, but
honestly, he's smitten. Sorry
to drop this in your lap on top
of everything else, but today
is the day for coming clean.

"I guess it is. So you know,
I have no freaking clue how
Dad managed to keep me
in the dark about everything.
Obviously I'm stupid."

That makes two of us. But listen.
There's more. After you left
and your dad took off, I stayed
and talked to Ms. McCabe
for a few minutes. You need
to know that she was awarded
legal custody of you. As her story

goes, one December morning
when you were very little she was
at work when Mark—I can't think
of him as Jason—picked you up
from daycare. He was in the army
when he took off with you, and
that made him AWOL. Now
he's considered a deserter.

Awesome

Just keeps getting better
and better. "So now what?
Is he going to be arrested?"

> She says she hasn't called
> the authorities. I believe her,
> though I can't understand

> why not. Or maybe I can.
> She doesn't want to take
> a chance on pushing you away.

"I'm not hers to push anywhere.
Why did she track us down now,
anyway? Why, after all this time?"

> Honey, she swears she never
> stopped looking for you, though
> the trail got cold after a while.

"What if she's making it all up?
How hard could it have been?
What about Ma-maw and Pops?

She must have known them,
and I stayed with them a few
times. Easy to find me there."

> I have no answer to that, or
> any opinion about why now.
> All I know is, this is complicated.

Complicated

Zelda is the Queen of Understatement.
I mean, what am I supposed to do?

Go home?
Home?
What's that?

Get up and go to work tomorrow,
as if nothing unusual has happened?

Unusual?
More like
mind-bending.

And then on Monday, do I go to school,
practice layups and free throws afterward?

Algebra.
Basketball.
Just another day?

How do I figure out my identity
when I don't even know my name?

Ariel?
Casey?
Who the hell

am I?

My Sonora Anchor

Seems pretty flimsy
at the moment, and
it occurs to me that
to Dad "attachment"
is a foreign concept.

"So what happened
with Dad? Did he say
anything?"

> *I can't repeat most*
> *of it. I try not to use*
> *language like that,*
> *but what he said*
> *to Ms. McCabe was*
> *totally inappropriate. . . .*

"That much I already
guessed. But what did
he say to you? Did he offer
any kind of an explanation?"

> *Denial, denial, denial.*
> *That's what he offered,*
> *and when I didn't swallow*
> *a word of it, he stormed*
> *off. Left the rest of us*
> *standing there gawking.*

The Word

That springs to mind concerning
Dad is "coward." I've never before
thought about him in that way.
Not sure why not. He was never

exactly hero material, but he was
all I had, so I guess I respected
him for that. I've lost all respect now.
"So what are you going to do?"

> Zelda shrugs. *The quickest*
> *way to destroy a relationship*
> *is dishonesty. I love your dad,*
> *or thought I did, and believed*
>
> *he loved me, too. Love can weather*
> *small deceptions, but this . . .*
> She shakes her head. *To have*
> *absolutely no clue who the person*
>
> *you've devoted eight months of your life*
> *to really is? That's hard to think*
> *about, and trusting him—or anyone—*
> *after this will be impossible, I'm afraid.*

Eight months of your life? What
about the entire seventeen years
of my existence? Still, I feel sorry
for her. She doesn't deserve this.

Nobody does.

Trying to Process

Everything will take
a while. A long while.
Zelda and I sit in silent
consideration.

Thoughts ping-pong
inside my skull, and the pain
of that is very real.
I've spent years denying
my mother's existence.
Years wading through
resentment, completely
sucked into the lie
that she didn't want me.

Years with absolutely zero
doubt I was Ariel Pearson.
What else don't I know?
That terrifies me.

I think about Maya McCabe.
The excitement in her eyes.
Eyes, as I recall them,
the approximate same shade
as mine. And her hair, though
it's straighter, is the exact
color of mine.

"I look like her, don't I?"

No hesitation. *Yes, you do.*

"I . . . I just . . . I don't . . ."

> *I know exactly how you feel.*
> *But now Zelda takes the time*
> *to study me. Nope. Wrong.*
> *I can't possibly know how*
> *you feel. I'm sorry, Casey.*

"Don't call me that! I hate
that name." I'm Ariel.

> *Really? I think it's cute. You*
> *should probably try it on for*
> *size. It sort of fits you, actually.*

Me? Casey?
Casey.
Casey.
Casey and Maya.

"Dad never called her Maya.
He called her Jenny, when
he bothered to call her anything
other than dyke, bitch, or whore.
Do you think that woman with
spiky hair is Maya's partner?"

> *Not her partner. Her wife.*

"So she *is* a lesbian."

> *Apparently. Does it matter?*

I Don't See How It Can

I might be a lesbian,
or at least halfway gay.

Why should it bother me
at all that my mother

is married to a woman?
But somehow it seems to.

I guess it's been such a big part
of Dad's chronicle for so long.

He made me choke it down—
a heaping spoonful of bitterness.

At the moment I just want to puke
it back up, spit it in Dad's face.

"How the fuck could he do this to me?"
My eyes sting and I burrow them

into the palms of my hands. "Holy
shit, Zelda! My entire childhood

is gone. He made me believe I was
someone I wasn't. He made me

believe he was all I needed. Not
friends. Not family. Not my . . ."

Mom

Mom.
I know the word.
Can't comprehend its meaning.

I've seen moms on TV.
Handsome women with scripted
senses of humor who forgive
their kids' mistakes, regardless
of how huge and in-your-face
the infractions are. Yeah, right.
TV moms don't count.

I've seen moms in the park.
Pushing their kids
on the merry-go-round, wearing
permanent smiles and texting
who-knows-who. Beneath
Sephora makeup and Pilates bods,
park moms are real
plastic.

I've seen moms at school.
Delivering forgotten homework
or lunches, or birthday cupcakes,
all decked out in fancy jogging
suits and perfect ponytails,
quick to hug, slow to scowl,
at least in that setting.
School moms know how
to make an entrance.

I've seen all these moms
over the years, and none quite
measured up to my romanticized,
highly stylized vision
of the mom I pretended
belonged to me.
I can still picture her:

She's young and pretty.
Her favorite outfit is well-worn
jeans, a soft angora sweater.
Her eyes are deep ponds
of wisdom. If I stare into them
long enough, I'll find the answers
I need. She's tough and bold,
but her lap is my haven,
and her hands are cups
of tenderness. When
she holds me, my thirst
for home is satisfied.

I imagined her.
Yearned for her.
Went to sleep crying
for her. Eventually,
I gave up on her.

What am I supposed
to do with her now?

I Leave Zelda

Quietly drowning
her bewilderment
in tumblers of alcohol.
I must not inherently
be a drunk, or I would
have joined her. Escape

seems preferable
to confrontation, but
it's the latter I go in search
of, and I have zero idea
what I'll face when I walk
in the door at home.

Passing the Triple G,
I spy the distant silhouette
of Gabe's GTO parked
in front of the house, and
a sharp sense of loss slices
into my solar plexus.

But I'm not sure
if Gabe is to blame.
I guess, thinking back over
the past couple of weeks,
he was pulling away,
but it was a subtle change
and not one I noticed.
What does that say
about me?

Oh, How I Wish

That losing Gabe
(who I never exactly
"had," or even wanted
to) was my biggest
problem. If I

concentrate

solely on that,
direct all my worry
and energy there,
will the too-immense-to-

imagine

problem just go away?
For years and years
all I wanted was
a solid home, and not
one I had to

invent

in my mind over
and over again.
But not in my wildest
dreams did I ever

envision

the scope of
Dad's deception,
and no matter what
I do or want, there's
no way my life won't

change.

Dad's at the House

When I get there. I expected that.
But the pandemonium inside

comes as a shock, don't ask me
why. I should've guessed.

Dad's running around in panic mode,
stuffing personal possessions into

a duffel bag. Three large suitcases
already clog the hall by the front door.

"What are you doing, Dad?" I ask,
though it's pretty damn obvious

he's making plans to disappear. Again.
Well, he's going without me this time.

>He pauses his packing long enough
>to answer. *We have to go now, Ari.*

>*I'm sorry, but you'll have to leave
>your car here. Too easy to trace.*

"Nope. Count me out. I'm staying
right here, along with my car.

I'm not running away, and neither
are you. Can we just get real for once?"

I am getting real, and we are getting
the hell out. This is all your fault.

Oh, you just had to get your ass on TV,
didn't you? You just had to fuck things up.

What the serious hell? "Me? You want
to blame this on me? Are you totally

out of your goddamn mind? You—"
I don't see his backhand coming.

It connects with my right cheek,
snapping my mouth closed around

the remainder of the sentence.
Shut the fuck up. Don't you dare

talk to me like that. Just who
the hell do you think you are?

The look in his eyes defies
anything human. "Nobody."

That's exactly right. He's pulling
in breath like it's an effort. *Nobody.*

His hands clench, and experience
whispers this could go from bad

to much worse.

I Lift My Hand

To my throbbing cheek,
hope to attract a small
measure of sympathy,
as I start a slow backward

creep, one foot behind
the other. He notices
and when he starts toward
me, I get ready to run.

"Is my name Casey Baxter?"
The simple question stops
his approach, and the concrete
set of his jaw softens.

>   *Not anymore.*

"Who is Ariel Pearson?
And Mark? Who is he?"
Dad's shoulders drop.
The tide of peril recedes.

>   *Look, Ari. There are things*
>   *you don't know, and shouldn't.*

"You mean, like you went
AWOL and officially now
you're a deserter?" Carefully.
Must play this carefully.

>   *Who the fuck told you that?*

Make It Personal

"Zelda. And what about her?
Is she just another use-
her-and-toss-her woman?
I thought she was different."

> *No such thing as different.*
> *All women are the same.*

"Come on, Dad. You don't believe
that. Zelda's special. I can tell.
Sonora's special, too, and I don't
want to leave. I love it here."

> *Too bad. We can't stay.*

"We can. Maya hasn't called
the authorities, and I don't think
she will, unless we disappear again.
She won custody of me, did you

know that? So I'm pretty sure
not only are you a deserter, but
technically you're a kidnapper, too."

> *No, goddamn it! She was leaving*
> *us for that woman, that Tatiana.*
> *The one who was with her today.*
> *If she really cared about you,*
> *she wouldn't have brought her.*

435

Spin

He's good at it, and I know
that, but what he just said
might contain an element

of fact. Still, I want to know
some things, the main one
being, "Who are Ariel

and Mark, Dad? Please
tell me the truth. I think
I deserve that much."

He sighs. *Okay. But then we leave.*
He plants his butt on the arm
of the sofa, waits for me to sit.

*You probably don't remember
because you were so little, but
a few weeks after we left North*

*Carolina we were in an accident
in Virginia. You were fine, but I got
pretty busted up. The woman who*

*stopped to help was named Leona.
We lived with her for several months,
while my broken bones healed up.*

"I remember her, but only bits
and pieces. She took care of me
while you were in the hospital."

*That's right. Well, Leona was
a widow. She lost her husband
and little girl in a train wreck.*

Oh my God. The lights snap
on. "Mark and Ariel Pearson.
I remember photos . . ."

*It was Leona who started calling
you Ariel. You reminded her
so much of her little girl, and*

*I think she was a tad tetched
in the head, which was why
she wasn't working right then.*

*She named her baby after Ariel
in that Disney movie, The Little
Mermaid, and she used to watch it*

*with you. You loved it because
you were the spitting image of that
mermaid. Well, except for the tail.*

Not sure if that's a weird
attempt at humor or if he's
serious, but I do have a vague

recollection of sitting in a woman's
comfy lap watching that movie
while she hummed along to the music.

Makes Sense

At two years old I absorbed the name
Ariel. Yeah, but what about Dad?

"So how did you become Mark?"
I can pretty much figure out the why.

> I needed a way to protect you,
> and he had no use for his identity
>
> anymore. Leona had everything
> necessary in her filing cabinet—
>
> social security cards, birth certificates.
> You and I became the Pearsons.

Calculating bastard. "I see, and
did Leona know you took them?"

> I think she kind of liked the idea
> of her family living on in some way.
>
> Like I said, she was messed up.
> In fact, at one point she tried to
>
> off herself. That's the main reason
> I decided it was time to leave.

There's truth here somewhere,
but I sense doublespeak, too.

One Question Answered

Truthfully or not,
others appear like
rabbits pulled out
of a magician's hat.

"What about Ma-maw
and Pops? They always
called me Ariel. Didn't
they know I was Casey?"

I can see the wheels
rotating in his head
and expect yet another
circuitous response.

> Instead he answers
> reasonably. *They knew,*
> *but went along with it.*
> *There was a lot at stake.*
>
> *They're good Southern*
> *Baptists, for one thing,*
> *and weren't about to let*
> *you go live with your mother*
>
> *and her female "friend."*
> *But they also knew sending*
> *me back to the army*
> *would've been the end of me.*

The End

Why not just spice up
the narrative with a big
dose of melodrama? "Come
on. Not like they would've
put you in front of a firing
squad for going AWOL."

Shit. Flipped his switch.

>   *That is not what I mean, girl.*
>   *You don't know the things*
>   *I saw, serving my country*
>   *in godforsaken third-world*
>   *armpits. You don't know what*
>   *it's like to duck when you hear*
>   *a sonic boom, to avoid July*
>   *Fourth celebrations because*
>   *fireworks trigger panic attacks.*
>
>   *You can't possibly imagine*
>   *what it's like to get turned on*
>   *by the scent of blood, to break*
>   *down at the smell of burning*
>   *rubber or singed hair.*
>
>   *Don't you dare lecture me as if*
>   *your life has been so fucking*
>   *miserable, when all I've done for*
>   *the last fifteen years is sacrifice*
>   *my needs in favor of yours.*

Dressed-Down

In proper military fashion.
"Sorry, Dad. You're right.
I wouldn't understand
any of those things."

Here I am, apologizing,
like I always seem to do.
There's something seriously
wrong with my psyche

because "sacrifice" paired
with "Dad" defines oxymoronic.
And I'm not sure exactly
what I'm sorry about.

> *Good. Then throw whatever you*
> *can't live without into a suitcase.*
> *I don't trust that bitch to keep*
> *quiet and I'm not going to jail.*

My head is shaking before
my mouth even opens.
"I already told you, no way."
It's the first time I've ever

straight-up defied my dad,
and it scares me that
he might in fact go and
leave me here alone.

"Look, Dad, I love you.
I really hope you'll decide
to stay and work through this.
It will be okay. Things don't

have to change, at least
not that much. For the first
time in my life I feel planted
somewhere. Please don't try

and uproot me again. Now
I get your reasons for relocating
so often, but that doesn't change
how hard it was. For once

I have friends, people I care
about. Commitments. A job,
even, though I've barely started
it yet. I have an actual life."

You call those people friends?
A Mexican—he spits the word—
and a boyfriend who's cheating
on you. Bet you didn't know that.

"But you did? Thanks for
telling me, and hate to spoil
the surprise, but I happen
to know about Gabe and Hillary."

I'm Glad I Do

He wanted so much
to hurt me with that.
He was almost giddy,
in fact. I dare to look
him straight in the eye,
and the storm of emotions
churning there almost
makes me back down.

Rage.
Pain.
Confusion.
Disgust.
Hate.
Overwhelming hate.

You want to be with her,
don't you? I can't believe
after all we've been through
together you'd choose that
goddamn whore over me.

"What are you talking
about? I did not choose
anyone over you. I just
can't stomach the idea
of living on the run.
How did I not realize
that's what we were doing?"

Lies, Lies, Lies

How could I have been
so freaking dense?

> Okay, fine. Desert me, then.
> That's how much I mean to you?
> Use me, then throw me away,
> like a snot-smeared Kleenex?

"Nice visual, Dad. Awesome.
But the honest-to-God truth
is it was you who used me."

> How do you figure that?
> Exactly how did I use you?

"You used me as revenge,
a pawn in your game
of payback. You used me
as a means to an end,
dangling me like a lure
in your meal ticket
fishing derby.

Mostly I think you used
me so you wouldn't spend
your life alone. Didn't you
realize at some point
I'd become an adult?

You can't own people,
and that includes me."

I'm Shredded

How do I reconcile loving
my father with despising what
he's done? What happens next?
And who are we now?

I can't stay here any longer.
He's masterful at what he'd call
persuasion, and I won't take
a chance on his coercing me
into leaving with him.

"You do what you have to do.
I'm spending the night with
Monica. It's her birthday."
I make up my mind without
even thinking it over.
She's my one constant.

I can see his brain at work,
searching for the exact
retort to turn me around.
And, here it comes.

> *Okay, then, Casey . . .*
> He hisses the name, malice
> shadowing his voice.
> *You run along to your beaner*
> *friend. I wash my hands of you,*
> *you ungrateful fucking brat.*

The Words Pierce

Like rusty tines,
and all I can do is bleed
silently, any verbal response
futile. I push past him and go
to grab clothes and my toothbrush.
Should I throw everything
into a suitcase, like Dad suggested?

If I don't and he takes off,
how long will I have to collect
it? I don't even know when
the rent is due or how it gets paid,
or what company provides
the power. I'm far, far away
from being anything like an adult.
I can't possibly live on my own.

Falling apart, I flop onto my bed,
cover my head with the pillow
I've slept on almost every night
since we moved in here.

In the space of a single
afternoon, the entire fabric
of my already fragile existence
has turned into tatters.
"I hate you, Maya McCabe!"
I scream into the pillowcase-
covered foam lumps.
"Why couldn't you
leave us alone?"

I Sink Into

The mattress and it sinks
into me that, whatever
her reasons, she has appeared

and, regardless, the only
direction I (or anyone)
can move is forward.

This day is almost over.
Tomorrow has yet
to materialize, but

that will definitely happen
unless I choose to end
it all right now, right here.

I've got way too much
to live for, and if that means
a fight, so be it. Dad might be

a coward, but that weakness
isn't genetic and I'll be damned
if I'm giving up now.

Pretty sure Dad's used
our entire luggage collection,
so I dig under my bed

for last year's secondhand
backpack, stuff in as much
as I reasonably can. I also grab

this year's new Walmart-special
backpack, which carries
my schoolbooks and supplies.

Whatever my living arrangements
stay or become, I plan on showing
up right on time for classes

on Monday morning. If I find
I don't have a bedroom here,
I'll stay with Monica or Syrah or,

who knows? Maybe Zelda will
let me move in. If all else fails,
there's my car or the tack room

at the barn. I'll go to work
tomorrow morning, not to prove
I'm too grown up to fail,

but simply because I need
to start earning my way. If Dad
disappears (oh, after everything

we've experienced together,
and so many times I feared
that's exactly what would happen?),

at least I'll have a measure
of independence. And then, one
day, one step forward, at a time.

Resolve

Is an amazing thing.
Too bad mine fails
almost immediately,
mostly because I totally
underestimated my father.

> *You've packed your things.*
> *That's good. I've loaded*
> *the rest in the car already.*
> *It's full, but there's room—*

"No, Dad! Haven't you
heard a single word I said?
I. Am. Not. Running. Away."

> He changes tactics, digs for
> some semblance of tears.
> *You hate me. I don't blame you.*

"I don't hate you.
It'd be easier if I did.
But I don't exactly
like you right now,
either. It'll take time
to sort out my feelings."

Not to mention the details
of the last fifteen years.
Every memory now requires
careful reexamination.

It'll be an exhausting,
but necessary, process
and once it's over
I'll have to let things go.
I can't launch a future
by wallowing in the past.

"I really wish you'd change
your mind and try to work
things out here. There's your
job to consider, and Zelda, and . . ."
As I watch, his demeanor
changes completely,
from injured pup
to rabid dog.

> *You're a liar, just like your*
> *mother. I know where you're*
> *really going. You're backstabbing*
> *me to take up with that cold-*
> *hearted whore, aren't you?*

"No, Dad, I'm not."
I sling a backpack over
each shoulder, hoping
he'll let me reach the door.
He does, but as I open it,

> *he says clearly and purposefully,*
> *I should've killed that bitch*
> *when I had the chance.*

Goose Bumps Lift

All over my body, and it
has nothing to do with exiting
the warmth of the house,
and everything to do with
the invisible menace that follows
me into the crisp starlit envelope
of this December night.

The tips of my nose and ears
sizzle from the cold, but it's
not far to the Focus, whose
engine is still warm. The first
thing I do is lock the doors.
Then I pump up the heater,
jack up the music, and take
a moment to text Monica,
let her know I'm on my way.

I've always hated this time
of year. The truncated days,
late dawning to early dark;
the claw of bitter air, when
often whatever secondhand
coat I called my own was
threadbare, hardly there.

Ditto the lumpy sleeping
bags that kept us from
freezing when we had to
sleep in the car, exhalations
painting frost pictures
on the window glass.

But worse was the holiday
cheer, which rarely touched
me personally. Other kids
went to shopping malls,
sat on Santa's lap, asking
for things their parents
already knew they wanted.

If I ever believed in Santa,
it was before my conscious
memory, and all those shiny
presents with big bows?
Rarely were there any for
me under a tree, and those
that did appear if we happened
to be living with one of Dad's
women were afterthoughts—
dollar-store dolls or teddy bears.

I've read that people often
choose this time of year
to die, and I don't wonder why.
Especially if they're alone,
or grieving, or just damn tired
of trudging through another
day, and the thought of crossing
the threshold into another year
sucks the soul right out of them.

I Turn Up the Radio

Just as the station goes to a break,
and the commercial happens
to feature my least favorite
Christmas song ever:

"Santa Claus Is Coming to Town."

I hate this song, always have,
and somewhere I've forever
understood it had something
to do with my mother. Mom.
Trying that one on for size, too.
Maya McCabe. I think she used
to sing that song to me, back
when she and I shared Christmases.

Were there only two?

Every December when Dad
and I stopped long enough
to notice, I'd see other kids
and their moms singing
Christmas carols together.
Only I didn't have a mom.

I wanted one then.

Wanted one more than anything,
as long as she wasn't a dyke
whore who tried to fool me
into believing she loved me

by doing regular mom stuff
like singing "Santa Claus Is Coming
to Town" and decorating
a cut-down-dead tree with
cheap homemade ornaments.

That, according to Dad.

How the hell could he do
what he did? To Maya McCabe,
who I don't even know,
but, more, to me? The life he built—
all that running, all those women,
every shredded chapter—

was pure fiction.

What am I supposed to think
now? Is it even remotely possible
that my mother—mom?—
will be here for this and future
Christmases? What am I supposed
to do? Go shopping with her?
Bake cookies together?

Talk about lesbian love?

Musing

I drive toward town
well under the limit,
unsure about wildlife
and my ability to miss it.

A vehicle approaches
from the opposite direction.
Fast. Too fast.
And swerving,
zigzagging side to side
across the white line.

As it nears, I recognize
Garrett's pickup truck,
and a stray thought
dashes through my head—
is that bottle still rolling
around in the back?

He passes now,
and his head rotates
toward the window.
Even though I can't see
his face, an outbreak
of anxiety strikes well
before I notice his brake
lights in my mirror.

Holy hell,
he's turning
around.

Whatever he's got
in mind can't be good.
What does
he have in mind?

I grab my phone
to keep it in close
reach, go ahead
and give the Focus
a big shot of gas.
Come on, baby.

Once I get off this road
and onto the highway,
mayhem will be less likely,
and I've got a decent lead.

Still, before long
here he comes,
screaming up over
a slight rise, bright lights
on and blinding.

I pick up speed,
but he's right on
my bumper and
and I don't know
what to do or how
to quiet the loud
percussion of my heart
thudding in my veins.

Flashback

Dad's driving.
It's a strange car.
I'm in the backseat.
With a dog.
Dog?
No, puppy.
No, somewhere
in between.
A young dog
with a silky golden coat.

I'm scared.
Crying.
The dog whines
at the lights in the rear
window. Bright lights.
I plant my face
into the dog's shoulder.
"Boo," I whisper.
Boo?

Dad cusses.
The car behind us honks.
Rides our bumper.
Starts to pass.
Dad swerves.
Slams on the brakes.
The other car goes sideways,
trying to avoid us.
Crashes.
Dad laughs.

Real Time

A vehicle starts to pass.
Close. Too close.
We're almost touching.

Only when I glance
to my left it isn't the hulk
of a pickup.

It's a car.
A familiar car.
Dad's LeSabre.

And it isn't Garrett
behind the wheel.

"Dad?"
I say it out loud,
but I don't know why.
He can't hear me.

Can he see me?
Surely he knows
it's me.
I honk once.

His head doesn't turn.

I honk again,
longer.
Still he stares
straight ahead.
Pass already, would you?

Suddenly,
he cuts me off.
I swerve.
Slam on the brakes.

Only this time
it's me who overcorrects.
Goes sideways.
Manages to avoid the ditch
on my right.

Barely.

Skids left.
Manages to avoid
the LeSabre's rear bumper.

Barely.

The Focus hits
the left-hand shoulder.
Sideways.

The Focus stops suddenly,
slams my forehead
against the steering wheel.

Brain spinning
inside my skull, I reach
for my phone—still
there on the seat.

Hit the first number
in memory. "Help me."

Dark Out Here

Dark.
But where is here?
Cold out here.
Cold.
But where is here?

I open my eyes.
Work hard to remember.

Car.
In my car.
Stopped.
Something's wrong.
Why am I sideways?

Ditch.
What ditch?
And why is my car
tilted into it?

Most of all,
why does my head hurt?

I reach up, touch
the spot above my eyes
that has swollen into
an awful knot.

Oh my God.
I remember.
Dad.

Headlights appear.
Approach.
Quickly.
Slower.
What if it's Dad?
Did he come back?

I should move my car.
I reach for the key.
The engine starts easily.
But the tires spin
uselessly.

I think I need
a tow truck.

The other car
brakes to a stop.
It's an old GTO with
a new paint job.

Gabe hurries over,
takes a good look
at the position of the car.
Opens the passenger door.

> *Ariel. Are you okay?*
> *Does anything feel broken?*

Everything but bones.

> *Holy shit. Look at your head!*

That Cracks Me Up

Not that anything's funny.
Not my head.
Not that I'm not okay.
"I'm great. How are you?"
Lame humor. Guess I'm not dying.

> *You don't look great.*
> *What happened?*

"Garrett was having
a little fun with me.
Except it wasn't Garrett.
Turned out it was my dad."

> *Garrett? Your dad?*
> *What are you talking about?*
> *Wait. Let's get you out of there.*
> *Can you unbuckle your seat belt?*

I fumble, but manage it,
and Gabe tugs me gently
across the seat and out
the door. He sits me
next to the car, wraps
me in the warmth
of his jacket to fight
the cold, and possible
shock. Uses a flashlight
to assess potential injuries.

"Hey. How did you know
to come looking for me?"

You called. Asked for help.
I didn't know you were
out here, though. I was on
my way to your house, and
to tell you the truth, I was

preparing myself to kick
your dad's ass. He studies
my face closer. Looks like
I should've gotten there
sooner. Bastard. Listen.

We should probably take
you into the ER. You could
have a concussion.

"Nope. Huh-uh. I've had
a shitty enough day. Not
going to deal with doctors,
too. Anyway, what would
they do for a concussion?
Keep me warm and make
me rest, right? I can do
that anywhere."

Ariel, I really think—

"No hospital! Other than
a headache, I feel okay.
I could probably even drive."

Yeah, Except

The Focus can't go anywhere,
and even if it could, Gabe
isn't about to let me behind the wheel.

       Take care of your car tomorrow.
       I'll drive you wherever you want.
       Can you stand up okay?

He helps me to my feet and into
the GTO, carefully, tenderly,
as if I might shatter. Maybe I will.

"Will you take me to Monica's?
She's probably worried about me.
That's where I was going when . . ."

I give him the lowdown,
at least what I can remember.
Everything's a little foggy.

       Your dad did this? Ran you
       off the road? On purpose?
       He could've killed you.

"I think that's what he had
in mind." The words exit
my mouth without conscious

thought. I can't quite believe
he'd hurt me, but what he did
was definitely deliberate.

Deliberate

De
li
be
rate.

Oh
my
serious
God.

My
dad
tried
to
kill
me.

Did he?
Maybe.
Maybe not.
Maybe
it was
an accident
after all.

So
why
didn't
he stop?

No.
No way.

Dad
has
many
faults
but
he
isn't
capable
of
homicide.

But now
his words
come back
to me.

I
should
have
killed
the
bitch
when
I
had
the
chance.

I Jerk the Door Open

Lean out as far as I can
before my stomach empties
itself of what little I've eaten
today. Gut clenching and
releasing, I heave and heave.

Finally, the nausea subsides
and I chance sitting up again,
shaky and, I'm sure, pale.
"Sorry. I think I managed to miss
your new leather seat, though."

> *Don't apologize! But thanks*
> *for avoiding the seat. I'll go*
> *put a note on your car. Do you*
> *have your phone, or did you*
> *leave it in the Focus?*

Phone? I called Gabe, at least
he says I did. . . . "I think it's on
the seat, or maybe the floor. Can you
grab it and both my backpacks, please?"
Most of my earthly possessions
are inside them. I'll have to go back

for what's left. But then what?
Because whatever Dad did
or didn't do tonight, he's gone.
He'll vanish like he did before
with one notable exception.

He Left Me Behind

Just like I always worried
he would when I was little.

Now, at least, I'm old enough
to take care of myself. Maybe.

Gabe returns, tosses my stuff
onto the backseat. All but my phone.

>That, he hands to me. *You can
>call the cops on the way to town.*

My head begins a slow right-
left motion. "Can't call the cops."

Run into the alfalfa fields. Hide.
No police ever. Programming.

>But Gabe's having none of it.
>*Why not? You can't let that bastard*

>*get away with this, Ariel. Who*
>*knows what he might do next?*

He's right. I'm wrong. As usual.
"But he's still my dad, Gabe.

If I call the cops and they catch
him, he'll probably go to jail."

>*Which is exactly where he belongs.*
>*Look, either you call 9-1-1 or I will.*

He Starts the Car

But waits for me to dial,
and I realize he's totally serious
about me doing this, so I comply.

"Hello? I've been in an accident."

The cop on duty asks
if I'm injured, and do I require
an ambulance, but when
I tell him I'm mostly okay,
he informs me that
this isn't really an emergency.

"What if I told you someone
purposely cut me off?"

He inquires if anyone else
saw what happened,
and when I say no,
he invites me to come in
and file a police report,
but without witnesses
it's my word
versus the other guy's.

Now he asks a series
of questions designed,
I think, to shift the blame
onto my shoulders.
He sounds like he thinks
I'm making it all up.

Have you been drinking tonight?

"Nope."

Are you sure another car was involved?

"Positive."

Could this be a domestic dispute?

"In a manner of speaking."

Were you fighting with your boyfriend?

"I don't have a boyfriend."

But you know the other driver?

"Yes."

Okay, who was it then?

Damn. Mistake. Can't say.

Hello? Are you still there?

"Uh-huh."

So, who cut you off?

"Never mind."

I Hang Up

Gabe shoots me
a *what just happened?*
kind of look.
I shrug.
"He said I need a witness."

It strikes me I might
have an unreliable one,
if I actually want
one, not that Garrett
would be likely to testify
even if he did see
Dad rocket by.

"Can we just go now,
please?"

> *They really won't do*
> *something about this?*

"Apparently not.
But I don't really care.
The last thing I want
right now is to confront
Dad, with or without
the police involved."

As Gabe eases the GTO
onto the highway, I realize
how true that is. And . . .
I'm crying. Damn.
"I can't believe any of this."

Gabe Reaches Across

The console, takes my hand.
I'm grateful for his touch. Remember
suddenly his touch is no longer mine.

> *I knew your dad was irrational.*
> *The look in his eyes when he went*
> *after your mother . . .*
>
> *And just now, when I saw your*
> *face, I realized he was abusive.*
> *I can't believe I didn't see it before.*

"Abusive?" Does running
me off the road count
as abuse? "What do you mean?"

> *I mean, I don't think that mark*
> *on your cheek came from your steering*
> *wheel. It looks like a fresh handprint.*

Beneath both forming bruises,
my face ignites embarrassment.
"It's nothing. He was upset."

> *Upset? You're kidding, right?*
> *You can't possibly be defending him.*
> *Ariel, that man is dangerous.*

It's true. He is. Maybe even
psychopathic. But then again,
"You're dangerous, too."

That Stops Him Cold

He doesn't say anything for a long
few seconds. Finally, he nods.

> I see how you might think so.
> I knew last night bothered you.
>
> Here's the thing. I absolutely
> have the ability to hurt someone.
>
> But other than sanctioned Golden
> Gloves matches, I've never gone
>
> looking for a fight. I will defend
> myself if I must, or someone who
>
> can't defend themselves if they're
> in trouble. But I would never, not
>
> ever in my lifetime, strike a woman
> unless she was out for my blood,
>
> and capable of drawing it. And
> hitting my own child? Impossible.

"Lots of parents hit their kids,
Gabe." Still sticking up for Dad?

> That doesn't make it right. Don't
> ever believe abuse is okay. It's not.

Abuse?

I'm not abused.
Am I?

Dad's only hit me
a few times.
Open-handed.

And only when I
deser—
Wait.

I really was thinking
deserved it.

But that's not right.
I never deserved it.
Never deserved
his ugly words, either.
Not to mention
what happened tonight.

Oh my God.
I'm a mess.

"Hey, Gabe.
You're right.
But can we
please talk
about something
else right now?"

I'm bending.
Don't want to
snap in half.

> He senses as much.
> *Okay. Like what?*

Thinking. Thinking.
Oh, right.
I've got it.
"Hillary."

> His Adam's apple
> bobs when
> he swallows.
> *How did . . .*
> *Zelda told you.*

"She told me first.
Dad confirmed.
Guess I was the last
one to know, huh?
Stupid me."

Stupid
abused
me.

He Starts to Sputter

So I relieve him a little.
"Hey. It's okay. I get it.
I just wish you would
have told me yourself.
I really felt like an idiot
for not noticing. Walking
around with my eyes
shut, as Pops used to say."

> *I'm sorry, Ariel. Truly I am.*
> *That's what I wanted to talk*
> *about after the game today.*
> *It blew me away how hard*
> *she and I hit it off. I mean,*
> *we have so little in common,*
> *and . . . Are you mad at me?*

"For what? Not like either
of us made any promises
to each other. I'll admit I
was a little hurt at first,
mostly because it felt like
you were sneaking around.
I never hid Monica from you."

> *Did you ever tell her you*
> *and I had sex?* Point-blank,
> he calls me out. Deservedly.

"No. But I plan to. Tonight.
It's the right time for honesty."

The Exchange

Is a good one. We come away
from it still friends, only no longer
with privileges. Okay by me.

I've got way too many supersize
complications to deal with anyway,
not to mention a small one or two.

"So . . ." I begin as he pulls up in front
of Monica's house. "I'm supposed to
be at work by eight tomorrow morning.

It's kind of early to bum a ride, I know,
but I'm not sure who else to ask. Syrah
might be able to, but she'd hate me."

> *You're planning on exercising horses*
> *tomorrow when your face looks like*
> *that? Might not be a good idea. I can tell—*

"I already missed today, and I'm going
to need the money. The horses won't
care how my face looks, anyway."

> *But maybe you're, you know, brain*
> *damaged or something. He grins.*
> *More brain damaged, that is.*

"Very funny. It's just a knot, and I've
always heard the real problems stem
from bumps that push in, not out."

If you say so. Okay, I'll pick you up
at seven thirty, drop you off, and do
something about your car. Sound good?

"Sounds early and generous and kind, and . . .
thank you. I'm lucky to have you
in my life, even with Hillary attached."

He's quiet for a moment. *Remember*
a while back when I told you I didn't
care who you loved? That wasn't true.

I might have thought it was then,
but once we spent some time together
I realized I wanted you all to myself.

You were truthful with me. I should've
returned the favor. Who knows?
Things might be very different now.

I really don't have the right to say
this, but your honesty is one of the best
things about you. Don't let go of it

in favor of the easy way out. Lies tend
to creep up and bite you in the ass.
I'm proof of that, and on a much larger

scale, so is your dad. I don't know what
he told you, but I listened in on Zelda
and your mom. Have you spoken to Maya?

I Assure Him

That I have not in a tone
of voice that denies the fact
that we're as close as we are—
or used to be. Were we?

"I don't know what to say.
I don't know what to do.
I don't know why she has
to show up now and make
a total disaster of my life."

> Force of habit, or honest
> affection, he laces our fingers
> together. *I know this came*
> *as a surprise. But while*
> *you're thinking about your*
> *life, have you considered hers?*

I yank free. "You calling
me selfish? Because here's
the thing. I've never, *not*
ever, had that opportunity.
What, in my lifetime,
has given me anything
to hold on to, to fight for?

The only valuable object
I've ever owned is the car
stuck in the ditch out there
in Bumfuckville. As for people,
the few true connections

I've been allowed are all right
here in Sonora. Now I'm
expected to sacrifice those,
because of the woman who
sacrificed me? No damn way."

> *Okay. Okay. But just so you*
> *know, "bitter" doesn't suit*
> *you. I'll shut up now because*
> *I don't want to upset you any*
> *more than you already are.*
> *Except one last thought:*
> *Maybe your anger is misdirected?*

Maybe. But does it matter?
"Thanks. I'll consider that."
I open the passenger door,
try not to slam it shut behind
me. Before I can stomp off
into the night, and up the walk,
Gabe pops out of the GTO.

> *Wait, okay?* He comes over,
> pulls me against him, hugs me
> tightly. *I don't want to leave*
> *while you're still pissed. Timing*
> *is critical. I'm sorry ours proved*
> *to be out of sync, my pretty Ariel.*
> *Or should I call you Casey?*

I'll Wrestle with That

For a while. Maybe a long
while. "No. Not Casey.

Not yet. It's sort of sinking
in that I'm not Ariel Pearson.

Facts are facts, whether
or not they make any sense

at the moment. The weird
thing is, I can more easily accept

the idea that Dad is Jason Baxter
than the theory that I'm Casey."

> He takes a deep breath. *Okay,*
> *I'm going to try this again,*
>
> *and please listen. You're reeling.*
> *I get it. I would be, too. But for one*
>
> *short minute think about how it*
> *would feel to go to pick up your child*
>
> *after work. Only she's gone, and you*
> *have no idea how to find her.*
>
> *Maybe your mom made mistakes.*
> *But she didn't deserve that. She loves*
>
> *you. I believe that. Why don't you*
> *give her a chance? Hey. Look at me.*

Beneath the Cool Glare

Of the streetlight
I look up into those
crazy eyes, realize
it just might be
the last time I do.

I understand Gabe's
not mine to kiss, but
I'm steamrolled
by lust and would
give pretty much
anything to be
with him right now.

I'm morally bankrupt.
I rest my cheek upon
the rippling sinews
of his chest, where
his heart drums in
primitive song, and
when he folds me in
tighter, tears well.

It occurs to me suddenly
that it's not sex I'm after,
though that would be
nice, and accomplish
what I need—the solace
of another's touch.

I Cry into His Shirt

For a solid five minutes,
wishing all the hollow spaces
would fill with the compassion
he offers. But now I remember

that only a few steps farther,
Monica is waiting, and she's exactly
what I need. I push him away. "Go
on. I'm not mad at you anymore."

> *Sure. Soak my shirt. Use me,*
> *then discard me. It's okay.*
> The echo of Dad's recent outburst
> is an unfortunate coincidence.

It makes me cringe, though I know
Gabe's only kidding. Dad wasn't.
The profound sense of loss I felt
earlier is shallower now, and

I'm grateful for that. "Don't stay
up too late. Early to bed, early to
rise. I'll see you at seven thirty.
Thank you for coming to my rescue."

Mine or not, I reach up and kiss
him. On the lips. But no tongue.
Okay, truth be told, I'm going to
miss tongue swapping with Gabe.

Asi Es La Vida

Such is life.
Monica answers the door
as soon as I knock.
She's been waiting for me,
expected me sooner.
I neglected to let her know
about my road-rage experience.

> The first thing she says is, *Oh
> Dios mio. ¿Qué pasó en la cara?*

"What happened to my face
was my steering wheel."
I avoid mentioning Dad.
"Can I come in? I need a mirror."

> *You need more than that.
> I'll get you some ice.*

She steps back, ushers
me into the warmth
of her home, and not just
temperature-wise.

The Torres family
might be celebrating
Monica's birthday
tonight, but the house
shouts Christmas.
I thought Zelda and Gabe's
attempt was pretty great.

But take their green-
and-red swag,
add
gold and silver,
purple and blue;

plus a very real,
ceiling-high
Noble fir
dripping ornaments
and tinsel;

throw in candles,
scenting every room
with gingerbread,
apples, and cinnamon.

The effort is obviously
well rehearsed.

"Tu casa es hermosa."
Her house *is* beautiful.
"Y tambien eres tu."
And so is she.
"Feliz cumpleaños, novia."

> *Gracias.* Her thank-you
> is rather cool. *Now let
> me get that ice. Are you
> hungry? We already ate,
> but there's plenty left.*

Am I Hungry?

I suppose I should be.
I haven't eaten a thing
since breakfast. "I'll nibble
on something, I guess."

I follow her into the kitchen,
where her parents and sister
are playing Conquian,
a Mexican version of rummy.

> Her mom looks up from
> her cards. *¡Ay! Tu cara.*
> *¿Estás bien? ¿Que pasó?*

While Monica puts ice
in a Baggie, I tell
everyone what happened to
my car, omitting
the circumstances
immediately preceding.
I'll confide the ugly
stuff to Monica later.

> *Here.* Monica hands me
> the makeshift ice pack.
> *I'll get you some posole.*

The bowl of spicy pork-
and-hominy stew satisfies
at least one of the hollow spaces.
I hope Monica can fill the others.

Post Posole

I thank Mrs. Torres for the stew,
Mr. Torres for his hospitality,
and Carolina for offering to
give up her bed to me.

> *It's okay. I like sleeping*
> *on the couch, especially with*
> *the Christmas lights on.*
> *Your head looks better.*

"Does it?" I reach up, explore
the bump, which does feel
smaller. "Ice is magic, I guess.
Hey, maybe that's where
Santa's magic comes from—
all the ice at the North Pole."

> *Carolina rolls her eyes.*
> *I stopped believing in Santa*
> *when Roberto got an iPod*
> *instead of a lump of coal.*

Smart kid. Amazing family.
Intact family, and that in
itself makes them amazing.
"I have to be up early for work
in the morning, so if you don't
mind, I think I'll go chill.
Monica, you coming with?"

She Seems Almost Reluctant

And that scares
the crap out of

me.

What if
she's tired of

me?

What if
she's sick of

me?

What if
she's done with

me?

In this moment,
I'm in desperate need of

her.

I've never had a friend
as close as

her.

I've never touched
someone like I've touched

her.

I'll never love
anyone like I love

her.

At Least I Manage

To segue from me to her,
though I guess in reality
it's still mostly about me.
Is that bad, considering
the kind of day I've had?

Reluctant or not, she escorts
me to the room she shares
with Carolina. Monica's family
lives simply in a plain three-
bedroom home that's always

welcoming and clean, despite
the number of people living
here, and the fact that both
of her parents work, and
her mom maintains two jobs.

The weird thing is, no matter
how hard they labor, they're
steadfastly cheerful. Must be
what it's like when love fuels
a family dynamic. "You're lucky."

> Monica flops down on her bed.
> *What makes you say that?*

I sit on Carolina's bed, cross-
legged. "I'm jealous of the way
everyone in your house cares
about each other. It's so weird."

Laughter

Puddles in her mouth,
warm and rich as caramel.
I want to taste it. Savor it.

> *We have plenty of arguments*
> *around here, that's for sure.*
> *But yeah, we love each other.*

"Do you think that would
change if they find out about . . .
you know, you and me?"

> She stops laughing. *No lo sé.*
> *I'm sure they'd still love me, but*
> *no creo que habían aceptan.*

"But if they love you, wouldn't
they have to accept it? What about
after high school? At some point,

will you come out?" Obviously
it's something she's considered.
Still, she stays quiet for a few.

> *No lo sé. But I've got lots of time*
> *to decide if, how, and when to tell.*
> *For now, es nuestro secreto, ¿no?*

It's our secret, yes, and one I'd
never reveal without her explicit
consent. Tonight is a bad night

to consider keeping secrets,
however, especially one as big
as this. But it's not my place to

out her. Instead, I'll come clean
and cop to one of my own. But
how best to approach the subject?

"Want to hear some unexpected
news? Or gossip? Or whatever?
Gabe and Hillary are going out."

> She cocks her head, looks at me
> as if I must be lying. *What? No way.*
> *I just saw the two of you . . .*

I jump from Carolina's bed onto
Monica's. "Way. What you just saw
was us confirming we're friends

but not friends with privileges.
I still think he's hot, by the way,
but not enough to sleep with him."

Go on. Go on. Don't chicken out.
"Sleep with him again. Because
we did have sex a couple of times."

> *I thought so. Did you like it?*
> Not what I expected, but then
> Monica often surprises me.

How Do I Answer?

Truth, remember? Truth.
"Okay, I'm going to be honest
here, because this is a good
day for coming clean.
I can't say I'll never lie
again, but it will be
a very long time."

I scoot closer, stroke
her arm gently, note
the knotting of her muscles
and the fact that her eyes
refuse to meet mine.
"Look at me, novia."
I rest the back of my hand
under her chin, tilt it up
so she has no choice.

"I did like having sex
with Gabe. But it's not
the same as making love
with you. I've come to
the conclusion that I
enjoy the physical act,
and I refuse to feel guilty
about that. But it's real
connection I crave, not
just body part to body
part, but heart to heart.
No amo a Gabe, te amo."

I Don't Love Gabe

I love her.

The door is closed,
so I chance a kiss,
this one *with* tongue,
and the wet satin
of her lips makes me
want a whole lot more.

Can't happen here,
of course, and there's
something kind of nice
about having to wait.
Like it's an experience
to anticipate. Still,
the stunning rush
of desire
makes me tremble.

That she returns
my kiss with the same
driving passion
tells me all
I need to know.

She loves me, too.
And I'm forgiven.
At least, mostly.

Panting

We pull ourselves out
of the what-will-be, return
to the what-is-right-now.
Which basically tosses
me smack back into
the what-happened-today.

"Just so you know,
Gabe is picking me up in
the morning and taking me
to work. I'm supposed to
be at the barn by eight."

> *Pretty good friend to get up*
> *so early for you on a Sunday.*

"I guess, and I'm grateful.
I need to make some money.
Dad's on the run. . . ." I fill
her in on the evening's ugliness.

> *Anxiety creases her forehead.*
> *What are you going to do?*

"I don't know, but I'll
figure out something.
For sure I'm not leaving
Sonora. I've got an actual
life here, which includes you.
It's a year before I turn eighteen,
but maybe I can emancipate."

You haven't talked to your mom?
I gave her your number.

It was Monica? "Why did
you do that? I figured it must
have been Syrah, not you.
And, no, I haven't talked
to her. I've got nothing to say."

　　She crosses her arms. Snorts.
　　Maybe not. But she's got plenty
　　to say to you. I don't get why
　　you won't listen. Don't you
　　want to know who you are?

Stamp "pissed" across
my face. "I *know* who I am,
Monica. I don't need Maya
McCabe to explain it to me."

　　You only know what your dad's
　　told you, Air. You don't even
　　know what your birthday is.

"What are you talking about?
My birthday's October ninth."

　　She shakes her head. That's
　　Ariel Pearson's birthday.

Bulldozed

October 9
is Ariel Pearson's
birthday. And

                                  I'm

not Ariel Pearson.

Meaning
October 9
is probably

                                  not

my birthday.

Spicy hominy
stew gurgles
in my stomach.
Churns acid.

My entire backstory
has been fabricated.
Birth certificate.
School records.

Driver's license.
Social security card.
All bear the name

                                  Ariel

Pearson.
But I'm
not
Ariel

                                  Pearson.

The Truth

When delivered so abruptly
is impossible to ignore.

I fall back on the bed, nestle
my head into the Monica-

scented pillow, and my best
friend settles beside me.

> *I know it's totally up to you,*
> *but my advice is to talk to her.*

A huge sigh escapes. "She left
my dad for a woman, Monica."

> *So what?* She reaches for my hand.
> *You left your boyfriend for me.*

"That's true." I have to smile.
"But I don't want to leave here.

I don't want to leave you. I don't
want to have to go live with her."

> *You don't have to go anywhere.*
> *Ariel might be seventeen, but*

> *Casey is eighteen. You were three*
> *when your dad took you away.*

This Revelation Sinks Like Lead

"What? No! That's impossible.
I might not know my birthday,
but I know how goddamn old I am."

Do I?

"There's no freaking way Dad
could convince me I was younger
than I was! That makes no sense."

Or does it?

I've always been considered
big for my age, but I always
thought it was because

of my height.

> Monica shrugs. *Remember that
> time with Zelda and the coffee
> and he told her he drinks it black?*

On my not-birthday.

> *You could tell she was all confused,
> like she'd never heard that before.
> But he swore she knew all along, right?*

How can I forget?

There's a word for what your dad
did. It's called gaslighting. If he could
convince her, how hard would it be . . .

"To convince a little kid."

Bits and pieces of memory flash
like multicolored neon—people,
mostly women, asking my age. Dad

correcting my fingers.

Until I finally got it right. Did I
argue my name with him, too?
Or was I simply content to become

the Little Mermaid?

My childhood is a jigsaw puzzle,
with chewed and misplaced
pieces. I've always known that.

What I didn't realize

is that even if every correct piece
was fitted perfectly into place,
the resulting picture would've been

interpretive art.

Gaslighting

A quick search on my phone
reveals a lot of information.
Gaslighting is:

> *a sophisticated manipulation*
> *tactic used to create doubt*
> *in the minds of others.*

Check.
The word comes
from an old movie
(and earlier play)
where:

> *(paraphrased) a shithead*
> *husband tries to convince*
> *his wife she's going insane.*
> *His tactics include isolation*
> *and making stuff disappear,*
> *then telling her she's to blame,*
> *though she can't remember it.*

Check.
There are many
ways to create
said doubt:

> *create self-doubt through*
> *intensity of conviction;*
> *if that fails, toss in a little*
> *self-righteous indignation;*
> *skew actual facts with*
> *distortions that can't be*
> *proved or disproved.*

Check.
Check.
Check.

At least until
someone who
might very well
disprove them
appears on scene.
And overall:

> *the best liars deceive*
> *by repeating stories*
> *that are mostly true,*
> *while leaving out (or*
> *adding) a fact or two*
> *that represents truth.*

That's my fucking dad, okay.
My father, master of lies,
who raised me with affection.
Except when he reminded
me, with sharp words and
the occasional slap across
the face, that I was, in truth,
little more than his possession.

What all this gaslighting
information neglects to
mention is the power of warping
love to accomplish a goal.

Which Begs the Question

Does anyone truly love
anyone else, or is every
supposed love relationship
fueled by some messed-up
desire to achieve or conquer?

Will I ever have a legitimate
answer to that question?
How long must I travel
to find it? Can I just start
right here, right now, or will

today's revelations make me
forevermore toss aside chances
in favor of assurances?
Would I even be asking
these questions if I still

believed myself to be
only seventeen, with a dad
who sacrificed everything
and a mother who left
me in her lust-fueled dust?

Goddamn it, I'm only a kid
(with or without the proof
of eighteen), so why is any
of this relevant to me?
Why can't I just

be?

I Fall Back Again

On Monica's pillow, only
this time I'm crying.

Fuck.
Fuck.
Fuck.

What good has crying
ever done?

"I'm sorry."

Not sure why.
Not sure who
I'm really talking to.

All I know is I'm sorry
and it isn't enough
for Maya
or Zelda
or Monica
or me
or anyone
involved in this
insane bullshit

created by my dad.

"Will you tell her
I want to talk?"
I can't do it myself.

Apparently

Monica and my purported mother
have been communicating today

while she and her partner, Tatiana,
traveled back to San Francisco.

Maya McCabe is actually some
hoity-toity network news anchor.

Which means she has weekday
commitments in the Bay Area.

Monica sets up a meeting here
in Sonora next Saturday afternoon.

In other words, I've got an entire
week to meander through, semi

brain-dead. I spend this night
in Carolina's bed after almost

getting busted seeking consolation
in Monica's arms. Good thing Carolina

was anything but quiet when she came
in, looking for her pajamas. I hope one day

in the not-so-distant future I won't have
to disguise the integral truth of who I am.

As I Lie Here

Listening to Monica's soft,
even breathing, I wonder
if I'll ever really know
the truth of who I am.

Is there truth in being two
people, all wrapped up in
one skin? If I accept that I am
Casey, what happens to Ariel?

Now that I seem to have
become fatherless, do I invite
a stranger in, embrace her
as my mother, when before

today resentment for her
infiltrated every waking moment
of my life? Does reconciliation
require forgiveness when

maybe, just maybe, she's done
nothing at all to forgive?
Perhaps an even bigger question
is what about Dad? Is it okay

to keep loving him despite
everything? How could I believe
all those lies? How will I ever
completely trust anyone again?

Sunday Morning

Gabe's right on time, honking
from the curb in front of the Torres
house. Monica's still drowsing
when I kiss her good-bye.

"Talk to you later. After work
I've got to go home, see if
it's still home or if Dad deserted
the place. Love you."

I dare to slip my hand beneath
the covers, cup one breast
and then the other, circling
her attention-seeking nipples

with one finger. "Wish we had
more time, not to mention
privacy. Te quiero, novia."
I do want her, and very soon.

> Ten cuidado. You be careful.
> Horses are big. Don't fall off.
> And stay out of your boyfriend's
> backseat in case he's changed his mind.

"Cross my heart. No backseat, and
no spills off sixteen-hand horses.
That would hurt, and my head
is just starting to feel better."

The swelling is down, the knot
a lot smaller. What's mostly left
is a huge ugly bruise on my forehead.
And another on my right cheek.

    When I reach the GTO, Gabe does
    a double take. *Wow. You look, uh . . .*
    That's some kind of contusion you've
    got going on. Does it still hurt?

"Only when I touch it, so I'm
trying to avoid that. Of course,
I haven't tried thinking real
hard." Mostly because that *does*

hurt. I hop into the passenger
seat and as we take off, I ask,
"How's Zelda doing? She was
pretty shaky yesterday."

    I wish I could tell you, but I really
    don't know. By the time I got
    home last night, she'd drunk
    herself into a stupor, and she was

    still sleeping it off when I left
    this morning. She's struggling,
    obviously, but that's to be expected.
    What about you? Better?

Better Is a Relative Term

That's what I tell him
before running down
all the new information
Monica made me privy to.

"I don't know what to do
with it, Gabe. One damn
lie piles onto the next
and now it's just a huge
stinking heap of bullshit."

> I wouldn't expect to shovel
> through that pile for a while.
> One good thing, though.
> Well, two, actually.

"Really? Do tell. I could
use some good news."

> Well, you are eighteen,
> which means you don't
> have to leave Sonora
> and move in with Maya.
>
> And, two, I'm glad you've
> decided to talk to your
> mom. It's important. If
> you don't, you'll never get
> to the bottom of the manure.

"I still don't think of her
as my mom. It's possible
I've managed to accept
'mother.' I've thought
and thought and can't

come up with one good
reason for a complete
stranger to contrive such
a complicated deception,
so I guess she must be for real."

*She's totally for real, Air.
You should've seen the look
on her face when she saw
you standing there in front
of the gym. I thought
she was going to pass out.*

*She seriously couldn't believe
she was that close to you.*

He stops to assess my sudden,
unbidden scowl. *Whoa. Wait.
You're not mad I said that, are you?*

Wow

Everyone's tiptoeing
around me. Way to go,
me. Ariel. Casey.
Whoever. This is not
how you treat friends.

"Gabe? I'm sorry I've been
so bitchy, okay? I really
don't know how to process
this. To have every single
thing you believe about
yourself be proven a lie?"

> *But that's not exactly*
> *true. You're still the same*
> *warm, funny, sexy-as-hell*
> *girl inside. No one knows*
> *who they are at seventeen.*
> *Or eighteen, or nineteen or*
> *maybe ever, for that matter.*

> *My dad used to say you learn*
> *something new every day.*
> *If that's true, don't you change*
> *a little every time? How can*
> *you learn something new*
> *and still be the same?*

"I don't know. But 'new' and
counterintuitive are two
different things. I prefer new."

As Accurate

As my response is,
his question
is valid.

I understand
that while
the definition
of the external
me

seems to
have changed,

intrinsically,

I'm the same
person I was
prior to . . .

yesterday.

How
is
that
even

possible?

Fortuitously

We've reached the Triple
G and I can think
about what I've got to do
now instead of what
might come afterward.

Gabe asks for the key
to the Focus, promises
to extricate it from the ditch,
then continues to the house.
Hillary is a lucky girl.

I arrive at the barn
with five minutes to spare.
Max, who has already saddled
a bay gelding, can't help
but notice my gorgeous face.

> *Boy, I hope whoever did*
> *that to you got it worse.*

"Actually, my steering wheel
looks a whole lot better than
I do. It was just a little accident."

> He's unconvinced, but lets
> it go. *You okay to ride?*
> *Superfly there is raring to go.*

"How can I turn him down?
No worries. I'll be fine."

The horse's name totally fits.
Wind sharp through my hair,
we circle the big paddock on
a well-used track. Trot to warm
up, urge him into a lope, and

after once around, when I give
him his head we are, indeed,
flying. The syncopation
of his gait; the warm puffs
of his exhales into the chill
air; the rising scent of horse
as he works up a sweat.

These things make sense, and
I'm grateful for their logic.

Slow him, walk him to cool
the heat of his exertion.
Return him to Max, who has
a sorrel filly ready to ride.

We work like this for two-
plus hours, and this time
when I return the young
stallion, Hillary's waiting
to talk with me. "Okay to take
a short break?" I ask Max.

He grins. *If my boss there says
so, and I imagine she does.*

I Hand Over the Reins

And go to join Hillary,
who's sitting on a soft bale
of straw. She takes a good,
long look at my face, winces.

> *Gabe told me what happened.*
> *I'm so, so sorry, Ariel. Oh, by*
> *the way, he's meeting the tow*
> *truck at your car. As long*
> *as it's okay to drive, they'll*
> *drop it off here for you.*

A sudden thought crosses
my mind. "How much do you
think it will be? I don't have
any money to speak of, and—"

> *Don't worry. I'll cover it.*
> *You can pay me back whenever.*
> *In fact, if you need a few dollars*
> *to hold you over till you get*
> *paid, I'm happy to loan it to you.*

"Wow, Hillary, that's really
nice. I'll let you know if I do."

> *Okay. But, listen. I . . . uh . . . wanted*
> *to talk to you about Gabe and me.*
> *I know you two had a thing, and*
> *since I'll be seeing a lot of you*
> *here with the horses—*

"Hey. Don't worry. I'm cool
with it. Gabe and I are just
friends, okay?" I don't feel
the need to confess anything
about special privileges,
even though her expression
tells me she definitely knows.

> That's what Gabe said, but
> I wanted to hear it from you.
> He also mentioned your mom
> showing up after the game.
> That must have been a shock.

"Hillary, that is a major
understatement. I truly
believed I'd never see
my mother again, and
honestly, I never wanted
to. I'm still not sure I do.
The only thing I feel
for her is resentment."

Even as the words leave
my mouth, I hear how
cold they must sound
to an outsider. Will I
ever thaw all the way out?

Hillary Nods Understanding

But now she says simply,
I'd give anything for a little
more time with my mom.

She doesn't add the part
about that being impossible,
but she doesn't have to.

I get what she's trying to tell
me. "I know, and I wish it were
in my power to give that to you."

Instead, I'll just give her my
not-quite-a-boyfriend. "As far
as my mother, we're supposed

to meet next Saturday after
I finish up here. I've got a week
to figure out what to say."

Another curt nod, and like
the last, it means she wants
to offer unsolicited advice.

Maybe you should just listen
and decide how to respond
after that. Not that you asked.

"I don't mind. You happen to be
right. Meanwhile, better get back
to work. I need to earn my pay."

Two more things. We're having
a holiday party next Saturday
night. Aunt Peg's planning it, so

it should be amazing. Lots of food
and a band from Sac. I'd love for you
to come, and you're welcome to

bring a date—or your mom—
if you'd like. Second, I'm aware
you might need a place to stay

for a while. We've got lots of spare
rooms if it comes to that. I'm serious.
At least till you figure things out.

First her car, and now this?
"For real? Wow, Hillary,
that's incredibly generous.

I don't know what I'm going
to do yet, but my options
are limited. I'll keep it in mind."

Please do. You don't have to
carry this alone. One last thing.
There's strength in forgiveness.

I Would Never Have Believed

I could like Hillary Grantham.
But she really is a decent human
being. I'm glad she and Gabe hit
it off. They deserve each other.

I go back to riding and she goes
back to whatever it is she's got
planned for the day after taking
the time to try and improve mine.

By the time I finish, my rear
end's sore, but my brain
is functioning on a higher level,
and that's a good thing because

now I've got to go and see what
remains of the place I've called
home for the last eighteen months.
The Focus is parked just outside

the barn, with a note on it saying
it's okay to drive, despite a few
scratches on the driver's side.
Just as I'm about to leave, Peg

arrives on scene, waves me over.
Oh my God. What did I do now?
And why is this the first
thought to pop into my head?

But she is kind. *Hillary confided*
what's going on with you.
I just wanted to affirm her offer
of a place to stay with us here.

Too kind. "Thank you. I really
appreciate it. I'll have a few
days to work out if that's
something I'll need."

Wonder exactly how much
they know. What did Gabe tell
Hillary, and what information
did she pass on to her aunt?

I understand the tenuousness
of your situation. Advice is cheap,
but for what it's worth, I don't
recommend hasty decisions.

You've lost the majority of your
life to subterfuge, but there are
a lot more years ahead of you.
Make the wrong choice now,

there might be no turning back
around. I speak from experience.
You've got all the time in the world.
Consider carefully. Regret is an illness.

I Drive Home Slowly

Thinking
about forgiveness.

Is there strength in it?
Idiocy?

Defeatism,
perhaps?

Where would I
even start?

Who would I
even start with?

Why would I
even want to?

Next, the concept
of regret.

This one
I've had no time for.

This one
I've had no need for.

This one
I'd rather not

make room for.

The Driveway Is Empty

No sign of Dad's car,
which offers both relief
and a sinking feeling.

For once the front door
isn't locked, and on the far
side of the threshold,

all the suitcases are gone
and the house is winter-cold,
no shoes lined up beneath

the thermostat. I wander
room to room, absorbing
what's left of Dad's presence—

the scent of his deodorant
over the sweat, oil, and booze
BO it never could quite conceal.

And more than a trace
of tobacco. It permeates
every room in the house.

There are even butts,
stomped on the floor. Why not?
It's not his home anymore.

He Didn't Leave

A good-bye note
except for seven words,
scrawled on the wall
by the door
in black Sharpie:

**FUCK YOU
YOU MADE ME
DO THIS**

Fuck who, Dad?
Fuck me?
Fuck Maya?

Fuck the whole
goddamn world?

And what did I, or
any of us, make you do?

Make you leave?
Make you kidnap me?
Make you decide
to try and kill me?

Oh, how I wish I knew
if that's what you
had in mind.

I Still Can't Quite

Bring myself to believe it.
Not enough evidence.
Not enough witnesses.
Way too much shared past.

Well, at least he eliminated
my need to decide whether
or not to move on. I crank
up the heat. Why not? Who's

going to tell me I can't?
That's the little kid left
in me. The emerging adult
does ask who's going to pay

the bill. Since it's in Mark
Pearson's name, it won't be
me. And it won't be Dad, either.
Should I feel guilty? All I feel

at the moment is warm. I go
into the kitchen, see what's
left to eat in the cupboards
and fridge. Not a whole lot,

but then there rarely was.
The alcohol, I notice, is all
gone, which is probably good.
If I'm going to do this on my own,

I'm damn sure doing it right.
That means getting up for school
tomorrow morning and practicing
basketball tomorrow night.

Suddenly I'm starving. I fix
a couple frozen burritos
out of the half dozen Dad left
behind. Wonder if Hillary's

invitation to move in includes
food. They probably wouldn't
let me starve. I'll figure something
out, because that's what people do.

I wolf down the mediocre
Mexican food, wishing it was
Monica's mom's tamales.
Then I shower off the horse

smell eclipsing my own nervous
stink, slip into some hammies,
call Monica to tell her I love
her. Her echoed *te amo* settles

gently against my pillow.
Good thing I'm exhausted.
I tumble toward slumber, hoping
my dreams aren't nightmares.

One Week

Until winter break, I plow
through schoolwork, finals,
basketball practice, and two
games—Monday away, which
we blow, and one at home
on Friday, in which we blow
the other team away.

Monday night I sucked.
Friday night, I kill it.

I've managed to regain
confidence and footing,
mostly because of my friends,
who've rallied around me,
offering support, ideas, food,
and a whole lot of love.

I haven't heard a word
from my absentee father.

The next two weeks will offer me
lots of time to ride and earn
some extra cash. Plus, Peg's
vowed to start my dressage
training. It'll be good
to have something new
to keep my brain occupied.

I can't not think about Dad.
I can't not worry about Dad.

Not One Word

Not even a call checking
up on me.
He doesn't care at all,
does he?
And I'm worried about *him*?

So why tonight
after the game do
I abandon my teammates
and very best friend,
leave them to celebrate
without me?

Why do I return
to the house I, for
the first time in my life,
thought of as home,
thinking maybe
he'll be here,
knowing
he won't. Why
do I sit here alone
and cry for my dad?

The dad who left me
reeling
six days ago, barely
enough time
for my bruises
to fade green.

The dad who never
allowed me a real family,
with a mom who I now suspect
might've loved me
all along.

The dad who constructed
our lives on a foundation
cemented with lies.

Where did he go?
What's his name now?
When he meets
his next woman,
will he even admit
there's a me?

He won't, will he?
No, he's excised me
from his fabricated
history.

I am raging.
I am wounded.
I am lost.

Saturday Morning

At the barn, Max, Peg, and I
discuss a possible schedule.
Understanding my situation,
they offer plenty of hours.

> *The horses—and we—will*
> *miss the extra attention when*
> *you go back to school, says Max.*

"Once I finish basketball I'd
love to come work after school.
I'd leave the team, but I'm not
a quitter." I realize that's true.

> *We wouldn't want you any*
> *other way, says Peg. We'll be*
> *able to give you as many hours*
> *as you want. Hillary's doctor*
>
> *insists she give up riding, and*
> *regardless, she's planning to start*
> *at University of the Pacific in the fall.*

"I thought she was going
to Stanford. Why the change
of plans?" But it hits me just

> *as Peg confirms, Gabe. UOP*
> *is in Stockton. It's kind of nice,*
> *really. She'll be closer to home.*

Quick Decision

Must be someone's idea
of love. I'd ask if she's already
been accepted, but I figure
if her dad can guarantee
Stanford, UOP is a no-brainer.
It's called connections.
Maybe one day I'll have some.

Max goes to saddle a horse
for me and I take the time
to ask Peg, "So when Hillary
goes, you're staying?
I mean, you could move
back to New York."

> I could do a lot of things,
> but I've made a life here,
> and just because one element
> will change doesn't mean
> I want to uproot myself again.

"I get it. But what about
your fiancé? No chance
at putting that back together?"

> He's married now, with three
> kids, but even if he wasn't,
> I wouldn't try to rebuild
> a relationship that was less
> than fulfilling to begin with.
> With age comes wisdom.

Wonder If That's True

For everyone.
I cycle through
the horses, and
with each, anxiety
about seeing Maya
in just a few hours
grows exponentially.

We're meeting at
the Diamondback
Grill, best burgers
in town, which means
Syrah will be our
server, at least
if she gets her way,
and she will.

After the last filly
is put away, I take
the time to run
home (how can I
still think about
it that way?) and
shower. No use
immersing Maya
in equine drift
while she picks
at her salad or
whatever. I doubt
her diet includes
cheeseburgers.

I Get to the Restaurant

At six exactly. Maya's already
there, and Syrah is, in fact,
taking care of our table.

I approach cautiously. Not sure
why. Not like she's going to jump
up and hug me. Oh God, please, no.

She does stand. But all she does
is take my cold hand into her warm
one and stroke it gently.

> She smiles. *Casey, sit down.*
> *I'm so glad you agreed to talk.*
> *No pressure, I promise.*

We slide into our seats and
Syrah comes over to take
our orders, or check up on me.

Or both. "I'll have my usual,"
I tell her, and am surprised
when Maya nods and says,

> *Whatever she's having, same*
> *for me. Oh, unless you're vegan.*
> *Sorry, but I'm a carnivore.*

> Syrah giggles. *Vegan? Ha!*
> *That girl is way into meat.*
> *The kind you eat, I mean.*

So Syrah, but it's okay because
the ice is now broken. "Thanks
for clarifying. Oh, and in case

you two haven't actually met,
this is my friend, SEER-uh, like
Sarah, but spelled Syrah."

> Maya smiles, and her teeth,
> of course, are perfect. *I see.*
> *Great information to know.*

Syrah hesitates, but when
her manager puts his hands on
his hips, she hustles off to do her job.

We sit, sizing each other up, for
a few long minutes. Finally, I say,
"This isn't nearly enough time

to work through everything
I've learned in the last week.
I don't have a clue how to feel

about you, just to be clear.
But I do know one thing, and
that is how important the truth

has become to me. If we can
start there, maybe the rest
will fall into place eventually."

Wordlessly

Maya studies my face,
feature by feature.

>Finally, she says, *I don't*
>*have time for lies, Casey.*
>*Wait, may I please call*
>*you that? You've always*
>*been Casey to me.*

All I can say back is,
"I don't know who I am.
Call me whatever you want."

She looks like I've slapped
her, and maybe I have.

>*Okay, listen. I get that*
>*you've been lied to, and*
>*believe me, I understand*
>*what an outstanding liar*
>*you father is. He's clearly*
>*a sociopath, not that I knew*
>*what that was when we met.*

"I don't want to talk about
Dad." Not yet. Maybe never.

>*Fine. This is on your terms.*
>*So, tell me about school. Love*
>*it? Hate it? Future plans?*

"Future? I have to concentrate
on the present. My only plan
right now is to graduate high
school, apparently a year late."

What do you mean?

"I mean, until last week,
I believed I was seventeen.
I had my birthday wrong, too."

*Oh, right. Monica told me.
I'm so sorry you were fed
a steady diet of deceit.*

We let that sit. "Have you
talked to Monica a lot?"

*Not a lot. But enough
to know she's worried
about you. Everyone is.*

Everyone except
my goddamn father,
who apparently
couldn't care less.

But I hold that inside.
I need to keep my parents
separated, at least in my mind,
for a little longer.

Luckily

The food arrives.
Syrah shoots me
an *are you okay?*
look as she delivers
big platters
of comfort food.

Here we go, ladies.
Can I get you anything
else right now?

In answer
to both the voiced
and unvoiced
questions,
I shrug.
Smile.

Ask for ketchup.
Mustard.
Pickles.
Added comfort.

Allowing
the dialogue
to move away
from Dad.

For a little while.

Over Cheeseburgers and Fries

(Fries!)
We talk
about (in no
certain order,
and sometimes
we return to
various subject
matter):

school (finals)
basketball (winning and losing)
horses
Hillary
Gabe
Syrah

Monica
         Monica
                  Monica
Maya suspects—
probably because
of how many times
I turn the conversation
back to Monica—
the depth
of our friendship.

But I don't
confess it.
Will I ever?

That Circles Us Around

To talking about Maya.
We start with easy stuff,
some of which I'm aware
of. Most, I'm clueless about.

She's originally from Texas.
(Yippee! I own a megadose
of Lone Star genes
because, as it turns out,
Dad isn't from Oklahoma.)

Both her parents are dead.
(Awesome. More family
lost to me forever.)

She lives near San Francisco.
(Right on the beach, which,
by the way, is cool and gray
more often than not.)

She enjoys her newsroom job.
(But prefers sports announcing.
My mom—did I just think that?—
is a world-class jock, or jock lover,
or something like that.)

She prefers alternative music.
(When she was young she listened
to country, but now she can't stand
it. It reminds her of Texas, where
she hopes never to return.)

We Avoid

Talking about Dad
for the longest time.
The subject hovers,
just out of reach,
because neither of us
wants to touch it.

Eventually, of course,
we must, and there's no
way around discussing
that fateful day fifteen
Decembers ago.
I was three.
Not two.
And my mother
was just twenty.
At my age, she already
had a baby.
She had one-year-old
me.

> *I'm not sure exactly*
> *what Jason told you*
> *about me, but I can say*
> *that on some level it was*
> *probably accurate.*
> *He's an expert at taking*
> *basic truths and twisting*
> *them into distortions*
> *that suit his purposes.*

So Far, So True

But I'm not quite ready
to agree with her philosophy,
no matter how accurate
it might be. "What he's told
me about you, over and over,

is that you left your family—
that would be him and me—
for your girlfriend. I assume
he was referring to the person
I saw you with at the game?"

> *Tati—Tatiana—is my wife.*
> *We've been together as partners*
> *since after your father took off*
> *with you, but we were friends*
> *for years before that. However,*

> *I did not leave you for her.*
> *She was there to support me*
> *when he stole you, and make*
> *no mistake about it, that's*
> *exactly what he did. This was*

> *never about me. It was always*
> *about him needing to manipulate*
> *everyone to suit his purposes.*
> *I'm sorry, but I'm afraid that*
> *included you. He's an evil man.*

Evil?

Don't think so. Self-centered,
certainly. Narcissistic, probably.
But spawn of Satan? Nah.
"He took good care of me."

> *Define "good."*

"Okay, he took decent care
of me. Most of the time.
Sometimes. Whatever.
But 'evil' is a strong word."

> *Casey, do you know where
> the names Ariel and Mark
> Pearson came from?*

"Yeah. Dad told me he took
them from a woman we lived
with. They belonged to her dead
husband and daughter."

> *Right. Leona Pearson. I did
> a little research last week.
> Turns out Leona died under
> suspicious circumstances.
> Ostensibly, she overdosed.*

> *But her brother claims she was
> not on the medication the autopsy
> revealed, and that at the time
> of her death she was living happily*

with a man and his little girl,
both of whom disappeared on
the day she died, along with her
deceased husband's car. It was
later discovered abandoned.

"No. He wouldn't." But now
bits and pieces of his story surface:

. . . tetched in the head.

. . . tried to off herself.

. . . why I decided it was time to leave.

"He needed a way to protect me."
That part slips out audibly.

> *I can't speak to motive, Casey,*
> *and maybe he didn't go that far.*
> *There's no way to prove it*
> *at this point. But it's a very*
> *real possibility. Leona's brother*
> *is convinced that it's true.*

It Can't Be True

Can it?

I know my dad.

Really?

He's not a killer.

Is he?

He's a liar.

Totally.

A gaslighter.

Definitely.

A narcissist.

Exceptionally.

A sociopath?

Probably.

But a murderer?

Please
don't
let
him
be.

My World

Just tipped, tilted
so hard on its axis
every rule of nature
has just been called
into question.

"I . . . uh . . ." I take
a gulp of water.
"He left, you know."

       I suspected he would.

"Said he was afraid
you'd call the cops.
Did you call them?"

       I wasn't going to. My main
       goal has always been to
       reconnect with you. If you
       only knew . . . She fights
       the lump that has formed

       in her throat. *When I finally*
       found you, revenge wasn't
       so important. I might've let
       it go. But when I learned about
       Leona, I had to alert the police.

"But why? Like you said,
after all this time, it
would be hard to prove."

Some things you can close
your eyes to. Others demand
serious consequences, or
the perpetrator is likely
to repeat them. I've been in

the news business for a while
and I can tell you that from
what I've seen, very few killers
and rapists act only once.
Besides, on the most intrinsic
level, Leona deserves justice.

Justice.
Right.

"Don't you think
you deserve justice?"

    She sighs heavily. Casey,
I wanted justice for years.
Wanted to see Jason locked
up for what he did to you
and me for as long as the law
would allow. That hunger
for payback has dissipated.

But I really wouldn't want
him to hurt anyone else.
It's my moral duty to do what
I can to see that doesn't happen.

As Pissed As I Am

At Dad, it's hard to reconcile
this information with how I've
always pictured him. But I only

saw what I wanted to, or what
he let me see. And if I came
too close, he knew exactly
how to manipulate me,

pull the blinders down over
my eyes. I hate that I've been
so naive. I despise what he's done.

To her, yes.
But mostly to me.

I can't blame Maya for
notifying the authorities.
"Did Monica tell you what
he did the night he left?"

> You mean running you off
> the road? Yes, and truthfully,
> it's also one reason I chose
> to report him. I was afraid
> if I didn't he might come back
> and hurt you worse than he did.

The implication is clear:
finish me off.

As much as I want to say
that's impossible, I really
can't. Last Saturday night
pops into view like a video.

Dad rode my bumper.
Passed. Too close. Swerved
in front of me. I can see
his profile clearly. I thought
then that he didn't look at me,
but when I jerked my car
sideways, barely missing
him, his head turned toward
me and for one instant
before my head hit
the steering wheel,
I caught his expression.

Satisfied.
He smiled satisfaction.
"Do you think they'll catch
him? What happens if they do?"

> *I don't know. At the very*
> *least he'd face a court-martial.*
> *I don't believe there's a statute*
> *of limitations on desertion.*

> *But Jason seems to be an expert*
> *on lying low. And without you*
> *in tow, he'll be damn hard to catch.*

God, I Want to Be Angry

With her.
        Not him.
                But why?

I think it's me
who's crazy.

Obviously my brain
needs rewiring.

Or, at the very least,
reprogramming.

        Are you okay?

Her hand sneaks
across the table,
meets mine, and
I don't pull away.

It's the first time
I've touched my mom
in fifteen years.

"Yeah, I'm okay."
Except tears
stream down
my face, and not
because of Dad.
I lift my eyes
level with hers.

They're the color
of mine and shiny
with tears, too.
"So, what now?"

> Oh, Casey! All I want
> is to know you.
> Your childhood is lost
> to me, but your adulthood
> is just beginning. Please
> let me be part of it.
> Maybe I can help you
> realize your dreams.

"I don't like to dream.
Every time I do I get
royally screwed."

> Maybe we can change
> that. I'd like to try.

Her voice is sincere
and she's so damn nice
and I really wish
I wasn't starting to like her.

> Okay, with your dad gone,
> where will you live? If you
> need a place, I've got room—

Now I Pull My Hand Away

"No. I couldn't." Too far,
too soon, Maya McCabe.
"I don't want to leave Sonora,

and besides, I can't move in
with a stranger." Mean, mean,
and it feels good, and now I'm sure

I'm crazy. "I've got options."
Actually, I know where I'm going.
Gabe's mom was released from

the hospital, and he's moving
back to Stockton. Zelda's invited
me to stay with her for now.

> Maya does her best not to act
> hurt. *I understand. Just know*
> *if you ever need a place to go*
>
> *my door is open. Maybe you*
> *could come for a visit at least.*
> *Aren't you on winter break?*

"I am," I admit, "but I've committed
to extra hours at work. I need
the income." Nothing but the truth.

> *Let's keep it an open invitation*
> *That includes Christmas.*
> *Oh, hey. I brought a present for you.*

Dollar-Store Teddy Bear?

But no. She cradles the gift,
which is wrapped in newspaper
with jute twine in place of ribbon.
When she hands it to me,

>she says, *I've kept this for you*
>*since you were born. I hope*
>*you'll treasure it as much as I*
>*have. There's a lot to go through,*
>*and I think it will explain much*
>*of what you're struggling with.*

"Should I open it now?" I feel
like a little kid on Christmas
Eve. She nods, and I untie the simple
bow, carefully remove the tape,
though the paper isn't worth
keeping. "A journal?"

>Your *journal*, she corrects.
>*I started it before I lost you,*
>*and kept it all these years.*
>*I wanted you to know, if I ever*
>*found you again, my own journey*
>*while you were missing.*

I dare to open it, and inside
are lots of entries, long and
shorter, plus photos of a young
Maya, Dad in his late twenties, and . . .

I've Never Seen Pictures

Of baby me. That fact smacks
me like Dad's open hand, hard
and stinging. "I . . . I . . . was cute."

> *You were adorable. Beautiful,*
> *in fact. And smart. And curious . . .*

Now her tears drip onto
the table, and some foreign
part of me wants to comfort
her, but sincerely doesn't know
how. Or maybe is afraid to.

I flip through more pages,
come across a faded photo
of a Christmas tree, toddler
me sleeping just beneath it,
with a golden-furred puppy.

"Boo." The name scratches
up from a buried dream.

> *Yes, Boo. Your father took her,*
> *too. She was a gift from Tati.*
> *Whatever became of her?*

"I . . . don't . . . remember."
I should,
shouldn't I?
But I can't.

You were very little. I hope
the book fills in some blanks
and that over your break
you'll have a little free time
to read it in-depth. I'm sure
you'll have questions. You
know how to get hold of me.

Syrah's been watching
the scene unfold and seems
to think we've reached
a conclusion (or maybe
they need the table; it *is*
Saturday night), because
she zips over with the bill.

Unless you want dessert?
We've got killer apple pie.

Maya glances at me,
the offer of pie in her eyes,
but I shake my head.
"I'm stuffed. But thanks."

She gives Syrah her credit
card and says to me, Tati
and I are staying in town
for a couple of days. If you're
so inclined and can make
the time, I'd love for you to
meet her. Maybe we could have

lunch or something. You could
bring Monica, too. If there's
anything you need—anything
at all—please don't hesitate
to give me a call. Okay?

There she goes again,
being oh-so-sweet, and
making me feel cared about.
"I have to work tomorrow,
but maybe we can catch
a bite after. Monica, too."

Her smile is genuine and
seems to melt a year or two
off her striking face.
My mom is pretty.

That sounds perfect. Text
me when you finish up at
the barn. Tati will be thrilled.
Let me finish paying and
I'll walk you to your car.

Outside

The December night
feels a little less frozen.
I even accept Maya's good-bye

hug. It's lingering, warm,
and promises I never have
to be alone in this world.

> You'll remember my open-
> door policy, right? Anytime.
> And Casey? I love you.

I don't say it back. I can't.
For me that bond was severed
years ago. But maybe it can be

regrown. For now, I nod. "I know."
The simple acknowledgment
seems to satisfy her. Smiling,

she turns, and I watch her go
before returning to my own car,
clinging to the journal she kept for me.

Before I start the engine, I check
my phone and sure enough,
there's a message from Monica:

WELL? HOW DID IT GO? TEXT
ME ASAP! I consider going over
to her house to dig deeper

into the journal entries. What an
amazing gift, one I'll share
with Monica eventually. But not

tonight. The initial exploration
is something I must do on my own.
I don't text. I call, to fortify myself

with the sound of her voice.
I let her know things are okay,
invite her to a late lunch tomorrow

with my mom and her wife, and
the lightning thought strikes that I
just might have someone I can confess

to about my love for mi bella novia
Monica. "Buenas noches, mi amor.
Dulces sueños." Good night, my love.

Sweet dreams. I need alone time
to process way too much
information, both good and terrible.

I point the Focus back toward
the house, no longer home, but home
is not a building. It's a harbor.

As I Drive

Images flurry, a hint
of snow before the blizzard.

Maya's hand, tentatively
reaching for mine
across the table, nervous
in its desire for connection.

Monica's hand, sensuously
tracing the outline of my face,
the peaks and valleys
of my anxious body.

Dad's hand, a lightning
strike against my cheek,
an outburst of rage,
undeserved, unnecessary.

Garrett's hand, viciously
snapping my head back
in his grotesque bid
to prove I'm straight.

Killers.
Rapists.
Justice.

I doubt I can find justice
by reporting an attempted
assault that's a week old,
but I think I have to try.

If not for me,
for the next girl Garrett
decides needs convincing.
At the very least, if I go public,
I'll have done what I can
to prevent a repeat performance.

The idea of confrontation
scares the hell out of me.
For my entire life,
I've been coached
to keep my mouth shut
about things I knew were wrong.

Enough.

It's time to stand
up for what's right.
I can't do it alone.
I'll lose my nerve.
But I've got people
in my corner who'll help.

Tomorrow.

Tonight I dive into
chapters of my history
I believed were lost to me.

I Read for Hours

Reread. Return again
to many passages.

Learn a lot I didn't know
and more I never expected.

Absorb information.

Build knowledge about
myself.

My mother.

Her wife.

And my father.

Much I still find hard
to believe.

Who.
What.
When.
Where.

And most of all,
why.

Taped on a page, beneath
an entry dated December 2001,
is a letter from Jason to Maya.

Maya, Maya, Maya,

You conniving whore. Well, fuck you and your dyke lover, too. You thought I didn't know, that I didn't see you kissing her in our living room, with little Casey sleeping right there on the floor? You're disgusting.

I saw you, and I heard you talking, too. Did you really believe you could desert me, run off with your "best friend," the one I can just see you finger banging? And you didn't even let me in on the fun. Oh, that would be a picture, wouldn't it? You and me and lezzie makes three?

I get it now. Marrying me was a farce, a way out of your miserable childhood. I guess I gave you that much, didn't I? Not to mention a home, a paycheck, and a baby girl. Well, guess what? You won't see her again. I'll be damned if I'll ever let you near me or my daughter.

I bet you hoped they'd send me over there to that hellhole, didn't you? I bet you hoped they'd send me back home zipped inside a body bag. Well, bitch, I'm not going over there again, and it will be a cold day in hell before you find a trace of Casey or me. Or the damn dog, either.

Boo

Oh my God.
I remember now!
Boo.
Sweet little Boo.
She traveled
with us for a while.

Dad always bitched
about having to feed her
and the messes she made.

But I loved Boo.
She was all I had left
of Mommy.

I must've said that
too many times
because one day
Dad let her out
of the car to pee.

He drove off
without her.

I cried and cried.
But he said it was best
for her because dogs
belonged running
free, and wasn't I
just a selfish little girl
to want to keep
a puppy cooped up?

The Sudden Insight

Zaps me like a stun gun.
Freezes in certainty
a watery concept
recently introduced
to me: gaslighting.

I go back to a paragraph
that won't let go of me:

Oh, to be given the gifts of the chameleon! Not only the ability to
match the appropriate facade to circumstance at will, but also the
capacity to look in two directions simultaneously. How much gentler our
time on this planet would be.

I think most people
are chameleons,
hiding pain and anger
beneath a mask of civility.

We call those who
aren't afraid to disguise
it dangerous, but I wonder
if hiding behind the facade
is not, in fact, the more
perilous pursuit.

I have lots of time
to dissect the past
fifteen years of my life,
look for clues to the man
behind Dad's veneer.

I Close My Journal

Lay it on the bed,
beside the pillow I sink
my head down into,
a cushion for my dreams.

Funny, but before all this
I didn't dare dream too far
into the future. It's like unlocking
the past freed me to move
into tomorrow in pursuit
of bigger goals than I ever
thought possible.

Thank you, Maya McCabe,
for never giving up
on finding me.
I inherited your looks.
I hope you've given
me your courage
and determination, too.

I'm still scared
to try and make it
on my own. But I don't have
to do it all alone.

I have friends.
I have Monica.
And I have a mom.

No More Tonight

I glance at the clock.
One a.m.
Seems I missed
Hillary's Christmas party.

Christmas.
Not my favorite holiday,
but this year, beyond
the drama, I find hope
in the gift Mom's given me.
Not just the journal
itself, but in what it represents:
moving into the New Year
blessed with the hindsight
of yesterday.

Looking two directions
at once.

I still don't know
exactly who I am.
But I'm a lot closer.

I'm Casey Baxter,
eighteen years old.
I'm in love with a girl
named Monica.
And I don't want that
to be a secret anymore.

I'm done with secrets.

Postscript

Held fast atop terra firma,
by a force not yet fully explained,
I gaze upon the electric waltz
of the aurora borealis and consider

          what

mystical Intelligence might in fact
have created such mad beauty.
From here the northern lights appear
random in flow, but I understand

          if I

could peer down from outer space,
I'd see how auroras crown the poles,
north and south, where the earth's
magnetic field is strongest. I

          am

amazed by the science. Probability.
But more intriguing is the design,
past in relationship to future.
Possibility flung from a faraway

          solar

plane. Sometimes I wonder if I am
only flesh, bone, and blood, or might
I be a spark of stellar fire, carried
through time on the tail of astral

          wind?

Maya's Journal
For Casey

November 2001

In the wake of the World Trade Center tragedy, every American life feels changed. Patriotism is running high. Red, white, and blue is a common theme. Flags fly in the usual places, but also on porch pillars, car antennas, and trees in yards and parks. I've even seen one hoisted above a doghouse!

Neighbors are helping neighbors. Families have bonded tighter. (Mine happens to be an exception, but some relationships can't be repaired.) Couples are holding each other closer. Your daddy and I even felt lovey-dovey again for a few days.

Things on base are a little crazy. Okay, a lot crazy. Rumors are flying about eventual deployment to the Middle East. Your daddy's gone a lot, with extra training and lots of drills. Any military installation could be the next target, so everyone's on edge. The hijackers took out part of the Pentagon, so it's not much of a stretch to think we could be in danger here.

It didn't take long to figure out who the hijackers were. The FBI found suitcases one of them left behind in Boston, where he took the jet. Inside was a list of every one of them, nineteen altogether. Most were from Saudi Arabia and had ties to some organization called Al-Qaeda.

I never heard of it before, but everyone's heard of it now. They hate the United States because of our friendship with Israel, and because we have our own problems here at home. But now they hate us because of our pr_nce in the Middle East. I think a lot of Americans were _ of like me—ignorant about all that. But now we've _me very aware of the wider world and how it views _s.

I mean, it had to take an oversize load _ to do what

they did. We still aren't sure how many people died that day. It will take a while to sift through all the wreckage. But it's thousands, including hundreds of the rescue workers who tried to save lives and a bunch of little kids in a daycare center. It's the saddest thing ever.

What if I lost you? You are the best part of every single day. You entertain me. Make me laugh. Make me learn, because you're always asking questions I don't know the answer to. Best of all, you keep me from being lonely.

Your daddy insists I need to go to work, that his paycheck isn't enough to cover all we need. I don't think that's true. We're doing okay, even if we can't afford to go out to dinner or buy a bigger TV. And the thought of leaving you with strangers scares me to death.

I probably shouldn't confess this here, but no one else will listen. When I told Jason I didn't want to work until you got older, we had the biggest fight ever. He'd been drinking, of course, though that isn't any kind of excuse for slapping me around.

Thank God you were asleep, and totally unaware of the ugly scene going down just beyond your bedroom door. I suppose I should be grateful he used an open hand instead of his fist, but I'll wear his bruises on my face for many days.

Oh, he apologized, swore it would never happen again, but something in his eyes says it will. And now I'm scared he might do the same thing to you. I can't take that chance, Casey. But I don't know what to do. I don't dare call the cops. From what I've heard other army wives say, military police hate domestic abuse situations, which could ruin the career of one of their comrades in arms.

No, I have to find another answer, and quickly. I won't ever let Jason Baxter lay a hand on you.

December 2001

Oh, Casey, I'm so excited. Auntie Tati is coming for a visit! Your daddy hates that you call her Auntie, but I couldn't care less. Daddy doesn't like a lot of things.

He finally got his way and I went to work part-time at the commissary. It's boring and doesn't pay very well, but I only have to put you in daycare two days a week. You like Miss Paula, which makes me feel a little better about leaving you there with her. And you really like playing with the other kids, which makes me feel worse. I kind of wish you only wanted to play with me.

I guess that's pretty selfish, and lately I'm feeling more and more like life as a military wife is not enough. I see the wives of lifers caught up in their snobbish cliques. They stick up their noses at girls like me, knowing some of us married soldiers under the misguided assumption that we'd be well cared for, living on the government dole. As if. But even those women still glued to their soldiers who are close to retirement don't look all that satisfied to me.

I'm not going to labor my life away for minimum wage and decent benefits care of Uncle Sam. What I want is college and a chance at a decent career. Tati always said I should be a lawyer because I'm so good at arguing, but I don't think I'd like that very much. What I really want to be is a sports announcer. Not too many women do that job, but I think it would be a blast.

Your grandpa, my daddy, introduced me to sports, not that your grandma put up with it. My mother (who you'll never, ever meet) got all sucked into this cultish church called Scientology. She said it was a religion, but I know better than that. God doesn't play a role in the theater of L. Ron Hubbard, and neither do football, baseball, or basketball.

Mom was a strict disciple, and her staunch adherence to weirdness is what drove my father out of the house. He was already into the bottle, something she wouldn't put up with. But after he left, his daily alcohol consumption increased steadily until it reached overdose levels. So you'll never know your grandfather, either. I'm sorry about that.

I wish I'd known him better, but he left when I was ten, and I only got to see him a few times afterward. I had to sneak out to do it, in fact. Mom said he was an enemy of the church. He told me that's because he knew about some of their creepier rituals, and they don't like that information getting around. Personally, I never believed any of that garbage, mostly because the friends I kept called me on it. It won't touch you.

I ran just as hard as I could as soon as I could. And I did everything I could to make the church—and Mom—not want anything to do with me. I turned myself into a regular party girl.

I met your daddy in a bar in downtown Austin. Me and my fake ID. I guess you could say I trapped him into marrying me, though when I told him I was pregnant with you, he didn't complain or haul buns in the opposite direction. He did what most decent Texas boys would do and asked me to be Mrs. Jason Baxter.

My mother? Oh, she threw a fit. (Like I cared.) Threatened to disown me. (That was the point.) The only glitch was convincing her to sign off on the marriage license. I pointed out that she no longer had to worry about me. (I'm sure that was a relief.) Oh, and if she didn't go along with my game plan, I, too, was privy to information she might not want me to share publicly. (She didn't.)

I totally got my way. Too bad your daddy turned out to be an even bigger player than I was.

December 2001

Casey, Casey, Casey, what fun we've had with Auntie Tati! Christmas is coming, and even though it's a little subdued this year because of the Towers and all, you and me and Tatiana are celebrating our time together. Oh, and Tati brought us a very special gift—a sweet little golden retriever puppy. You named her Boo, and when you called her the very first time, she came running to you.

Your daddy got all pissed off, of course. He hates dirt and disorder, and he's sure the pup will chew the furniture and leave hair all over and soak the carpet with pee. But I'm going to keep her. Some things are worth fighting to hold on to. We'll give her bones to gnaw and vacuum the hair and take her outside to do her business. After only two days, she's almost housebroken already, like she wants to make us happy.

Between Boo, Tati, and you, this is the happiest I've been in a long, long time. I wish it could be the four of us together, somewhere—anywhere—besides North Carolina. It's not the state I hate. It's the call to war, and it's coming soon, though it's supposed to be all hush-hush. Ha. Like you can be immersed in army life and not understand the focus on deployment.

You don't know this, but your daddy's a whole lot older than I am. I didn't want to marry a total grunt. I set my sights on a soldier who'd been in ten years or more, and Daddy joined up at twenty. He'd already been to the Middle East for Operations Desert Storm and Desert Shield, so when I met him, his rank was E-5. I know that means nothing to you, but to me it meant a decent monthly paycheck, at least if you figured in benefits and base housing. I never thought about another war, and it's almost here.

But Santa is coming soon, so we've put up a tree. We can't afford lots of ornaments, so I bought a few and made a whole lot more. Who knew your mommy was crafty? Tatiana knew, that's who. It's not like you care that popcorn strings circle the tabletop pine instead of tinsel. You love the little twinkling lights, and seeing you smile at them makes everything else worthwhile.

Right now you and Boo are napping together on a big quilt spread across the floor. Both of you are snoring, and that makes Tati laugh. I love the way she laughs. It reminds me of times we spent together when we were still in high school. I dropped out so I could escape my mom, but Tatiana stayed, and now she's at the University of Texas in Austin. She wants to be a teacher.

Tati says I can get my GED and go to college, too, that she'll help me figure it out. We're going to make a secret plan because your daddy wouldn't support me in this. He's happy with me making minimum wage at the commissary.

But here's the thing, my beautiful angel. That's not good enough. Not for me, and definitely not for you. I don't have to give you the universe, but I want to share the world with you. One day we'll travel to Paris together, and tc Rome, and Japan and Argentina, or wherever you have the hankering to see. (One day I'll quit using words like hankering. There's still too much Texas in me.)

Allow me to revise. One day you and I will travel wherever your heart desires. (Yes, much better, if a little cliché.) Until then, I'm making plans, and our dear auntie Tati is coaching me. It might sound like I'm being selfish, but everything I'm striving for revolves around you. Okay, we can include Boo, too.

Funny, but I've never owned a dog, though I always wanted to. One time I begged my mom to let me keep a stray who found me on the playground. She took it to the pound, which pretty much sums up the way Mom felt about suffering creatures, despite claiming to be a caring Christian. (In case you're wondering, Scientology has nothing to do with God.)

But we'll take extra-good care of Boo to make up for that, and I don't give a darn what your daddy says. Next to you and Tati, that little pup means everything to me. I wish every person in the world had a beautiful child, a lovable dog, and a stellar best friend to love. That would be the merriest Christmas ever.

December 2001

What has he done? Where have you gone? How could he do this? To you? To me? Maybe he'll change his mind. Bring you back. How can I find you? Why would he take you away from me? I'm your mommy. You're my baby. He's ripped me in two.

I was doing just what he asked, working cash registers at the commissary, when your daddy picked you up from daycare. Told Miss Paula he was taking you to visit your grandparents. He loaded you in the car and drove away without saying a word. He took my puppy, too.

I went by Miss Paula's after work, like I always do, but you weren't there. I didn't know about any trip. I got scared and hurried home. But you weren't here, either. The house was empty, Casey. No Jason. No Boo. No you. Just a note on the dresser where your clothes used to be, bragging that I'd never see you again. I gave a copy to the investigators, but I'll put the original here in your book, where it will be safe.

See, your daddy was supposed to deploy to Afghanistan in a week. For such a big, tough guy, he was freaking out, even though as a mechanic he probably wouldn't have gone anywhere near the front lines. I think his whole excuse for running off was nothing but a lie, no matter how close to truth some of it might have been.

Oh, Casey. Where are you? You've been missing for two days now, and nobody cares except Tati and me. I've called everyone, pounded on doors—military police, Jason's commanding officer, off-base cops, even the FBI. No one will help. The problem, they say, is he's your father. Like it or not, he has the right to take you away from me, at least until I can see a judge about custodial rights. By then, who knows where you'll be? Oh, Casey. My baby.

Your daddy's in big trouble when they catch him. He's AWOL now. More than twenty-four hours without reporting for duty makes him absent without leave. For some totally messed-up reason, the fact that he kidnapped you doesn't matter as much to the base authorities as his hitting the road without permission. The longer he's gone, the worse it gets. After thirty days, he's an official deserter.

Oh God, why didn't I leave sooner? Tatiana and I planned for me to move in with her once your daddy deployed. He must've guessed that part after he found your auntie Tati and me in what some people might call a compromising situation. It was only a kiss, I swear. Nothing dirty. Nothing ugly. I just needed to feel loved. Not like furniture, the way Jason makes me feel.

I've been in love with Tati since I was twelve, but no way could I ever do anything about it when I was living at home. Then after I met your daddy, I believed I could hide that seed of me, bury it so deep it could never sprout again, never take root and grow. But if love is real, you can't bury it, Casey. You can't. I tried to explain that to your daddy, and swore that no matter what I'd stay married to him, stay true to him, but he knew those were lies.

I just wanted to make a home filled with happiness for

you. Joy. We would never have experienced it living with your daddy. And now what will I do? I can't stay here very long, but what if he changes his mind, brings you back, turns himself in? I have to be here.

I can't work. What little brain I have left thinks only of you. I can't eat. If I try, it churns in my stomach, comes right back up. I can't sleep. If I do, I dream of you, and when I wake up to an empty house, I tumble down into a deep, dark pit.

I sit by the phone, hoping for news, holding the baby blanket that's perfumed with you. A few of your toys are scattered across the floor. I leave them there, hints of you. Sometimes I swear I can hear you in the other room. But I know it's just a ghost, laughing inside my head.

Oh, Casey. Where are you? Are you afraid without your mommy? Tell Daddy to bring you home.

March 2002

You've been gone almost three months now. It seems like longer! It seems like forever! Everything is different. Everything is crazy. Everything is lonely, even though I'm living with Auntie Tati in Texas. I still can't believe you're gone. Still can't believe your daddy could just drive away with you, disappear without a trace.

Well, not exactly without a trace. Detective Morella located your daddy's Chevy. He tracked down the license plate when the guy Jason sold it to changed the title. That was in Virginia. Maybe that's where you are. The man remembered you and Boo, so guess that means you're safe. At least I have that to hold on to. He said your daddy had his eye on a different car and sold the Chevy cheap for cash.

Detective Morella is with the Cumberland County

Sheriff's Department. I had to go off-base to find help, and even there the law's complicated because your daddy and I are still married, and so there was no custody order in place. I filed for an emergency order and was granted temporary custody until things can get settled. That means you belong to me. All I have to do is find you!

Good thing your daddy was stupid and left that note. It's evidence that he planned to conceal you. That's how the law reads in North Carolina—with or without custody, it's kidnapping if the parent who takes a child out of state tries to keep her hidden from the other parent.

Now your daddy's not just AWOL. He's a deserter. That happens at thirty days of unauthorized absence. So the federal database has his name. If he gets stopped for a traffic ticket or has anything to do with the police, they'll know to arrest him. That's my biggest hope of getting you back quickly. But it's three months already. Actually, ninety-six days, emptied of you, each lonelier than the last.

I didn't want to leave North Carolina, in case your daddy changed his mind, but his paychecks stopped right away, and they wouldn't let me stay in base housing. At first they even believed I might have been part of his plan to disappear. Like I'd send my baby off to God knows where with a man who is obviously crazy. He must be crazy.

Tatiana came and helped me pack everything and put it in a U-Haul truck. The Christmas tree was still up. I left it there, decorated. Those ornaments would only remind me of how temporary happiness can be, and of the weight of sadness. Some days I can barely find the strength to drag myself out of bed in the morning. But I know I have to so when you come home I can be the best mommy ever for you.

I'm taking classes to get my GED. I thought about going back to high school and doing credit recovery to earn an actual diploma, but one trip to the campus made me realize I'm not a kid anymore, and that goes way beyond being twenty. Besides, I hated school when I was sixteen. Pep rallies and proms? What are those to me?

Tati says college is different from high school, and I hope she's right. But even if I hate it there, too, I'm determined to get my degree. For you, yes, but also so I'll never have to rely on another person to make my way in the world. I want to be independent, at least financially. I need to be able to take care of myself. And you.

It's weird being in Texas. I thought I'd never come back to this place. At least my mother's gone—moved out to California, and that gives me a small sense of relief. I couldn't stand running into her, and having to admit how wrong I was about your daddy. She warned me he was no good. But even she couldn't see he was evil.

A couple days after I arrived, I drove out to your grandparents' ranch, the one your daddy said he was taking you to. They swore they hadn't seen him. Hadn't heard a word. But my visit put them on edge, I could tell. I think they were lying. I gave them my number, begged them to call if he contacted them. They promised they would. I think maybe they're scared of him.

I have a place to live, and someone who loves me. I love Tati, too. But without you, everything's gray. You were the light in every one of my days. Sometimes I see other mommies get mad and yell at their kids. I want to tell them to stop and think about how empty their life would be if something bad happened to their babies. What if their angels flew away?

April 2004

Please forgive me for not keeping up with your journal. You're not a baby anymore. It's been more than three years since you vanished. That makes you six. What do you look like? Is your hair still the color of a bright copper penny? Does someone put it up in a ponytail, like I used to once in a while? I hope it isn't cut short. When I dream of you, I see it down in soft waves around your giggling face.

I do still dream of you, my Casey. And you are mine. It took months of work and too much money, labored for and borrowed, but I won custody of you and legally divorced your father. There are ways to do that without actually serving papers on the person who disappeared from your life. It was complicated and time-consuming, but it's done.

Every once in a while Jason calls, just to taunt me. He doesn't use his own phone, if he even has one. Because he's now in violation of court orders, I can involve law enforcement. The few times they've managed to trace his calls, the phones he made them from came back as stolen. Big surprise. And they've been from different parts of the country.

Which makes me wonder. You should be in kindergarten. But did he even let you start school? I worry about that because school would be one way to find you, so he might not enroll you. But you have to go, you must. You are such a bright little girl. Are you reading? Do you love books? Can you use a computer?

I finally learned. I had to for school. Tati and I moved to Phoenix a year ago. She transferred to Arizona State University, and I'll start there next year. Right now, I'm on track to get my associate of arts degree in communications at the end of the current semester. I've still got my eye on a career as a sportscaster, and it's my plan to get my bachelor's in com-

munications at ASU. That won't assure my dream job, but at the very least, it will help me find work in a related field.

Meanwhile, I've got a marketing position at a local TV station. It isn't on-air, but it does allow me access to the newsroom, where I'm making friends. I'm targeting the assignment editors, one of whom might one day allow me a shot at reporting, or maybe even doing live broadcasting from a Cardinals or Diamondbacks game. I've let them know I'm interested if there's ever an opening, and as a station employee, I've got an "in."

One thing I'm discovering is the value of relationships, both professional and personal. Sometimes I go out after work with people from the station, most of whose company I do enjoy, although a few are fueled by superegos. You have to massage their overinflated self-esteems, though, because they are the ones with the most power to either help or hinder your own goals. A few know about you, Casey, and I've asked them to alert me if a news story relating to Jason happens across their desk.

On the personal side, Auntie Tati and I are more than just friends now. We're partners. It took some time for me to accept the idea of commitment again. Your father (not going to call him your daddy anymore) totally destroyed my trust supply, which was never very big anyway. Tati had to work really hard to rebuild it, and thank God for her patience. Accepting love is hard, but she's taught me how worthwhile it is.

Wouldn't it be awesome if you could redecorate your past? How I wish I wouldn't have thrown away three years of my life—given them to a man whose heart was black and intentions were evil. I won't say I wish I never got pregnant, because that feels like I'd be jinxing you. You deserved life. But I deserved to keep you in my life, too.

I'll never give up looking for you, hoping for some small clue that will reunite us, mommy and daughter, together again. You know what I do sometimes? I comb obituaries, searching for the name Jason Baxter. Is it awful to yearn for someone's death? I suppose it is. Tati tells me to quit, that bitterness makes people old. But how can I not be bitter?

Oh, Casey, do you even remember your mommy? I think about you every single day. Sometimes I cry for you at night. Your baby blanket? I keep it folded under my pillow, unwashed because it still holds the faint scent of you.

Through the relentless motion of time, I discovered a certain momentum and attained goals far beyond any I thought within reach. The haunts of my past played a role in that, drove me into a comfortable present, at least as measured by personal success.

September 11, 2006

It's your birthday, darling Casey. I hope wherever you are whoever you're with is celebrating your day in a big way. I know you might never see these updates, but I decided to write them on your birthday so I'll always remember to do them. I'll never forget the importance of this day. Or give up on spending future birthdays with you.

Not a whole lot has changed in the past year and a half, except I did start at ASU, which added a lot of work to my already busy life. But it will be worth it in the long run. Oh, I am doing some weekend reporting at the station, which means now I have to keep in shape so I look svelte on camera. Svelte. Cool word, yeah? And whoever would have thought I'd use it in reference to myself?

Doesn't matter. I look good enough for Phoenix, apparently.

It's weird, but I actually get come-on e-mails from viewers. Men, of course. There's a certain satisfaction that comes from that. Once I was pretty watery about my sexual identity, and even now I can't say I'm not attracted to good-looking men.

Who knows? Had I been attracted to the right man, rather than the handful I dated (especially your father), maybe I'd be married to one, and have a passel of kids to care for. I loved being a mommy. Don't know what kind of mother I'd have made. Some people believe ambition is a bad thing for a woman to own. I don't know what to think. All I know is Tati is more than enough "partner" for me. I just wish you were here, too.

September 11, 2007

Happy birthday, nine-year-old. You must be getting so big. Are you tall? I never mentioned it, and you surely can't remember this, but your mommy (that's me!) is five foot eleven. That's pretty tall. Tati calls me Everest when she wants to tease me, though that's kind of a stretch. Ha. Get it?

I've got one more year to finish up my communications degree. Tati is ahead of me. She got her criminal justice degree last year and is taking special coursework to become a credentialed victims' advocate. She wants to help people, and she says I inspired that desire. She watched me suffer because I lost you. Can you imagine how many people like me there are in the world?

It might be hard to believe, but I still dream about you. My favorite is the Christmas dream. We're decorating the tree and I'm singing that silly song I made up: Eggnog and beer make for too much good cheer, but you can bet the sleigh knows the way, so Santa please don't sweat it. Dumb, I know, but you're only three, frozen there in time, and you laugh and laugh, even if you only understand the gist of my words. That makes me laugh, too, and I am filled with happiness. It's a joyous Christmas.

But then the dream ends when your father walks in, pissed off, and slams the door behind him. I hate when dreams get real.

September 11, 2008

Ten years old today. I can hardly believe it's been an entire decade since that incredible day you came into the world. I run a finger along the C-section scar faded into a silver thread below my belly button, remember the first time I held you, all plump and pink and perfect. You looked up at me, and in your eyes was recognition. You knew me! Our connection, independent of a physical cord, was complete in that moment. We're still connected, Casey, wherever you are. Jason can't take that away from us. Ever.

So what's up with me? Well, your mom's an official college graduate. Finishing school definitely freed up my schedule. Now Tati and I actually have a little of this thing called "spare time," and we're using it to mountain bike. I love going outside the city and cruising back roads and trails. It's a different adventure every time we go.

Speaking of going, Tatiana and I are moving to California! She got a job. I got a job. Both of us were lucky enough to find work in the same city: San Diego. I hear it's beautiful, and am looking forward to leaving the desert in favor of the ocean. Not only that, but the TV station I'm going to work for is going to let me do sports! Chargers and Padres, woot-woot!

Oh, some bad news. I've tried to keep in touch with your father's family, just in case. I'm not sure if you're acquainted with your Uncle Drew, but he was a policeman. I say "was" because one of the bad guys killed him. I'm sorry about that. I liked Drew, even though I only met him in person once. When I'd call, asking about you, he could never offer any updates. But he was always kind, unlike your grandparents. Do you know them? I suspect you do, though they've never admitted it. Keeping us apart is more than callous. It's unforgiveable.

September 11, 2009

Happiest birthday, my sweet Casey. Will you have a party and a cake with eleven candles? What kind of presents will you get? Maybe an iPod? Do you love music? I think you're into hip-hop, don't ask me why. Jay Z, perhaps, or Rihanna? When I was your age, I was all into country, but I left that behind in Texas. Are you in Texas? I hope not. I want more than that for you.

Tati and I have been in San Diego for ten months. Have you ever been here? It's amazing! Perfect weather. Pacific Ocean. Big city, but not so big that you can't live comfortably in the suburbs. And the people! Oh, Californians, at least most of them, embrace the motto "Live and let live."

I mean, of all the states, with the possible exception of New York, California must be the most progressive. It doesn't matter what color your skin is or who you're in love with. As long as you embrace "Live and let live," you can find happiness here. It's refreshing, especially after the other places I've lived.

Of course, it's not totally peace and love, or there wouldn't be such a big need for victims' advocates like Tati. Lots of crime in Southern California, though we haven't seen a whole lot of it in our decent neighborhood. Working in the newsroom, I hear about it, though. I'm still a sports reporter, and loving my job.

I hope wherever you are (even if it is Texas) you're happy there, too.

September 11, 2010

Oh, Casey! You're twelve. I was thinking that if I saw you on the street I probably wouldn't recognize you, and that made me so, so sad. But also mad! This giant bolt of anger, electric and white-hot, surged inside me. I wish I would've been angrier nine years ago. Wish I would've screamed from rooftops, knocked down doors, begged for TV airtime to take our story public. Instead, I passively waited for something to happen—for Jason to make a mistake, or for the cops to find him, or even for fate to bring you home to me.

That was my upbringing, Casey. That was my marriage. That was having self-respect beaten out of me. Learning the hard way not to question authority. I'm sorry I wasn't tougher. I'm a different person today, and if—when—we're together again, I'll never let you down.

What are you like today? Do you still have coppery hair, or has it gone blond from the sun? Or maybe it's even turned darker. Are you gold? Ginger? Auburn?

Are you athletic? Do you play soccer or softball or basketball? I wish I could take you to games with me. One of the best things about my job is watching from the sidelines. Best seats in the house, even if I'm mostly standing. I hope you like sports. I hope you're a strong girl. I hope you're happy. I hope you wonder about me.

September 11, 2011

Casey, my Casey. You're officially a teenager today. Do you feel different having been awarded that designation? I remember when I was twelve I thought being a teen would magically change everything for the better. It didn't, by the way.

Where has the time gone? Today is the tenth anniversary of the World Trade Center destruction. They've been rebuilding for a while now, and the plans for the new structures are grand! The replacement towers climb higher and higher, and One World Trade Center will be one of the tallest buildings on the planet once it's complete. This morning, the memorial opens on the site and tonight the towers will be swathed in red, white, and blue lights.

Across the country, people can't help but remember that terrible day. I know I'll never forget it, not only because the events are seared into my memory, but also because it reminds me of you.

You've been gone for almost a decade. I've hunted and hunted for clues. But it's as if a spaceship came down out of the sky, zapped you aboard, and flew away.

But I know you're still on earth. My heart swears you're here, and so I'll keep chasing after every clue, no matter how small, until I find you.

September 11, 2012

Sweetest Casey. Another year has passed without you. Another year lost to us, twelve long months. Eleven years total. Funny, but I keep looking for signs—some whisper of fate to tell me this is the year, this is the month, this is the week I'll find you.

Poor Tati. She must grow tired of my fretting. But if she does, she never lets on. In fact, whenever I feel like giving up, she's the one who nags at me not to lose hope. She decided this year we should celebrate your birthday somewhere special, so I'm writing this on the beach on the Big Island of Hawaii, wearing leis and drinking piña coladas, which are way too sweet for me, though Tati loves them.

Have you been to Hawaii? For all I know, you might even live here. Then maybe you'd be a surfer. Do you ride? I've covered some surfing events. They're intense.

Speaking of intense, my love for Tati has grown in intensity. She had a little skin cancer scare not long ago, and the idea of losing her freaked me out. It was okay in the end, but we spent several anxious days until we got the good news.

How I wish I'd get good news about you. I watch the heave of the ocean, listen to its crash and moan, hoping to hear that message from the ether. Will this be the year? Will this be the month? Will this be the week I find you?

September 11, 2013

Happiest birthday, Casey. I wish I could reach out and touch you, or at least pick up the phone and call to let you know not a day goes by that I don't think of you, if only for a brief moment or two. I imagine how you look, what you're doing. I imagine the joy of hugging you, wish for more than attachment by the slenderest thread of memory.

To move or not to move? That is the question of the day. Tati and I have been in San Diego for five years now, and I feel like it's time for something new. I was offered an anchor position at the station, and have been considering it. It would mean more money, but a lot less freedom, and money isn't everything.

So I've put out a few feelers, looking for work in different cities. The problem is, San Diego is a great market, and I love California. Plus, there's Tatiana to consider, though she thinks it won't be hard to find a job wherever I might end up. We'll see.

How many times have you moved? I think it must've been many to have kept you so well hidden. Are you still with Jason? Sometimes I wonder if maybe he gave you away. Anything to keep us apart. The man is a monster.

September 11, 2014

Sweet sixteen. I guess you've probably been kissed by now. I hope whoever he—or she—is, that person treats you right. Don't settle for less than the best partner, Casey. Don't allow yourself to be used or abused. And never glom onto someone you don't really love, thinking it's a means of escape.

The person I escaped from is gone for good. My mother passed away last June. You know how I found out? I happened to read her obituary. She was living right here in San Francisco. Just as well I didn't know, but I have to wonder if she ever saw me on TV, and if she did, whether she even recognized me—her daughter, sixteen years since we'd last seen each other. And that brings me right back to you.

I'm in San Francisco now, where it's cooler than San Diego, and more expensive. Tati and I live in a little house near the beach, south of the city proper. I don't cover much surfing up here, but there are sailing events, and I've discovered how much I love the sport. Not just watching it, but experiencing it. Skimming the water, powered by the wind, is pretty darn close to heaven.

We'll sail together one day, you and me. I'll show you the ropes. Ha-ha. I wonder what you can teach me.

September 11, 2015

Oh, Casey. Every year on this day I wake up and almost immediately see some kind of 9/11 tribute. A responder's untold story, or a where-is-this-survivor-now article. The first thing I think of is you. That unimaginable event will forever be linked in my mind with my little girl's disappearance.

That's good and bad, I suppose. The World Trade Center destruction was an immense catastrophe, but to me, losing you was the greater tragedy, one I've never been able to reconcile because a huge piece of my heart went missing.

You know what I do? I get a cup of coffee and turn on my computer and do a web search for your name. I've found thirty Casey Baxters, but none of them is you. They're either too old or too male.

Do you ever look for me? Do you even know my name? What has Jason told you about me? Oh, how I wish I knew. If I did, it might lead us to each other.

September 11, 2016

You're eighteen years old today! All grown up, and on her way. You must be a high school senior this year. You'll gradu-ate in the spring. Do you have plans for college? Oh, you must! Don't be a late bloomer like me. And don't get married. Not for a while. Find out who you are first.

I guess that's weird advice, considering I've been with Tati, like, forever, and when we first got together I had no clue who I was, other than your mommy. And then you were gone.

You know, I've no idea why I'm doing this anymore, other than to prove to myself I still believe we'll find each other one day. It's hard, baby. So hard. But I can't forget you. Refuse to give up all hope. Instead, I'll close my eyes and toss a birthday wish to the universe.

November 16, 2016

Oh my God. Did my wish come true? On slow news days, one of our producers pores over stories from the wire, Internet posts and articles from Northern California newspapers that might make good fillers. Today Randy handed me a copy of the Union Democrat, a paper in Sonora, which is not so very far from here. He pointed out a story about Charles Grantham's daughter falling from her horse. Two teens had come to her rescue. I might not have thought twice about Ariel Pearson, except I recognized the man standing behind her.

He was identified as Ariel's father, Mark Pearson. But even fifteen years couldn't age Jason Baxter's face enough to disguise it completely. I took another look at the tall, ginger-haired girl. It's possible I'm wrong, but I don't think so.

Ariel Pearson is you, Casey. I can hardly breathe! But now what do I do?

December 2016

Oh, to be given the gifts of the chameleon! Not only the ability to match the appropriate facade to circumstance at will, but also the capacity to look in two directions simultaneously. How much gentler our time on this planet would be.

I've spent almost half my life staring back over my shoulder at years I can't regain. Years filled with regret for situations not in my power to change, vital things lost forever now. Years shadowed by anger at someone not worthy of even that emotion. Years emptied of you, dearest Casey.

That's not to say they were empty. My best friend, lover, partner, and now wife coaxed me forward, one day draining into the next. She never let me despair completely, despite so many glimmers of hope snuffed out and promises shattered into lies.

It was Tati who stood me up when I fell on my knees, begging a God I didn't believe in for your safe return. Tati who reminded me no force of Good was responsible for your disappearance; it was an instrument of Evil. Tati who urged me to keep going when I was certain I couldn't take another step without you.

But I had to trudge on, didn't I? Had to forge ahead, to have any chance at all of holding you again. How I've dreamed of that reunion, over and over again.

Just recently I found a shaky belief in luck.

Today, for the first time in a very long time, I dare to project myself into a future no longer devoid of you. All I want—all I've ever wanted—is to find you, my darling daughter, and to share my tomorrows with you.

It was totally random happenstance that led me to know your whereabouts. Ironically, you're not very far from me, and neither is your father. I'll have to play my cards carefully, but play them I will. I'm making plans to get you back into my life just as soon as I can.

AUTHOR'S NOTE

My personal experiences often inspire characters or story threads, and once in a while they are the driving forces behind one of my books. This is one of those books. When my youngest daughter was three years old, her father (my ex) picked her up from daycare and, in defiance of my custody orders, took her out of state. I lost her for three years.

During that time, he moved around the country. This was pre-cell-phone days, and I'd receive collect calls from time to time, always with the promise that I could talk to her, but really he just wanted to taunt me. The calls came from New York, Hawaii, Virginia, wherever. When he decided she should start school, he settled back in his hometown, and at that point one of his relatives called to let me know where she was. Even after I found her, it took months to get law enforcement help and finally a judge in California told me to "kidnap her back," because as soon as we left the county he lived in, there wouldn't be a problem.

Under threat of "getting our heads blown off if we showed up," and with the aid of my ex's grandmother, my husband and I flew back, picked her up from school, and were across the county line before my ex could carry out his threat. He did, many years later, tell my daughter he wished he had killed me when he had the chance.

There's a lot more to that story, and I'll write it extensively one day, but those years without my daughter remain frozen in my mind. That one parent could take a child away from the other parent, all in the name of revenge, is unbelievably cruel. But according to missingkids.org, more than 200,000 children per year are victims of family abduction. Here are some statistics.

- Of the 203,900 children who were victims of family abduction in one year, 53% were taken by their fathers, 25% by their mothers, and the rest by other relatives, including stepparents and grandparents.
- Of those children, 44% were younger than age six.
- Law enforcement was contacted in 60% of those cases, to locate or help recover a child from a known location.
- In the cases where families did not contact the police, 23% resolved the issue within the family, 15% didn't believe police could help, and 10% knew the child's location. Other reasons for not contacting the police included dissatisfaction with prior police contact, fear that the child would be harmed, and the resolution of the issue with an attorney.
- Only 30% of abducted children were gone for more than one month, with the majority gone between one day and one month.

A Reading Group Guide for
The You I've Never Known

by Ellen Hopkins

About the Book

For as long as Ariel can remember, it's been just her and Dad. Ariel's mom disappeared when she was a baby. Dad says home is wherever the two of them are, but Ariel is now seventeen and after years of new apartments, new schools, and new faces, all she wants is to put down some roots. Complicating things are Monica and Gabe, both of whom have stirred a different kind of desire.

Maya's a teenager who has run from an abusive mother right into the arms of an older man she thinks she can trust. But now she's isolated with a baby on the way, and life's getting more complicated than Maya ever could have imagined.

Ariel's and Maya's lives collide unexpectedly when Ariel's mother shows up out of the blue with wild accusations: Ariel wasn't abandoned. Her father kidnapped her fourteen years ago.

What is Ariel supposed to believe? Is it possible Dad's woven her entire history into a tapestry of lies? How can she choose between the mother she's been taught to mistrust and the father who has taken care of her all these years?

Discussion Questions

1. This book begins and ends with a rumination on "the gifts of the chameleon." Why does the author choose to bookend the story with these almost identical sections? Does the poem "To Begin" offer any foreshadowing of the story? How does the last segment of Maya's diary help to tie up loose ends? How do the differences between the two passages reflect the differences between the two women who wrote them?

2. In what ways is Ariel's father abusive? Is his abuse limited to Ariel, or do other people experience it as well? Why does Ariel love him anyway?

3. What role does addiction play in the characters' lives? Does witnessing others' dependence on substances have any effect on the behavior of Ariel and her friends? Is Maya's mother's devotion to Scientology a form of addiction?

4. Ariel talks about getting free from her father's influence, but at one point says, "but what if I'm the kind of captain who can't avoid sideswiping the glacier and sinking the ship?" Do you think that this is a common feeling for someone Ariel's age? Does her lack of confidence have anything to do with her father's treatment of her?

5. Why does Ariel think that psychology might be a good career choice for her? Does her psychology elective help her have insight into the things that happen around her? Do you think the events of the story will bring her closer to this career or drive her farther away?

6. When faced with the prospect of a romantic relationship, Ariel says, "Lacking anything like a role model, commitment isn't something I understand." Has she ever had a good relationship role model? Is this a problem she will be

able to overcome? Does the fact that she realizes it's a problem say anything about her ability to have a committed relationship?

7. How is Ariel's kiss with Monica different from her kiss with Gabe? What does she get from each of them that the other can't give her? Does Gabe relieve Ariel from having to make a decision between the two, or had she already made up her mind?

8. Why does Ariel's father say such nasty things during the Thanksgiving dinner with Gabe and Zelda? What is it about this family holiday that makes him need to lash out? Does Ariel's reaction make the situation better or worse?

9. Maya writes about 9/11 in her journal, and Hillary's mother and brother were killed when the twin towers fell. What effect does this terrorist attack have on the characters when it happens? Are they still feeling the repercussions in the present day? Do the characters who were too young at the time to register what was happening feel changed by that day?

10. Hillary's aunt Peg says that she won't leave Sonora when Hillary goes to college because "All that I am is right here." What does she mean? Is this true of any of the other characters?

11. Zelda and Ariel both feel betrayed by Mark/Jason. How does this help them interact in the aftermath of Maya's arrival? Does Zelda have the right to feel betrayed? In what ways are the lies that he told the two women similar, and in what ways are they different?

12. What is "gaslighting"? Who does Mark/Jason do this to, and how? How does knowing about this technique help Ariel wrap her head around what has happened to her?

13. Will Ariel be able to forgive her father? What regrets might she have if she doesn't forgive him? How would you react if you were in this situation? Would you be able to forgive your father? Is there anyone else whom Ariel needs to forgive?

14. Why does Ariel love Monica? Why is it so difficult for her to admit that she loves Monica, and to take the next step in their relationship? Even though their family situations are so different, why is it also difficult for Monica to come out as a lesbian to her loved ones?

15. How can Ariel be attracted to both Monica and Gabe? Why is she also hesitant to identify as a bisexual? Do you think that it's possible for a person to be attracted to both men and women equally? Moving forward, do you think that Ariel will identify herself as bisexual or a lesbian?

16. There are several points in the story when Mark/Jason and those who love him use his life as a soldier to excuse his behavior. Are there parts of his personality that make him a good soldier? How does his identity as a soldier change from when he meets Maya to when he leaves her?

17. Even before she finds out about being kidnapped, Ariel struggles with her identity. What defines her as a person? Can her father's past actions erase who she truly is? What parts of her past and her personality will she take with her moving into the future?

18. The author structures her poems so that the title also serves as the first line. Why do you think she does this? How would the book be different if the individual poems didn't have titles? Are there any instances where the title serves in the traditional sense, as opposed to being part of the "story" of the poem?

19. Why are there two narrators telling their stories? Did you notice parallels to the two stories, even before you understood the connection between them? How would the story have been different if there had been only one narrator?

Guide written by Cory Grimminck, Director of the Portland District Library in Michigan.

This guide has been provided by Simon & Schuster for classroom, library, and reading group use. It may be reproduced in its entirety or excerpted for these purposes.

HAVE YOU READ IT YET?

TURN THE PAGE FOR A LOOK AT THE
#1 *NEW YORK TIMES* BESTSELLER

IDENTICAL

by Ellen Hopkins

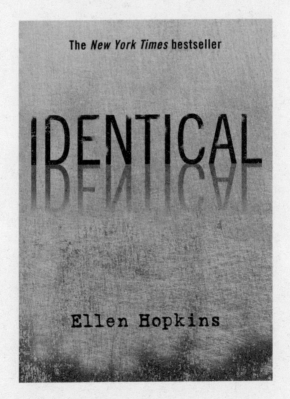

Raeanne
Mirror, Mirror

When I look into a

mirror,

it is her face I see.
Her right is my left, double
moles, dimple and all.
My right is her left,
unblemished.

We are exact

opposites,

Kaeleigh and me.
Mirror-image identical
twins. One egg, one sperm,
one zygote, divided,
sharing one complete
set of genetic markers.

On the outside
we are the same. But not
inside. I think
she is the egg, so
much like our mother
it makes me want to scream.

Cold.
Controlled.

That makes me the sperm,
I guess. I take completely
after our father.

All Daddy, that's me.
Codependent.
Cowardly.

Good, bad. Left, right.
Kaeleigh and Raeanne.
One egg, one sperm.
One being, split in two.

And how many
souls?

Interesting Question

Don't you think?
I mean, if the Supreme
Being inserts a single soul
at the moment of conception,
does that essence divide
itself? Does each half then
strive to become whole
again, like a starfish
or an earthworm?

Or might the soul clone itself,
create a perfect imitation
of something yet to be
defined? In this way,
can a reflection be altered?

Or does the Maker,
in fact, choose
to place two
separate souls within
a single cell, to spark
the skirmish that ultimately
causes such an unlikely rift?

Do twins begin in the womb?
Or in a better place?

One Soul or Two

We live in a smug California
valley. Rolling ranch land, surrounded
by shrugs of oak-jeweled hills.
Green for two brilliant
months sometime around spring,
burnt-toast brown the rest of the year.

Just over an unremarkable mountain
stretches the endless Pacific.
Mornings here come wrapped
in droops of gray mist.
Most days it burns off by noon.
Other days it just hangs on
and on. Smothers like a wet blanket.

Three towns triangulate
the valley, three corners, each
with a unique flavor:
weathered Old West;
antiques and wine tasting;
just-off-the-freeway boring.

Smack in the center is the town
where we live, and it is the most
unique of all, with its windmills
and cobbled sidewalks, designed
to carry tourists to Denmark.
Denmark, California-style.

The houses line smooth black
streets, prim rows
of postcard-pretty dwellings,
coiffed and manicured from curb
to chimney. Like Kaeleigh
and me, they're perfect
on the outside. But behind
the Norman Rockwell facades,
each holds its secrets.

Like Kaeleigh's and mine,
some are dark. Untellable.
Practically unbelievable.

But Telling

Isn't an option.
If you tell

a secret

about someone
you don't really know,
other people might

listen,

but decide you're
making it up. Even if you
happen to know for a fact

it's true.

If you tell a secret
about a friend, other people

want to hear

all of it, prologue
to epilogue. But then they

think

you're totally messed
up for telling it
in the first place. They

think

they can't trust you.
And hey, they probably
can't. Once a nark,
always a nark, you

know?

Kaeleigh
I Wish I Could Tell

a secret,

       But to whom could
       I possibly confess

       any secret? Not to my mom,
       who's never around. A time
       or two, I've begged her to

listen,

       to give me just a few
       precious minutes between
       campaign swings. Of course

it's true

       the wrong secret could take her
       down, but you'd think she'd

want to hear

       it. I mean, what if she had
       to defend it? Really, you'd

think

       she'd want to be forewarned,
       in case the *International Inquisitor*
       got hold of it. Does she

think

       this family has no secrets?
       The clues are everywhere, whether
       or not she wants to

know.

There's Daddy

Who comes
home every
day, dives
straight into
a tall amber
bottle, falls
into a stone-
walled well
of silence, a
place where he can tread
the suffocating loneliness.
On the surface, he's a proud
man. But just beneath his not-
so-thick skin, is a broken soul.
In his courtroom, he's a tough
but evenhanded jurist, respected
if not particularly well liked. At
home, he doesn't try to disguise his
bad habits, has no friends, a tattered
family. A part of me despises him,
what he's done. What he continues
to do. Another part pities him and
will always be his little girl, his
devoted, copper-haired daughter.
His unfolding flower. But enough
about Daddy, who most definitely
has plenty of secrets. Secrets Mom
should want to know about. Secrets
I should tell, but instead tuck away.
Because if I tell on him, I'd have to . . .

Tell on Me

How I'm a total
            wreck. Afraid to
let anyone near.
            Afraid they'll see
the real me, not
            Kaeleigh at all.

                        I do have friends,
            but they don't know
                        me, only someone
I've created to take
                        my place. Someone
sculpted from ice.

                        I keep the melted
                                    me bottled up
            inside. Where no
                        one can touch her,
            until, unbidden, she
                                    comes pouring out.

            She puddles then,
upon fear-trodden
            ground. I am always
afraid, and I am vague
            about why. My life
isn't so awful. Is it?

We Live in a Fine Home

With lots of beautiful stuff—
fine leather sofas and oiled

teak tables and expensive
artwork on walls and shelves.

Of course, someone used to
such things might wonder

why there are no family
photos anywhere. It's almost

like we're afraid of ourselves.
And maybe we are, and not

only ourselves, but whatever
history created us. There are no

albums, with pictures of graying
grandparents, or pony rides

(never done one of those)
or memorable Gardella family parties.

(The Gardellas don't do parties,
not even on holidays.)

No first communions or christening
gowns. (We don't do church, either.)

Of course, no one ever comes
over, so no one has ever wondered

about these things, unless it's our
housekeeper, Manuela. Have to have

one of those, since Mom's never home
and Daddy often works late, and even

if he didn't, he wouldn't clean house
or go to the grocery store. Normal

parents do those things, right? I'm
not sure what normal is or isn't.

But It Really

Doesn't matter. Normal
is what's normal for me.
I've got nice clothes,

nicer than most. Pricey
things that other girls would
kill for, or shoplift, if they

could get away with it.
I have a room of my own,
decorated to my taste

(okay, with a lot of Daddy's
input) and most of the time
when I'm home, I hang out in

there, alone. Listen to music.
Read. Do my homework.
What more could a girl ask

for, right? I mean,
my life really isn't so bad.
Is it?

I Clearly Recall

Once upon a time, long
ago, when everything
was different. Mom

and Daddy were in love,
at least it sure looked
that way to Raeanne

and me. How we used
to giggle at them, kissing
and holding hands.

I remember how they used
to joke about their names.
Ray[mond] and Kay

How fate must have been
a bad poet and wrote them
into a poem together.

Then Raeanne or I would beg
them to tell—just one more time—
the story of how they met.